Book 1 of the Parallel Ops series

I0654180

THE
SCIENTISTS

R.J. ARCHER

NWIDI Press ~ La Paz, BCS, Mexico

THE SCIENTISTS

This book is a work of fiction.
All names, characters and incidents are either
the product of the author's imagination or are used fictitiously
and any resemblance to any persons, living or dead,
is entirely coincidental.

For more information on the Parallel Ops series, visit:
www.ParallelOps.com

Library of Congress Control Number: 2011960324

823.0876

"The Scientists" by R.J. Archer

p. cm.
ISBN-10: 0-9779109-4-6 (softcover)
ISBN-13: 978-09779109-46
Science Fiction, general

Published 2011 by NWIDI Press, San Ysidro, CA, 92143

Cover design by Diseño International, La Paz, BCS, Mexico.

Manufactured in the United States of America.

"R. J. Archer scores a mega hit with his latest novel, *The Scientists*. This spellbinder will launch mystery fans on a riveting adventure ride as they race through the pages. Readers accustomed to the works of David Baldacci or Clive Cussler will find they now have a new author to put on their bookshelf."

William Beck
Author of the Bryson McGann novel series

~|~

"Ancient artifacts, government conspiracies and a world traveling anthropologist form the rock solid core of Archer's gripping adventure-thriller, *The Scientists*."

Rick Chesler
Author of *kiDNApped* and *Wired Kingdom*

~|~

"R.J. Archer has done it again. If you like mysteries with a SciFi twist then *The Scientists* is your cup of tea. In *The Scientists* Archer brings back one of the main characters of the popular *Seeds of Civilization* series and spins a fantastic yarn that makes you question if the story is fact or fiction. Well done R.J."

Mike Monahan
Author of *Barracuda*

Acknowledgements

Significant portions of **The Scientists** take place in and around Munich, Germany, and I would like to thank Dr. Elisabeth Schuhmachers, of Munich, for her review and suggestions regarding the German locations. Her efforts helped me keep the factual portions of this book true and accurate.

I would also like to thank Bruce and Kathleen Bennett, owners of Allende Books in La Paz, BCS, Mexico. Not only did they read the manuscript and make several important suggestions, but they allowed me to host my eBook Release Party in their brick-and-mortar bookstore.

A Special Thank You

While most writers acknowledge the contributions of their spouse in the opening pages of their books, my wife, Marty, deserves much more than an obscure mention because she is actually part of the creative team. She reads (and corrects) every chapter the minute it's finished; she gets invested in the story line; and she helps with plot development. But more than that, she keeps me going when I would like to throw in the towel and quit. And that's especially true with this novel and this series. Although *Parallel Ops* was started before we left the United States—back when we still had a regular routine—most of the writing was done during a time when I was trying to figure out what retirement was all about in a foreign country where I didn't speak the language. The challenges of our new lifestyle have been significant and the distractions plentiful, but when I finally typed, "THE END" it was an awesome feeling—one I would never have experienced without constant encouragement from my wife, partner and friend, Martha (Marty) Olver.

Author's Footnote

Although this novel is purely a work of fiction, it is based on a great deal of factual information. I consider myself a fanatic for detail and, whenever possible, I make my fiction fit the facts, rather than the other way around. Many readers will be surprised to learn about the Navy's *Atlantic Undersea Test and Evaluation Center* (AUTEC) but I encourage you to check it out. AUTEC is a facility similar to the Air Force's "Area 51" except for one big difference—AUTEC is located on foreign soil!

For more information about this series, please visit http://www.ParallelOps.com.

THE SCIENTISTS

Prologue
(Monday, December 9, 2002)

"Linda, are you there?" asked Jim Barnes. "Linda! Please answer me!"

The line had gone dead and someone was ringing the bell at his lab door, so Jim hung up and went to see who was there. It turned out to be a delivery of some supplies he'd ordered from the U.S. weeks ago. Jim thanked the Navy seaman and started to close the door, but then called after the man.

"Seaman, have you heard about any telephone problems on base today? Specifically calls to the mainland?"

"No sir," replied the young man. "Everything seems to be fine over at HQ."

"Okay, thanks," replied Jim as he closed and locked the door.

Before their call had been cut off in mid-sentence, Jim had been in the process of warning Linda McBride and her new husband, Javier Reyes, that they might be in serious danger. He had cautioned Linda that her calls might be monitored—but now he wondered if the interruption had been on his end, so he redialed Linda's Cancun number. He let the phone ring more than a dozen times before finally giving up.

Jim paced the floor of his windowless lab at the U.S. Navy's AUTEC research facility on Andros Island, The Bahamas. Since his line seemed to be working, he had to assume that something had happened to Linda's phone. Jim was convinced that their mutual friend and NWIDI team member, Tony Nicoletti, had been abducted by a man named Buzz Edwards a week ago in Cancun. Linda and Javier had been on their honeymoon in Cabo San Lucas until today, and now Jim feared they might have been picked up, too.

"Think, Jim, think," he said out loud.

Moving to his computer station, he browsed his contacts for an idea. In the three months that Jim had been at AUTEC he'd met a lot of visiting scientists and researchers from all over the free world because the Navy made their facility available to many countries friendly to the United States. Its location on the east side of Andros Island made AUTEC uniquely qualified for the testing of underwater weaponry and electronics. Since much of this research was classified, AUTEC was the perfect place to conduct his examination of the mysterious triangles he and his NWIDI team members had recovered from the ruins of an underwater city off the northwest tip of Cuba. Jim's work was top secret and only a handful of people in the world knew about the alien artifacts he was studying.

As he scrolled through his list, the name Carmen Lopez came into view. Carmen was a librarian Jim had met on his first outing with NWIDI. He and Frank Morton had traveled to Mexico's Yucatan in search of some unusual spheres and Carmen had provided them access to a private library that helped them greatly. Jim and Carmen had stayed in touch during the past eighteen months, even after Carmen had moved to Cancun.

Jim grabbed the phone and dialed the long international number as fast as his fingers would move. In a few short minutes, Carmen was on her way to Linda and Javier's apartment to check on them and Jim breathed a sigh of relief.

Jim went back to work on his latest triangle theory and an hour later, when his phone rang, it startled him from his deep concentration.

"Hi, Carmen," he answered, recognizing her number in his caller ID display. "Were you able to deliver my message to Linda?"

"No, I'm afraid not," she replied. "There was no answer at their door, but you sounded so concerned about them that I decided to check with the apartment manager. She said she saw them getting into a taxi with four large suitcases, but didn't you say they had just returned from a trip?"

"Yes I did," smiled Jim, "and I'm glad they took my advice and went on another one. Thank you, Carmen, you've been a great help. I have something I need to take care of right now, but I'll call you in a few days and we can chat."

As Jim hung up the phone, he couldn't help wondering where Linda and Javier were headed—or if he'd ever see them again.

Chapter 1
(Wednesday, April 16, 2008)

Jim Barnes handed his boarding pass to the British Airways ticket agent and forced a smile. He used to enjoy traveling, but ever since the 9-11 enhanced security measures had been put into place airline travel had become a real pain. He much preferred remaining in his air conditioned lab back on Andros Island and taking advantage of the U.S. Navy's sophisticated video conferencing technology. But this trip was necessary, he reminded himself.

Once on board, Jim eased himself into the wide seat in the last row of the first class cabin and smiled—this time for real. During the past five and a half years his status within the scientific community had gradually improved and first class travel was only one of the many perks he now enjoyed. Jim accepted a ginger ale from the flight attendant, rested his head against the supple leather of the seat and closed his eyes in thought.

A former professor of anthropology at Seattle's University of Washington, Jim Barnes was now a respected speaker on the subject of ancient civilizations—knowledge he was continuing to expand through his study of the alien triangles locked away in his lab. He was deeply grateful for the research opportunities he had been provided, but he often felt guilty because his good friend and former boss, Frank Morton, had given his life during the team's mission that had produced the triangles more than five years earlier.

The mission had come to the team from "the highest levels of the US government" and the decision to accept the project had been entirely Frank's but Jim still felt a certain amount of remorse every time he removed the triangles from the small vault the Navy had installed in his lab. And yet, Jim knew that Frank would have wanted him to pursue his research and find out how—and why—the triangles had ended up 2,100 feet below the water off the Cuban coast.

"May I take your glass, Sir?" asked the flight attendant gently. "We're about to take off."

Jim opened his eyes and handed her the glass. "Ah, yes, back to reality," he thought.

About a month ago, Jim had received a phone call from Karl Schmidt, a professor at the University of Munich—the host of the conference Jim was on his way to attend. Schmidt had opened with the normal pleasantries exchanged between academics unknown to each other, but his tone had quickly turned serious.

"Dr. Barnes, it's very important that I meet with you privately while you are in Munich," the German had said softly.

"Well, I suppose I can arrange something," Jim had replied. "I'll be staying at the Hilton Munich Park, which I believe is just across the English Garden from the University. Would you like to meet me there on Thursday or Friday? I think they left my schedule open on both of those afternoons."

"Not on Thursday and not at the hotel, but perhaps in the park. I'll get a message to you with the necessary details. Shall we say 3:00 p.m. on Friday, April 18th?"

In the month since the mysterious call, Jim hadn't heard anything more from Professor Schmidt and he had no idea why anyone would want to meet with him so urgently, but the call had certainly changed his attitude about flying all the way across the Atlantic to speak at a conference. He was actually more interested in his meeting with the professor than attending the conference.

The overnight flight from Miami to London was uneventful and Jim was able to get a decent night's sleep, thanks to the ergonomically designed beds in the747's first class cabin. A quick change of planes, another two hours in the air and he was in Munich for the first time in his life. As he exited the customs area with his luggage, he spotted a young woman holding a sign that said "Dr. Barnes." He waved and headed in her direction but collided almost immediately with a traveler headed in the opposite direction.

"I'm terribly sorry," said the other man, as he held out his arms to steady Jim while he regained his balance.

"No, it was my fault, replied Jim. "Sorry!"

When he reached the woman with the sign, he introduced himself and she looked surprised. When she realized her own reaction she blushed.

"Please forgive me, but I was expecting someone much...older. My name is Sophie Hoffmann and I'm a graduate student at the University. If you'll follow me, I have a car waiting to take you to your hotel."

Jim nodded and obediently followed the woman out through the terminal doors and down the wide sidewalk toward a silver Mercedes sedan. The trunk was already open, so Jim tossed his suitcase and garment bag in and returned to the side of the car where *Fräulein* Hoffmann was holding the rear door open for him. As he settled into the seat, he heard the trunk close, and simultaneously the driver and the graduate assistant entered through the doors on the driver's side.

"Welcome to Munich, Dr. Barnes," smiled Jim's hostess. "I'm sorry for the abrupt departure, but we weren't supposed to park where we did and the driver was anxious to get away from the curb. I assume you'd like to go directly to your hotel, correct?"

"Yes, that would be fine. I'd like to unpack and freshen up before I do anything else," replied Jim.

"Certainly. Here's the telephone number of the Campus Hosts office. If you need anything during your stay, please don't hesitate to call. There's someone on duty twenty-four hours a day and we're there to make sure your stay is as comfortable as possible. We can provide information, arrange transportation and even assist with translators, if necessary. And please let us know when you plan to return to the airport so we can arrange for a car."

Jim accepted the business card and put it in his shirt pocket. As he did, it caught on another piece of paper already in his pocket. He pulled the paper out and tried to read it, but the tinted windows in the car made the interior too dark. He shrugged and put both the card and the paper back.

"So how do graduate students end up chauffeuring around old fuddy-duddy professors?" asked Jim.

"Oh, it's strictly a volunteer opportunity but personally I find it very interesting to meet visiting dignitaries from all over the world. And as a student of foreign languages, I find it also helps me improve my speaking skills."

"Interesting," replied Jim. "Which languages do you speak?"

"Well, I'm studying the languages of northern Europe but I also speak French, Spanish and Italian. And, of course, I speak a little English," she laughed.

"*Fräulein*, your English sounds perfect to me and I wish I had your talent for languages. The few I've tried my hand at have been a real struggle."

"And what languages do you speak?" asked Sophie.

"Well, it's not so much speak, as read," smiled Jim. "My primary discipline is anthropology and I'm a student of several Mesoamerican languages such as Mayan, Aztec and Olmec."

"Oh, wow!" exclaimed Sophie. "That puts my modern language work to shame. It must be very exciting to study passages that might not have been read for thousands of years. I absolutely must attend your lecture this weekend!"

"Well, you know my lecture isn't really about the Maya or Aztec, or even the Olmec," explained Jim. "These days I'm putting forth the theory that our current civilization—the one that began with the Sumerians about 5,000 years ago—is only one of many civilizations that have risen and fallen in the history of Earth. If it wasn't for some undeniable physical evidence, I'd be laughed out of Munich in a heartbeat."

"Really! What evidence?'

"Ah, well, that's what my lecture is for, isn't it?" teased Jim. "I'm speaking Saturday morning at 10:00 a.m. and I believe there are still a few tickets left."

"Tickets? I thought the lectures…"

"Kidding, Sophie! The lectures are open to anyone with the courage and fortitude to sit through them. I look forward to seeing you there, but please be advised that you may be the only person in the hall. Like I said, my theories aren't very well accepted in the scientific community. Most of the conferences I attend are pseudo-science, at best."

In a matter of minutes the car eased to a stop in front of the Hilton and a bellman opened the door for Jim while the driver unloaded his baggage and placed it on a cart. Sophie also exited the car and came around to the passenger's side to say her goodbyes.

"I'm going to hitch a ride back over to the campus with the driver, but I can't wait to hear your lecture Saturday morning," she smiled. "And don't forget to call the number on that card if you need anything from the Campus Hosts."

With that she climbed back into the car where Jim had been sitting and closed the door. As the car pulled away, Jim patted his pocket and waved.

The room the conference organizers had reserved for him was actually a very well appointed suite with a living room and a separate bedroom. The fully stocked wet bar at the far end of the main room was equipped with a small refrigerator, a microwave and a sink for hosting small cocktail parties. A huge fruit basket on the bar contained a note that read, "The University of Munich Convention Committee welcomes Dr. Jim Barnes."

Jim unpacked his suitcase into the large armoire in the bedroom and hung the two suits he'd brought along. He'd been in his clothes for nearly eighteen hours, so he undressed to take a shower before exploring the hotel and the neighborhood. As he unbuttoned his shirt, he remembered the business card Sophie had given him and when he pulled it out he rediscovered the folded piece of paper. He didn't recognize the paper and couldn't imagine where he'd picked it up, but he tossed it onto the small table next to the bed along with Sophie's card, his wallet and his passport. He started for the bathroom but returned, unfolded the paper and read it out loud.

"Dr. Barnes. Thank you for agreeing to meet me tomorrow, Friday, in the *Englischer Garten*. I propose that we meet in front of the Chinese Tower at 3:00 p.m. I will be wearing a dark wool suit and a dark derby hat but you can recognize me by the white rose I'll have in my lapel. I'll stay off to myself to help you find me. Please don't tell anyone about our meeting. After we've spoken, you'll understand why."

Jim reread the note a second time and then put it back on the table. The old Jim would have gone running to the police or the U.S. Embassy or somewhere else for help, but his year with NWIDI and the past five years of top secret work at AUTEC had steeled his nerves a lot. Frank Morton and Tony Nicoletti, two of his NWIDI team members, had been military Special Forces soldiers in their younger years and they were both inclined to dash off into danger without a second thought. Maybe some of that bravado had rubbed off on Jim, because right now his attention was focused on how the note got into his pocket, rather than what might await him at a mysterious rendezvous in a strange country.

He wrinkled his brow and thought back over his morning minute by minute.

"The guy at the airport!" he yelled out loud.

The traveler he had bumped into (or had it been the other way around?) must have slipped the note into his pocket when he reached out to keep Jim from tripping. Mystery solved, he thought to himself. And now he knew how he was going to spend his first afternoon in Munich—at the University library checking out the mysterious Professor Karl Schmidt.

Chapter 2

Jim didn't leave the University of Munich library until almost 5:00 p.m. and his afternoon's research consisted of just a handful of sheets he'd photocopied from several University publications. It seemed that the mysterious Dr. Karl Schmidt was neither famous nor infamous. He was simply an average professor of biology doing some minor research in nanotechnology. As far as Jim could tell, Schmidt's only published work was a couple of articles in University-based scientific journals and they were in German so he couldn't even read them.

After a short taxi ride back to his hotel, Jim poured himself a glass of wine from the bar and sat down in a large, over-stuffed chair in his suite's living room area to ponder the information he'd collected at the library.

Schmidt had received his PhD in biology from the University of Munich in 1982 and he had immediately accepted a teaching position on the university staff. His most recent published work was a paper on the relatively new science of *blink microscopy*, but Jim hadn't run across any additional material on the subject and Schmidt was now working with a large group on a University-funded nanotechnology project.

Thinking that there might be some clues in the German articles, Jim went into the bedroom and retrieved the Campus Hosts card Sophie had given him. When a male voice with a heavy accent answered the phone, Jim introduced himself and inquired about German-to-English translation services.

"I'm afraid there isn't anyone available at the moment," replied the man politely, "but I'd be happy to have someone call you in about an hour. May I have your phone number?"

Jim gave the man the information and hung up. He switched on the large flat-panel television across the room and stepped through the channels, finally settling on BBC World News. He had almost drifted off to sleep when the loud

European-style ring of the telephone next to him startled him awake.

To Jim's surprise, it was Sophie Hoffmann, the graduate student who had met him at the airport earlier in the day.

"Oh, hello, Sophie! I called earlier about getting a few pages of German technical articles translated but this really isn't urgent, so maybe I could just have the front desk fax them over and someone could give me a call tomorrow morning. I'd like to know what they say before a 3:00 p.m. meeting I have tomorrow."

"Well, that someone would be me," laughed Sophie. "I'm the only one on duty this week that can do German-to-English technical work and I have classes all morning tomorrow, so how about if I meet you in the lobby of you hotel in about an hour? I'm finished here at 7:00 p.m. and I can stop by on my way home."

"Oh, no, it really isn't that important!" replied Jim. "I don't even need a written translation, just someone to scan a few pages and give me an overview. Maybe I can get someone here at the hotel to give me a hand."

"It's quite all right, Dr. Barnes!" insisted Sophie. "I drive within a block of the hotel on my way home and the bellman at the hotel is a friend of mine so I'll just double-park in front, run in and translate for you. Really, it's no problem and in exchange you can reserve me a front row seat at your lecture. I'll meet you in the lobby in about an hour."

Before Jim could protest, the line went dead, so he hung up and browsed through the room service menu on the large ornate coffee table in front of him. As he read down the list of delicious sounding items, he realized that he hadn't eaten since breakfast on the short flight from London to Munich. Since he had an hour to kill before Sophie would be arriving, he decided to check out the hotel's dining room rather than order room service. He gathered up his copies from the library and put them in the thin, leather portfolio he had carried on the plane because it also contained his passport and conference ID—which he didn't want to leave behind in the room.

As he drained his coffee cup for the third time, the waiter approached his table and leaned down to whisper discretely.

"Dr. Barnes?"

"Yes," nodded Jim.

"Dr. Barnes, there's a young lady in the lobby to see you," said the waiter softly. "Shall I show her to your table?"

Jim glanced at his watch and couldn't believe it was already 7:15 p.m.

"Wow!" he exclaimed. "I was enjoying the meal so much I completely lost track of time. Yes, please show her in!"

As soon as the words were out of his mouth he thought better of it.

"No, wait, I'll meet her in the lobby. Could you bring my check, please?"

"Of course," smiled the waiter. "I took the liberty of bringing it with me when I learned that you had a visitor. Just sign and put your room number right here. Thank you for visiting us at Tivoli Restaurant and I hope you enjoy the rest of your evening."

Jim rushed into the lobby to find Sophie chatting with a young man in an ornate hotel uniform trimmed in gold cords.

"That must be her friend, the bellman," Jim thought.

When Sophie saw Jim heading her way, she said something to her friend and he zipped away.

"Sophie, I'm so sorry!" apologized Jim. "I…"

"It's quite all right. The front desk tried your room and when there was no answer, they suggested I inquire in the dining room. I'm sorry to have disturbed your meal."

"No, no, actually I was done some time ago. I was just sipping coffee. Shall we sit?"

Jim indicated a small couch to one side of the lobby and retrieved the papers from his bag.

"Thank you very much for taking your personal time to do this. It's just these few sheets and I'm only interested in the general content. I'm meeting with the author tomorrow afternoon and I want to sound like I've done my homework," he lied.

Sophie took the pages and started to scan the top sheet.

"This is by Professor Schmidt!" she said, surprised.

"Yes, that's correct. Do you know him?"

"Well, I don't actually know him. I mean, I'm not sure I would even recognize him, but everyone on campus knows his name. He's considered a little, ah, 'strange'," Sophie stammered.

"Strange in what way," questioned Jim. "Does it have to do with his research work?"

"Oh, no, nothing like that," replied Sophie as she continued scanning. "He claims to have had encounters with aliens—the kind from outer space."

Jim's jaw dropped and his reaction must have showed.

"I know, it's crazy, huh? This paper seems to be about some process for detecting a defect in a DNA strand. I don't begin to understand all the science here, but it sounds like it would be an important discovery if it's ever made."

"What do you mean '*if*'?" asked Jim, only half listening. He was still stuck back on Sophie's comment about aliens.

"This is a paper on a theoretical process. Professor Schmidt is saying that *if this, then that*, but at the time of its writing the process hadn't yet been achieved in the lab. This was published about six months ago, so that's probably still the case."

"I see," frowned Jim. "And what about the other paper?"

Sophie scanned.

"Same deal. Another theoretical process to do a different job, but until someone actually makes it happen in the lab, these are just scientific pipe dreams. I wonder where he comes up with this stuff."

"Maybe the aliens told him," laughed Jim stiffly. "I'm just kidding, of course."

"Maybe," laughed Sophie. "Professor Schmidt is considered a bit strange socially because of his 'close encounter' stories, and it looks like he has the same problem in his research. Do you have anything more?"

Jim's mind was far, far away, but he managed to mumble "Ah, no, thank you, Sophie. You've been a great help, and I'll see you Saturday morning."

"Don't forget that front-row seat," she smiled. "Oh, and I asked my friend Alex to look after you. If there's anything you need, just ask him, okay?'

"Yes, I will," nodded Jim, "and thank you again."

By the time he got back to his room, Jim's head was reeling with possibilities about his meeting with Schmidt the next day. Had Schmidt really had any alien encounters or was he a whacko, as Sophie believed? And what about his nanotechnology theories—were they fact or fiction? As Jim finally slipped into a fitful sleep that night, he had no idea that, elsewhere in Munich, sinister forces were asking the same questions about *him*.

***

"Are you sure?" demanded BKA Bureau Chief Wilhelm Kruger. "Are you absolutely positive it's the same person?"

"Yes, Sir, it's Barnes, all right," replied Max Becker. "He's been working inside a high-security military facility in the Bahamas for most of the past five years, but it's the same Jim Barnes that visited *Loltún*, in the Yucatan, and the Yonaguni site in Japan. He definitely knows—or at least he *knew*—Frank Morton."

"I thought the whole NWIDI operation folded up when Morton died in that diving accident five years ago, so what's this guy doing here in Munich?" demanded Kruger again.

"He could be here speaking at a conference, just like his visa states, Colonel. According to our source at the university, Barnes was invited to attend and actually refused the invitation at first, so it doesn't sound like he came here with his own agenda."

"Well, you know the drill. I want to see a list of every place he goes and every person he comes in contact with while he's in Munich. I will *not* have an incident on my watch, so put out the word that screw-ups will not be tolerated."

"Understood," replied Becker, as he stood to leave the Bureau Chief's office. "What about electronic surveillance, Sir?"

The older man ran his fingers through his white hair and thought for a minute.

"Let's hold off for now," Kruger finally replied. "If he's involved in classified work for the Americans, they may be keeping an eye on him, too, and we certainly don't want to tip our hand to them. Let's do this the old fashioned way for now."

Becker returned to his own office down the hall and told his secretary to hold his calls until further notice. Pulling his inner office door closed behind him, he slumped into his chair and sighed. Just what he needed was another busy-work project to satisfy his boss' paranoia. It seemed to Becker that Kruger was getting the BKA far too involved in minor matters lately. "Maybe the old man is finally losing it," thought Becker as he unlocked his desk and retrieved a private, hand-written address book.

Kruger had come to him nearly eighteen months earlier with a "top-priority, classified project" that seemed at the outset to be a waste of time. But Becker reluctantly accepted the assignment and spent days researching an American non-profit group named NWIDI. The group had been involved in some pretty far-fetched work, to be sure, but nothing that effected Germany in any way.

In the summer of 2001, they had uncovered some evidence of a culture that had existed in the Yucatan centuries before the Maya. It was interesting, but certainly no threat to Germany. In early 2002, the same group of four individuals showed up on a tiny speck of land at the southern end of the

Japanese islands and discovered that the three highest points on the island were actually buried pyramids built by an unknown culture more than ten thousand years ago. This was even more interesting, but it, too, had no impact on Germany. The following fall, the rogue band of adventurers discovered the ruins of an ancient city on the ocean floor just off the western tip of Cuba but rather than stay and explore it fully, they took off for Andros Island, in the Bahamas. It was there that the team's leader, Frank Morton, disappeared along with a local hotelier named Miles Adderly.

And, as far as Becker had been able to determine, that was the end of the story. The remaining members of the original NWIDI team had gone their separate ways and slipped into obscurity. Jim Barnes had resurfaced a couple of years later when his articles about ancient civilizations were picked up by the popular media but there was no indication that he'd reconnected with his former teammates. "And even if he had, so what?" Becker reminded himself. They were nothing more than a lucky bunch of amateur investigators. Certainly no threat to the German government!

One after another, Becker dialed phone numbers from his address book and put together a team to provide twenty-four hour surveillance of Dr. Jim Barnes. "What a waste of time," he thought.

***

Friday morning was filled with welcoming events at the University which Jim somehow managed to smile his way through. By noon he had shaken a hundred hands and forgotten as many names. At the luncheon, he was seated at the traditional round table with two other guest speakers, two faculty members and a thin, mustached man who smiled a lot but said very little. Jim hadn't caught the man's name when they went around the table with introductions.

The minute the luncheon was over, Jim excused himself and fled to his hotel room, a half-mile off campus. He'd gotten used to the lectures and presentations that went along with scientific conferences, but he absolutely hated the socializing that was a part of these events.

In the solitude of his room, his thoughts immediately turned to his scheduled meeting with Karl Schmidt. Jim felt uneasy about the mysterious circumstances the man had used to contact him and Sophie's suggestion that the man was "a bit strange" didn't help his comfort level. Jim hated traveling with his laptop computer but right now he wished he had one so he could do a little more digging before his meeting. After a quick call to the hotel's business center, he was off to find out as much as he could in the two hours he had left before his rendezvous with Schmidt.

Despite getting tangled up in traffic twice, the taxi dropped Jim off at 3:00 p.m. on the dot about 100 yards from the Chinese Tower in Munich's famous *Englischer Garten*— the English Garden. He walked briskly towards the five-story structure until he was closer and then he slowed to a more natural walk so he wouldn't attract any attention. All day long he'd had the strange feeling that he was being watched but he knew it was just his imagination making something out of this strange meeting arrangement.

He scanned the area in front of the tower and immediately spotted Schmidt pacing back and forth to the left of the main entrance. The man was dressed exactly as he had said he would be and he looked nervous.

"Professor Schmidt?" asked Jim, as he approached the man.

The small, stout man jumped at the sound of Jim's voice but forced a smile when he recognized the face.

"Yes, good afternoon, Professor Barnes, and thank you for meeting me under these circumstances," replied Schmidt. "And please call me Karl."

"Well, I have to admit that I've been a bit curious ever since I first received your telephone call, but this setting is quite beautiful, so I'm glad I accepted your invitation. And please call me Jim. I do so little teaching these days that 'Professor' isn't even appropriate anymore."

"As you wish, Jim. Please allow me to get right to the point of our meeting. How much do you know about me?"

"Well, apart from the two hours of library research I did yesterday and the two hours of Internet research I did just before coming here, I hardly know anything about you," laughed Jim. "I'm not usually so nosey, but under the circumstances…"

"I understand completely," nodded Schmidt. "So I assume you know a little about my theories and I also assume you've heard about my alleged alien encounters."

"Alleged?" interrupted Jim. "So the encounters didn't really happen?"

Schmidt paused for a minute, as if working through a problem in his head. Then he smiled.

"Your question says a lot about you, Jim. Probably more than you realize. Most people would have assumed the stories were fiction but you obviously believe the opposite. That tells me that I've come to the right person. But I digress.

"Yes, the encounters did happen, but not the way they've been reported in the media. I never intended for any of that information to become public but on my last birthday some friends insisted that I join them for a few beers and I'm afraid I got pretty drunk. Someone overheard me talking and the next thing I knew the story was all over campus and it even spread to a local tabloid. Most unfortunate, I'm afraid."

"Yes, I can see how it would be," sympathized Jim. "And I take it this occurred after your nanotechnology theories were already published. It would be easy for someone to put two and two together and publish a headline like "University professor steals technology from aliens."

"Exactly!" said Schmidt emphatically. "I see you found that article in your research, too. Well, no matter— what's done is done. The unfortunate truth is that I did publish information that I acquired from alien sources, but I felt it was important and I couldn't very well cite aliens in my footnotes, could I? But that has nothing to do with why I wanted to meet with you."

Jim raised his eyebrows, wondering how much more bizarre this conversation was going to get.

"So why *did* you want to meet with me?"

"I got your name from an associate in London, Jim. I've been looking for others who might have had contact with alien technology and I believe you are one of those people. But my…"

"What? Why would you think I've had contact with alien technology?" said Jim a little too loudly.

Schmidt hushed Jim and looked around to see if anyone had overheard. Convinced that the secret was still safe, he replied.

"Let's just say that my friend knows someone who served aboard the merchant ship Atlantic Protector and this person saw you holding some objects that were retrieved from deep beneath the waters near Cuba."

The triangles! Jim tried not to show his shock, but he was sure it was apparent.

"But that's not what I want to discuss with you," continued Schmidt. "What you do with the knowledge you have acquired is up to you. I came here to warn you about a group that may pose a great danger to you and your associates. You called yourselves NWIDI, if my facts are correct."

"Whoa, back up the bus!" objected Jim. "I don't know what you're talking about, my friend."

"I think you do, so please let me finish. The aliens who provided you and me—and probably many others—with various technologies are trying desperately to save civilization from self-destruction. However, there's a multi-national group known simply as 'the Six' that is determined to maintain control of the world's future for their own purposes, even if they destroy the planet in the process."

"Wait a minute, here," replied Jim. "How do you know all this? And who's this *Six*, as you call them?"

Once again, Schmidt looked over both shoulders before answering.

"*The Six* is a group of individuals who secretly manipulate the governments of the United States, Great

Britain, Russia, Mexico, China and South Africa. They work outside all laws and without the knowledge of their elected leaders. And they are very, very dangerous. That's why I had to warn you."

"And the aliens?" asked a dumb-founded Jim. "Do they have a name, too?"

"As a matter of fact, they do. They are known as *the Teachers* and someone has to protect them, or our culture—and this whole planet—will be destroyed. I've made contact with a few others like us, but there's no plan or leader. I was hoping you would…"

"As I've said," Jim interrupted sternly, "I don't know what you're talking about, and I'm definitely not interested in becoming part of your ghost busters club! I think this meeting is over."

Jim turned and started to walk away, but Schmidt called after him in an uncharacteristically loud voice.

"Be careful, my friend. They have eyes everywhere."

Chapter 3

The next morning Jim was at the University early for the 7:00 a.m. meet-and-greet breakfast and to attend the 9:00 a.m. presentation that preceded his own in the same lecture room. The topic was "Mars in the Ancient Past" and the presenter was a colorful old guy from Cornel University who had worked with Carl Sagan and shared a lot of the deceased astronomer's humor and no-nonsense approach to science.

In the hallway between sessions, Jim ran into Sophie and several of her friends whom she'd talked into attending Jim's presentation.

After the introductions, Sophie pulled Jim aside and asked, "How did your meeting with Spock go?"

Confused, Jim replied, "Who?"

"You know—Professor Schmidt. Everybody on campus calls him 'Spock' because of the alien thing. Anyway how did it go? Did you hear that he didn't show up for his team's presentation this morning? Isn't that something he…"

Jim held up his hand to slow the young student down.

"Wait a minute. Did you say he didn't show? Are you sure?"

"Positive! One of the girls I just introduced you to is a grad student on the same project and Schmidt was supposed to have a few minutes to discuss one of his hypothetical theories. The team leader had to fill in for him and I guess he wasn't prepared to do so. It's not going to go well for Spock when they catch up with him."

"Interesting," puzzled Jim. "He was fine yesterday afternoon. Maybe the poor guy just overslept. I need to get in there before the introductions begin but let me know what you find out about Schmidt, okay."

Much to Jim's surprise, the lecture room was about three-quarters full—probably a hundred people or more—and there were some thought-provoking questions when he finished speaking. One, in particular, caught Jim off guard.

"How is it that you and your three friends happen to be lucky enough to stumble upon all this remarkable evidence of ancient civilizations, Dr. Barnes? Of all the investigators in all the thousands of years, why did all the good luck go to the four of you?"

Jim mulled the question over for a minute, wondering if the man was a jealous researcher or if he was challenging the evidence itself.

"That's an excellent question, Sir, and one the four of us have asked ourselves many times. I don't know much about the early days of the first investigation, but I believe we were successful on the second and third outings because our team leader, Frank Morton, already believed what our discoveries would eventually confirm. He looked at things in a different way than I would have without his influence. There were many situations where I would have interpreted something incorrectly due to preconceived notions and pre-programmed 'knowledge' acquired during my 'education.' As a very skilled space engineer, Frank didn't have that problem and he had a knack for looking at things from a completely different angle. And maybe that's a lesson we should all take away today. Sometimes, the answer is right there in front of us but we're just too educated to see it."

Jim's response prompted a round of applause from the attentive audience and then the house lights went up, indicating that his time was up and he needed to yield the room to the next session.

As Jim and his audience moved out into the hallway, a number of attendees stopped him to ask questions or get clarifications on certain points. Finally, the group dispersed and Jim was left standing there with just Sophie and her three friends.

"Wow!" he said to no one in particular. "That's the biggest group to ever attend one of my talks, and they actually seemed to be interested in what I was saying. I'm blown away!"

"Oh, sure," laughed Sophie. "I'll bet you get even bigger crowds in the United States. I was absolutely fascinated, Dr. Barnes, and I had no idea that real, physical evidence of previous civilizations actually exists. Why don't we hear about this stuff in school?"

"Yes," chimed in the lone male member of Sophie's group. "I took three terms of anthropology last year and they never mentioned this once—not even once!"

"Well, that's why I'm here," laughed Jim. "I have to run to a meeting, but maybe we can pick this up again before I leave, if you're interested. Sophie, don't forget to let me know if you hear anything about Karl Schmidt. Bye!"

The rest of Jim's Saturday was consumed by conference functions and other lectures he wanted to attend. By the time he reached his hotel it was after 9:00 p.m. and he was really beat. The only thing on his mind was a hot shower and a good night's sleep.

"Dr. Barnes?" called a voice from behind him as he made his way across the large hotel lobby.

He turned to see Alex, the bellman jogging in his direction.

"Yes, what is it?" he replied with a yawn.

"Dr. Barnes, I'm Alex Fischer, Sophie's friend. She asked me to give you a message."

"Hi, Alex," said Jim, yawning again. "I'm sorry, but I'm really tired. What's the message?"

"She said to tell you that '*Spock is no longer aboard the Enterprise.*' Does that make any sense to you? I tried to reply to her text message, but she's apparently turned her cell phone off."

In his fatigued state it took Jim a minute to process the reference to Spock, and then it hit him—Schmidt was missing!

"Uh, yes, Alex, and thanks. Goodnight!"

Jim fast-walked his way to the elevators and punched the button for his floor. Riding up, his head swirled with questions. "What happened to Schmidt? How does Sophie know he's missing as opposed to out for a walk? Why did Sophie think it was necessary to pass the information in code?"

As Jim passed from the living room into the bedroom portion of his suite, he stopped dead in his tracks. The inner room had been "tossed" and it was an absolute mess. Drawers had been pulled out of the dresser and night stands and thrown onto the bed, which no longer had any bedding on it. His clothes had been pulled out of the closet and thrown into a pile on the floor along with his luggage. Even his toiletry bag had been dumped into the bathroom sink. Only his leather portfolio, which still contained his passport and his research on Karl Schmidt, was untouched because he had carried it with him all day long.

Frozen by the scene, Jim listened for any sounds in the room. Slowly, he backed out of the doorway and moved to the telephone on the end table next to the couch.

Moments later there was a loud knock on his door.

"It's security, Herr Barnes. Are you okay?"

By the time hotel security and the local police left, it was nearly midnight and Jim could barely hold his head up. The front desk had offered to send a maid up to put the room back together, but Jim declined. He just wanted to get some sleep.

He spread a sheet across the mattress, dug a pillow out from under the pile of bedding and lay down fully dressed. The lights in the outer room were still on, but he didn't care. He closed his eyes and took one deep breath, waiting for sleep to come.

The ringing phone on his night stand dragged him back from the edge of sleep and scared him so much that he yelled out loud.

"What now!" he shouted into the ornate mouthpiece.

"Professor, it's Sophie! I have to talk to you right now. What room are you in?"

"Sophie? What's the problem? Do you know what time it is? Call me tomorrow—I need to get some sleep."

"No, wait, Professor! Don't hang up—this is really important. Please, what room are you in?"

Five minutes later Jim opened the door to a disheveled and panting Sophie.

Waving her into the room, he scolded, "What are you doing out at this time of night? And what's the big urgency?"

Catching her breath, Sophie poured herself a glass of water at the bar and drank it down.

"Dr. Barnes, I'm twenty-four years old and I frequently stay out all night. As for the urgency, I thought you might like to know that your new best friend Karl Schmidt was picked up by the BKA early this morning—that's why he didn't show up at the conference."

"The BKA?" asked Jim.

"Our national police—similar to your F.B.I. Doesn't it seem a little odd that he would be picked up just a few hours after meeting with you? My friends and I were at a bar not too far from here when I heard the news and I ran all the way here to warn you. *That's* the big urgency!"

"Sorry," apologized Jim, "but I've had a little excitement of my own this evening. Let me show you something."

When he motioned her towards the bedroom, Sophie raised an eyebrow, but followed cautiously. When she gazed into the room, she gasped.

"The police have come and gone, but they didn't seem too confident they would figure out who did this. I'm more hopeful that the hotel security cameras may have caught something. The Chief of Security promised to let me know tomorrow."

"I'll bet they don't! I predict that tonight's recordings will mysteriously disappear or get erased or something like that. I'll bet this is the work of the same BKA that's holding Schmidt, and that means they're watching you, too. You have to get out of here and you have to do it right now!"

"What?" exclaimed Jim. "Even if I could hide someplace, sooner or later I'm going to have to leave the country and that means a trip to the airport where there are a million security cameras and almost as many cops. I refuse to believe that Schmidt's detention and this mess are related. And just how do you know that this BKA bunch has him, anyway? Is it already posted on the Internet?"

"No, of course not! But the student underground here in Munich is extensive and things like this have a way of leaking out. There's hardly an office in this city that doesn't have at least one student intern or staffer. Trust me, the BKA has Schmidt! And I still think they're responsible for turning your hotel room upside down. I would be willing to bet they've been watching your every move since your meeting yesterday afternoon."

"Well, if that's true, then they're now watching you, too," frowned Jim, "because they would certainly have seen you run in here in the middle of the night."

"I know, but I felt it was important to warn you and you weren't answering your phone, so I decided to come in person. Now that I see this," Sophie said, indicating the bedroom mess, "I guess that wasn't such a smart move. We need a plan."

Jim laughed out loud.

"Well, *my* plan is to get about twelve hours of uninterrupted sleep before I deal with any more crises. As I told the police, it doesn't look like anything was taken and with the safety latch secured I think I'll be fine for the night. Now if you'll excuse me..."

"No, I can't go out there! Like you said, they're probably after me, too, now that I've been seen associating with you. No Sir, I'm staying right here tonight and I'll figure some way to sneak out tomorrow morning."

"Suit yourself," replied Jim tossing her the comforter from the bed. "You can sleep on the couch, but I warn you, I snore. There's a half-bath to the left of the bar. Good night."

And with that, Jim gently eased the young woman into the living room and closed the bedroom door behind her.

When Jim opened his eyes the sun was beating in and he realized that in all the commotion of the night before, he'd forgotten to close the floor-to-ceiling drapes. He rolled out of bed and made his way to the bathroom. He was half way through brushing his teeth when he remembered Sophie.

With the tooth brush still in his mouth, he leaped over the pile of clothes and pillows on the floor and yanked open the door to the living room.

"Sophie?"

There was no answer, but in the middle of the living room there was a serving cart with a note taped to it.

"Dr. Barnes: My friend Alex helped me out on the bottom of one of these carts. I'll contact you later today or you can call my cell at 0172.309.8502. You should assume that every move you make is being watched, so please be careful! – Sophie"

Jim lifted the lid on the cart and discovered a full breakfast being kept warm by one of those Sterno cans used on buffet lines. Since he was starving, he decided not to let the food go to waste so he sat down and ate. When he was done, he took a quick shower, dressed, collected his portfolio and headed off to another long day of sessions and the dreaded conference luncheon.

He stopped by the front desk to let them know he was leaving for the day so they could clean up the mess from the night before and put his room back together.

"Oh, Dr. Barnes, there's an envelope here for you. It arrived last night, but with all the excitement the night staff neglected to bring it to your room. I'm terribly sorry."

Jim accepted the envelope, slid it into his portfolio and thanked the clerk. Once he was situated in the back seat of the taxi and headed towards the University, he opened the envelope and thumbed through the pages inside. On top of the small stack was a hand-written letter from Schmidt.

"Dr. Barnes: I had hoped that you would be more receptive to joining our growing group, but I understand your reservations completely. In the hopes that you will change your mind—and because I fear that I'm under surveillance by my own government—I've decided to trust my initial instincts about you and send you all the information I've been able to gather thus far. I assume you'll know what to do with it. Respectfully, Karl M. Schmidt"

"No!" shouted Jim out loud.

"Excuse me," questioned the cabby. "Is there something wrong, Sir?"

"Yes!" exclaimed Jim. "Ah, no, but I've changed my mind. Please take me to the American Consulate instead of the University."

"We just passed it, Sir," replied the driver. "It's right on the edge of the *Englischer Garten* so I'll have to turn around."

Jim had to wait thirty minutes to see anyone and then it was a third-level administrative staffer, not the Consul General, as he had requested.

The young man shook his head.

"I'm sorry, Dr. Barnes, but it's not our place to interfere in local matters unless they directly involve an American citizen."

"Well it may involve one—me! I have reason to believe that whoever has Schmidt is also monitoring me. I could be the next one to go missing and I'm demanding some protection!"

Ten minutes later, Jim was sitting in front of the Consul General's desk and the older man was not happy.

"Dr. Barnes, we simply cannot provide a private security detail to every American who shows up in Munich. If you have proof of your allegations, then…"

"I've already told you," replied Jim. "I have reliable information that Schmidt has been picked up by the BKA and this same source tells me that I'm also being watched."

"I'll make some inquiries, but I can't promise you anything. Even if the BKA does have your friend in custody, it's none of our business and they are under no obligation to tell us if or why they have him. How long will you be staying in Munich?"

"I fly out Tuesday afternoon," frowned Jim. "That is, *if* I'm not locked up in some German concentration camp by then."

"I think you're being a little melodramatic, don't you? And just for the record, we've been aware of your presence in Germany ever since your plane landed Thursday morning.

No one with a security clearance like yours travels overseas unannounced. Now, if you'll excuse me…"

Jim hailed a taxi in front of the Consulate and instructed the driver to take him to the University. During the short trip, he couldn't help keeping one eye out the back window to see if he were being followed.

By the time he arrived at the conference center he'd missed the whole morning program and the 11:00 a.m. sessions were just breaking for lunch. Since he had recently eaten and hated the luncheons anyway, Jim found a chair in a quiet part of the foyer, dug Sophie's note from the breakfast out of his bag and dialed her cell.

"*Guten Morgen,*" said Sophie's voice.

"Sophie, it's Jim Barnes. I took your advice and went to the American Consulate to see what they could tell me about Karl Schmidt, but they won't get involved in a domestic issue and they don't believe there's any threat to me. Any suggestions?"

"Well, like I said last night, I think you should get out of that hotel but I'm tied up for another hour over at the University. Where are you now?"

"I'm at the University, too, over in the building where the conference is taking place," replied Jim. "It's lunch time, so almost everybody is in the ballroom eating. I'm out in the front foyer."

"Perfect!" shouted Sophie. "Listen very carefully, okay? In ten minutes make your way down the hall that runs along the left side of the ballroom. Go past the restrooms until you come to a door on your right that says *Küche.* Make sure no one can see you and then slip inside. That's the kitchen they're using to serve the conference luncheon, so don't be alarmed if it's full of people. Stay right near the door and my friend Manny will meet you and get you out of the building without being seen. Got it?"

"Uh, yes, I have it," stuttered Jim. "How will I know this Manny?"

"He's the one you met yesterday after your seminar, but he'll find you. Just stay close to the door and if anyone approaches you except Manny, act like you're lost. But whatever you do, don't go back out into the hall."

Jim slipped the cell phone back into his pocket and checked his watch. After five minutes had passed, he casually made his way down the hallway Sophie had indicated and stopped at the men's restroom where he killed five more minutes pretending to comb his hair and wash his hands—in case he were being watched or followed. At the appointed time, he re-entered the hallway, looked carefully back in the direction of the foyer and then quickly located and entered the kitchen.

The place was a madhouse, with two dozen serving staff rushing this way and that. No one paid him any attention at all until the young man he recognized from the prior day suddenly appeared at his side dressed like a cook.

"Here, put these on and follow me," he said as he handed Jim a white cook's jacket and hat.

The jacket was a little snug over his sport jacket, but it covered well. The only tell-tale evidence was his portfolio, but there wasn't anything he could do about that. As soon as he put the hat on, the man Sophie had called Manny took Jim's elbow and led him towards the back of the large room. In a flash they were out of the kitchen and into a small utility truck with the University logo on the side. Driving way too fast for Jim's comfort, Manny negotiated a series of alleys that ran between several campus administrative buildings. At the end of one such alley, a garage door was open and Manny flew through the opening and screeched the vehicle to a stop.

"Out!" was the only word he said during the entire trip.

By the time Jim was out, Manny was already on his side of the truck and helping him out of the cook's coat. Manny threw his own cook's gear into the front seat on top of Jim's and motioned for Jim to follow.

They were inside a large warehouse and Manny moved quickly to a small cargo van similar to a Volkswagen mini-bus.

"In," the man said.

After another hair-raising ride, this time through the city streets of Munich, the van finally lurched to a stop in front of a large, three-story stone building with a steeply-pitched red roof.

"Inside," barked Manny as he scrambled out of the van.

As Jim was led up the stairs to the front door, he caught a glimpse of the shady, tree-lined street and realized that they had already driven down this street at least once since leaving the warehouse.

"What have I gotten myself into now?" Jim asked himself.

Chapter 4

Manny led Jim to the second story of the apartment building, opened a door near the stairway and motioned Jim inside. The building turned out to be the apartment building where Sophie and a number of her friends lived and it was only a short distance from Jim's hotel.

"Please wait here. Sophie will be up to see you as soon as she returns from the University. I have to get back to the conference, but there's beer in the frig. Please don't leave the room until Sophie gets here, okay?"

Jim nodded. "Thanks for helping me out, Manny."

The other man smiled and then he was gone. Jim locked the door behind him and looked around the small but comfortable studio apartment. The refrigerator contained a six-pack of a German beer Jim had never heard of and a wedge of cheese. On the counter he found a loaf of dark bread and what appeared to be a clean knife so he helped himself. Maybe it had been a mistake to skip lunch, he thought.

The television only received three channels, all in German, so Jim picked a talk show and settled back on the couch. Forty-five minutes later, there was a knock on the door.

"Who is it?" he asked tentatively.

"It's Sophie. May I come in?"

Jim unbolted the door and opened it. Behind Sophie stood the group from the conference—minus Manny—along with several other people he hadn't met. Sophie introduced them all by name and then swept her arm around the room.

"So how do you like it?" she asked.

A little confused, Jim replied, "Like what?"

"Your new apartment, silly! This is where you'll be staying until you leave for the United States. The real tenant is away studying in China for several months, so it's yours for as long as you need it."

"Oh, I can't do that! Besides, I need to be at the conference today and tomorrow or people will wonder what's happened to me."

"Not a problem," smiled Sophie. "One of us will get you there and bring you back whenever necessary. One of our comrades at the hotel will make sure your room looks like it's being lived in and when you're ready to check out we'll sneak you back into the hotel so you can make a normal exit."

"And why are you doing all this?"

"Well, I'd like to tell you it's because you're such a brilliant scientist and we all admire your work so much, but..."

"But what?" demanded Jim.

"Well, we're actually doing it because we object to the way the BKA operates, especially here in Munich. The local bureau chief is a former army colonel who runs the federal police force as if it were the Gestapo and we feel it's our duty to protest his behavior. Obviously we can't challenge him in the open, so we've created an underground movement to harass the BKA until things change."

"Isn't that dangerous?" questioned Jim. "Because it certainly sounds dangerous to me."

"Yes, but we all feel pretty strongly about this. In the past, several students have been taken in for questioning and never heard from again and others have been deported for no apparent reason. We've tried to take our concerns to the federal officials, but nobody wants to listen to a bunch of college students. So until Colonel Wilhelm Kruger is replaced, we're committed to keeping him under control."

"Really!" challenged Jim.

"Yes, really," insisted Sophie. "The BKA will never expect you to be here and I seriously doubt if they will bother you at the university. A bunch of us are getting together down in the study on the first floor this evening if you'd like to join us. In the mean time, please don't go out on the street by yourself. If you need something, let one of us know. I'm down the hall in 2-G and Manny is right below you in 1-C in case I'm not in. If you get hungry, there's a pizza place a couple of blocks away that delivers, but have it sent to apartment 1-A. That door bell is wired to ring in several apartments and someone will get it and bring it to you—don't go down to the door yourself."

"So what you're telling me is that I can be held prisoner by the German state police or by a bunch of college students—either way, I'm still a prisoner," declared Jim only partly kidding.

"Well, that's one way of looking at it, I guess, but we'll torture you with pizza and beer, whereas the BKA tends to use entirely different techniques. Suit yourself, though."

Jim held up his hand.

"No, I'm sorry for being so unappreciative. It's just that I didn't expect to attract so much attention from so many people. Thank you—all of you—for your concern. I'll try to be a good house guest. And, yes, I'd love to join you later but only if you let me make a significant contribution to the party fund."

Once everybody had cleared out of his room, Jim settled down for a quiet afternoon. Using the small dining table as a desk, he opened the envelope he had received from Karl Schmidt and spread the papers out. He set the hand-written letter aside and studied the rest carefully. The first item was a one-page typed list of names, addresses and other contact information. It was titled "Those Who Know" and Jim was surprised to see his name near the bottom of the list and circled in red. The address listed was that of his AUTEC laboratory on Andros Island and it even included his personal cell number.

Several other names on the list looked familiar but most were people with whom Jim wasn't familiar.

The next page was titled "The Six" and contained a centered, double spaced list of the six countries Schmidt had mentioned during their meeting on Friday: United States of America, United Kingdom, Russia, Mexico, China and South Africa.

Stapled to this typed page were seven hand-written pages that appeared to contain randomly organized names and contact information. Jim thumbed through them scanning for anything that looked interesting. His eyes widened when he saw a name that was all too familiar: Wilhelm Kruger! In the margin next to the name he found a reference to the BKA and a string of numbers that meant nothing to him.

"But Germany isn't even on the list," he said out loud.

Intrigued, Jim read on. It was like reading a stranger's diary; the comments were interesting, but they didn't really mean much. And then, on the next to the last page, he spotted a name that shocked him: Michael "Buzz" Edwards. Next to the name Schmidt had written "USA" followed by another string of numbers. There was also an address in Washington, D.C. and several telephone numbers.

"Edwards!" he said out loud again. "And he knows everything about us!"

Jim leaned back in his chair and slumped. Edwards' name on this list probably meant that he had been using NWIDI from the very beginning for some sinister purpose. They had all been duped, especially Frank, who had trusted Edwards even when the rest of the team had their doubts.

Jim closed his eyes and thought back through NWIDI's three missions together. The first one, which got started by accident, took them to Las Vegas, where Tony had first encountered Edwards and a Department of Energy agent named Gene Carlson. Tony had been handed a mysterious black sphere one night in a bar and he had passed it on to Frank, who had sought out Jim's assistance in decoding several hieroglyphs etched into the surface. Edwards had showed up again in Mexico after Jim and Frank had flown down to seek out the origin of the sphere. Several other spheres had been found on a restricted area not far from Area 51. Although the information was still highly classified today, the NWIDI team had established that the spheres were all of alien origin.

Jim had always thought the team's second mission—to Japan's Yonaguni Island—was Frank's idea, but now he had his doubts. Just prior to leaving for Japan, Edwards had helped Frank purchase a Learjet from the Department of Defense. The plane had been confiscated from a notorious drug dealer and for some reason the DOD had wanted it off their books.

They had even helped Frank obtain a new tail number for the aircraft so it couldn't be traced.

During the course of the mission to Japan, Jim had discovered three ancient buried pyramids from a civilization previously unknown to the scientific world. This discovery and Jim's subsequent work in decoding several large murals had instantly rocketed him from relative obscurity to the top of the list of "lost civilizations" experts in the world.

Their third, and last, mission had been entirely the work of Edwards. He had summoned the team from Seattle on very short notice, briefed them in a super-secret underground complex at the Cancun airport and sent them off in search of the source of mysterious underwater signals near the western tip of Cuba. With the help of a vessel equipped for deep underwater exploration, the NWIDI team had located and partially explored the ruins of what appeared to be an ancient city more than two thousand feet below the surface. It was here that they had found the triangular "coins" that now occupied much of Jim's time in his AUTEC laboratory. Following a geological trail along the sea floor, the team had found themselves in the Bahamas and it was here that Frank and a former Navy SEAL named Miles Adderly had disappeared five and a half years ago. Looking back on it, Jim now realized that Edwards had been involved in everything NWIDI did, almost from the beginning. He now wondered if it had been Edwards that had sent that first sphere their way. Had he somehow orchestrated the formation of NWIDI by manipulating Frank?

Jim desperately wanted to research the names on both the "Those Who Know" list and on this list of apparent "bad guys" but he needed a computer and Internet access to do that. Sophie had said to let her know if he needed anything, so he walked down the hall and around the corner until he found the door marked 2-G.

Jim knocked three times to no avail and was just turning his back on the door when it was flung open by a short, dark-haired girl with wet hair in a robe.

"Oscar, you're early!" she exclaimed before she realized that it was Jim at the door.

"Oh, I'm sorry," apologized Jim. "I must have the wrong apartment. I was looking for Sophie."

"Uh, hello," blushed the girl. "She's not in just now. I'm her roommate, Angela. May I ask how you got into the building, Sir?"

"I'm Jim Barnes and I'm a temporary guest down in apartment 2-C. I'll come back…"

"Dr. Barnes! I'm so sorry. Sophie has told me all about you but I've been incredibly busy working on my thesis and I haven't had a chance to meet you. I'd invite you in, but…" smiled the girl glancing down at her own robe.

"No, no, I'm sorry to intrude. I'll just see Sophie later. Please forgive me."

"Well can I at least give her a message?" asked Angela.

"I was just hoping to borrow the use of a laptop to do a little research on the Internet," replied Jim. "But it's not urgent. I can talk to her later, really."

"My friend Oscar should be here any minute and he's our in-house computer guru, so I'll see what he can dig up for you. You said you're in Marco's place?"

"Uh, I don't know. It's 2-C, if that helps."

Back in his apartment, Jim returned to the packet he had received from Karl Schmidt. There was one final item he had almost missed. Two type-written pages titled "The Teachers" provided a rambling narrative about a group that was apparently trying to save human-kind from self-destruction by repeatedly intervening at just the right moment and pulling civilization back from the brink of extinction. During their meeting Schmidt had used this same name when referring to the aliens who had provided technology to Jim, Schmidt and "many others." These would be the individuals mentioned on the first list titled "Those Who Know."

Jim studied the document closely trying to wrap his head around the implications of what was going on in the world behind the backs of almost every living soul. If

Schmidt's information was correct—and that remained to be seen—then somebody would have to step up and pursue this just as Schmidt had suggested in his letter. But who could Jim trust with this kind of information? Who could take this task and run with it? No matter who Jim considered, he kept coming back to one person—Frank Morton.

He leaned over the table, rested his chin in his hands and stared at the papers spread out before him.

"Frank, where are you when I need you?" he said out loud. "And why have I suddenly started talking to myself?" he thought.

"This task is yours, Jim."

Jim snapped upright.

"Frank?" he asked, already realizing that it was a stupid thing to say.

Jim leaped out of his chair and scanned the room.

"Who's there?" he demanded.

There were precious few places in the small apartment that anyone could hide, but Jim searched anyway. He checked the small closet near the door and he even pulled down the Murphy bed but, of course, there was no one else in the room. As he passed the table and glanced at the papers strewn about, he realized that he'd let himself get too involved in the possibilities they presented and had just imagined Frank's voice in his head—there hadn't been any sound at all.

Grinning at his own childish behavior, he sat back down and organized Schmidt's papers back into their original order and slid them into the envelope.

Jim wondered what had caused Schmidt to collect all this information. Was any or all of it true? If it *were* true, what should the next step be?

Jim was still trying to figure this out when there was a loud knock on his door.

"Who's there?" he asked before unbolting the door.

"It's Oscar, Dr. Barnes. Angela said you were looking for a computer."

Jim opened the door and greeted a young man in his early twenties with short, black hair and a goatee.

"Come in, please," welcomed Jim. "But I did tell her that this isn't an emergency."

"It's no problem at all. I keep a couple of spare laptops around in case somebody's primary machine craps out on them." Handing Jim a laptop, he added, "This isn't the fastest race car on the track, but it should get the job done for you. It's all set up to connect to our wireless network here in the building, so you shouldn't have any problems getting to the Internet. I'm sorry I don't have any spare printers, but if you need to print something, use the default device I set up. That's the photocopier down in the study—the room we call '1-A'."

Reaching into his jacket pocket he retrieved the AC adapter. "It's all charged up, but you'll probably want this, too."

Jim accepted the computer and charger gingerly and smiled, but before he could say anything the other man was already backing out the door.

"Sorry to run," he apologized, "but Angela has been working for weeks and tonight is our first real date in a long time. Good luck!"

And with that, Oscar was headed down the hall.

Jim pushed Schmidt's envelope to one side and set the laptop up on the table. The power adapter's cord didn't quite reach the nearest outlet, so Jim moved the table closer to the wall and turned the computer on. While he waited for it to boot up, he removed Schmidt's papers from the envelope and planned his course of action.

It was nearly 8:00 p.m. when a knock on his door broke Jim's train of thought for the first time. During the three and one-half hours he had been working he had generated six pages of notes about individuals whose names were on Schmidt's "Those Who Know" list and it turned out that Jim was in some very good company.

"Who is it?" he called from the table as he scrambled to collect Schmidt's papers and his own to stuff them into his briefcase.

"It's Sophie," came the reply. "Are you ready for some pizza and beer?"

Jim opened the door and invited Sophie in. She was carrying Jim's toiletry bag and a small suitcase he didn't recognize.

"I thought you might like to have your own things, so we stocked your room with some new stuff and gathered up yours. I hope you don't mind."

That evening Jim was introduced to more than a dozen graduate students from the University of Munich. Although he only recognized a few, they all seemed to know about him and his work. Apparently Sophie had become a big fan after his presentation the previous morning and she had done her best to spread the word.

It soon became evident that Sophie was the unofficial leader of the group and she seemed to accept this role with ease and grace.

"So, this is the infamous apartment 1-A, huh?" asked Jim, trying to make conversation.

"This is it," smiled Sophie. "It's actually our study and library but we use it as a multi-purpose room. Tonight it's a party room but tomorrow when everybody's back in classes it will take on a much more serious tone."

"I take it from conversations I've had with others tonight that you're not all studying the same curriculum, so what brings you together? How do you filter prospective tenants?"

"I guess that's my job," smiled Sophie. "I own the building right now, so I get to decide who lives here."

"You said 'right now'—do you plan to sell the place soon?" asked Jim.

"Well, not this year, but when I graduate I will pass ownership on to someone else, sure. I bought the building from my predecessor for $1 about three years ago and I'll sell it for the same amount when I leave the University. This building has been passed down that way for decades ever since a former student inherited it while he was a grad student at the University."

"What a unique idea!" exclaimed Jim. "And what a cool legacy. By the way, I want to thank you for putting me up here for a couple of days. The more I've thought about it, the more I'm glad I'm not at the hotel."

"You're quite welcome, but it was a group decision," smiled Sophie. "Every tenant has an equal say in everything we do here, including how we spend the rent, but the decision to offer you a room was unanimous. It's not often we get celebrities, you know."

"I wish my academic status were as high elsewhere as it seems to be here in Munich," laughed Jim. "I could double my speaking fees!"

"Sorry, but I didn't mean that," Sophie said, suddenly serious. "I meant you're a celebrity because you're on the BKA watch list. But many of us find your theories on ancient civilizations interesting, too. I'll be right back. I see a stein of beer that's about to take a spill."

Jim turned to survey the room and almost spun into Manny, the driver who had rescued him from the conference at noon.

"Oops, sorry, Manny. How did the rest of the lunch go?"

"Good evening, Dr. Barnes. It was just your typical conference luncheon. The only interesting thing going on was all the whispering about Professor Schmidt. If people knew how much waiters overhear, they'd spend a lot more time eating and less time talking."

"Really?" asked Jim. "And what was all the whispering about?"

"Well you probably know that he's been picked up by Munich's version of the Keystone Cops, right?"

Jim nodded.

"Well, the favorite lunch topic seemed to be why he was picked up. Speculation ran from tax evasion to divulging state secrets. Crazy, huh?"

Jim winced.

"Yeah, crazy. Excuse me a minute."

Jim caught up with Sophie and latched on to her elbow.

"Can I talk to you in private, please?" he insisted.

Out in the hall, Jim told Sophie what he'd just heard from Manny.

"As you know, I met with Schmidt on Friday. If they're serious about this state secrets thing, they may suspect that I'm involved, too. I think I should go in and make sure they know I'm not involved."

"No, you should absolutely *not* do that!" replied Sophie adamantly. "First of all, you have no idea what the BKA's real issue is with Karl Schmidt. All you have are rumors from a luncheon. And even if they did haul him in on treason charges that might be just a ploy so they can hold him indefinitely without filing more specific charges. That's how it works here."

"But what you don't understand," confessed Jim, "is that I actually do have access to classified material—*very* classified material. And if your BKA knows that, and if they implicate me with Schmidt, I could be in big trouble back home."

"Wow! In that case, maybe you should go talk to your people again, but I can't stress enough that you should have nothing to do with the BKA—at least not here in Munich. There isn't anything we can do tonight, so let's go back in and enjoy the Sunday night bash. I have an early morning class tomorrow, but as soon as it's over I'll come back here and take you wherever you think you should go."

"The Consulate," nodded Jim. "I was there this morning and they weren't very cooperative, but I think I should try again. And they're already aware of my security clearance, so maybe they'll understand my concerns this time."

"Okay, and overnight I'll see if I can find out more about Schmidt's status. Let's go back in."

At 10:30 p.m. Jim excused himself and went back to his temporary room on the second floor. Still fretting over the BKA's apprehension of Schmidt, Jim dug the missing professor's envelope out of his case and shuffled through the pages several times hoping an answer would magically appear. When it didn't, Jim decided to call it quits for the night.

As he was sliding the papers back into the envelope, his eye caught something written in pencil on the back of the last page of the stack—the second page of the "Teachers" ramblings. Turning the envelope over, he slowly slid the packet out until he could read the one-line hand-written note.

"Frank Morton, 17-SEP-2002 ???"

Slowly, Jim laid the envelope and its partially exposed packet of papers down on the table and leaned back. Finding Frank's name in Schmidt's work was shock enough, but why would the German professor also have recorded the exact date of Frank's disappearance? And was the hastily scrawled information just a quick note on a convenient piece of paper or did it actually have something to do with *the Teachers*?

Chapter 5

Jim finally fell asleep on the couch sometime after 2:00 a.m. and was startled awake by a knock on his door. As he struggled to sit up, he realized it was daylight.

"I'll be right there," he called, running his fingers through his hair.

"Hi," smiled Sophie when he opened the door. "Ah, are you okay?"

"Yes, but I'm afraid I spent the night on the couch and I'm not ready yet. Can you give me a few minutes?"

"Of course," she replied. "I'm done until this afternoon, so just knock on my door when you're ready. Have you figured out what you're going to do yet?"

"No, not really," frowned Jim. "Would you mind if we stopped someplace for breakfast while I think about it?"

"Not at all. I've already eaten, but I can always use more coffee and you must be starved. Just let me know when you're ready."

Jim showered, shaved and rummaged through the suitcase that Sophie's friends had brought from the hotel looking for clean clothes. When he was ready, he packed everything back into the suitcase and set it by the door. He collected Schmidt's papers from the table and slipped the envelope into his briefcase. Giving the room one last glance, he picked up the suitcase and walked down to Sophie's room.

Sophie chose a small cafe near the University for breakfast. Once they were seated in a booth and Jim had ordered his meal, she leaned towards the center of the table.

"So what have you decided, Dr. Barnes? It looks like something is bothering you."

Jim smiled sheepishly.

"Guilty as charged," he replied. "I'm concerned about Professor Schmidt, of course, but I'm also pretty worried about being implicated in anything he may be mixed up in. Did your friends find out anything new?"

"No, nothing," shrugged Sophie. "And that's odd because if he were being held in any of the normal detention cells, we'd have located him. Maybe it's something personal between Schmidt and the Colonel."

Jim winced at Sophie's last statement and she spotted it.

"What's wrong?"

Jim was silent for a minute and then decided he could share a little of what he knew with his new friend.

"When I met with Schmidt on Friday, he tried to convince me that a multi-national group of thugs was up to no good and he tried to get me to join his cause against them. I refused, of course, and ended the meeting rather abruptly. But the next night—the night my hotel room was ransacked—he had an envelope delivered to the front desk. I didn't receive it until yesterday due to all the commotion, but among Schmidt's notes I found Wilhelm Kruger's name and notes indicating that he is part of this group."

"Get out!" exclaimed Sophie. "If Kruger has his own agenda, apart from normal BKA business, that would certainly explain the rogue behavior he's exhibited. And it probably explains why Schmidt hasn't surfaced as part of the normal BKA business. Kruger probably has him!"

"I'm afraid it looks that way, and now I'm concerned about my own safety. You asked me what I've decided to do and I think I'm going to have you drop me at the Consulate and hope they will take me in until I fly out tomorrow afternoon. I hate to blow off the rest of the conference, but I don't think I should take any chances until I know more about Schmidt's allegations and I don't want to put you or any of your friends at risk."

"I'm afraid I have to agree with that. What else did Schmidt have to say?"

"Sophie, I really appreciate everything you and your friends have done for me, but I can't tell you any more until I have a chance to verify some of Schmidt's information and I may not be able to share any more even then. Here's my card. I've written my personal cell number on the back. If you hear any more about Schmidt, please call me collect day or night. And be very careful about interfering with Kruger until we learn more about him. I promise I'll let you know the second I have something concrete, but don't take any unnecessary chances until you hear from me."

Sophie pulled a pen out of her small purse, wrote a long phone number on the restaurant napkin and slid it across the table to Jim.

"That's my cell number as you would dial it from the United States," she said. "Call me the second you get home and again whenever you have news about Kruger. You've seen a small part of the organization we have here in Munich and we're at your disposal if you need ears and eyes here or anywhere else in Europe. If Schmidt's claims are correct, you're going to need all the help you can get."

"Thanks, Sophie, I will definitely keep that in mind. I'm not going to share the Schmidt documents with anyone else until I've had a better chance to study them, so please don't tell anyone they exist."

"You have my word," she replied as the waitress brought Jim's food.

Later, Sophie eased her car into the taxi zone in front of the American Consulate and turned to Jim.

"It's been interesting, to say the least," she smiled, "but it's been far too short. I hope you have a chance to get back this way soon, Jim."

The fact that she called him by his first name for the first time since they had met wasn't lost on him.

"Me too," nodded Jim. "And if you ever get across the pond, be sure to give me a call. Thanks again for everything."

"You're quite welcome. We'll have your things from the hotel sent here unless we hear otherwise from you this evening. And if they won't take you in, please call me immediately and then wait here—I'll come back and get you."

The honk of a waiting taxi behind Sophie's car ended the good-bye and Sophie was lost in traffic soon after Jim's feet hit the sidewalk.

Inside, Jim began what he expected would be a long series of bureaucratic shuffles. He presented his passport to the guard just inside the heavy glass door and prepared to take a seat in the waiting area.

"Right this way, Dr. Barnes," said the guard crisply. "The Consul General will see you now."

When the door closed behind the guard, the short silver-haired man behind the desk motioned for Jim to be seated in one of the straight-back chairs in front of him.

"So, we meet again, Dr. Barnes," said Jeffrey Hartford in a slow, even tone. "It seems that I may have been a bit hasty the other day and I'd like to offer my apologies. We now have reason to believe that you are being followed by a person or persons unknown and we'd like to suggest that you remain here until your plane leaves tomorrow afternoon."

"So the BKA does have Schmidt!" exclaimed Jim.

"We have no information on Professor Schmidt," frowned the Consul General, "other than the fact that a missing persons report has been filed with the local police. Regrettably, the BKA has not responded to our inquiry, but Schmidt isn't really our concern—you are."

"That wasn't what you told me the last time I was here," snapped Jim.

"True, but that was before this new information came to light. And again, I do apologize for denying your earlier request but we have very strict State Department guidelines. The information you presented during your first visit just didn't warrant any involvement on our part."

"You said 'person or persons unknown' are following me," replied Jim, calming down a bit. "Do you have any idea who they are or who they represent?"

"No, none whatsoever. However, they don't seem to be any of the Munich 'regulars' such as city police officers or local BKA agents. I suppose they could be from another region, but that seems like a lot of effort to go through. Besides, they're a bit amateur in their tactics. After all, we picked up on their activities almost immediately. Our best guess is that they are part of someone's private security force.

Have you angered any German locals during your short five days here, Professor Barnes?"

"I don't think so," replied Jim. "Other than some college students who attended my conference presentation, the only other people I've said more than a few words to have been Karl Schmidt and the staff here at the Consulate. Exactly how did you find out I was being followed? Other than the fact that I told you so, I mean."

Hartford smiled thinly at Jim's jab.

"As I mentioned when we last spoke, no one with your level of security clearance travels abroad unmonitored, Dr. Barnes. Because of the concerns you raised I was able to enlist the help of a local CIA agent who, in turn, spotted those watching you.

"And I must say," Hartford continued with a smile, "your escape from the luncheon yesterday was brilliantly played. These amateurs I referred to are still watching your hotel, waiting for you to head off to the conference. They have no idea that you spent the night in a university housing facility."

Jim was floored! Not only was he being followed by two different groups, but the CIA agent even knew about his association with Sophie and her friends.

"Listen, those students were just trying to help. They…"

"They are well known to us," interrupted Hartford, "and they're mostly harmless. We even solicit their help from time to time, but usually without their direct knowledge. You need not worry about them, I assure you. However, given the circumstances, I'd much prefer that you stay with us, rather than with them. At least inside this building we can keep an eye on you until you're safely on your way back to the United States. Given your clearance, I'm a little surprised they let you travel alone, but that's not my call."

"You've mentioned my clearance several times," replied Jim. "What's so special about my security clearance? I work in a facility that, among other things, deals with experimental military weapons, but I'm not directly involved in any of that. I was granted a Top Secret clearance when I first started working there, but I'm sure it was just routine bureaucratic stuff due to my location. They sent me a letter, I think, but I just filed it away"

The Consul General laughed out loud.

"Oh, I'm sure they sent you a letter! Yes, you have a Top Secret security clearance—so do I and so do lots of people. But yours has more acronyms after it than I've ever seen before. *SAP* I recognize—that's Special Access Programs. And *SCI* stands for Special Compartmental Intelligence—also a common designation. But the rest of this stuff is Greek to me. Here take a look at this."

The Consul turned an open file folder around and pushed it to the edge of his desk so Jim could see it. He pointed to a line that extended almost the entire width of the typewritten page.

"Wow!" smiled Jim. "That makes me look really important. I wonder what all that stuff means? I don't really do anything that significant—I just happened to be assigned to a Navy facility where a lot of important stuff takes place."

"Yeah, right!" grinned the Consul as he spun the folder back around and moved it back to his side of the large desk.

Secretly, Jim suspected that all additional codes tacked onto his clearance had to do with the alien technology he'd been exposed to during his involvement with Frank Morton and NWIDI. The spheres from the Mayan caves in Mexico, the buried pyramids on Japan's Yonaguni Island and the mysterious triangles from the "Lost City" off Cuba's western tip were all highly classified government secrets known only to a small handful of people in the world. Jim smiled as he realized that thanks to him, the U.S. Government had probably been forced to make up some completely new security clearance codes.

"So here's what we're going to do," stated the Consul, leaning back in his chair. "A couple of floors below me there's an apartment designed to house myself and my immediate staff in case of an emergency. I'm going to ask you to spend the rest of today and most of tomorrow with us. We'll get you to the airport tomorrow just in time to catch your flight in the afternoon. I'll have someone make sure you are brought meals but you are to stay down there until we take you to the airport. It's not as bad as it may sound, though, and I think you'll find the facilities quite pleasant."

"So basically, I'm under house arrest?" questioned Jim.

"I'd prefer to call it 'protective custody' but either way, you're staying with us until you leave Germany. I don't have the manpower to protect you out on the street and we don't have any idea who we're dealing with. Downstairs, you'll be comfortable and safe. There's Internet access in case you have any work to catch up on and there's satellite television from the States. I'll also have the place stocked with plenty of beverages and snacks. I see that your flight leaves Munich at 4:10 p.m. tomorrow, so please be ready to leave for the airport at 3:10 p.m. sharp. One benefit of staying with us is that we'll get you around all the lines at the airport using a diplomatic pass. You'll go right from the town car to the jet way with no stops and no hassles. Now if there's nothing more…"

Jim rose, shook hands with the Consul and started for the door.

"Oh, one more detail," said Hartford. "We'll collect your belongings from the hotel and bring them to you within the hour, but I'm afraid we have no practical way of recovering whatever you may have taken to the apartment building. Please feel free to call your friends and ask them to drop your things off here, but you'll need to make that call before you get in the elevator because there's no cell or landline service downstairs."

"I brought everything from the apartment," replied Jim, "and they offered to get the stuff from the hotel."

"Not necessary," replied the Consul. "That's being handled as we speak."

Outside the office, Jim was met by another young man in a dark suit.

"This way, Sir. I'll show you to your quarters."

When they got off the elevator two stories below the main floor they were in a wide hallway that looked like the service halls in a large hotel. The man led Jim to the left a short ways to where the hallway ended at a wall with a large metal door. He entered a code into a keypad next to the door and stepped back. There was a hissing sound and then the door slowly slid open, disappearing into the wall. They stepped through into a space approximately six feet on a side and the man pressed a button on the back wall. The open door closed, there was another hiss, this time with the faint hint of antiseptic, and then the entire back wall slid sideways revealing a comfortably appointed living room.

"This is obviously the main sitting area," explained Jim's escort. "There's a small kitchen and eating area through that door on your left and those two doors back there are bedrooms. Please choose whichever one you prefer. There will be some staff members coming down to stock the flat, but they will announce themselves first using this intercom. To open the inside door, simply press this button. Once I leave, no one will be able to enter without your expressed permission, so please listen for them because they will have the food and beverage items Mr. Hartford mentioned. The phone on the desk connects to a similar device upstairs. Please feel free to call us if you need anything. On the desk you'll also find menus from several nearby restaurants. When you get hungry, just make your selection and call us. Please allow about forty-five minutes for it to arrive. Do you have any questions, Sir?"

Jim looked around and shook his head but then had a second thought.

"I was told I might have Internet access to catch up on some work."

"Ah yes, I almost forgot," said the aid. He keyed something into a numeric pad next to the intercom and said, "There, you now have wireless access anywhere in the suite. However, you should be aware that all your activity passes through automated filters built into the Consulate Data Center, so…"

"Yes, I get it," frowned Jim. "But I don't have a computer."

"You'll find a laptop in the center drawer of the desk right over there, Sir. Is that all?"

Jim nodded and the aid quickly left through the large, nearly invisible door they had used to enter the suite. As he looked around, Jim was frustrated and angry about his situation but also a little relieved to be "off the street" and in the relative safety of the Consulate. He checked out the suite, poking his head in each room. The kitchenette was small but well furnished and included a small table and four chairs. One bedroom had twin beds and the other a king, so he tossed his suitcase on the king bed and kicked off his shoes. Returning to the living room, he retrieved the laptop from the drawer, placed it on the desk and turned it on. As he was connecting the A/C adapter to an outlet next to the desk, a buzzer sounded from the intercom.

"Yes?"

"Dr. Barnes, I have a delivery requested by Consul Hartford," came the reply.

Jim pressed the door button and turned to face the sliding wall. When it retracted, two men in kitchen staff uniforms wheeled a cart containing two large plastic tubs through the door.

Jim raised his eyebrows and smiled.

"Wow," he said. "All for me?"

The men wheeled the cart to the kitchen door and quickly unloaded the contents of the two tubs into the refrigerator and an adjacent cabinet.

On their way out, one of the men said, "One more trip, Sir. Your belongings from the hotel just arrived. We'll bring them right down and then we'll stop bothering you."

* * *

Kruger was fuming and Max Becker wished he could be anywhere else on the planet instead of on his way to his boss' office. A call from Kruger's office had awakened

Becker in the early morning hours and he was tired and confused. But worse, he had nothing to report to Munich's BKA Bureau Chief. There was no explanation or excuse for what had happened and yet Kruger was going to expect both.

When Kruger had ordered Professor Karl Schmidt brought in for questioning, he had insisted that Schmidt be handled "off the grid" so most of the BKA office staff was unaware that the eccentric professor from Munich University was even in custody. Becker had questioned the decision to hold Schmidt in a private interrogation room that was part of the Bureau Chief's executive suite. In fact, he'd questioned the need to bring Schmidt in at all, but Kruger had insisted. Now Schmidt was missing and Becker was going to have to explain why and how.

Becker had examined the windowless interrogation room and verified that it had a solid ceiling and air ducts that were far too small to accommodate a human, leaving the single, guarded door as the only possible way Schmidt could have escaped.

During his questioning of the two agents assigned to guard Schmidt, Becker had tried to pit the men against each other but they had both stuck to their stories and insisted that no one had gone in or out of the room until they opened the door for a routine check and discovered that the room was empty. As Becker approached the Colonel's office, he could hear the older man yelling at the top of his lungs. Apparently the guards were being questioned again!

***

When his clothes from the hotel were hung in his closet and the Consulate staffers had left, Jim relaxed for the first time. He turned on the flat-screen TV mounted opposite the couch and found CNN. The reporter was detailing the gruesome statistics about the Iraq War, a military action Jim just didn't understand or support. He listened for a minute and then wandered towards the kitchen to check out the "snacks" that had been delivered. Just as he reached the door, he heard a different TV reporter say "UFO" and he spun to see what was going on.

"There have been unconfirmed reports of UFO sightings all across western Europe," the reporter continued. "We're still waiting for additional information, but these reports seem to be centered on Munich, Germany where the alleged sightings took place late Sunday night and early Monday morning, Munich time."

Chapter 6

Jim raced to the couch and flopped down, but the reporter was already wrapping up and suggesting that viewers should visit the network's website for more information.

He quickly moved to the desk, navigated to the CNN site and scanned the screen for a link to the UFO story, finally finding it at the bottom of a long list of articles in small print on the "World" page. When he clicked the link, instead of the story, he was presented with a dark blue screen that had the seal of the U.S. Department of State in the center and the words "Content blocked by server" in white letters across the bottom.

Jim grabbed for the telephone on the desk and buzzed upstairs.

"May I help you, Dr. Barnes?" asked a friendly male voice.

"Yes you may. I'm trying to look up some information on the Internet but instead of the Web page I get a screen indicating that the content has been blocked."

"I'm sorry, Sir, but I can't help you with that type of problem. May I connect you with the Information Systems department?"

"Yes, of course!" replied Jim, already growing impatient with the bureaucracy of the Consulate.

A few seconds later, another male voice answered.

"This is Dan Sloan speaking. I understand you're having Internet problems, Dr. Barnes. How may I assist you?"

"I'm trying to look up an article on CNN's website and apparently your servers are blocking it. The Consul General assured me I would be able to catch up on some work while I was here but I can't do that if my Internet access is blocked."

"I'll look into it and get right back to you, Dr. Barnes. As far as I know, we're not blocking anything to your suite, but let me check."

Jim continued to watch the news report on television, but the UFO story had come and gone and probably wouldn't be replayed for another thirty minutes. Returning to the laptop, Jim did a search for "UFO" and "Munich" to see what he could find but the story was still too new to be listed by the search engines. Just then the telephone rang.

"Mr. Barnes, I'm sorry to tell you this, but the information you're interested in is being blocked worldwide by the State Department in Washington D.C. and there's nothing we can do locally to alter that. I'm afraid you'll have to work on something else while you're here in the Consulate. Is there anything else I can help you with?"

Jim fumed but he knew when he was beat.

"No, that's all. Oh, wait! Do I have access to my office network back in the States? I work at a military complex called AUTEC in the Bahamas."

"Let me check, Sir," replied the IT person. A few seconds later he said, "Yes Sir, we can provide Level 3 secure access to your facility if you would like. All your communications with AUTEC will be encrypted so you may work as if you were in your own office. Is there anything else?"

"No," smiled Jim to himself. "Please enable the Level 3 link and I'll start catching up on my work back home. Thanks for your help."

As Jim watched the laptop screen, it flashed black and when it returned to the normal desktop there was a new icon visible that was titled simply "AUTEC." Jim double-clicked on it and after a brief delay he was presented with a log-on screen identical to the one he would see if he were back home in his office. Within seconds he was reading the CNN story by accessing the Internet through the encrypted link to his office computer. Apparently the Department of State and the Department of the Navy had different ideas about censorship.

Unfortunately, the story CNN was running on their website didn't include much more information than Jim had heard on the television so he dug out the envelope he had received from Schmidt and browsed through it again. When he came to the page titled "The Six" he went back to the laptop and tried several searches. The only interesting thing he came up with was an article about the Six Nations, also known as the Iroquois Confederacy, and the role they played in the new American government of Benjamin Franklin and Thomas Jefferson. Next Jim performed searches using all six countries Schmidt had mentioned during their meeting on Friday: the United States of America, the United Kingdom, Russia, Mexico, China and South Africa. Again, nothing interesting turned up. Eventually he tired of the delays resulting from the encryption and the trans-oceanic communications to his office so he logged out of his secure connection and shut down the laptop. There would be time enough for research when he got back to his own computer at AUTEC.

Jim passed the rest of the day and the evening reading a book he found on a bookcase next to the desk. Titled *1491: The Year China Discovered America*, the book put forth the theory that Chinese admiral Zheng He had actually discovered the Americas seventy years before Columbus. As a trained anthropologist, Jim found the "facts" that supported the book's theory amusing, but he had to remind himself that things he had seen in his three missions with the NWIDI team were far more incredible and far less believable—and yet he knew them to be the truth.

***

Trying not to look disrespectful, Max Becker dropped into a chair in front of his boss' desk and waited for him to finish a telephone call. Becker had tried to use the call as an excuse to come back later but Colonel Kruger had issued a firm hand gesture and insisted that he stay. Max couldn't tell who was on the other end of the line, but Kruger was being much more polite than he was with any of his subordinates, including Max.

Finally, Kruger hung up and slowly slumped into his high-back leather chair.

"Have you seen the news today?" asked Kruger.

"No, Sir, I haven't," Becker replied softly, "and I gather from your side of that conversation that Professor Schmidt hasn't been found yet."

"CNN has just broken a story about multiple UFO sightings over Munich! And no, Schmidt has not been found yet. To make matters worse, our visiting professor from the United States has apparently been granted shelter at the American Consulate until he leaves the country tomorrow afternoon. That means we have no way to know what those two talked about on Friday when they met at the *Englischer Garten*."

"Well the good news is that Barnes will soon be back in the United States and then he'll be someone else's problem," smiled Becker. "The American authorities should have no problem grabbing him if they feel it's necessary to coax some information out of him. That leaves us with just the Schmidt disappearance to resolve."

"And that brings us to your new assignment, Becker," said Kruger angrily. "And this assignment comes from people much more powerful than me, so listen very carefully. You are to do whatever it takes to find Schmidt, dead or alive and return him to this office. Alive would be preferable, of course, but either way he is to be brought back here. You will have all the resources of the BKA at your disposal because we're going to put out the word that Schmidt is wanted on suspicion of treason. We're also going to add him to our list of Most Wanted so others in this office and elsewhere won't question the resources we're going to throw into this man-hunt. Any questions so far?"

Becker took a minute to absorb what he was being told before replying.

"Why me?" he protested. "Certainly there are others that are more qualified to conduct a search of this magnitude. I haven't worked in the field for several years."

"And that's exactly why you are going to head up this investigation, Becker! I want a fresh perspective and some new thinking. It's imperative that Schmidt be brought here, to my office, and that he not fall into the hands of another agency or even into the hands of another branch of our own agency. Is that clear?"

"Yes, of course," nodded Becker. "So I take it he's not really wanted for treason. It might help me find him if I knew what he was really up to, Sir."

"Conspiring to provide information to a foreign agency or government," replied Kruger.

"But isn't that treason?" challenged Becker.

"Okay, let me rephrase that—conspiring to provide information to an *alien* agency or government."

***

After being mostly ignored by the Consulate staff for more than twenty-four hours, Jim was given the royal treatment Tuesday afternoon as he made his way to the airport and boarded the British Airways jet that would take him to London's Heathrow Airport. Just as the Consul General had promised, Jim was escorted from the government town car directly to the aircraft long before regular boarding began in the terminal. As he and his escort reached the bottom of the metal steps that led up to the top of the jet way, the other man shook his hand.

"This is where our VIP services end, I'm afraid," said the other man. "Your luggage will be loaded shortly and tagged for transfer in London according to your ticket. Once you arrive there, you'll be just another traveler, so be sure you check in with the airline."

When Jim reached the top of the stairs and opened the door, a female flight attendant was waiting to greet him and show him to his seat in First Class.

"General boarding doesn't start for another fifteen minutes, so may I get you a beverage while you wait, Mr. Barnes?" asked the young woman.

"Sure," smiled Jim. "I'll take a ginger ale, if you have any."

"Of course, Sir. That's quite a coincidence because that's what the other gentleman is drinking, too," quipped the attendant nodding her head towards the rear of the cabin.

After the attendant zipped off to the galley, Jim stood up and took off his jacket while he scanned the cabin for other passengers. Jim was seated on the right side of the plane in row ten, about two-thirds of the way back in the First Class cabin. Trying to look casual, Jim opened the overhead compartment and looked to his right. The only other person he could see on the plane was a thirty-something man wearing a dark suit and tie and a pair of metal-framed sunglasses popular with pilots and military types.

"CIA," Jim said to himself.

When he turned to return to his seat the flight attendant startled him.

"I'll take that, Sir," she said indicating his jacket. "We have a closet for our first class passengers. Here's your ginger ale. Please let me know if there's anything else I can get you before the rest of the passengers come aboard."

Jim had a two-hour layover in London, so he found a sports bar and had supper before his nine-hour red-eye flight to Miami. While he waited for his food, he glanced around the restaurant for the CIA agent who had been on the flight from Munich but he didn't spot anyone that seemed to fit the stereotype. Jim had been among the first passengers off the plane and he had hung around the gate until people stopped coming out of the jet way but he never did see the agent again.

Jim made it a point to be at his departure gate well in advance of the scheduled boarding time because he wanted to be one of the first onboard. From his seat, this time near the front of the first class cabin, he examined every passenger that came aboard to see if he were still being followed but none of the more than three hundred other passengers looked like what Jim would characterize as a federal agent and he decided that once he was safely on his way back to U.S. soil they had called off their surveillance.

While the mass of passengers in the coach cabin were still stowing their carry-on baggage, Jim's cell phone rang.

"This is Jim Barnes," he said.

"Dr. Barnes, I'm so glad I caught you before take-off! It's Sophie, from Germany."

"Sophie! I didn't expect to hear from you so soon, but I'm glad you called. What's up?" asked Jim silently apologizing to the man in the seat next to him.

"Have you heard the latest about Schmidt? Apparently he managed to sneak away from the BKA facilities and now there's a massive man-hunt underway to find him!"

Jim could actually hear the glee in Sophie's voice as she described the situation and the embarrassment it must be causing the BKA.

"No, I hadn't heard about that," he replied. "The Consulate kept me pretty isolated while I was there and even censored my Internet access. Did you hear about the UFO sightings over Munich a couple of nights ago?"

"Sure, that story is all over the local news, but we hear about UFO sightings all the time," laughed Sophie. "I've even seen one or two, I think. "Oh, wait, you don't think they abducted poor Professor Schmidt, do you?"

She was laughing so hard Jim could barely make out the last part of the sentence.

"No, of course not," replied Jim trying to fake his own laughter. "Well, they're making the announcement about turning off all electronic devices, so I have to go. Thanks for the Schmidt update and let me know how the man-hunt goes, okay?"

"Of course," replied a more serious Sophie. "Have a safe flight and call or email when you get settled back wherever it is that you're going. Bye for now!"

Jim smiled and turned off his iPhone before slipping it back into his shirt pocket. It made him feel much better knowing that Karl Schmidt, a man he had only really met once, had somehow managed to escape Germany's version of the FBI but he also wondered how long Schmidt's freedom would last before the BKA tracked him down.

Nine and one-half hours later, the British Airways 747 touched down at Miami International Airport right on schedule and by late Wednesday afternoon Jim was back in his own office at the AUTEC facility on Andros Island in the Bahamas. He had never felt so glad to be "home" in his life!

After texting Sophie that he had arrived safely, Jim started going through the stack of mail that had accumulated during the few days he had been away and then he powered up his Navy-supplied desktop computer to check his email.

Among the dozens of routine messages from colleagues and scientific organizations, Jim found one that actually made him gasp. Dated April 19, 2008—the previous Saturday—it simply said, "*J: free at last. Beware of Edwards. More later –T*" and it was from *xtnq6prd@gmail.com*, a seemingly random email address that Jim didn't recognize. If Jim hadn't recognized the word "Edwards" he would have probably deleted the message without a second thought, but he knew immediately that this message was from Tony Nicoletti, his teammate and friend from NWIDI. Tony had been silent for more than five years and Jim had feared he was dead but now here he was, sending cryptic email messages warning about Buzz Edwards!

Jim stared at the message for a long time, reliving his NWIDI adventures and remembering that Tony had always been the "muscle" of the group—the one who got things done, one way or another. Tony had been an Army Ranger in Viet Nam and had met NWIDI's team leader, Frank Morton, behind enemy lines during some covert operation or another. After the Army, Tony had leveraged his pre-military truck driving experience into a contract job hauling classified freight for the federal government. It was on one of these trips that Tony had been handed the strange black sphere that started the whole NWIDI thing in the first place.

"Tony's alive!" shouted Jim out loud.

Grabbing at his keyboard, Jim pounded out a quick reply to Tony and clicked "Send." Within seconds, his message bounced back from the Gmail server with an error indicating that the email address Tony had used no longer existed. So, even though Tony's message said he was "free at last," he was obviously still hiding from someone—probably from Edwards and his friends.

Jim was elated to know that Tony was okay but he was also frustrated that he couldn't communicate with the other man and find out where he'd been for the past five years. He was determined to find a way to reach Tony.

AUTEC was an unusual place for many reasons, not the least of which was the fact that small groups of researchers from various companies and countries were always coming and going. The complex housed dozens of small one- or two-person labs similar to the one that had been assigned to Jim. Other than casual conversation in the base dining hall, independent researchers rarely spoke to each other because each were on tight time tables and were working on their own proprietary—and often classified—projects. Jim had initially been assigned a Navy Ensign to assist him but as his work on the triangles became more and more bizarre, whoever was overseeing Jim's project had decided that the fewer who knew about it the better and the Ensign had been reassigned. However, Jim and Stan Mallory had remained in contact and periodically met at the base Officers' Club for an afternoon beer. Among other things, Ensign Mallory was a computer wizard and he often helped Jim get some new piece of software running. Maybe he could figure out how to track down Tony.

"Here's to Wednesday," toasted Mallory, sarcastically, "and one more day into the log books. How's your research going, Jim?"

"Oh, I'm still muddling my way around, but they haven't pulled my funding yet, so I'm still here," smiled Jim.

Even though they had worked together for nearly a month, Mallory knew very little about Jim's research. He had seen the triangles, of course, but back in those days they were considered just ancient artifacts that exhibited unusual chemical properties. When Jim began to zero in on the real origin of the objects, Mallory was removed from the project and Jim's work was moved to a Top Secret, "need to know" classification. And as far as Jim had been able to determine, he was the only one on the base that needed to know. He electronically filed monthly status reports to some obscure agency in Washington, D.C. and otherwise reported to no one. When he first arrived at AUTEC he had been given the civil service position of Research Scientist with a pay grade of GS-14, the equivalent of a Lieutenant Colonel in the Army or a Commander in the Navy. Technically, this meant that Jim outranked Mallory by a lot, but Jim never paid much attention to the Navy's protocols and he had always insisted that Mallory call him "Jim" rather than "Sir."

"However," continued Jim, "I need some more of your computer expertise. I have an old friend who sent me an email message but I was out of town and he apparently cancelled his email address before I had a chance to reply. I really want to get in touch with this guy and I was hoping you might have some ideas."

"Where was the email account?" asked Mallory.

"The address ended with 'gmail.com' so I assume that's Google, right?"

"Yes, and that's a dead end, I'm afraid. There's no way to pry any information out of those guys without a federal court order. If this is AUTEC-related business you might ..."

"No, it's personal," interrupted Jim. "What if he were to contact me again? Is there any way to shoot a reply back to him before he has a chance to cancel his account?"

Mallory thought for a minute and then nodded.

"Sure! You could set up what's called an *auto-responder*—also called a *vacation response* or an *out-of-office reply*—that will automatically send a pre-stored message the instant his message is received. The only problem is that it will go out to everyone who sends you email, not just your friend."

"Could we put some kind of filter on it?" asked Jim. "I get very few emails from Gmail accounts and I could design the reply so it wouldn't make sense to anyone but him."

"Did this email come to your AUTEC email account?" asked Mallory.

"No, I use an account at Yahoo for my public speaking activities and that's where this message was sent," replied Jim.

"Perfect! Yahoo lets you send a custom message to email from specific domains, so I think we can make it happen."

Mallory pulled a tiny laptop-like computer out of his backpack and opened the lid.

"What the heck is that?" asked Jim. "It looks like a toy."

"Oh, it's no toy, I assure you. In fact, if you're going to be doing a lot of traveling, you should get one for yourself. The size is only one of its benefits. Here, log into your Yahoo account and let's give this a try."

Fifteen minutes later Jim's Yahoo email was configured to catch incoming email messages from all Gmail accounts and fire back an auto-response message that read *"T: Received your update but must talk ASAP. Call number on website where you found my email address. –J."*

"There!" said Mallory proudly, "If he sends you another message your response should get back to him before he can delete the account. Anything else?"

"As a matter of fact, yes," smiled Jim. "Would you help me pick out one of those little laptop things?"

By the time Jim got back to his lab it was 9:30 p.m. and he was anxious to check his email to see if Tony had tried to contact him yet. The telephone number his email responder referenced was his personal cell phone, so he was sure Tony hadn't tried to call, but there was no guarantee he could or would, even if he received Jim's message.

There wasn't anything from Tony that night or all day Thursday or on Friday, either. By Saturday morning, Jim was getting worried that Tony's email might have been a one-time event. He rescanned every email he'd received since returning from Germany, but there was just the single message from Tony. However, Jim did find an unusual message in his "official" AUTEC Inbox on Saturday morning. It was addressed to "Dr. James Barnes" and it read "Pending further investigation of a security breach, you are hereby requested to confine yourself to your current duty station (AUTEC) for your own safety." The message was signed "G. Wellington Armstrong, Director, Office of Science, U.S. Department of Energy."

Chapter 7

Jim stared at the email message, his anger rising by the second. How dare they tell him where he could and couldn't go? In his five and a half years at AUTEC this was the first time he'd had any sort of restrictions placed on his activities and he didn't like it one bit! He scanned the message for a telephone number or email address, but there was neither. He typed a reply asking for clarification and hit Send but almost immediately he received a reply indicating that the originating address did not accept incoming mail and suggesting that he use "proper channels."

The normally mild-mannered Jim slammed his fist down on his desk and swore. Grabbing his sun glasses, he stomped out the door of his lab and started down the street in the direction of the base administrative offices. It was a Saturday, so he didn't expect to find many people there, but there should be an orderly or an Officer of the Day on duty and he intended to find out why he was being confined to the base. As he turned the corner onto the wide avenue that connected the base's main gate to the administrative buildings he was nearly run down by a Navy Shore Patrol jeep traveling at a high rate of speed. The back of the jeep was stuffed with extra SPs and they all appeared to be heavily armed.

"Get inside!" one of them yelled to Jim.

Across the circular area that contained the base flag pole, Jim could see armed SPs standing guard in front of the entrance to the administration building and he decided that maybe this wasn't a good time to go yell at them. As he surveyed the scene around him, he saw a lot of intense, fast-paced activity—something was up and it was obviously being taken very seriously by the military component of AUTEC. He quickly weighed his options and decided that he'd prefer to sit out this event in his lab rather than in the small room that served as his living quarters so he retraced his steps back down the narrow side street to his lab as fast as he could without breaking into a run. Inside, he locked the door and pulled down the shade to cover its small, rectangular window. Since the military was obviously occupied and he knew very few other civilians on the base, he decided to spend some quiet time investigating the papers he'd received from the now missing Professor Karl Schmidt.

Jim retrieved the manila envelope from his lab's small safe and laid the papers it contained out on his desk in four piles. On the far left he placed the hand-written letter from Schmidt. Next was the one-page list titled "Those Who Know" which included his own name. In the third stack he placed the typed, doubled-spaced list of the members of *the Six* along with Schmidt's seven pages of hand-written notes that included Edwards' name. In the right-most stack he placed the two pages of typed narrative titled "The Teachers" that described an alien race that was apparently trying to save civilization from self-destruction and *the Six*.

"The good, the bad and the alien," Jim said out loud as he was reminded of Clint Eastwood's classic western film.

In Germany, Jim had made it clear to Schmidt that he didn't want any part of this crusade and yet here he was, staring at what might be the only set of recorded information connecting the Six to *the Teachers*. With no obvious place to begin, he decided it might be a good idea to learn more about his allies before taking on the Six, so he decided to concentrate on the single "Those Who Know" page.

He turned to his computer and created a new Excel worksheet. In the left hand column he entered the seventeen names, exactly as they appeared on Schmidt's list. In the next column, he entered any available contact information. Sometimes this was a complete address, sometimes it was a phone number, sometimes it was *both* and in a few cases it was *neither*. One thing every entry had, though, was an email address and this Jim entered in a separate, third column. To satisfy his own curiosity, he used a fourth column to record the country location of each individual. He got this information either from the address or by looking up the telephone number's country code on the Internet. Of the five entries that had neither, he was able to catalog three based on the domain portion of their email address, leaving just two unidentified entries.

When he sorted the list by country, he was a little surprised by what he found. First of all, the seventeen entries included fifteen different countries that spanned the entire globe: The United States, Canada, Mexico, Costa Rica, Argentina, Australia, Indonesia, Japan, China, India, Egypt, Italy, Great Britain, Russia and Germany. The lone German entry was none other than Karl Schmidt himself.

Secondly, the only country with multiple entries was the United States. His name was there, of course, along with two others that sounded familiar: Alan Thompson and Benedict Kingston. Another name, the only one listed for Mexico, also seemed vaguely familiar. Where had he heard the name Prof. Alfonso Torres before?

Jim leaned back in his chair and clasped his hands behind his head. With his eyes closed, he repeated the three names over and over, trying to stir some memory, but nothing came.

Suddenly his computer emitted a series of shrill beeps and the screen flashed solid yellow. Large black letters appeared at the top:

"This is not a drill. The AUTEC facility is under YELLOW ALERT. Seek shelter inside and do not leave until you hear the All Clear signal – a long, continuous tone from the base warning siren. Repeat, this is not a drill."

"Holy Cow!" thought Jim. "This must be serious."

Aware that he was in possession of some potentially history-changing alien artifacts, Jim closed and locked the safe to protect the triangles from any physical danger. Not knowing what to expect, he made sure the more potent chemicals he kept on hand were secure and not where they could tip over or fall onto the floor if the ground shook. The sky had been clear when he had headed for the base headquarters, so he didn't think the alert was due to an impending hurricane or tropical storm, but he wondered if one of the many rumors about a "killer" tsunami might be materializing. Since AUTEC, and

Andros Island where it was located, were virtually at sea level, a serious tidal wave would be a big problem.

Back at his desk, he tried to forget what might be going on outside and concentrate on Schmidt's list. Personally, he knew of three different types of alien artifacts: the twenty black spheres from Mexico's *Loltún* Caverns, the twelve *tsubutes* he had discovered under Yonaguni Island and the five triangles currently stored in his safe. If there were at least sixteen other people who had intimate knowledge of alien artifacts, how many different types of objects could there be? Dozens, maybe? Or maybe several individuals knew about a single artifact, in which case the number could be quite small.

Jim thought back over his three specific cases. The entire NWIDI team knew about all three of them, of course, but only his name was on the list. As he rewound his mental tape of the *Tractrix Project*, it suddenly occurred to him who Benedict Kingston was! Jim had known him as Ben, not Benedict, but he was the young Department of Defense exobiologist who had been on loan to the Department of Energy when he and Jim had first met. Ben was the lone investigator of an alien craft that had apparently brought the *Loltún* spheres to Earth long before the Maya culture evolved. And there had been another individual that Ben had mentioned working with—of course! Al Thompson, the strange old guy who had given Tony the sphere that launched the *Tractrix Project* in the first place. And just that fast Jim had identified two of the familiar names on Schmidt's list. Now what about this Torres guy?

He worked his way backwards through the *Tractrix* timeline, back to the few days he and Frank had spent in the Yucatan. He smiled briefly, remembering his chance meeting with Carmen, the librarian at the University in Merida. She had given Jim access to some research done by a professor named…Torres! That's how he knew that name! Jim had later determined that Torres had discovered the secret hiding place of the spheres and then mysteriously gone missing, never to be found again. So that made four people, at least, who knew about a single type of artifact. Granted, two of them were now dead, but Jim had no idea how old the list was. Conspicuously missing from the list was the DOE agent, Gene Carlson, who had originally introduced Ben and Jim. And there must be others within Gene's close circle of confidants who also know about the spheres stored a thousand feet below the surface at the Yucca Mountain complex north of Las Vegas. And what about the Mexican father and son team, Alfredo and Ricardo, who had led him and Frank through the *Loltún* Caverns and eventually to the secret hiding place of the twentieth and final sphere?

Something just wasn't adding up. If numerous people who know or knew about one or more of the artifacts weren't on the list, then maybe "Those Who Know" didn't refer to artifacts at all. Some of the people he had just mentally listed not only knew about the artifacts but also knew they were of alien origin, so that couldn't be it, either. Jim scratched his head and wondered what else the seventeen people on Schmidt's list had in common.

As he concentrated, his eyes wandered across his desktop, eventually coming to rest on the rightmost pile—the two page summary of "The Teachers" and their apparent mission. And then it hit him—*the Teachers*! Could that be what the "Those Who Know" list referred to? Did all of these people know that an alien race was actively working to save human civilization from destruction? Jim had only just recently learned about *the Teachers* from Schmidt, but that might explain why his name was at the bottom of the list and circled in red. Suddenly, Jim remembered something he had discovered back in the little apartment in Munich. Slowly he turned the two pages on the far right over, knowing what he would find on the back—Frank Morton's name and the date he disappeared scrawled in long-hand.

For as long as Jim had been associated with NWIDI he had known about Frank's theory that one or more ancient civilizations had existed long before the Mesopotamians and that they had vanished without a trace. In fact, it was Jim's discoveries that had confirmed Frank's theory. In the last days of NWIDI's final mission Frank had come to the conclusion that numerous civilizations had existed and that they had each been jump-started by some alien influence. When pressed on the subject, he always pointed to the Maya. "Why," he would ask, "would the Maya need a calendar that spanned more than five thousand years when their own civilization lasted less than a thousand? And how and why did a culture that never learned to use the wheel for transportation develop such an incredible knowledge of astronomy and mathematics?" Frank's theory was that the calendar and the astronomy knowledge were both gifts from an alien race and Ben Kingston's research on the excavated space craft seemed to bear that theory out. At least it proved that the spheres had arrived here on Earth from somewhere else.

But none of this addressed the question at hand. Why wasn't Frank's name on the "Those Who Know" list and why was it written on the back of the information about "The Teachers?"

One at a time, Jim Googled each of the other sixteen names on the list. A few produced hits but most of them didn't. Of those that did, none really stood out as significant. Most were unknown scientists or researchers, except for a woman from Italy who had a doctorate in theology from the prestigious St. John's University in New York.

What was it that bound this group of individuals together? Had they all just stumbled onto something, the way Jim had, or had they been chosen for some reason? Since his Internet search wasn't turning up anything worthwhile, the next logical step seemed to be individual contact. Jim began the process of creating a mailing list with the intention of sending some sort of vague inquiry to each person on the list just to see what kind of response he would get. Based on the responses, he would decide how next to proceed. He had just started typing when he heard the long wail of a siren in the distance.

"All clear," he thought, looking up at the clock. "Whatever the fuss was all about, it only lasted an hour."

Before he could resume work, the familiar chime of his computer told him he had new email and he glanced up at the screen to see who was bothering him this time. When he saw the random string of characters followed by "@gmail.com" he almost fell out of his chair.

"Gotcha!" shouted Jim.

With any luck, the canned auto-response message Ensign Murphy had set up for him would have already fired off its reply to Tony and he would see it before he had a chance to log off and delete his email account.

He grabbed his mouse and opened the message as quickly as he could.

"J: escaped mx2 in March. Edwards on my trail now. Alert others if you can. More later. –T"

Jim puzzled over Tony's short, staccato message. Did it imply that Tony had been held in MX-2, the secret military installation buried deep beneath the ground near Cancun International Airport's main runway, for more than five and one-half years? Was Edwards personally pursuing him or did he have others doing that? Tony's short message left many more questions than it answered.

As he pondered Tony's message, the computer chimed again and, again, this message, too, was from an anonymous Gmail account.

"Tony, you old dog, are you back already?" he laughed.

But his laughter turned to shock as he read the text.

"J: I know we should have contacted you long ago, but we couldn't for reasons I hope to be able to explain someday. For those same reasons, I'm using an anonymous email account that I will cancel as soon as I click Send so you won't be able to reply. I'm sorry, but that's the way it has to be. I just wanted you to know that we've learned, indirectly, that T is alive and apparently well. We've also stumbled onto a stream of data from an international group that's obsessed with the UFO sightings over Munich. Thought you might know something about that. Our data also indicates they are

planning something significant in your area very soon – in fact it may already be underway. Heads up! –L"

"Linda!" Jim shouted out loud. "Where are you?"

Almost immediately he realized that the auto-response message would have been sent to Linda because she was also using Gmail.

"Oh well," he thought, "at least she'll know that I'm also aware of Tony's status."

Jim assumed that Tony must have contacted Linda the same way he had reached out to him, but the "how" didn't matter, as long as there were some communication. Jim reread the last sentence of Linda's message again. Had she somehow stumbled onto the same group that Schmidt had called "the Six?" And did the "significant operation" she referred to have anything to do with all the craziness going on outside his laboratory?

His desk phone startled him out of deep thought and back to the reality of his lab.

"This is Jim Barnes," he answered.

"Dr. Barnes, this is Lieutenant Cannon, the Officer of the Day. Captain Gregory would like to see you in his office as soon as possible."

"Captain Gregory as in Base Commander Captain Gregory?" stammered Jim.

"Yes Sir. Shall I send a vehicle for you?"

"No, that's not necessary. I'm just a couple of blocks away and I'm leaving right now."

Jim didn't know or care much about military protocol but he knew that if the base commander wanted to see him it was serious business. Within a minute, he was out the door and headed up the street to the main administration building.

"Please sit down," motioned the Captain from behind his large desk. "I don't believe we've ever met, have we?"

"No, Sir, I don't believe so. I was one of many in the crowd at the reception when you took command a couple of years ago, but I never managed to get through the well-wishers to introduce myself."

"So you've been here, ah," the Captain said, opening a manila folder on his desk, "five and a half years, more or less, is that correct?"

"Yes, Sir. I was sort of 'drafted' while here on Andros with some friends conducting a rather unusual investigation."

"Yes, I can see from your file that your work is highly classified but that's not why I wanted to speak with you. I'm sure you're aware that the base was just on alert. It's not the first time AUTEC has been threatened, but it's the first time since I've been here and I didn't want to take any chances. I hope it didn't interrupt your work too much."

"Ah, no Sir," replied Jim, astounded that the Base Commander would even care about his work. "Did you say threatened?"

"Yes, the boys up at the Pentagon picked up a lot of chatter that seemed to reference us so we were already on our toes and then an unidentified vessel approached the entrance to our secure harbor area and refused to respond to hails. Our closest air support is the Naval Air Station in Jacksonville so I decided to lock things down here until help could arrive. However, as quickly as the blip appeared on our perimeter defense systems, it disappeared. With the federal budget being what it is, I called off the jets as soon as the target vanished."

"Did anyone see the intruder?" asked Jim.

"Well, no because it was submerged. It's not unusual to have submarines in our waters because a great deal of the research conducted here has to do with weapon systems to be used on or against submarines. However, all our vessels were accounted for, so this one caused us some concern.

"Wow," said Jim. "I realize there's a lot of secret stuff here, but it's all still in development. Why would anybody want to threaten AUTEC?"

"That's exactly what I would like to ask you, Professor. You see, along with AUTEC, your name was also mentioned in that chatter!"

Chapter 8

"Me?" replied a shocked Jim. "Why would my name…wait, you don't think I had anything to do with this, do you?" As an afterthought, Jim added, "Sir."

"No, Dr. Barnes, Navy Intel actually thinks you may have been the primary target and AUTEC was merely your unfortunate host. I've been ordered to debrief you and file a report by seventeen hundred hours today. However, I need to remind you not to divulge any classified information to me unless it relates directly to the safety of AUTEC and its personnel. May we proceed?"

Dumbfounded, Jim nodded his head. "Of course, Captain Gregory, but I don't know where to begin."

"Well, let's work backwards, beginning with your recent trip to Germany. I understand you sought asylum in the U.S. Consulate. What was that all about?"

"I was invited to speak at a scientific conference hosted by the University of Munich. I have some unique and somewhat controversial theories about the existence of ancient civilizations and that was the subject of my presentation in Munich. Just prior to leaving AUTEC, I was contacted by a professor over there who requested a private meeting with me, so I obliged. Soon afterward my hotel room was ransacked and I learned that I was being followed by both the CIA and some other group. Naturally, I sought help from the Consulate until it was time to fly home."

Gregory scanned the documents in front of him and then looked up. "Yes, that all matches what I have here except for one thing. What about the package that was delivered to your hotel—the one that was left with the desk clerk?"

Jim's heart skipped a beat. How did they know about that?

"Ah, well, yes, a mysterious envelope arrived the night my hotel room was torn apart, but I didn't receive it until the next day. It was just some scientific papers."

"From whom?" asked the Captain.

Jim paused for a second. He had to be very careful not to cross the "need to know" line here.

"It was from the professor I had met with the day before—ah, no, by then it would have been two days prior, I guess."

"That would be Professor Schmidt, I believe," replied the Captain without looking up. "Are you aware that he's currently missing and a wanted fugitive?"

"No," lied Jim. "In fact, I have it on good authority that he's in the hands of the German BKA."

"He was, but apparently he managed to get away and he's now the subject of a nationwide manhunt. You wouldn't happen to know where he is, would you?"

"Of course not, Captain! I only met the man for a few minutes and it didn't take me long to decide he was a nut case. I was surprised to receive the package from him because I thought I had made it very clear that I didn't want to have any more to do with him."

"What was in the package, Dr. Barnes?" asked the base commander looking up and directly into Jim's eyes.

Jim paused again. "I think we've reached the point where I should not answer your question due to the classified nature of the answer, Sir."

"Suit yourself. Let's try another approach. Before coming to AUTEC you were associated with a private research group called NWIDI. Where are the other members of your group now?"

"Well, as your report probably indicates, the leader of our group, Frank Morton, disappeared in a diving accident near South Bimini Island in September of 2002. I haven't seen the other two since then."

"Two?" challenged the Captain. "My information indicates there were three others. Nicoletti…"

"Oh, you probably have Javier Reyes listed there, too," interrupted Jim. "He wasn't really a part of the organization, although he probably would have become a member since he and Linda were married a few months after Frank's disappearance."

"That's correct," nodded the Captain. "And you haven't seen or heard from either Linda McBride or Javier Reyes since 2002?"

"No, Sir! In fact I was the one who urged them to…"

The Captain smiled. "Urged them to do what, Dr. Barnes?"

"To disappear, Captain, but I think we've come to another point where I can no longer answer questions on this subject."

"Fair enough. I only have one more thing for you. I'm going to say a phrase and I want you to look directly at me as I do it. Please don't say a word, just look at me."

Jim shrugged. "Okay."

"The Teachers," said the Captain slowly.

Jim was thrown off guard by the words and he was sure his shock was obvious to the Captain.

"That will be all. Your laboratory has been temporarily sealed so please return to your quarters and don't leave the base until further notice. You should hear from me by tomorrow morning."

"Hear about what?" questioned Jim. "What is it that's being decided, Captain, and by whom?"

"That will be all, Dr. Barnes," replied the Captain sternly as he closed the folder in front of him.

Jim turned and started for the office door feeling like a scolded school boy.

"And you are not to mention a word about this to anyone," called the Captain as Jim turned the knob.

Slumping into the only chair in his small sleeping room, Jim shook his head. What had just happened? Why would his name be mentioned in "chatter" intercepted by Navy intelligence? What was going to happen to him now? What about his highly classified research on the alien triangles? Jim stared at the tiny television for hours pondering these and many other questions.

***

Max Becker sat alone at the corner table in the café where he'd taken lunch almost every day since he started work for Colonel Kruger, Munich's BKA Bureau Chief. As he sipped his coffee and waited for his meal, he wondered how long it would be before he'd be able to return to his office—the one place that brought him comfort.

Just a short few minutes ago Kruger had sent him on a mission to find the escaped Professor Karl Schmidt, from the local university. Schmidt was something of a local legend because of his public claims that he'd encountered aliens from outer space and accepted scientific knowledge from them. He was a little out of touch with reality, maybe, but no more so than many of the academic types that Becker had run into. And now he, Becker, was about to lead a manhunt for this professor that should never have been arrested in the first place. The one who should be locked up, thought Becker, is Kruger. He has been acting more and more paranoid each day and Becker attributed it to pressure from something Kruger seemed to be obsessed with outside his normal BKA duties. Becker didn't know much about Kruger's personal life but he knew that the older man was acting stranger by the day.

Kruger had hand-picked Becker as his personal assistant nearly ten years earlier when Becker was a rookie BKA agent recently assigned to the Munich bureau. Back then it seemed like the chance of a lifetime but lately Becker wasn't so sure he'd hitched his wagon to the right star, to paraphrase an American saying. If Kruger were up to something fishy and he implicated Becker, Becker would be a dead man—a BKA agent inside a prison had a very short life expectancy.

During the past year Becker had tried to find out what was driving Kruger but his investigation had turned up very little. He'd scraped together some bits of information, but not enough to know what was going on. Perhaps his new assignment would allow him to get out from under Kruger's constant watch and do some real detective work. Who knows, he might even locate the mad professor and get to the bottom of his UFO stories!

Becker ended his meal in a much better mood than he had begun it and he even had an idea where he would start looking. He had heard about an apartment building near the University of Munich campus that housed a number of the more radically-thinking students. That sounded like the perfect place to begin a wild goose chase.

***

The telephone in Jim's sleeping quarters finally rang at 8:45 a.m. the next morning. He had spent most of the night in his chair and had slept fitfully in bed for only a couple of hours.

"Captain Gregory will see you at 0900 hours," stated the voice on the line. "Please be prompt."

Jim acknowledged and the line went dead. Fifteen minutes later, Jim was sitting in front of the Captain's desk again, right where he'd been the afternoon before.

The career naval man looked up with a frown.

"Well, I'm sure this will be AUTEC's loss, Dr. Barnes, but it seems that you'll be leaving us. The boys in Washington have decided that our facility can't provide the level of protection you and your research require, so you're being transferred, effective immediately. I argued against this decision, but I was overruled. You have about three hours to pack your personal belongings, your research notes and, of course, your triangles. I'll send a jeep…"

"You know about the triangles?" interrupted a shocked Jim.

"A little bit, yes. Most of it I learned during the past twelve hours, but there's always been a short file on you here at AUTEC—just enough to justify why we were providing you with a lab and living quarters on a more or less permanent basis."

"So where am I going?" scowled Jim.

"I don't know, and that's the truth. Your departure will be a closely guarded secret, as will your arrival at your final destination. I will not be told where you've gone and the individual in charge of the receiving facility, wherever that is, will not be aware of your origin. It's for your own safety."

"But I'm a civilian," Jim protested. "I'm not some sailor you can just order around at will. Besides, my research is at a critical stage right now and this disruption could set me back months"

"I'm sorry, but this decision is not mine nor is it entirely the Navy's. Your fate is now in the hands of a small group of very select individuals, both military and civilian, and you have no choice in the matter. Your transfer is being done in the interest of national security and that's all there is to it. You'll either go willingly or unwillingly but you *will* go so I suggest you opt for the former rather than the latter."

"I can't believe this is happening," complained Jim, now standing in front of the Captain's desk. "I demand to see my Congressman!"

The Captain laughed. "I'm afraid he or she wouldn't have the necessary security clearance to even hear your case, Dr. Barnes. Please take my advice and go with the flow here. I can assure you that those who have made this decision have only your safety in mind. Now go pack and be ready for the jeep when it arrives at your lab at noon, sharp."

"I thought my lab had been sealed," replied an angry Jim.

"It is now unsealed, but you are the only person authorized to enter until all your research materials are safely off our facility."

When Jim arrived at his room, a new, dark blue Navy duffle bag had been placed on his bed, so he loaded it with his clothes and his few personal items. He packed the two new suits he'd purchased for the Munich conference into his suit case and struggled down the stairs to the main door of the barracks facility. At the bottom of the stairs a Shore Patrolman rushed to his aid.

"I'll take those, Sir. I have a jeep outside to take you over to your laboratory."

At the lab, the SP carried Jim's two bags to the door and then excused himself. Jim muscled them inside and locked the door.

Two hours later he had transferred all his relevant computer files onto CDs and packed them, along with his written notes, into a small carry-on bag. He rolled and packed his suits into the duffel bag and set the empty suitcase aside. His last act was to place the five triangles back into the original metal-like container where they had been found and carefully store it in the carry-on bag with his other research materials.

Jim looked around the large rectangular room that had been his workplace for more than five years and realized that he hadn't exactly come here willingly, either, but it hadn't been so bad. A little lonely, maybe, but he was a solitary kind of guy. He wondered what he would find at the other end of the trip on which he was about to embark.

The jeep that picked him up at his lab a few minutes later delivered him to a small building at the edge of the facility's waterfront. The SP helped him move his duffel bag into the otherwise empty room and then turned to leave.

"Someone will be here for you in just a few minutes," he said. "Please stay inside until they arrive."

Jim heard the jeep drive off and almost immediately he heard a slight hissing sound behind him. He turned to see an otherwise invisible elevator door open and reveal a sailor dressed in typical ship-board denim pants and blue shirt.

"Welcome aboard, Sir," greeted the man. "Please step to the back of the car and I'll collect your bag for you."

Five minutes later, Jim was shocked and amazed to be stepping into the very first submarine he had ever seen.

"I didn't know these things could be boarded underwater!" he exclaimed.

"Yes Sir," smiled the sailor, "but it's something we don't like to advertise. This way, Sir."

During the ten-hour trip aboard the submarine, Jim was locked in a small state room obviously intended for a junior officer. The room had a small in-wall refrigerator that was stocked with bottled water and a variety of soft drinks and twice a sailor delivered a tray of snack foods and sandwiches, but otherwise Jim was sequestered and alone. He departed from the submarine through an underwater system similar to the one he had used to board at AUTEC and he was transported to a large military hangar in the back of a canvas-covered truck.

As Jim climbed out of the back of the truck, he spotted the most beautiful aircraft he'd ever seen. The blue and silver jet had a narrow, pointed front topped with a long canopy. Two short, stubby-looking wings protruded from mid-plane and the rear contained twin upright tail pieces.

"She's a real beauty, isn't she?" asked an airman who had approached the truck to help Jim down. "It's a Javelin MK-20 Trainer. Someone will be along to get your bag, but please take any classified material with you and keep it in your possession at all times."

Jim grabbed the carry-on, which now contained the metal box of triangles, his CDs, the Schmidt file and his hand-written notes and followed the airman across the hanger to a series of offices on the far side.

"Please wait here while I get you some clothes," said the airman, indicating a chair in the first room they approached. "I'll be right back."

When the young man with a crew cut returned, he was carrying what appeared to be a pilot's jumpsuit.

"Please try this on while I get you some boots. You can leave your pants and shirt on the table for now. Size eight, right?"

Dumbfounded, Jim nodded. When the airman returned, he was still trying to figure out some of the jumpsuit's fasteners.

"Not bad," said the airman as he stepped back to admire his outfitting job. Pointing the insignia on Jim's shoulders and the nametag over his left pocket, he added, "For the next few hours, you are Major Smith, USAF. Have a safe trip, Sir."

The man disappeared out the door and Jim stood there staring at his boots.

"Good evening!" boomed a middle-aged man dressed in a flight suit similar to Jim's. "Ready to go flying?"

Jim's jaw dropped and he stammered. "I don't know where I am, much less where I'm going. Are we going to fly in that…"

"Javelin MK-20 Trainer," finished the other man. "That's right, but I'm going to do all the flying tonight, Major. We need to go over some safety items, so please follow me. Oh, and stuff your clothes into your carry-on, there. We'll find some way to squeeze it into the cockpit with you."

At exactly 11:31 p.m. a colonel with no name tag on his flight suit, a terrified "Major Smith" and a sleek MK-20 jet flashed into the sky, climbed to twenty-five thousand feet and leveled off at 425 mile per hour.

Chapter 9

Seated in the instructor's seat behind the Colonel with no name, Jim was in a state somewhere between shock and awe for the next two and one-half hours. In front of him was a mirror image of the instrument panel the Colonel was using to control the aircraft and the pilot had used the intercom built into their helmets to point out several lighted displays, but Jim was too fascinated with what was going on around him to listen. Instead, he focused his attention on the spectacular star show above the jet's canopy. Based on a rudimentary knowledge of astronomy he soon deduced that they were flying in a generally north or northeast direction. Below was only blackness, so he sat back and enjoyed the thrill of the ride.

Eventually Jim felt the plane make a sharp bank to the left and begin to lose altitude.

"Are we there?" he asked tentatively.

"Almost," said the voice in his helmet. "We'll be on the ground in about fifteen minutes. How are you doing?"

"I'm blown away, actually," replied Jim honestly. "It's such an incredible perspective from up here! Do you ever get used to it?"

"Well, I've been flying for almost thirty years but I still love every second of it," replied the Colonel. "Looking down at the ground makes you remember just how tiny we humans are, but flying a machine like this also makes you realize how much we've accomplished."

"Well put," agreed Jim, "and for me this has certainly been a day to remember. I started out in…"

"I don't need to know that information!" interrupted the pilot. "My job is to deliver you from Point A to Point B. Everything else about you is to remain private until you are debriefed later today. I'm going to be busy for the next few minutes, so sit back and enjoy the rest of your ride."

And with that, the earpieces inside Jim's helmet went dead and he assumed the pilot had turned the intercom system off.

Outside, he could now see lights spread out on both sides of the plane and he realized they must be approaching the east coast from out over the Atlantic. As they descended, the lights grew brighter and more numerous until the entire surface below the plane seemed to be lit up. A sharp turn to the left followed by a sudden and sustained decrease in altitude almost cost Jim his lunch and he instinctively grabbed the sides of his seat. While he was wondering what he would do if he had to vomit, he heard the thump of the wheel bays opening and the plane began to level off. His stomach returned to its normal place and he stole a glance over his left side as the pilot made another course correction. Seconds later the plane touched the runway in a crescendo of screeching and bumping. When the jet finally eased to a stop, Jim released his grip on the seat and sucked in a deep breath.

"Sorry about that," apologized the pilot, "but we were instructed to remain at altitude until the last minute and then drop in 'unannounced' to minimize the amount of time we spent on commercial radar screens. Welcome to Andrews Air Force Base, Major Smith. A flight crew will be here to help us out in just a minute."

Jim was helped out of the plane by three young airmen and escorted to a dark blue golf cart with the Air Force insignia on the side. Clutching his overnight bag, he watched them unload his duffel from a compartment behind his seat and place it on the cart. As he was driven across the huge tarmac to a small building, he looked around and tried to take in as much as he could. In the distance, he recognized the distinctive shape and color of Air Force One bathed in light from a dozen huge halogen work lights. He was in Washington D.C.!

The senior airman unlocked the door to the small, windowless out-building and indicated that Jim should proceed inside. Another airman followed with the duffel bag.

"Someone will be along in a few minutes to pick you up, Major, but while you wait, please change back into your civilian clothes and leave the jumpsuit and boots in here. The door will lock behind you so be sure you have all your belongings before leaving."

A few minutes later he heard the loud thump-thump-thump of an approaching helicopter and he opened the door a crack to see what was going on. As the large, gray craft settled to the ground fifty yards away, a crew member jumped to the ground and trotted his way.

"Right this way, Sir," greeted the helmeted Navy crewman. "I'll get your bag. Please keep your head down."

Aboard the helicopter, the crewman who had carried his duffle bag helped Jim into a shoulder harness and then sat down on a bench-type seat opposite him. The crewman's helmet had a mirrored face shield covering the front but it was obvious the person behind the shield was communicating with someone using a built-in system similar to the one in the helmet Jim had worn on the jet.

The crewman gave Jim a "thumbs-up" and the helicopter lurched off the ground and into the air. Jim had been strapped into the center position on the wide seat and it was impossible to see out the side windows, so he tried to relax. He still had no idea where he was going, but he had the feeling that he was nearing the end of a very long day.

After a few minutes, Jim felt the helicopter set down and the crewman across from him came to assist with the harness again.

"Keep your head down and go straight into that building!" he yelled above the still spinning rotors. "I'll be right behind you with your bag."

Jim opened the door that had been indicated and stepped out of the way so the crewman could enter with the duffel bag. Before Jim had a chance to say "thank you" the man was gone, dashing across the helipad to the waiting craft.

"Good morning," said a voice from behind the counter.

Startled, Jim spun to face a young Air Force Lieutenant.

Glancing at his watch, he frowned. "Yes, I guess it is morning, isn't it. It's been a long, long day. Where the heck am I, anyway?"

"Welcome to Bolling Air Force Base, Dr. ah, Smith," he said, scanning down a log sheet he held. "If you'll just sign in here, I'll get someone to take you to your quarters immediately so you can get some rest."

Jim was fed up with all the cloak-and-dagger activities but he was too tired to argue so he signed "Dr. James Smith" where the other man indicated and handed the log sheet back. From somewhere under the counter the Lieutenant produced a thick brown military routing envelope and handed it to Jim.

"This contains some initial paperwork you will need to fill out as well as your schedule for the next few days but you have nothing scheduled until eleven hundred hours, so there's plenty of time to look at that later. The car that's pulling up out front right now will take you to your residence. Welcome to Bolling, Dr. Smith."

Jim looked over his shoulder to see an Air Force staff car rolling to a stop at the door.

Thirty minutes later, Jim was alone in a small, two-bedroom apartment that the driver had described as a "Mixed Service Guest Residence." The unit was completely furnished, right down to linens, dishes and silverware and there was even a modest supply of beverages and non-perishable foods provided but all Jim cared about was getting some sleep. His watch read 3:15 a.m. meaning that he had been up for more than twenty hours. He tumbled onto the bed, pulled a folded blanket over himself and crashed.

**

Max Becker sat slumped down in his car across the street from the brick apartment building that was known to be the home of a number of student activists. He had watched people come and go for nearly an hour, and he had to admit that they didn't look like a very dangerous crowd to him. He checked the BKA dossier he had copied before leaving the office to make sure he had the right address but everything checked out. With no real plan in mind, he crossed the street and walked up the half-flight of steps to the building's main entrance.

In the small foyer, one wall was lined with call boxes for each unit. Becker scanned the names, mentally checking off several as being ones that appeared in his dossier. But when he came to the one labeled "S. Hoffman" he smiled and stopped scanning. He had read a great deal about *Fräulein* Hoffman in his BKA file and he was convinced that if anyone knew the whereabouts of the missing Professor Schmidt, it would be her. According to the BKA, Sophie Hoffman was the closest thing to a leader this group of misfits had.

When there was no answer after the third ring, Becker began to think his day wasn't going to go so well after all.

"Can I help you?" asked a female voice through one of the other call boxes.

"Ah yes, I was hoping to talk to *Fräulein* Hoffman, but apparently she's not home. Perhaps I should come back later. Do you happen to know when I might find her home?"

"No." replied the voice bluntly. Then, in a friendlier tone, "May I tell her who called?"

Now Becker had to think fast because he was off his game plan.

"Ah, she wouldn't know my name, actually. I'm looking for a friend of mine and I had hoped that *Fräulein* Hoffman might have some information that would help me locate him. He's missing and I'm very worried," lied Becker.

"Well, I can let her know you stopped by, if you want. What's your friend's name?"

"Karl Schmidt," replied Becker. "He's a professor over at the University."

"Stay there! I'll be right down!" replied the voice.

Surprised but pleased, Becker did as he was told. Soon a young woman Becker recognized from her dossier photo as Sophie Hoffman came down the hallway towards the glass door that separated the foyer from the rest of the interior.

She opened the door and motioned for him to come in.

"We can talk in here," she said, leading Becker into the first room on the right.

After she closed the door, she invited him to take a seat at a large table in what was obviously some sort of multi-purpose room. Sophie took the chair opposite Becker.

"Now what's this about Professor Schmidt?" she demanded. "And why would you be looking for him here? I'm Sophie Hoffman, by the way."

"But I rang your bell several times and..."

"I was next door and didn't hear the bell at first," interrupted Sophie.

"Ah, well I'm glad you finally did," smiled Becker. "As I said, I'm a friend of Karl's and I haven't been able to reach him for more than a week. I'm worried but I don't want to go to the authorities if he's away on personal business."

"And why would you be looking for this missing professor here?" Sophie repeated.

"I asked around over on the campus and several people told me that you know about everything that happens on and off campus," lied Becker. "You have quite a reputation, young lady. And I mean that in a good way."

"I've never seen you on campus before. How do you know Schmidt?" pursued Sophie.

Making up his story as he went, Becker replied, "I'm a private researcher, not associated with the University. Professor Schmidt and I are collaborating on some research and we generally meet over dinner somewhere. When he stood me up a week ago Sunday I was surprised but I figured something had come up at the last minute. But when he didn't show again last night, I got very worried. This has never happened before."

"Well, I'm sorry, Mr.... I'm sorry, I didn't get your name."

"Weber," lied Becker, falling back on his mother's maiden name. "I'm Max Weber and anything at all that you might know or have overheard would be appreciated very much. Although we never talked about it, I understand Karl was interested in UFO sightings. Do you think that might have anything to do with his disappearance?"

"I'm sure I don't know, Mr. Weber. I know of Professor Schmidt, of course, but I don't believe I've ever met him and I'm sure I wouldn't recognize him. I've only seen pictures of him in the local newspaper and I've read some of his fantastic claims but I'm afraid I can't help you. He's a legend around campus, but not a celebrity."

Putting on his most disappointed look, Becker shrugged.

"Well, thank you for your time. I sure hope he didn't get mixed up with that American that was here last week. A while back Karl mentioned that he was meeting with someone from the United States and this morning I heard that an American who spoke on campus last week is the subject of a nationwide BKA investigation. Again, I thank you for your time, *Fräulein*."

Standing up, Becker went through the motions of preparing to leave.

"Wait," said Sophie, biting her lip. "Was this American you mentioned the one who spoke on the existence of ancient civilizations?"

"It could be," nodded Becker. "Why? Do you know him?"

Now it was Sophie's turn to lie.

"No, of course not, but I attended his talk with some friends of mine. One of my classmates is studying anthropology and we actually went to heckle the guy, but he turned out to be a very interesting speaker. Why is he wanted by the BKA?"

"I have no idea," replied Becker, "but I sure hope Karl isn't mixed up in anything dangerous. Listen, if you hear anything—anything at all—will you give me a call? For the next few days I'll be at the Hotel Dolomit, Room 412."

"Of course," replied Sophie, moving towards the door, "but I really don't think I'll be of much help. Good luck in your search, though."

After Sophie had showed the man out and made sure the front door had locked behind him, she returned to the room and looked directly at a painting on the far wall.

"Did you get all of that?" she asked.

"Of course," replied a male voice from a speaker on a nearby bookshelf. "He was parked across the street for almost an hour before he came to the door and he looks to me like BKA."

"Oh, I'm sure of it," nodded Sophie. "And it's obvious that they've lost Karl Schmidt. What I want to know is how they connected him to me. Are you sure you weren't followed the day you brought Dr. Barnes here?"

"I'm positive, Sophie. I used every trick in the book getting here from the University and I hung around outside for fifteen minutes after he came inside to be sure nobody was cruising through the neighborhood."

"Well, it's too late to worry about it now, anyway. Check out the hotel and see if you can find out who he really is, but be careful. Even the BKA aren't without their resources. His story about Jim is probably a lie, but I need to warn him anyway."

"Jim?" asked the voice in the speaker.

"Dr. Barnes," corrected Sophie as she blushed and left the room.

***

After a fitful night's sleep, Jim awoke just before 9:00 a.m., showered and dressed. After exploring what was apparently his new residence, he poured himself a glass of orange juice and sat down at the table in the dining area. The information packet was still there where he had tossed it the night before, so he opened it and browsed through the sheets inside. The top page was his itinerary for the next few days and the only item for today simply said "Commander's Briefing, 11:00 a.m.—please wait for a staff car to pick you up."

As his eyes scanned down the page, he learned that tomorrow he would be attending a "New Staff Orientation" in the morning, followed by a "Workplace Safety Seminar" in the afternoon. On Wednesday his only task appeared to be "Lab Assignment and Familiarization" which probably meant that he could finally get back to work.

The rest of the documents were confidentiality agreements, non-disclosure agreements, and waivers of several different types. He vaguely remembered the desk clerk who had given him the envelope saying that he needed to complete them before his 11:00 a.m. appointment, so Jim read and signed all of them without understanding half of what he was reading.

At exactly 10:45 a.m. he heard a car pull into the driveway and honk one short "beep." He picked up his carry-on bag, took a quick look around, and stepped outside. After locking the front door he proceeded to the Air Force staff car and climbed into the back seat. He had learned the night before to *never* sit in the front seat with the driver!

"Good morning, Sir," greeted the young driver.

"Good morning," replied Jim.

No other words were spoken during the short, ten-minute drive because Jim was totally absorbed by his new surroundings. He hadn't been able to see anything the night before, but in the daylight, he was taking in everything he could.

The car wound through what appeared to be a small residential area, with many identical buildings each containing two to six units like the one in which he had just spent the night.

Soon the car came to what was obviously a military gate or checkpoint of some sort and after being waved through by a military policeman it turned right onto a frontage road. To his left, Jim could see a busy Interstate highway, but the car paralleled it and soon turned right again, stopping at another gate. Out the right side window, Jim saw a large sign that read "Naval Research Laboratory" in huge block letters.

After a short conversation between the Airman and a naval policeman, the car proceeded through the gate and down a wide street lined with office buildings and windowless structures that looked like warehouse facilities. Eventually the one-way street made a right-angle turn to the left, passed in front of a large office building and appeared to make another left turn and head back towards the gate. However, the car stopped in front of the large building at the end of the street.

"Here you are, Sir. Someone will show you where to go once you're inside. Don't forget your bag."

Jim thanked the man and walked into the building with a great deal of apprehension.

"What have I gotten myself into?" he asked himself.

Jim was led to an office that had the words "Captain Stukey, Commanding Officer" neatly painted on the heavy wooden door. Inside, a female secretary sat behind a large "L" shaped desk protecting a door on the right. At the far end of the room, several small couches were arranged against the three walls facing the door.

Jim exchanged pleasantries with the woman and she asked for his packet. After glancing at the name printed on the envelope, she suggested that he make himself comfortable at the far end of the room until the Captain could see him. Several minutes later the phone on her desk buzzed and she called to Jim.

"The Captain will see you now. Right through here," she said, indicating the door beside her desk.

As Jim stepped through the threshold, he felt like he had stepped into a time machine. The inside of the Captain's office was finished in dark wood and military memorabilia was on display everywhere. As he glanced around, his reaction was apparently obvious.

"I'm a bit of a history buff," smiled the distinguished looking man seated behind the desk.

Jim had been so impressed by the décor that he hadn't even noticed that anyone else was in the room.

"Yes, I can see that!" replied Jim honestly. "Good morning, Sir, I'm Jim B.., er Smith."

The Captain smiled and stood to shake hands.

"You'll get used to that name soon enough, Son. Please sit down and let's chat for a bit. Would you like some coffee or tea?"

Jim declined both and waited for the Captain to sit down before taking his own seat.

"I expect you've had an interesting thirty-six hours, Dr. Smith, and I apologize for all the secrecy and military protocol you've no doubt been subjected to. You'll have to trust me when I say that it was necessary to protect you—and the knowledge you possess.

"First of all, let me start by welcoming you to the United States Naval Research Laboratory in Washington D.C. This will be your new work place and we hope you will find it a pleasant place to continue your research. We'll get you settled into a laboratory equipped with whatever materials you need in the next day or two after you've become acquainted with our facility. Although the NRL was originally an arm of the Navy, we now support research programs for all branches of the military as well as other agencies of the federal government and I believe you'll find our facilities more than adequate. If that's ever not the case, please let me or one of my senior staff members know immediately.

"We've arranged housing for you at the adjacent Bolling Air Force Base facilities. As you no doubt noticed this morning, you have to leave Bolling and travel a short distance on a civilian road in order to access NRL. I wish that weren't the case, but it is. However, we would like you to limit your travel in the civilian world to that short trip back and forth, at least for the time being. Between the two facilities, you will find a wide variety of recreational activities, dining establishments and two base exchanges for shopping. And, of course, you'll have access to Bolling's very nice Officer's Club, with all that it has to offer."

"So I'm restricted to the base?" interrupted Jim.

"Well, it's actually two bases, but yes, that's it in a nutshell. This will make more sense to you in time, but I assure you these actions are for your own safety and protection. And that brings me to the next thing I want to discuss with you this morning, Dr. Smith.

"I'm sure you realize the scientific importance of the objects you are carrying in your bag but what you haven't been told, until now, is that they have become a matter of national—even international—security. And so have you, since you are the only one that even begins to understand how and why they work. They—and you—have been declared national assets that are to be protected at all cost. However, we also need you to continue your work in as much freedom as possible so that's why you are here at NRL."

Jim started to interrupt again, but the Captain cut him off.

"There's something else you should know, Dr. Smith, but this information must never be repeated outside this office, is that understood?'

Jim nodded.

"The people who arranged for you to be here are very concerned about your safety, but they're much more concerned about the safety of our nation. They believe that an international group is working from inside our own government—and possibly others as well—to manipulate world events and further their own interests. Your benefactors also believe that this international group is now highly focused on acquiring you and the objects in your bag for some unknown purpose. The reason for all the secrecy during the past few hours is because we don't yet know who these individuals are."

Jim smiled and relaxed for the first time since leaving the AUTEC facilities.

"I believe the group you're referring to is called 'the Six.' They've already infiltrated the governments of the US, the UK, Russia, Mexico, Japan and South Africa and they're working on Germany as we speak."

As the Captain's jaw dropped, Jim continued.

"And if I were you I'd start by having a talk with a Department of Defense staffer named Buzz Edwards."

Chapter 10

Captain Stukey glared at Jim for a second and then leaned forward onto his desk.

"Dr. Smith, I don't know where you got that information, but if any of what you just told me is true it is hereby classified Top Secret, do you understand?"

"Yes, Sir, Captain, and I believe it's true. I haven't had time to research the data yet, but if the U.S. Navy will leave me in one place for a few days and provide me with unrestricted access to the Internet, I can probably get you a verdict by this week-end. That is, if you are authorized to receive such information. The Commander of my last duty station apparently wasn't on…"

"I assure you, Dr. Smith, I *am* authorized to receive the information," interrupted Stukey. "In fact, I'm going to ask you to tell me everything you know about this but before I do I need to tell you something that very few people in this country know. What I'm about to tell you is classified, of course.

"Because of my position as director of this research facility, I sit on a special Presidential advisory panel made up of military and civilian folks from a number of different disciplines. As I mentioned, our internal intelligence people intercepted some disturbing chatter that led us to believe that a person or persons inside our own government were collaborating with individuals overseas in an effort to manipulate world events. I can't go into more detail than that, but suffice it to say that this became a concern at the very highest levels. If you have information that will shed light on this topic, I need to hear it but so do some other members of the panel and I want them to hear it directly from you. If you would be so kind as to wait in the outer office, I will set up a secure conference call so you only have to tell your story once."

Overwhelmed, Jim nodded. "Yes, of course, but as I mentioned I haven't really had a chance to study the material in detail yet."

"I understand, but the others need to know what we're dealing with. I'll let you know when the call has been set up—it shouldn't take very long."

Jim collected his bag, which was feeling heavier by the minute, and removed himself to the outer office. As he passed the secretary's desk, she was apparently already on the phone with the Captain because Jim heard a lot of "Yes, Sir" replies from her.

While he waited, he thumbed through the papers he had received from Karl Schmidt just over a week before. Although he hadn't actually studied them in detail, he had done a lot of thinking about their significance and what the various lists meant.

Ten minutes later the secretary indicated that the Captain was ready to see him again and Jim re-entered the inner office. There was a black, star-shaped device in the middle of Captain Stukey's desk with a wire attached to a jack on the wall.

"Ladies and gentlemen, Dr. Smith has just joined us. Dr. Smith, I'm sure you'll understand if I don't make the traditional introductions. I'd like you to repeat what you told me earlier and then explain to us how you came to possess the information. I'd also like you to describe any other information you may have relating to this topic. Please begin, Dr. Smith."

For the next fifteen minutes Jim spoke without interruption. He repeated his statements about the Six and Buzz Edwards; and then he went on to describe his meeting with Karl Schmidt, the professor's unusual request and the arrival of the packet at the hotel in Munich. He described the contents and even referred to the actual documents a couple of times so as not to confuse the details. He closed by describing Frank's diving accident and the fact that Frank's name and the date of the accident had been written in pencil on the back of the two-page document titled "The Teachers."

"That's all, I think," concluded Jim.

"Before I open this up to questions," said the Captain, "I'd like to review a few things you've just told us. You say there are three separate documents—"The Six," listing the countries you mentioned; "Those Who Know" which contains your name; and "The Teachers" which, among other things, has your former teammate's name penciled onto the back. Is that correct?"

"Yes it is," answered Jim loud enough for the device on the desk to pick it up.

"And you believe that a member of the Department of Defense named Buzz Edwards is somehow involved with this group called 'the Six'?"

"That's also correct," replied Jim. "I believe he used my group to obtain information of a highly sensitive nature for his own use—or at least for use by his group."

"Thank you Dr. Smith. I'm sure there are some questions, but to keep us from stepping all over each other, please allow me to call on each of you, one at a time, using the number I gave you when you dialed into the conference call. Let's begin with number 1."

"First of all," said a lady's voice from the speaker built into the device on the desk, "let me thank you for coming forward with this information. I understand you have also been working on some rather remarkable research in another area, is that true?"

"Ah, yes, ma'am," stammered Jim. "But I've been told not to discuss that information with anyone unless I have expressed written permission from the director of the Office of Science. I'm sorry, but…"

"This is the Director, Jim," interrupted another voice from the box. "You are hereby authorized to share whatever you know about the artifacts with this group. I just faxed a written authorization to Captain Stukey's office. You may continue as soon as his secretary hands you that letter."

Surprised, Jim replied, "Well, then you also know my name isn't really Smith, too, so why does everybody keep calling me that?"

"Because I'm the only one in this group who knows your real name and we've all agreed to compartmentalize our information until we know more about our adversaries and the extent of their infiltration. Please continue when you are ready."

The secretary had opened the door and handed Jim a single sheet of paper while the Director was speaking.

"Okay, I have the letter. I recognize the signature as one I've seen on other documents, so I'm going to assume that I have authorization to speak. In response to the lady's question, yes, I have been studying some artifacts for the past five years and I have made limited progress in understanding their origin and the mechanics of how they work; but I still have no idea what their purpose is or how they came to be located where they were found."

"By 'artifacts' you mean alien artifacts, don't you, Dr. Smith?" asked the female voice.

"Yes, Ma'am," replied Jim without elaboration. "And I believe that everyone on Karl Schmidt's 'Those Who Know' list is also in possession of alien artifacts. I think that's the thing we know—that aliens have visited earth in the past and…" Jim's voice trailed off.

"And what, Dr. Barnes," prompted the Captain.

Jim took a second to collect his thoughts.

"And that they are probably still here. I believe they are *the Teachers* mentioned in Schmidt's notes and that the Six intends to interfere with whatever they are doing."

There was a long silence in the room before the male voice that had identified itself as Director of the Office of Science spoke.

"And just how do you plan to proceed, Dr. Smith?"

"Proceed?" questioned Jim. "I don't know what you mean. This is all national security stuff now. My research on the artifacts was just harmless science that hasn't actually led to anything very earthshaking. But Karl Schmidt's file is a whole different matter. It doesn't have anything to do with me."

"Oh, but it does," said a vaguely familiar voice from the box. "It has everything to do with you. In fact, you may be the only person on the planet who can pull this all together and make some sense out of it. Ladies and gentlemen, I suggest we ask Dr. Smith to put together a team and begin investigating both the artifacts and the Schmidt file immediately. Does everyone agree?

A dozen voices said, almost in unison, "Yes, Mr. President."

Jim shot a glance at the Captain, who put his finger to his lips to silence anything he might say.

After an awkward silence, the voice now inadvertently indentified as the President of the United States finally said, "That was my fault, people. I promised I would remain silent and I didn't. But maybe it's good that Dr. Smith knows that he has the full support of my office. Dr. Smith, will you accept this challenge as a personal favor to me?"

"Of course, Mr. President," stammered Jim. "Of course!"

"Thank you. I'm going to drop off the line now, but I'll leave it to the rest of you to work out the details and provide whatever resources the good doctor needs to get us some answers. I don't need to remind you how vitally important this is."

There was a short silence while the other members of the conference call waited for the President to disconnect and then Captain Stukey resumed his role as moderator.

"I know we hardly got started with the questions, but given what we all just heard, I suggest that members of the panel put their questions in writing and forward them to my office. I'll get them to Dr. Smith and he can prepare a response before we meet again. Shall we say a week from today at 0930 hours?"

There were no dissenting votes, so the call was terminated and Captain Stukey leaned back in his chair and frowned.

"Well, my friend, you just took on a huge responsibility and I think you should get started immediately. You can throw away that agenda we put in your welcome packet because from here on out, everything moves at the speed of light. We have a lab prepared for you, but I think I'd like to move you to larger quarters, given the dual nature of your new mission. I'll get you a room in this building for today so you can start developing a plan and we'll have your permanent facilities ready by tomorrow morning. Can you have a list of supplies and equipment worked up by 4:00 p.m.?"

Jim's head was swimming with all that had transpired and he barely heard the Captain.

"Did I just talk to the President?" he asked.

"Yes, yes, now what about that list? 4:00 p.m.?"

Jim nodded but his mind was far, far away.

***

As soon as Sophie had the digital recording of the interview with the BKA agent on her laptop, she emailed it off to Dr. Barnes. She included the name and hotel information the man had given her but warned Jim that they might both be false. She also included her opinion that the BKA might have lost Schmidt.

"We'll follow up on this end," she closed the email. "Please let me know how I can help."

That evening Sophie called a meeting of her "crew" in the multi-purpose room and played the video for everyone to see.

"The fact that they came here at all means they've made some connection, so we all need to be extra careful. However, beginning tomorrow morning I want to launch our own investigation into the disappearance and possible current location of the infamous Karl Schmidt. I'll get the University newspaper to agree to run an article on the eccentric professor and that will give us some minimal cover to ask around about him. When we don't find him, we should be able to escalate the biographical sketch into a full-blown investigative story about the 'missing' professor and what that means to campus security, etc. That will create enough smoke to let us continue our search without too much suspicion."

After the meeting broke up, Manny hung around to talk to Sophie in private.

"Have you heard from the American?" he asked.

"Not yet," she frowned. "If he hasn't replied to my email when I get back upstairs, I'm going to call him. It will be almost noon where he is and I think he needs to know that the BKA is hunting for him."

"Agreed, but you shouldn't use your own phone in case it's tapped. If you can give me about fifteen minutes, I'll set up an anonymous VPN connection to make it look like you're calling from the United States and you can use that Internet phone I brought back from my trip to Chicago last Christmas."

"You're a genius, Manny. Thanks!

"Agreed," he smiled.

***

Captain Stukey had escorted Jim to a small conference room down the hall from his own office and a staffer had provided him with several yellow pads, a stack of Number 2 pencils and a half dozen bottles of water.

"Restrooms are down the hall to your left. Don't wander around or leave the immediate area until I return because that visitor's badge will get you in big trouble if you leave this floor. I'll be back before lunch time with your permanent credentials and someone to show you around. And whatever you do, don't leave your bag unguarded. If you go to the bathroom, take it with you. And don't forget that list, Dr. Smith. I can't provide what I don't know about."

After the Captain left and closed the door, Jim opened a bottle of water and breathed a deep sigh. Since leaving AUTEC things had been non-stop crazy and it felt good to just relax for a minute.

He had no idea what Captain Stukey wanted in the way of a list, so he just began jotting down things he had found useful in his lab back at AUTEC. On a separate page he did his best to sketch the glass and stainless steel enclosure the AUTEC folks had fabricated to allow him to create artificial atmospheres and study their effects on the triangles. It was this device that had helped Jim to establish the alien origin of the artifacts.

When he couldn't think of any more items to list, he pushed that pad aside and grabbed a fresh one. Reaching into his bag he retrieved the Schmidt folder and began to ponder, for the first time, what the information meant and what Schmidt had intended to do with it.

One thing was certain—Jim was going to have to find a way to contact every single person on the "Those Who Know" list and get them to talk about their artifact. Maybe if Jim had a complete list he could piece together their individual and collective purpose. As he scanned the seventeen names, he was reminded that one, in particular, had the most obvious alien artifact possible.

He had met Ben Kingston, a Department of Defense exobiologist, on his first outing with the NWIDI team. During their brief few days together, Jim had learned that Ben was working alone in a lab built into a mountainside overlooking Area 51 and that he was studying the properties of an alien craft that had been found buried under a mound in the Maya region of Mexico's Yucatan.

Jim was also familiar with two other names on the list—Alan Thompson, now deceased, was the individual who first introduced NWIDI to the alien spheres near Las Vegas. Professor Torres had apparently been studying the same spheres in an underground cavern complex in Mexico before his disappearance. So, Jim actually had first-hand knowledge about four of the names on the list, but two of them were dead or presumed dead.

In addition, Jim and his teammates had discovered twelve alien artifacts shaped like *tsubutes*—ancient ninja throwing weapons—under a mountain in southern Japan. Like the spheres, the *tsubutes* had been confiscated and locked away by Edwards and his men under the pretense that they presented a threat to national security. Jim now wondered if anyone else in the government was even aware of those discoveries. With Edwards and his bunch now in control of the spheres and the *tsubutes*, it was no surprise that they wanted the triangles, too!

When Jim's cell phone rang, it startled him because the conference room and the building in general were so quiet.

"Dr. Barnes, this is Sophie from Munich. Sorry to bother you, but did you get my email message?"

"Hi, Sophie! Ah, no I've been traveling and I haven't had access to a computer in a couple of days. What's up?"

"Well, I sent you a video that you're going to want to watch, along with some backup information, but let me summarize it. This morning a man stopped by the apartment building looking for information about Karl Schmidt. He asked for me by name, which is a little discomforting, but he also mentioned your name. In fact he told me that the BKA is conducting a country-wide man-hunt for you. Were you aware of that?"

"No, absolutely not!" exclaimed Jim. "Why would the BKA be looking for me? And if they were, I'm sure they would have made an inquiry through official channels by now. I was in a meeting earlier today with some people who would surely have known of any such inquiry."

"Well, that's why I wanted you to know. We suspect the man was BKA, but he obviously wasn't telling me the truth. And there's something else. We now think that the BKA did have Schmidt at one time but we also think they've somehow lost him. The visit this morning was probably just a fishing expedition."

"What about you, Sophie? Are you concerned that this guy knew about you and where to find you?"

"Not really," she replied. "We've been pretty open about our opposition to BKA tactics and I'm sure my name has showed up on more than one watch list down at their headquarters."

"Well, listen, if you need help or sanctuary you get yourself to the U.S. Consulate and ask for Jeffrey Hartford. If it helps, mention my name."

"Thanks, but why would the American Consul help me? I'm German."

"I know, Sophie, but he's aware of you and your friends and he's sympathetic to your cause," explained Jim. "He mentioned it when I met with him. I'll also ask someone from here to make sure he's prepared to provide you protection if it comes to that."

"Well, okay, thanks, but I can't imagine that things will get that serious. You mentioned that you had been traveling. Where is 'here' these days?"

"I'm probably not at liberty to say," laughed Jim, "but I guess my status has been elevated a little, because I suddenly have some very important friends. Say, I didn't recognize the phone number you called in on but it looked like a U.S. phone number. How did you pull that off?"

"Remember Manny? He did some Internet magic in case my cell phone has been tapped. Don't bother storing that number, though, because we don't leave it connected."

"So how can I reach you?" asked Jim.

"I guess you'll have to call my cell and hope it's not being monitored. But don't leave any detailed messages or discuss anything important. Just say 'Call me' and hang up. Then I'll get Manny to connect up this system again and I'll call you back."

"Okay, you be careful over there! I'll look into the BKA thing and let you know what I find out. Bye."

While Jim was pondering the phone call, Captain Stukey returned with a young Marine dressed in a snappy Class C service uniform and wearing a holstered side arm.

"Doctor Smith, this is Sergeant Miles," said the Captain. "He's going to be your new best friend for a while. The sergeant is a member of the security detail here at the NRL but I'm assigning him to you until we sort out this matter of the intelligence chatter that mentioned your name. You should consider him the first member of your new team and you may trust him with any information you deem necessary. Sergeant Miles will be your driver, your personal security detail and beginning tonight, your roommate. I understand they put you in a two-bedroom residence, correct?"

A little shocked by this turn of events, Jim nodded. "Yes, Sir, but is all this really necessary? After all, this seems to be a pretty secure place."

"It's a *very* secure place," insisted the Captain, "but I'm not taking any chances with your safety—not while you're on a mission for the President of the United States!"

The sergeant's eyes widened and Jim guessed he was hearing that bit of news for the first time.

"Well, Sir, then there's something you—and the sergeant, here—should probably know. A few minutes ago I received a call from an acquaintance in Munich, Germany, who was told that I'm the subject of a country-wide man-hunt ordered by the BKA, the German..."

"The German version of the FBI," finished the Captain. "I haven't heard anything about this, but I'll look into it. In the mean time, do not leave Sergeant Miles's side. I suggest the two of you get to know each other over some lunch, but stay on base and come back here after you've had a chance to look around. I'll meet you both here at 1600 hours with the final details about your lab facilities and you can get back to work beginning tomorrow morning. Understood?"

"Yes, Sir!" replied both Jim and the Marine in unison.

The Captain handed Jim a very official-looking laminated identification badge attached to a neck lanyard.

"Wear this at all times when you are on NRL property. It will grant you access to places you don't even know you need to go yet. I'll see you both in exactly three and one half hours, gentlemen."

After the door had closed behind the Captain, Jim smiled and shook his head.

"He's a little intense, isn't he?"

"Sir?"

"He's a little gung-ho or whatever you call it."

"He's a Captain in the United Sates Navy, Sir, and he has a lot of responsibility. It's his duty to be focused on his mission at all times, just as it is mine."

"Oh, brother," moaned Jim. "Let's go get some lunch while I try to teach you not to call me 'Sir.'"

As Sergeant Miles led the way out of the conference room, Jim noticed for the first time a thin, clear wire that ran from the Marine's ear down to his collar, where it disappeared into his short-sleeved, open-neck shirt.

"I'm a prisoner of my own government!" thought Jim in silent anger.

Chapter 11

For most of the afternoon, Marine Sergeant Danny Miles escorted Jim around the central part of the Naval Research Laboratory's main campus to help the newcomer get acquainted with the facility. They started with lunch in the main cafeteria on the ground floor of the central administration building where Captain Stukey's office was located. From there they walked across the grassy mall to another large building that housed offices on the main floors but which was also home to a health club and a respectable-sized swimming pool in the basement.

As they neared the admin building, Jim stopped and examined a plaque at the base of the huge flagpole.

"Let's have a chat before we go back inside," Jim said. "I'm not very comfortable with our new situation, Sergeant, but I want you to know right up front that it has nothing to do with you. I've apparently become a prisoner of the U.S. Government and I don't like it. However, there's probably nothing I can do about it, so let's talk about how this is going to work."

"Certainly, Sir," replied Miles. "However, I was just given this assignment a few hours ago and I don't know as much about it as you do."

"By 'assignment' I assume you mean me. And you know a lot more about the military and the military way of doing things than I do, so help me out here. Am I a prisoner?"

"No, Sir!" replied a shocked Miles. "At least not as far as I know. All I've been told is that you are a high-value asset and that there are some hostiles who have an interest in you. My primary responsibility is to protect you from harm while you're a guest here at NRL."

"Okay, so you're my body guard. How much do you know about me or my recent work?"

"Not a thing, Sir. The Captain called you Dr. Smith, so I assume you're a scientist of some kind and I also assume your real name isn't Smith," replied the Marine. "Beyond that,

I don't know a thing about you, why you're here or where you came from."

"Interesting. Well, the Captain also said that I should consider you the first member of my new team, so welcome aboard. Having said that, I have to tell you that I have no idea what this team is going to do or who else is going to be on it, but welcome aboard anyway. I guess you're in charge of security, huh?"

Danny Miles smiled for the first time since Jim had met him.

"Well, since I have a gun and you don't, I guess that makes sense, Sir."

The marine's attempt at humor caught Jim completely off guard and made him laugh out loud.

"That's better! Now please stop calling me 'Sir!' I understand that you have certain protocols in the military, but if we're going to work together and live under the same roof, you absolutely must call me Jim. Understood?"

"Yes Sir," replied Danny. "I mean, Jim."

"Now there's one more thing I want to get out in the open before we go back inside. You heard the Captain mention the President and from the look on your face I'm guessing you hadn't been briefed on that, right?"

"No, Sir, that was quite a shock but I assume I'll be brought up to speed at the appropriate time."

"From here on out, you are to 'speak freely,' I think you call it. If you have a question, ask. If I really am in danger, you need to know what's going on so you can be prepared. So here's what I know. I was called into the Captain's office this morning for the typical Commander's welcoming speech but during the course of that talk I mentioned something that apparently stirred up a hornet's nest. The next thing I knew I was on a conference call with a bunch of high-powered government types. They hadn't been introduced to me by name on purpose but during the call the President slipped up and identified himself. By the end of the call I had accepted a mission from the big guy and now you're a part of that mission, too. Tonight, over some pizza, I'll fill you in on the details, but I just wanted you to understand that you and I, and whoever else joins the team, are working under the direct authority of the President of the United States."

Danny stiffened his back slightly and seemed to come to attention, at least mentally.

"Yes Sir!"

Back inside the conference room that was serving as Jim's temporary office, the two new teammates waited for the Captain's return. Jim showed Danny the list of supplies and equipment he had made, but since Danny didn't have a clue what Jim had been doing for the past five years, he could only shrug and nod.

Jim flicked his hand, indicating the room they were in and said, "It's probably best not to discuss too many details here. Is there some way we can have the house scanned to make sure it isn't bugged?"

Danny stared at Jim for a second and then his eyes widened.

"You're serious aren't you?"

"I'm deadly serious, my friend, and we'll have to perform the same process on the lab when we find out where it is. Once I bring you up to speed on our mission, it isn't to be discussed anywhere except outdoors or in those areas you personally know to be secure."

"Understood," nodded Danny. "If I may make a quick call, I'll get some wheels in motion right now."

Using a very military-looking cell phone, Miles placed a call and talked for several minutes. When he hung up, he had a look of bewilderment on his face.

"What's wrong?" asked Jim.

"Wow! That was weird! As soon as I mentioned my name he was all business and falling all over himself to get me anything I wanted."

"It sounds like the word is already out," frowned Jim.

"Yes, but I know that guy! We play basketball together once a week over at the gym."

Before Jim could reply, there was a knock on the door and Captain Stukey let himself in without waiting for an invitation.

Looking first at Jim he asked, "Do you have your list?"

Jim nodded and stood to hand him the list he had prepared earlier.

"Good," nodded the Captain. And then to Miles, he said, "Your orders are being cut as we speak but officially you report directly to me now. However, as a matter of daily routine you'll be working for Dr. Smith. Oh, one other thing— effective immediately, you are promoted to Staff Sergeant."

He handed Miles a sheet of paper and then continued.

"That's the office and laboratory complex we've assigned to your team. I'm sorry it couldn't be closer, but I think you'll find this facility very acceptable. Dr. Smith, I'll give you a day or so to get settled in but then I'll need to see your staffing roster. If you have any specific people in mind, please note their names next to the job titles. For the remaining slots, we'll work together to select compatible individuals from the NRL staff whenever possible. If that doesn't work, we'll cast our net as far as necessary to get you the people you need. Any questions?"

Dumbfounded, both Jim and Danny shook their heads but then Jim spoke up.

"Captain, when you said specific people, who exactly does that include?"

"Dr. Smith, I can get you just about anybody in the free world below the pay grade of O-7. So as long as you don't need a Rear Admiral or a General on your team, your options are wide open."

"What about outside the military? For example, could I request someone from the Department of Defense?"

"As long as their civilian pay grade is less than the equivalent of O-7, I can have them here on the next available flight," boasted the Captain. "Why? Do you have someone in mind already?"

"Maybe, but I'd like to work up a complete list before I name any names. I was just wondering if I could look outside of NRL."

"Alright, gentlemen, I think that's it for today. I suspect you'll need to make a stop at the Navy Exchange on the way back to your quarters, so why don't you take off for the day. Tomorrow morning please report to your new facilities and get started. I'll have as much of this equipment delivered by 0600 hours as I can. The rest will arrive just as soon as it can be acquired. And remember, the President is counting on you!"

And with that, the Captain was gone.

Danny looked at the paper he had been handed and whistled.

"Well, well, well! We're moving to the high-rent district, Dr. Smith. This building is at the other end of the mall and it was just re-opened about a month ago. It was closed for renovation for almost two years and I hear it's now the most sought-after location at NRL. Nice work!"

At the Navy Exchange, Jim and Danny filled a shopping cart full of groceries and other household supplies before returning to the house. Jim was still getting his bearings, but when he realized that the house was just a couple of streets over from the Exchange, he commented about how easy it would be to walk over if they needed anything.

"Yes, but never, ever, do that alone," cautioned Danny.

"Are you kidding me? How dangerous could it be here on the base?"

"Hey," reminded Danny, "you're the one who wants the house swept for listening devices."

As Jim stepped through the front door with two heavy bags of groceries, he nearly tripped over a stack of large equipment cases.

"And speaking of sweeping the house," commented Danny, "there's my gear, right in the middle of the floor."

When the supplies were stowed and the frozen pizza was in the oven, Danny began opening and inspecting the cases. Jim watched with interest but said nothing. After several minutes, Danny had assembled a device that reminded Jim of a military-grade metal detector. From another, smaller, case he removed a device the size of a marble and placed it on the glass coffee table.

Finally unable to remain silent, Jim asked, "What's that?"

"That, my new friend, is one of the most sophisticated eavesdropping devices in the free world." Picking it up between his thumb and index finger, he motioned for Jim to hold out his hand. "Here, you go hide this somewhere down there and I'll see if I can find it. That way we'll know for sure the equipment is working and we'll sweep the house at the same time."

Gingerly, Jim accepted the small sphere and headed toward the bedrooms and guest bath that were joined to the living room by a short hallway.

When he returned, Danny was wearing an olive-drab set of headphones and he was already at work on the living room. Jim gave him the thumbs up and flopped into an overstuffed chair in the corner. Methodically, Danny moved the disk-like scanning head over every square inch of the room and its furnishings. Twice he stopped suddenly, made an adjustment to some control on the handle of the device and then rescanned a particular area. As the Marine worked his way down the hall, Jim became bored and retrieved the manila envelope he had received from Professor Karl Schmidt back in Munich. He had moved to the couch and spread papers all over the coffee table when Danny returned smiling.

"Professor Plum did it in the library with a candlestick," he reported.

"What?" asked Jim, missing the reference to the classic game of Clue.

Danny opened his hand, palm up, to reveal the object he had asked Jim to hide.

"Between the mattress and box springs in the guest bedroom," Danny replied proudly. "But this is the only hit I got, so I believe this area is free of any and all espionage devices. Now…"

The marine was interrupted by the door bell and after a quick look through the peep-hole he opened the door.

"Thank you, Seaman. You can just drop it right over there."

The sailor placed a dark green duffle bag on the floor just inside the door and extended a clipboard so Danny could sign a piece of paper. With a simple "Thank you, Sir" he turned and left. Danny immediately fetched his bug-sniffing gadget and thoroughly examined his own bag.

"All clear," he announced after a minute. Seeing the surprised look on Jim's face, he explained.

"If you want me to guarantee the security of these quarters, we'll have to check everything that comes into the house. And I mean everything! Groceries, mail, anything that hasn't already been scanned or that has left your possession since it was last scanned.

"So be it," acknowledged Jim. "At least until we know who and what we're dealing with. I think the pizza smells done, so let's serve it up and then let me tell you about this mess I have here on the table.

Two hours later, Jim had explained how he had come to have Schmidt's packet and what he currently thought it meant. It was clear that the Marines had not prepared Danny to process information about UFOs or aliens from outer space because his eyes were the size of quarters and he was speechless.

"And that's just half the story," continued Jim as he retrieved the metal box containing the five triangle-shaped objects that had been recovered from the ocean floor off the northwest tip of Cuba.

He opened the lid and tilted the box slightly, so Danny could see inside. The Marine's eyes widened as he stared at the dull, metallic objects. They were equilateral triangles about three inches on a side with a smaller triangular hole in the center. Between the edge of the hole and the outer perimeter the surface was covered with small, raised symbols that reminded Danny of ancient hieroglyphics he'd seen in movies.

"I've been studying these artifacts for more than five years and I'm absolutely convinced they came from a planet outside our own solar system," commented Jim. "I believe they were given to an ancient—and as yet unknown—civilization that once inhabited the Caribbean.

"So, Sergeant Miles, our mission is two-fold. On the one hand, we need to unravel this work by Professor Schmidt and figure out who 'the Six' are and what they're up to. On the other hand, we need to decipher the ever-changing symbols on these triangles and figure out what they're trying to tell us. Are you ready to get to work?"

Miles stared at the triangles for a moment longer, shook his head in disbelief, and then smiled.

"Yes, Sir!" he proclaimed as he looked up at Jim."Sign me up for the duration!"

"Excellent!" replied Jim. "I've already explained what I think the next step should be with the Schmidt documents, and I was hoping you could run point on that for me while I get back to unraveling the science of these triangles. I also have to prepare some sort of job description list for the Captain and I should start working on a game plan to present to the committee I talked to this morning."

"I'll get started first thing in the morning, Sir. But I have one favor to ask, if you don't mind."

"Anything, if it will make you stop calling me 'Sir'" nodded Jim with a smile.

"This Buzz Edwards guy sounds like he's not only dangerous to you and your friends but also a threat to our country and he's a traitor. When we locate him, he's *mine*."

***

When Max Becker had interviewed Sophie Hoffman at her apartment building the prior day, he had been convinced she knew a lot more than she had admitted to, but he hadn't pressed it. There was no need to panic her and drive her underground. The BKA had an extensive dossier on Sophie and her group and Becker knew that if she wanted to disappear, she probably could. Instead, he would try to use her without her knowledge and the tiny listening device he had planted in the multi-purpose room had already proved useful. For one thing, he knew she had videotaped their meeting. He also knew that she had already emailed a copy of that video to the American named Jim Barnes—the same Jim Barnes that had met with Karl Schmidt just before his disappearance. So while Becker's visit to the apartment house had probably blown his cover, it had established a positive connection between Sophie Hoffman, the American and Karl Schmidt. He didn't yet know how these three were linked but he would solve that puzzle soon enough. Today, though, he intended to focus on Schmidt.

Becker pulled away from the curb in front of his condo, which was also serving as his new temporary office, and drove straight to the University. Today he wouldn't be hiding his BKA identity—he would be capitalizing on it.

As he approached the receptionist in the main administration building, he dug his badge and ID holder out of his jacket pocket and laid them on the counter facing her.

"Special Agent Max Becker, BKA. I would like to talk to the University President, please."

"Ah, well, he's not…just a moment please!" stammered the woman before she disappeared through a door in the wall behind the counter. Seconds later, she returned with a middle-aged man dressed in a dark suit.

"Dr. Schwab is out of the country at the moment," replied the man in the suit. "I'm Vice President Häfner, the acting President. How may I assist you?"

"Good morning, Mr.—or is it Dr.—Häfner, I'm Special Agent Max Becker. I'm investigating the disappearance of one of your faculty members and I'd like to talk to anyone who might have had contact with Karl Schmidt before his disappearance. I want to start with his co-workers, but I may also want to speak with any students with whom he worked closely."

"It *is* Dr. Häfner," replied the man, "and we were under the impression that your people picked up Professor Schmidt on unspecified charges a week ago yesterday."

"I don't know where you get your information," frowned Becker, "but I certainly wouldn't be looking for him if he were already in custody, now would I?"

"No, I suppose not. Not unless…"

"Unless what?" demanded Becker.

"Nothing, nothing. Well, Professor Schmidt rarely ever visited this side of the campus, so I suggest you start your interviews in the Biology Department That's where his office is located."

Dr. Häfner grabbed a preprinted campus map off a stack behind the counter and made two circles on it.

"You are here," he continued, indicating the first circle, "and the Biotech Center is here. The Biology Department's office is on the second floor, just as you get off the elevator. You can't miss it. I'll call ahead to let the Dean know you're on your way over."

"That's not necessary," insisted Becker. "I might stroll around campus for a bit on my way over there. Thank you for your help, Doctor. Here's my card. Please call me if Professor Schmidt contacts this office for any reason. Good day."

As soon as Becker had exited the office, Häfner pointed to the security camera high up in the corner of the office and said, "Have Security pull a still photo off that tape and get a copy out to every officer on campus. I want to know every move this guy makes until he's off University property. Have them fax a copy to Sophie Hoffman, too."

***

As Jim and Danny made their way down the wide corridor the next morning, they both saw the armed guard standing against the wall.

"That must be us," commented Danny.

When they reached the guard Jim checked the room number next to the door against the orders Captain Stukey had given Danny the previous day,

"Yup, that's us!" he replied as he handed the paper to the guard.

After inspecting the two men's identification, the guard opened the outer door, handed Jim a single key and excused himself. Jim and Danny entered the office and locked the outer door behind them.

"Wow!" was all Jim could utter.

Danny's appraisal of the new facilities the day before had been correct—it was an incredible place! The renovations had actually involved gutting the structure back to the concrete shell and rebuilding the most state-of-the-art research facility Jim had ever been in. And the office/laboratory suite assigned to his new team was perfect. Visitors entering from the hallway found themselves in a small reception room completely sealed off from the rest of the area by a floor-to-ceiling wall. Only after checking in with a receptionist and being "buzzed in" could they open an inner door and gain access to the main office area where a dozen spacious cubicles awaited Jim's staffing. The back portion of the space was a clinical-looking laboratory that was also sealed off by a floor-to-ceiling wall—only this one was glass. A number of high-tech work areas occupied most of the lab space but about a quarter of it was consumed by a separate glass-walled "room" that was Jim's personal lab. Jim could see that workers had already installed the vacuum chambers in both lab areas for the continuing study on the effects of alien atmospheres on the triangles. Adjacent to each of the chambers stood a row of color-coded cylinders containing the gases necessary to simulate the various atmospheres; and cryogenic containers along the back wall of the main lab held supplies of liquid oxygen, helium and nitrogen. There were other pieces of equipment, too, but he could only guess at their purpose. One looked like a very deluxe version of the gas chromatography mass spectrometer he had used back at the University of Washington. Jim's personal work area had a glass door that opened into the rest of the lab and another one that opened directly into his office. Both doors opened by sliding to the side when his specially coded identity badge was held close to a sensing pad.

As he sat, staring out into the office space, he saw newly promoted Staff Sergeant Danny Miles lean out of his cubicle to take in his surroundings.

Jim smiled and pressed a button on the base unit of his fancy new phone.

"Sergeant Miles, please report to my office immediately!" boomed his voice through the office intercom system.

Danny spun his head back towards Jim's office and almost fell out of his chair laughing. When he arrived at the open doorway to Jim's office he snapped to attention and presented a sharp salute.

"Sergeant Miles, reporting as ordered," he said stiffly before bursting into laughter again.

"At ease, soldier," laughed Jim. And then, sounding more like a teenager than the head of a super-secret, super-important research team, he added, "Is this cool, or what?"

"Yes, Sir, it most definitely *is* cool," agreed Danny. Eyeing the glass door at the back of the office, he asked, "Do you have your own lab?"

"I do!" replied Jim, removing his ID badge from his shirt pocket. "Let me show you something."

Jim opened the door and held his badge over the sensor until Danny had stepped through and then he followed. When the door hissed closed, Danny's eyes got wide.

"Just like Star Trek," he grinned.

Jim had moved to the back of the glass room and was kneeling in front of the vacuum hood.

"Down, here," he said, pointing to the front of an industrial-strength safe.

When he had Danny's attention, he continued.

"A note on my desk indicated that this is a titanium vault where the artifacts are to be stored anytime I'm not actively working with them. Since you're officially in charge of team security, I thought you should know about this, too."

Mention of the triangles switched both men back into a more serious mood and Danny nodded.

"Got it. And I noticed a couple of heavy-duty file cabinets out in the office that have similar-looking combination locks on the top drawers. I assume that's where we'll keep the Schmidt papers."

Jim shook his head. "Essentially, every piece of paper we generate in here will be classified Top Secret but it goes without saying that some things, like Schmidt's stuff, need special care so the original file will be kept in here with the triangles.

"Well, I suppose we should quit acting like kids in a candy store and get to work. Why don't you take a first pass through the Schmidt file while I get started on a personnel roster? When I've done all I can on it, we'll go over it together and see how much I've missed."

An hour later the two new teammates sat at the small, round table in Jim's office and studied his first draft.

Danny scanned down the list nodding and then stopped with his finger on an item near the bottom.

"Linguist?" he asked. "What's this for?"

"I just thought it might be useful to have someone around who is fluent in the more common European languages."

Danny nodded and smiled.

"And this name you have written beside this job title— is that the same Sophie Hoffman you told me about last night?"

Chapter 12

"Sophie called me yesterday to tell me that the BKA—the German version of the FBI—is looking for me and I think they know that she and I met several times when I was in Germany last week. I think she could be in real trouble because of me and I need to get her out of there, if I can. But that's just between you and me, okay? As far as Captain Stukey is concerned, she's just a very talented linguist."

"Got it!" smiled Danny. "And what about this name? Is Ben Kingston another friend in trouble?"

"No, he's on one of the lists you have in the Schmidt file. He's an exobiologist who works for the Department of Defense out in Nevada. I'm not actually going to ask him to work with us here, but I'd like to bring him in for a meeting or two and get his input. He's been investigating a very sophisticated artifact for more than eight years and he will surely have some suggestions that will save us time."

"What kind of artifact?" asked Danny as he continued to scan the personnel roster.

"Well, actually, it's a flying saucer," replied Jim, watching the other man's face for a reaction.

Danny was silent for a second and then his eyes widened and he snapped his head up.

"A *what*?" he exclaimed.

"You're going to have to get used to the unexpected if you're going to work around here," smiled Jim. "Kingston has been the sole investigator working on an alien spacecraft that was found buried in an ancient mound east of San Luis Potosi, Mexico. It turns out that the spheres my team found and the craft Kingston is studying are somehow connected and I'm beginning to think that maybe all the artifacts are connected—or are at least of a common origin."

"The Teachers!" exclaimed Danny.

"That's right, *the Teachers*. We already have examples of artifacts from civilizations separated by vast distances and time, but I believe they all came from the same source and were used for the same purpose—to impart some critically needed information to an emerging culture at just the right time."

"Wow, all of this," he waved his arms at the office and lab area, "is pretty awesome, but this alien stuff is unbelievable. It's like a science fiction movie or something."

"Except that it's not fiction, my friend," smiled Jim. "And one of your tasks will be to get the other people on the list of 'Those Who Know' to come forward and tell us about their deepest, darkest secrets. Are you still up for this mission?"

"Yes Sir!" replied the Marine without apology. "Yes Sir, I am!"

***

"This actually came from Campus Security?" asked Sophie, as she examined the fax. "Now that's a switch, isn't it—them sharing information with us?"

"I know, I couldn't believe it either, but there it is," smiled Manny. "And there's no doubt that the person in the photo is your new best friend from the BKA. But check out the message below the picture!"

"Attention Campus Security Officers!" read Sophie out loud. "The individual pictured above is a Special Agent with the Munich BKA. Please report any contact with this individual to the President's Office immediately and do NOT provide any information that isn't specifically requested."

"It sounds like the University administration and the BKA are on the outs again," nodded Sophie. "Good! That could work in our favor. In fact, this might be a good time to call over there and tell them about the piece I want to do on Schmidt's disappearance for the campus newspaper. We might as well get the ball rolling sooner rather than later."

"I'm pretty sure President Schwab is away at a conference," frowned Manny. "That means you'll have to deal with…"

"Häfner!" finished Sophie. "Well, that complicates things, but maybe his issues with the BKA will overshadow his issues with me. Will you call a meeting of the senior team for this evening? If I can get the approval from Häfner, I want to get our own investigation started as soon as possible."

Twenty minutes later, Sophie was seated in the Vice President's waiting room. Much to her surprise, Häfner had not only agreed to see her, he had even suggested that they meet immediately.

A buzzer on the secretary's desk sounded and she said, "You can go in now, Ms. Hoffman."

When Sophie closed the door behind herself, the thin graying man looked up from some papers on his desk and indicated that Sophie should be seated in front of his desk.

"So, *Fräulein* Hoffman, we meet again. I trust you've been staying out of trouble since we last spoke."

"Er, yes, Dr. Häfner, most of the time." Sophie forced a stiff smile and laid the fax down on the Vice President's desk facing him. "As you can imagine, I'm very curious why you sent this to me. I didn't know you even had my fax number."

Häfner closed the thick file that was open on his desk and held it up for Sophie to see.

"I know quite a lot about you—and your friends," he replied coldly. "But for once, I think we're on the same side. I understand Agent Becker has been to see you recently. I assume he was asking about our wayward Professor Schmidt, correct?"

Sophie nodded. "Yes and his appearance at my apartment building caught me a bit off guard because we had information from a reliable source that the Professor was already in BKA custody regarding his UFO claims."

Häfner leaned forward and lowered his voice to almost a whisper. "I had similar information and probably from the same source. Is it possible that our mild-mannered Professor managed to escape from BKA custody?"

"We're almost certain of it!" exclaimed Sophie. "How he did it is quite another matter, but why would they be looking for him if they still had him in custody? We would like Administration approval to launch our own investigation into his disappearance under the pretense that we're developing a story for the campus newspaper. If the BKA had him and then lost him, there has to be more to this than we first suspected."

Häfner leaned back in his supple leather desk chair and folded his arms across his chest.

"I'm curious what your interest is in Schmidt, *Fräulein*. You and your friends have a lot of interests," he said tapping the folder on his desk, "but the University's faculty hasn't been one of them, until now."

Sophie studied her long-time adversary across the wide desk for a moment before deciding to put all her cards on the table.

"You're absolutely right, Dr. Häfner, but I have a connection to Professor Schmidt that you may not be aware of. During the University's recent archaeology conference the Professor sought out a visiting lecturer that I happened to be assigned to as a Campus Host. After a secretive meeting, Schmidt passed a folder to a Dr. Barnes—the visiting lecturer I mentioned. The next day, someone ransacked Dr. Barnes' room, obviously searching for something, and soon after that Schmidt went missing."

"And what's become of this Dr. Barnes?" asked Häfner.

"He has already returned to the United States, but I don't think the BKA knows that because they were asking questions about him when they paid me a visit."

"And what was the subject of Dr. Barnes' presentation?" probed Häfner, relaxing a bit behind his imposing desk.

"Ancient civilizations," replied Sophie without hesitation. "He has some amazing theories and he presented evidence to support the claim that many ancient—and now lost—civilizations existed prior to the emergence of our own culture some five thousand years ago."

Häfner pondered Sophie's answer for a minute before replying.

"So it would seem that the connection between Schmidt and your new friend has more to do with Schmidt's crazy UFO stories than with his nanotechnology research, wouldn't you agree?"

"Absolutely!"

Leaning forward once again, Häfner smiled for the first time since Sophie had entered the room.

"You have permission to launch your investigation with the condition that anything and everything you learn will be communicated to me, personally, in a timely manner. What you share with the public is up to you, but you must share everything with me. Are we clear?"

"Understood, Dr. Häfner, but why the personal interest in this case?"

"Are you going to tell me what was in the folder Schmidt gave to your friend?"

"No," replied Sophie without hesitation.

"Then the reasons for my interests shall also remain a secret. Good day, *Fräulein* Hoffman, and good luck." He opened a desk drawer, removed a business card and wrote on the back of it. "This is the information you will need to contact me personally. I will expect regular updates on your progress—or lack thereof—but please do not contact me at the University about this."

***

The first day on the job was an interesting one for Jim and Danny. Just before 9:00 a.m. a technician arrived and scanned both men's thumb prints using a hand-held device. The data was then downloaded to the office security system and the system was initialized. From that moment on, only Jim and Danny had access to the facilities beyond the small reception area. All the inner doors had small thumb print readers mounted next to them and each one could be programmed to allow or deny access to anyone in the system's database. When Jim asked how new staff members would be added, the technician just shrugged and mumbled something about only being responsible for the initial setup.

Danny spent the rest of the morning studying the Schmidt file while Jim poured over his staffing requirements list. He had never managed a team before and he was finding it hard to delegate specific responsibilities. His instinct was to write his own name beside every job description but, of course, he couldn't do that.

After a short break for lunch in a nearby cafeteria, they returned to find a standard pink message form taped to the outer door.

"'Delivery waiting. Please call X7398'," read Jim aloud. "Must be more of that stuff the Captain ordered for us. Would you mind taking care of this?"

He handed the note to Danny and headed for his office, not eager to get back to his roster project.

"Hey, what about scanning this stuff for bugs, bombs and the like? Shouldn't we take the same care here that you asked me to set up at the house?"

Jim stopped dead in his tracks. He just wasn't cut out for these covert missions.

"Yes, of course! I guess that's why the Captain put you in charge of security. Order whatever gear you need and leave the delivery out in reception until you're satisfied it's safe to bring in."

"Will do, boss," replied Danny as he settled into his new desk and lifted the telephone handset.

Jim slumped into his new-smelling leather chair feeling very overwhelmed. He suddenly realized the importance of the roster he had been developing and he returned to it with a new sense of urgency. If he expected his team to accomplish anything, he would have to surround himself with exactly the right people because he obviously couldn't do it alone.

***

Sophie was on her way to the apartment building's study room to meet with some of her closest friends when her cell phone rang. Stopping just short of the door, she answered.

"Sophie? Hi, it's Jim Barnes. Did I catch you at a bad time?"

"Hi, Dr. Barnes! I was just going into a meeting, but it can wait a few minutes. What's up?"

"Well, I can't go into a lot of details, especially on the telephone, but I've been asked to put together an international team to…"

"I'll call you right back," interrupted Sophie.

She dashed into the study and signaled for Manny to join her in the hallway.

"What's up?"

"I need you to set up the Internet phone as quickly as you can. I just got a call from Dr. Barnes. And can you stall for me in there?" she asked, nodding towards the study.

Five minutes later, Sophie was listening to a phone ring thousands of miles away.

"So you were telling me about a team, I think?" asked Sophie when Jim answered.

"Yes! I've been put in charge of an international team to look into the Schmidt file, among other things, and it occurred to me that since Schmidt did most of his writing in German it might be a good idea to have a linguistics expert on the team. Are you interested in spending some time in the United States?"

There was a long pause before Sophie answered.

"Wow, Dr. Barnes, I'm very flattered, but my friends and I are just launching a local investigation into the whereabouts of Schmidt, and we even have the blessing of the University. Something very odd is going on here in Munich and I need to be here to see this through."

"Sophie, I think you could be in danger because of me and this is the only way I know of to help. I have permission to draft anyone I wish and I could arrange for you to be on the next military flight out of Munich. Please let me do this."

Again, there was a long pause.

"I appreciate the concern—really I do. But the folder you have is only part of the puzzle. Knowing where all that information came from would answer a lot of questions and the only person who can tell us that is Karl Schmidt. You follow-up on the file and I'll find the man who gave it to you. And please don't worry—I'll be fine."

Disappointed, Jim sighed heavily. "I wish you'd reconsider, but at least promise me you'll check in often. And if you get into trouble and need to get out of there, you call me immediately. Understood?"

"Understood!" replied Sophie. "And thanks again for your concern, but I just feel that I can accomplish more here than I could in an office in the Bahamas."

"Well, actually, I'm not in the Bahamas anymore, but that's another story. If I can't change your mind, I guess I'll let you go back to your meeting, but be careful, okay?"

***

Disappointed, Jim laid his cell phone down on the desk and noticed that the message light on his desk phone was blinking. He looked up to see Danny standing outside his office door and he pressed the button to unlock the door.

"I didn't want to bother you while you were on the phone, boss, but I need to talk to you about the supplies. It seems that the delivery includes a lot of computer equipment—laptops, printers and even a server. Did you know all this was coming?"

"No, but I guess it makes sense. Our team will obviously need computers and I guess they should be Government Issue, right?"

"Sure," nodded Danny, "but that creates a whole new security problem for us because I assume you'll want to allow your team to access the Internet for research purposes."

"Ah, right! Hackers, spam, spyware and all that stuff! Well, security is your department, what do you suggest?"

Pointing to Jim's desk, Danny replied, "I suggest you add another position to your roster. We're going to need a network engineer who's also a security hotshot and I know just the guy."

By 4:00 p.m. Jim had finalized his initial staffing list and he called Danny in to review it before turning it over to Captain Stukey.

"Well, here it is," sighed Jim as he turned the paper so Danny could read it. "Sorry I don't have another copy for you, but until we get all that gear unpacked…"

"Tomorrow, I promise," interrupted Danny, as he scanned the list. "Well, I agree with your first two choices—you and I sound perfect for the job!"

Danny continued to browse the list for a couple of minutes and then counted the job positions Jim had selected. Then he turned and visibly counted the workstation locations in the inner office and the lab area.

"It looks like you're going to have some empty spots, Doc."

"I know, but I want some space for visiting temps, like Ben Kingston, and I'm sure we'll think of some other positions once we get cranked up. Did I miss anything obvious?"

"Well, let's see. A receptionist, three data analysts, two lab technicians, a chemical engineer, a metallurgist, your exobiologist friend from Nevada and my network security guy. Counting us that makes twelve and you've already mentioned that one of them will be here part-time, so you really only have eleven staffers. I count sixteen spots out there so there's plenty of room to grow, that's for sure. Do you think the Captain will go for it?"

"I hope so. I want to start small with something manageable. If any of our work pays off, we'll add positions where necessary. We may need a couple of public relations types just calling on folks from the 'Those Who Know' list who aren't willing to talk to us by telephone."

"Good point, but what you have there is a good start. Wait—what about your linguistics friend? I don't see her name here anymore."

"Well, I called her earlier and she has, for the moment, declined. She and some friends at the University are out looking for the mysterious Professor Schmidt. I'm concerned about her, but it certainly would be nice to have him around to fill in all the missing details in that file of his."

"That's for sure," agreed Danny. "But I wouldn't expect to see him in the reception area anytime soon. He made a specific point to meet with you and to get you this file. I think he knew then that the two of you wouldn't be sitting around a conference table having a chit-chat."

Jim thought about that for a minute.

"You're right, of course. In our meeting, when I refused to get involved, he as much as told me that someone else would have to take over his work and that he had decided it would be me. Later, when the file showed up at my hotel by messenger, I was angry but as I got into the contents, I became hooked. But he had no way of knowing whether I'd follow up or not and he took a huge risk by sending me the file. He wouldn't have done that unless he knew he was out of options."

"Well, I'm not so sure about that," smiled Danny. "I think he had a pretty good idea you'd follow up. I think he knew you better than you give him credit for, but I do agree that he knew his time with the information in the file was over. Do you know if he was ill?"

"Ill? Do you mean terminally ill? No, I have no idea, but that's probably something Sophie should look into. During our brief meeting he seemed afraid, but not like that. He acted very secretive and guarded like he thought someone was watching him. Later, when he was picked up by the BKA, I just assumed he had known they were on his trail."

"And they probably were," nodded Danny. "But maybe they weren't the only ones. Or maybe the BKA is somehow connected to the file Schmidt gave you."

Jim considered Danny's comment and reviewed the sequence of events in his mind. He had met with Schmidt on Friday afternoon. Schmidt was first noticed missing Saturday morning when he didn't turn up for a presentation at the conference. Jim's room was trashed by known BKA agents sometime before 9:00 p.m. that same day. Also sometime that day an envelope containing Schmidt's file was delivered to Jim but held at the front desk since Jim was away at the conference.

"You're absolutely right," replied Jim. "One of Sophie's friends eventually confirmed that Schmidt had been picked up by the BKA Saturday morning and my room was gone through after he was apprehended but before I physically had the file. Fortunately, they came up empty-handed but they knew we had met and they certainly suspected I had the file. And, just to clarify, '*they*' is definitely the Munich BKA!"

"Can I make one more suggestion for your personnel list?" asked Danny. "I think you should include a trained intelligence analyst from one of the major agencies—CIA, FBI, or NSA—someone who has the training and the contacts to dig into this BKA connection."

Before Danny had finished his statement Jim was adding the position to his roster. As he wrote, he couldn't help noting that newest member of his team was number thirteen.

Chapter 13

Thursday morning Jim met with Captain Stukey to present his staffing roster and to give the naval officer his first mission update.

"Obviously, we're just getting started, Sir," acknowledged Jim, "but Sergeant Miles received his security scanning equipment early this morning and he's busy processing the large delivery of supplies that arrived yesterday. There's a lot of computer equipment on the packing list, Captain, so it would speed things up a lot if Sergeant Miles' friend Chip Davis could join us sooner rather than later."

"Of course," nodded Stukey, scanning Jim's roster. "I only see one other name on your list, and it's marked part-time. Is this the Department of Defense scientist you mentioned the other day?"

"Yes, Sir, Ben Kingston is assigned to a special project at...er..."

"That's okay, Son, we can track him down if he's on the DOD payroll. We don't need an exact location if you don't know it."

"No, that's not it, Sir. I *know* where he works I just don't know the official name of the facility. Ben and I met at the Nevada Test Site, north of Las Vegas, but his lab is actually a few miles away at...well, it's at Area 51, Sir."

"Are you sure about that? I thought that place was just a name made up by our friends over at the Department of the Air Force to throw all the UFO nuts off the trail."

"No, Sir, I assure you it's a very real place—as real as the Navy's AUTEC facility in the Bahamas. In fact, Ben has been studying a UFO at Area 51 for several years. I've never been to his lab, of course, but I understand it's built into a cave system in the hillside overlooking the Area 51 runway."

As much as he tried, the Captain couldn't hide his surprise.

"Okay, we'll look into it and have him here tomorrow unless he's on leave or otherwise unavailable. And what about all these other positions without names beside them? I can fill the receptionist, data analyst and lab tech positions from our own labor pool here at NRL and I can also snag a senior intel analyst from here in Washington D.C. However, even if we have a chemical engineer or a metallurgist on site I'm sure they're already assigned to a project so I'd prefer to go outside for these two. Do you have any preferences?"

"Both of them will be working closely with me on the artifacts, so I need folks who are open-minded and willing to think outside the box. Maybe academic researchers would be better choices than industry types, but I don't know what security issues that might present. I assume all these people will have Top Secret clearances, right?"

"Yes, but just this morning the committee you spoke to decided to create two new SCIs—that stands for Sensitive Compartmented Information—which will be used for your team and your team only. Officially, you, Sergeant Miles and anyone who joins your group will be granted a security classification of TS/XA1/XA2 and will be required to sign non-disclosure agreements with the United States Government. Only individuals with XA1 classification are authorized to see or handle the artifacts currently in your possession or any additional artifacts you may acquire. The XA2 classification applies to the original Schmidt file and any additional documents you add to it. As you begin to make inquiries, please remember that a simple Top Secret clearance is not enough—one or both of these SCIs must also be issued before an individual can be granted access to the respective classified materials. For your own staff, you will have the authority to grant interim SCIs onsite. However they will still have to go through a more formal approval process to get a permanent classification and all outsiders must be cleared by my office."

"Wow, this is getting complicated! How will I know who has the correct clearance and who doesn't?" asked Jim.

"Never hesitate to ask for a person's credentials. As a member of the military, Sergeant Miles will receive a formal, written order upgrading his clearance later today. Ask to see his, so you know what you are looking for. As custodian of these classified assets, it is your responsibility to limit access to approved individuals only. I don't think I need to tell you how dangerous this information could be if it fell into the wrong hands."

"No, I get that," replied Jim. "I just never thought that I would end up with all this responsibility back when my friends and I were running around the globe picking up strange objects. This is becoming a bureaucratic nightmare."

"Well, I'm sorry about that, but you are the one person uniquely qualified to lead this group. We will provide all the support you need, but this is your ball game. And speaking of that, let's get back to your list. So, no preferences for these lower-level positions?"

"No, but in light of this security clearance requirement, I guess I would prefer people who can get approved quickly," frowned Jim.

"I think that's a wise decision, Dr. Smith. Let me go get started on this list. I'll let you know later today, but I should be able to get people cleared and reassigned today so they can be at your door-step by 0800 hours tomorrow morning."

Jim shook his head and laughed.

"Did I say something funny, Dr. Smith?"

"No Sir!" replied Jim, suddenly serious. "I just don't understand how you can make all this happen so fast. I mean, there's a dump truck load of equipment sitting in my reception area and now you're going to locate, process and reassign nine people in less than twenty-four hours? How is that possible?"

"Apparently you still don't realize how important this project is to the nation, Dr. Smith. I'll talk to you later today."

As Jim stood to leave, the Captain added, "It's going to be a wild ride so hang on tight and try not to fall off."

"Yes, Sir!" mumbled Jim as he reached the door.

***

Max Becker had talked to everyone on campus with any connection to Professor Karl Schmidt. He'd interviewed research associates, graduate students, and staff members but he didn't know much more than before he started. Schmidt was clearly an odd individual with very few friends and, so far at least, he had left a very small mark in the academic world. His nanotechnology research was interesting but probably years away from being commercially useful, according to his colleagues. Not a single person Becker had interviewed had any contact with Schmidt off campus and no one knew even where he lived. Becker did, of course, because he had the dossier the BKA began compiling when Schmidt first started making his wild UFO claims.

The third-story walk-up was in a modest apartment building less than a block from the University's main building but it took Becker several minutes to find the entrance, which faced a narrow alley. The small courtyard contained several bicycles of various styles and colors and it was obvious that the gray, concrete building had seen better days.

When Becker reached the door marked "304," he stopped and listened for sounds of activity inside the apartment. Hearing none, he removed a lock pick from his inside jacket pocket and opened the door in a matter seconds. Cautiously, he opened the door part way and then stepped back. The apartment was dark and appeared to be unoccupied. After a glance up and down the hallway to make sure he wasn't being observed, he slipped his Beretta automatic out of its concealed holster, entered and silently closed the door. Facing the interior of the room, he located the light switch beside the door and flicked it on with his left hand while his extended right arm held the Beretta ready to fire at anything that moved.

Across the dingy room a single floor lamp came to life, illuminating a worn, wooden rocking chair and a pile of reading material more than a foot high. As he scanned the room he detected movement out of the corner of his eye and felt something brush the inside of his left calf. He spun a full one-eighty into the room and took aim at the floor—and into the yellow eyes of a large black cat.

After an appropriate amount of cursing, Becker refocused on the situation at hand. He wasn't a big animal lover, but he knew enough about cats to know that Schmidt's ten-day absence should have left the cat starving or worse and yet he appeared healthy. A quick sniff told him the cat either had access to the outside or someone was keeping a litter box very clean.

Becker made his way to the small kitchen. A few dishes were arranged in the drainer but the room was otherwise neat and tidy. A plastic placemat next to the refrigerator held a nearly full bowl of water and a dish of dry cat food.

"Someone is taking care of this cat!" Becker whispered to himself.

With his handgun still extended, he searched the rest of the apartment. Like the kitchen, the bedroom and the bathroom were clean and tidy. As he was going through one of the two night stands that flanked the bed, the cat brushed his leg again and gave him another start so he chased the animal out of the room and closed the door. The large armoire that stood in the corner of Schmidt's bedroom contained a section of drawers and Becker noted that everything was neatly organized and folded—not at all what he would have expected from a middle-aged bachelor.

Returning to the living room, Becker slid the deadbolt on the front door and sat down at Schmidt's small writing desk. Several unopened envelopes were neatly stacked on one side and several more opened ones were arranged in a letter file near the back of the desk. Becker checked the postmarks on the opened ones and confirmed his suspicion. They had all been mailed—and opened—after Schmidt's detention by BKA and after his subsequent disappearance!

A search of the desk's center drawer revealed nothing of interest, so Becker moved to the stack of reading material next to the rocker. As he lowered himself into Schmidt's chair the obnoxious black cat surprised him again by popping out from behind an ottoman but it disappeared when he hissed at it.

Two hours later, Becker was still scanning the odd assortment of scientific journals, technical papers and magazine article reprints that spanned a broad range of subjects. Most of it was way over his head but some of the articles detailing recent UFO sightings were fascinating and he had to admit that the material made a convincing argument for the existence of something in the skies over Germany. Maybe the professor wasn't so crazy after all!

When the material in the stack became mostly physics and nanotechnology, Becker turned his attention to the large bookcase that stood behind the chair. Here he found numerous text books, a wide selection of classic literature and one spine that stood out from all the bound books. Opening the ornate appointment book, Becker turned to the current date and worked his way backwards until he found writing. The last entry, on the page labeled April eighteenth, had a simple message written in the 3:00 p.m. slot.

"Turn over files to Dr. Barnes," read Becker aloud.

But he knew no documents had changed hands at the meeting in the *Englischer Garten* because BKA agents had monitored that event from several angles and later they had thoroughly searched Barnes' room and found nothing of interest.

Becker ripped out the page and placed the appointment book back on the shelf where he had found it. As he started to fold the piece of paper, he noticed something written on the back and unfolded it again. There, in capital letters and underlined were the words "THE SIX."

Becker stared at the words for several seconds before reaching for his cell phone. Pressing one of the speed dial buttons, he waited for an answer.

"Yes?" said the voice at the other end.

"I'm in Schmidt's apartment and I just found a note he wrote that mentions something called 'The Six.' Do you have any idea what that means?"

***

The next morning Jim and Danny stopped at the base gym for a workout and when they arrived at their new office/laboratory facility there were several people milling around outside the locked door. Jim introduced himself and apologized for their tardiness while Danny unlocked the door and turned on the lights.

"I'm afraid our waiting room isn't very big but it's as far as you can go until we get you cleared," he frowned.

"Perhaps I can help, Dr. Smith," offered a young black man at the back of the small crowd. "I'm Chip Davis, your new tech support guy and I've also been trained on your internal security system. Once you've reviewed each individual's paperwork, I can add them to the system and get some proper ID badges printed."

"Well, I guess I need to start with you, then, Mr. Davis. Join me at the receptionist's desk and let's take a look at your credentials. If the rest of you will be patient, we'll get this done as quickly as possible. Once you've been admitted to the office area, please have a seat and we'll do a formal briefing for everybody at once."

Thirty minutes later Jim had met eight of the eleven people he had requested less than twenty-four hours earlier. Each of them had presented Jim with a sealed government-issue envelope that contained a standard *Curriculum Vitae*, a one-page Temporary Duty Order signed by Captain Stukey that assigned the individual to Project *CHALK FLYER*, a copy of a signed non-disclosure agreement and a sheet of four one-inch by one-inch color photos. The TDY orders elevated each individual's security clearance to Top Secret, effective immediately, but made no mention of the SCIs that Captain Stukey had cautioned Jim about the day before. Apparently this task really was going to be left to Jim to manage.

"Okay, thanks for your patience, and again, I apologize for our tardiness this morning. Just for the record, I'm a civilian and by that I mean a *real* civilian, not a government employee, so we'll be using the clock as a guideline, not a rule."

Jim paused for the few chuckles before continuing.

"You've each been hand-picked by the base commander here at NRL to join a very special project. From your orders, I see we've been named 'Chalk Flyer,' although I have no idea what that means. This project will actually be divided into two very distinct and separate investigations and initially most of you will be on one side of the fence or the other. This is due to the highly classified nature of the information and materials we will be investigating. Each investigation requires a separate SCI amendment to your security clearance and I will be authorizing those shortly. I should also point out that there will be two more people joining us very soon and a third person will be popping in and out as necessary. As the project unfolds, we may add even more staff, but the objective is to keep this work as compartmentalized as possible.

"I guess the next order of business should be getting you a permanent place to sit. As you can see, there are workstations on both sides of the room and I'm going to assign you a side of the room based on which investigation you will be participating in. I'll leave it up to you to select a spot that suits you and if one spot doesn't work out, please feel free to move around as long as you stay on your assigned side of the room.

"As I call out your name, please identify yourself and select a spot. Oh, except for this person. Where's Norma Massey?"

"Here," replied a middle-aged woman off to Jim's left.

"Ladies and gentlemen, this is Norma and she's going to be our receptionist and logistics guru. She will handle the switchboard, keep us supplied and perform other routine office functions. She will not be your maid, your mother or your janitor! Norma, your workstation is obviously on the other side of the wall in the outer office, but please don't leave us just yet.

"Where's Andrew Jones?"

"I'm here," answered a man that looked to be in his mid-fifties.

"Andrew, you're going to be our linguistics expert and you'll actually have two work areas. I'd like you to pick out a spot on the right side over here where we'll start Team 2, but you will also be spending considerable time in our lab, behind that glass wall.

"Now where's Justin Burgess?"

A young man who was probably in his late twenties raised his hand.

"Justin, please join Andrew on the right. You will also be spending most of your time back in the lab, but you'll need a place out here to do paperwork and research. You and Andrew will soon be joined by a chemical engineer and a metallurgist and the four of you are going to be helping me with some research I started about five years ago. Hopefully we will also be collecting additional specimens for you to analyze but I'll get back to that in a minute."

"Okay, can I have Albert Lund, please?"

"Here," replied a balding man in his late forties.

"Welcome Albert! Do you go by Al or Albert?"

"I prefer Albert," was the reply.

"Albert it is. Albert is going to be our lead data analyst and it says here that he comes to us from the Office of Naval Operations. Albert, I'd like you to move over to the left side of the room where we'll create Team 1. Albert will be assisted by Sharon Williams and Miguel Garcia. I'm guessing you are Sharon, right?"

Jim had pointed to the only remaining unidentified female in the room and she smiled and nodded.

"And which of you is Miguel?"

"That's me," replied a Hispanic man who was probably in his early twenties.

"Great! Would the two of you please take spots over there with Albert? Some of you have already met Chip Davis. Chip, please wave your arm. He's busy getting you all entered into our high-tech security system. Chip will be our go-to guy on all things technical and that includes everything from your telephones to your computers. Chip, if you'll take that desk on the right just in front of the lab, I'll get you an extra table so you'll have a place to take things apart."

"And that means you must be William Blass, our intelligence analyst," smiled Jim.

"That's correct," replied the older man, "but please call me Bill."

Jim scratched something on the paperwork he had been holding and nodded.

"Duly noted. Bill. You'll be working primarily with Team 1, so I'd like you to set up on the left side. Because we'll be working together a lot, I'd like you to take the cubical in the back, just outside my office.

"And now, allow me to introduce our team security specialist, Staff Sergeant Danny Miles. In addition to protecting the project's various physical assets, he's also been charged with keeping me out of trouble and out of harm's way. My name is Jim…er…Smith and I've been selected to be your project leader. Once upon a time I was a professor of Anthropology at the University of Washington in Seattle but that seems like a hundred years ago. About five years ago three friends and I made an incredible discovery in Mexico's Yucatan region and that discovery has been born out twice more since then. Because of the classified nature of the material, I'll go into more detail with Team 2 this afternoon, but I want you all to know that one half of our mission here will be to investigate some ancient artifacts—artifacts of an alien origin that were brought to Earth long before the rise of our current civilization. Our goal will not only be to discover the origin and purpose of these objects but also to learn something about the ancient, unknown civilizations that originally received the objects."

Jim waited until the buzz in the room subsided before continuing.

"In what initially seemed like totally unrelated events, I recently came into the possession of some documents that will be the focus of Team 1's work. Again, I'll save the details for a Team briefing later today, but you should all know that another part of our mission is to track down a number of individuals who may have additional artifacts and convince them to share that information with us—and us alone. The reason these two investigations are taking place here, under a single roof and with a single Project leader is because I have reason to believe that Team 1's artifacts and the ones we already have all came from the same alien race—a race that I believe is still here today!"

Chapter 14

"He knows about the Six?" demanded Colonel Wilhelm Kruger, director of the BKA's Munich branch. "The Six is a very sensitive project I'm working on and I'm one of just a small handful of people who know of its existence. How could he possibly know about the Six?"

"I don't know, Sir, but I'm in his apartment right now looking at something he wrote in an appointment book and it clearly says, 'The Six' and it's even underlined. And the other side of the page lists his *Englischer Garten* appointment with that American, Barnes, and it mentions turning over a file. I think Schmidt intended to tell Barnes whatever he knew about your project."

"But he didn't hand off any file," objected Kruger. "We had eyes on the entire meeting, right?"

"That's correct, and our men searched Barnes' room several hours after the meeting, just to be sure. But I'm sure that was Schmidt's intent. Maybe he found some other way to pass the information along. Maybe it was an electronic file and he managed to slip Barnes a flash drive without our knowledge. All I know is that he wrote the words 'The Six' on a piece of paper that shares Barnes' name."

"Okay, let's back up for a minute," replied Kruger. "First of all, we don't know for sure that any information was actually passed along. Secondly, we don't know how much, if anything, Schmidt really knows. The fact that he even wrote the words 'The Six' is disturbing, but he couldn't possibly know many details. However, in light of your discovery, finding Schmidt quickly is now more important than ever. I want you to come back to the office and run this manhunt from here. We have plenty of agents to put on the street but I need you to coordinate them and maximize their efforts. Get back here as soon as you can and come directly to my office. We'll discuss this matter more then."

The line went dead and Becker cursed under his breath. He had always hated working under Kruger's thumb and this covert operation was a chance to do things his way, out of the depressing BKA office atmosphere. Kruger micro-managed everything and everyone and Becker was sure he would end up being blamed for anything that went wrong and forgotten when things went right.

As he contemplated his sudden misfortune, he heard the front doorknob turn and the door rattle slightly.

This went on for a few seconds until a female voice finally called, "Professor? Are you in there? I thought you were out of town!"

Becker had to think fast. "I got back earlier than expected," he called back in German, hoping he was coming reasonably close to Schmidt's voice as he had heard it on tapes back at BKA headquarters.

"Is everything okay?" called the voice. "Would you like me to tidy up?"

"No, I'm exhausted from traveling. Please come back tomorrow."

There was a long pause.

"Okay, Professor. I'll come back tomorrow at my regular time. Are you sure everything is okay?"

"Yes, yes, I just need some rest. Tomorrow, please."

"Okay, bye!"

Becker breathed a sigh of relief and simultaneously realized why everything in the apartment was so tidy and how the cat was getting fed—Schmidt had a maid!

Becker quickly re-traced his steps to make sure he hadn't left anything out of place and then slipped out the front door, down the three flights of stairs and out of the building. As he passed through the small foyer to reach the outer door, he spotted a young couple kissing near the mailboxes but he turned his head the other way and shielded his face so they wouldn't be able to identify him later.

When he was out the door and away from the building, Sophie released her grip on Manny and apologized.

"Sorry about that," she smiled sheepishly, "but I had to make sure it was Becker. It looks like he beat us to the punch and he probably got away with any useful information, but at least he thinks there's a maid coming in on a daily basis. Maybe that will keep him away for a while. Let's go up and have our own look around, just in case he missed something."

***

The new staff of Project Chalk Flyer spent the afternoon getting settled in and familiarizing themselves with their respective tasks. Jim held two team briefings using the glass-enclosed lab as a "secure" meeting room. Since the lab area was totally sealed off from the rest of the office it actually worked pretty well except for the transparent wall.

After he loaded everybody's information, including their thumb prints, into the security system, Chip Davis began setting up laptops at the workstations each project member had selected. All the computers had been delivered identically configured but as the new team members signed on for the first time the server required them to make up a unique password and then it downloaded various applications Jim had previously selected for each team and, in some cases, for specific team members.

Neither team briefing had provided actual hands-on access to the objects that would be investigated. Instead, Jim had electronically transferred a portion of Schmidt's "Those Who Know" list to each of the three data analysts and asked them to find out as much as they could about the individuals on their respective sub-lists. Similarly, he had given his new lab tech a list of minerals and asked him to learn as much as he could about them by the end of the day. What he hadn't shared with the tech was that each of the minerals exhibited some of the same qualities exhibited by the triangles when they were exposed to specific "alien" atmospheres.

As a way of evaluating the linguist's skill level, Jim had given him a photograph of one of the Yonaguni murals and asked him to provide a brief assessment.

That left only intelligence officer Bill Blass and Jim put him to work determining whether or not the German BKA agency had any interest in an American professor named

James Barnes. Of course, Jim didn't mention that James Barnes was actually the same person the project staff knew as their not-so-fearless leader, Dr. Smith.

For the time being, Jim had assigned Danny Miles to Team 1 and asked him to collate any useful information the three analysts might come up with and provide a daily summary of their progress. Meanwhile, Jim needed to get his notes in order so he could bring the lab team up to speed on his work of the past five years.

When his watch faintly signaled the passing of another hour, Jim glanced at it and then at his growing staff on the other side of the glass wall. He saw several of them glance up at the large, military-issue wall clock and realized he hadn't set any specific office hours during his two orientation sessions.

Opening his office door, he said, "May I have your attention, please? I know I told you this morning that we would be using the clock as a guideline, rather than a rule, but you were all here early this morning and I think it's time to call it a day. The early mornings and late nights will come soon enough—there's no need to rush it. I understand Chip has installed a badge reader on the outer door, so please let yourselves in Monday morning and pick up wherever you leave off today. When you've gone as far as you can with your current assignments please let me know and we'll figure out our next step. I'm sorry to seem so disorganized, but this entire project was only conceived three days ago. Things will begin to make more sense soon, I promise! I'll see you all Monday."

As some of the inner office staff members began to shuffle things around in preparation for leaving, Jim signaled for Blass, the intelligence officer, to come into his office. Meanwhile, he picked up the telephone and repeated his end-of-day message to the new receptionist, Norma, who was at her desk in the outer office.

"Have a seat, Bill. I won't keep you long, but I'm curious if you were able to learn anything about the BKA's interests in…er…Dr. Barnes."

"I don't have all the details yet," began the no nonsense former CIA analyst, "but I'm pretty sure there is at least an unofficial interest. I've reached out to some of my contacts in Europe and the word on the street is that the Munich office, in particular, considers Barnes a 'person of interest' in some recent espionage activity. The Munich office seems to be keeping this fairly close to their vest but that's not unheard of, especially if they don't have any hard evidence."

"Any idea what type of espionage activity they suspect?" asked Jim, trying not to act too interested.

"No, but I should have better intel in a day or two. May I speak freely?"

Surprised by the request, Jim replied, "Of course!"

"Please excuse my candor, but it's obvious that you're new to this whole secrecy thing. I've been in this game for a long time and I can spot a rookie a mile away."

Not sure what to say, Jim simply nodded.

"When you asked me to dig into the mysterious Dr. Barnes you probably didn't know where I'd look or what I'd be looking for so it may not have occurred to you that I would obtain a detailed description, including recent photographs, as a routine part of my background work."

Jim's eyes widened but he let the other man continue.

"There's a remarkable similarity, Dr. *Smith*," the former agent said, placing an accent on the word Smith. "In fact, based on this picture I pulled down from a security camera in a Munich park, I'd say Dr. Barnes could be your twin brother."

Blass slid a black and white photo across Jim's desk so he could examine it personally.

Jim glanced at the photo and opened his mouth to speak but thought better of it so he closed his mouth without uttering a sound. Instead, he leaned back in his high-back office desk chair and closed his eyes briefly.

"Do you need a minute?" asked Blass, genuinely concerned.

"No, I'm fine and you're right, of course. I *am* a rookie and this government security crap really bugs me. I'm not used to lying or answering to fake names, especially with my comrades. My former teammates and I…"

"That would be Frank, Tony and Linda—your NWIDI teammates?" interrupted Blass.

Shocked, Jim nodded. "Yes, it would. My God, how much did you find out in just one day?"

Blass smiled again. "Well, you gave me a good start with the name Barnes. It was just a matter of connecting the dots to find the other three. And there's also a Mexican named Javier Reyes and a husband-and-wife flight crew named Fitzgerald, if my research is correct. It's all pretty much a matter of public record, Doctor…"

"Okay you got me, it's Barnes! But I'm sure we aren't allowed to use that name out loud. I don't think the base commander even knows my real name."

"You're probably right, but there are currently eleven other Dr. Smiths working here at NRL, so I'm pretty sure he knows that Smith isn't your real name, too. You're secret is safe with me, but I would suggest that you take the file I'm preparing for you and classify it 'Top Secret.' Lock it away in a vault somewhere and don't ever ask anyone else to look into Dr. Barnes again. The connection is just too obvious."

"I understand," frowned Jim, "but I have another problem. One of the people I've asked to come here and work with us knows me from my prior life. That is, he knows my real name and a lot of my history. His name is Ben Kingston and he works for the Department of Defense out in Nevada."

"The DOD, huh? I assume he has a security clearance."

"Oh, most certainly!" exclaimed Jim. "He's working on a project that I would guess is even more secret than this one."

"Okay, good. Let me talk to him when he gets here. We'll wrap this whole identity thing with a special security classification and get him to sign a non-disclosure. And I really think you should encourage the staff to call you by your first name so someone who knows better doesn't slip up and say 'Dr. Barnes' by mistake."

"I like that idea, anyway," smiled Jim. "When you get the final word on Barnes versus the BKA, I'd like you to take on a couple of other projects. The data analysts are running down some folks who are of special interest to me, but while they collect the routine data I've asked them for, I'd like you to check your intel sources and see what turns up. I expect most will be dead ends, but I need to know for sure before we bring them in for interviews."

"Of course," nodded Blass. "You mentioned there were a couple of other projects."

"Yes, but one of them is personal. Since you know all about NWIDI, I'd like you to do some additional digging for me. I haven't seen any of them in more than five years, but I have reason to believe that one or more are alive and living with new identities."

"And you'd like to contact them?" assumed Blass.

"Yes, but I don't want to put them at risk, either. I—or at least the Dr. Barnes version of me—was living pretty much out in the open but Tony and Linda completely disappeared shortly after Linda's wedding in the fall of 2002. I recently received some information that leads me to believe they might have gone underground to hide from a very secret and very dangerous global terrorist organization. And that brings me to your third—and possibly most important—assignment. Only a few people in the United States know this group exists and it appears that they have infiltrated several major governments around the world. I'd like you to devote your time here to finding out who these people are and what they're up to."

This time, it was Blass' eyes that widened.

"You just made this a very interesting day, Doc! Can I assume the rest of the staff won't be working on this?"

"That's correct," replied Jim. "Your findings are for my eyes only. Sergeant Miles is aware of the group and he's the only other person to have seen the entire Schmidt file, but I have other things for him to do. Based on your work today, I think you're better qualified to take on the Six."

"The Six?"

"That's apparently the name they've given themselves. Have you heard it before?"

"No," frowned Blass, "but I'll keep an ear out for any chatter in the intelligence community. Do you want me to get started on this tonight?"

"No, the same clock policy that I mentioned earlier also applies to you. In fact, it's time for us all to clear out of here. Monday will be another day."

***

Early Monday morning found Becker back at his BKA office for the first time in days. He slumped into his chair and stared at the pile of paperwork in his basket. With a dozen field agents now reporting directly to him, he had more important things to worry about than routine office correspondence and Kruger never let him handle anything really important, anyway.

The large computer monitor on his desk displayed the location of everyone under his command—a new technology that even the field agents didn't know existed. Their agency-issued cell phones were equipped with a tiny beacon that sent a unique identification code, along with the current GPS coordinates, back to BKA once per minute. If a transmission weren't received at the appointed time, an alert would be sent to Becker's screen indicating the agent as "off line."

The BKA software also kept a permanent record of the minute-by-minute locations of every beacon so Becker could single out a specific agent and see what he'd been up to for any specific period of time. This early in the manhunt Becker was primarily interested in making sure every part of the city was being covered, so he used these tracker beacons to make sure agents didn't wander out of their assigned grids.

Scanning a list on his desk, Becker located the beacon code for Agent Braun and displayed her movements for the past hour. Klaudia Braun had been with the agency for eight years and Becker had selected her to take over the search of the University area, including Schmidt's apartment. His monitor indicated that she was very close to the apartment building so he keyed her telephone number into his handset and initiated a call.

"Becker, here. Can you talk?"

All agents wore small blue-tooth earpieces and their phones were configured to answer silently. If the agent wasn't in a position to speak, they simply touched the "End Call" button as a signal to the caller. The phone recorded the caller ID and the agent could return any ignored calls when it was convenient and safe.

"Braun, here. Yes, I'm outside the building in a little courtyard but I'm just about to go inside."

"Any luck at the University?"

"No. In fact, it's as if somebody has put the word out not to talk to strangers about Schmidt. Everyone I talked to claims they haven't seen him for a couple of weeks, but I wouldn't trust any of them. We might have to start pulling people in for questioning."

"It's a little early for that," replied Becker. "Call me back when you get into the apartment, but be very careful you're not spotted making entry."

"Understood. Braun out."

Becker switched his monitor back to the city-wide view and clasped his hands behind his head. Braun was carrying a tiny video camera in her coat pocket and soon he would be able to compare the condition of the apartment today to that of two days ago.

Meanwhile, he had agents quietly showing Schmidt's picture in every corner of the city. The professor's disappearance had not been reported to the general media, and all it would take was one small tip—someone who had seen Schmidt at the airport, the train station or other public place—to close the net and grab him.

***

On the other side of the campus Sophie detected movement on a special video monitor Manny had installed in her apartment over the weekend. A tiny wireless camera had been transmitting the same static image for hours but as Sophie raced to her couch she saw movement on the screen again—someone was in Schmidt's apartment!

Sophie dialed her cell phone and waited for an answer. "Manny, get down here! We have activity."

Sophie watched as a thin, well-dressed woman closed the apartment door and turned the dead bolt. As she moved about the living room it was obvious that she was looking for something. It was also obvious that this wasn't her first search.

"Who is it?" asked Manny, as he sat down beside Sophie and handed her a beer.

"I don't know, but it's a woman and she knows what she's doing. I'm guessing she's BKA. Maybe we scared Becker off before he had a chance to finish his search."

"Maybe," replied Manny, "but she isn't going to find anything useful because we spent two hours in there and didn't turn up anything."

"Well, except for this," smiled Sophie as she picked up Schmidt's appointment book and opened it to where the page for April eighteenth was supposed to be.

"Ha!" laughed Manny out loud. "She's looking for it on the shelf and she can't find it! You're right, she is BKA. How else would she have known there was something of interest back there? She knows exactly what she's looking for!"

The woman on the monitor stopped her search, retrieved a small device from her coat pocket with one hand and dialed a cell phone with the other hand.

"Time to call the boss," observed Sophie. "What is that thing in her right hand? Oh, wait; it must be a video camera. She's not only calling in, she's giving someone else a look-see. I'll bet you a hundred marks she's talking to Becker."

"I wish I'd had time to install a camera with sound, but you didn't give me much advance warning and that cheap unit was all I had available."

"I know, sorry about that. I wish we could talk to her because I'd like to..."

"Hold on, what's that!" exclaimed Manny. "Did you see that?"

"See what?"

"Watch right here," he shouted, dashing to the monitor and pointing to an area in the lower left corner. "Look! There it is again!"

"Oh, my God," said Sophie, "there's somebody in there with her!"

"Yes, and I'll bet whoever it is didn't come in through the front door."

And with that, the monitor in Sophie's apartment went blank.

Chapter 15

"I hope you were recording that," said Sophie, after staring at the blank screen for several seconds. "What do you suppose happened to the camera?"

"Of course I was recording it," replied Manny, "and my guess is that our mysterious visitor somehow spotted the camera and disabled it. The camera could have failed at the exact time that person entered the view, but that seems like a little too much coincidence for me."

"I agree. Okay, can you rewind it a bit and play it again in slow motion?"

"I can step through it frame by frame, if that's what you want, but in order to do that I have to stop recording the incoming feed and if the camera suddenly were to come back on, we'd miss whatever is going on. How about if we give it a few minutes? If it stays off, we can probably assume it's dead and then we'll stop recording and play back what we have."

"Yes, you're right, of course," admitted Sophie, "but in the mean time that woman could be in real trouble. She didn't appear to have a clue that someone was sneaking up behind her."

"Well, you could always call the BKA and let them know they have an agent in trouble," smiled Manny. "Wouldn't they be surprised to learn that we were spying on their spies?"

"Given our history, I'm not ready to help the BKA quite yet, but I am concerned for the person involved," frowned Sophie. "Can you rig up a way for me to make an untraceable call?"

"Sure, just give me five minutes. Who are you going to call?"

"The Munich Police department," mumbled Sophie.

***

At his desk, Becker stared intently at the live feed from agent Klaudia Braun's hand-held mini-cam.

"No, it was a little more to the right...there! That's where I found it and that's where I put it after I finished with it," said Becker into his speaker phone."

"Well, it certainly isn't there now," replied the field agent. "And it's nowhere in sight. Are you..."

Suddenly the mini-cam feed disappeared and the phone line went dead.

"Agent Braun! Klaudia, can you hear me?"

There was no answer and Braun's avatar on Becker's screen blinked red several times before being replaced with the word "Offline."

Becker quickly returned his monitoring software to the city-wide view, contacted the three closest agents and dispatched them to Schmidt's apartment. All he could do now was to wait for a first-hand report.

***

Sophie hung up the telephone and nodded a "thanks" to Manny.

"Well, Munich's finest are on their way to Schmidt's apartment. Did I sound convincing enough?"

"Like you were actually being attacked," laughed Manny. "There's a police substation just a couple of blocks away and I'm sure the air around the University is screaming with the sounds of sirens right now."

"If they find your camera they won't be able to..."

"Not a chance!" interrupted Manny. "I wiped everything down very carefully and that particular camera is the standard variety sold at most computer stores."

"And the serial number?"

"Skillfully removed by yours truly," smiled Manny. "Hey, it's been more than five minutes since we went dark. Shall we have a look at that video?"

Once the equipment was reconfigured, they actually did step through the last minute of the video frame by frame.

"There," said Sophie as they began reviewing the final few seconds of the recording. "Whoever it is enters our view from the right. Isn't that the direction of the kitchen?"

Manny mentally reviewed his brief time in the apartment and nodded.

"Yes, but there's a door at the far end of the kitchen. I never did open it, but it must be a closet or something. Maybe our intruder was hiding in there."

"Maybe," contemplated Sophie. "Earlier in the recording we saw the agent leave the screen to the right at least once, probably to check out that area, and she would have seen anyone hiding in the small kitchen. A person would have to be pretty quick to react to the noise of the front lock being opened and get all the way back to that door, but I suppose it's possible."

While she was considering the possible hiding spot, Manny had been repeatedly stepping forward and backward through a series of three frames.

"What do you see?" she asked.

"Watch right here," he replied, pointing to the screen and stepping the video again. "Do you see it?"

"The shadow? Yes, I see it. That's why we're watching this video."

"No, look right here very carefully." Again the video went through the same three frames.

"A hat!" exclaimed Sophie. "It looks like the shadow of the brim of a man's alpine hat!"

"That's what I see, too" nodded Manny.

***

Becker watched his three agents close in on Schmidt's apartment. When the closest one was about a block from the University, Becker's telephone rang and startled him.

"Sir, it's Neumann. We can't get near the apartment building without tipping our hand. Munich PD has the entire block sealed off."

"What? Hold on a minute!" barked Becker as he dialed Munich Police Headquarters on another line. Seconds later he was back on with his agent.

"MPD says they received a call from a woman claiming that she was being attacked in what turns out to be Schmidt's apartment! Because of the proximity to the campus, they've scrambled everything they have in the area."

"An emergency call to the local police doesn't sound like the Klaudia Braun I know," replied the agent.

"No, and it's certainly not standard protocol, either," replied Becker. "Besides, her phone is down and it has been since before the police were called. They say they weren't able to trace the call."

"Agents Klein and Richter just joined me, Sir. How shall we proceed?"

"Stand by—all three of you," replied Becker. "We need to know what really happened in that apartment, so I'm going to call MPD and tell them the truth—sort of. I'll say that we had an agent interviewing a person of interest in the apartment and that we suddenly lost communications with her so we've sent backup to the scene. Once I get the groundwork laid, you three present yourselves to the onsite situation commander and ask to be allowed into the apartment. Call me as soon as you're inside."

While Becker was explaining the scenario to his contact inside MPD, the map being displayed on his monitor suddenly zoomed out. He watched in amazement as agent Braun's avatar reappeared and blinked green, indicating that her phone was back online and working properly. However, it was now thirty miles from Schmidt's apartment, at the south end of Lake Starnberg!

"Ah, never mind. My agent just checked in, so I guess it wasn't her that called you guys. Thanks anyway."

Becker quickly dialed Neumann's cell phone.

"Neumann, disregard my last order." Becker had to be careful here, because his agents didn't know he was tracking their every movement. "Braun just checked in so I want you to stand down and return to your original assignments. I'll fill you in later."

Returning his attention to the monitor on his desk, Becker dialed Klaudia Braun's phone and held his breath.

Ring one. Ring two. Ring three. Ring four, and then a click as the phone connected.

"Agent Braun! Klaudia, are you okay?"

Silence, and then another click as the line disconnected. Seconds later, the avatar representing Braun switched back to the word "Offline." Becker stayed on the line but he knew it was futile. Braun's phone was either powered off or it had been destroyed and no one was going to speak to him, no matter how long he stayed on the line.

He grabbed his coat and a small back pack he kept under his desk and dashed for the parking lot. On the way past reception, he checked out but gave no destination or estimated return time.

Once he had his car headed south on the *Garmischer Autobahn*, Becker called the office and officially signed out. Kruger was going to be furious, but this was something Becker had to investigate personally. Something about Lake Starnberg rang a familiar bell, but he couldn't quite place it. He'd visited the north end of the lake a few times, but he'd never been to the south end where Braun's phone had momentarily reactivated. As far as he knew, that area was a mixture of picturesque old farmhouses and lavish new country estates built near the water.

The further he drove, the more certain he was that he'd recently read or heard about the lake. But for the past several weeks, the only thing he'd read was Schmidt's BKA dossier—and then it hit him. Schmidt's dossier! Lake Starnberg was one of the locations where Schmidt reportedly made alien contact. And more specifically, it was at the south end of the lake where Schmidt claimed to have seen saucer-shaped objects streaking out of the water and into the sky at impossible speeds. The UFOs—or USOs in this case—were initially reported by several locals but no one was willing to talk to the press about them except Schmidt.

Becker pressed the accelerator harder, flying down the highway as fast as his BKA-issued compact car would go and smiling from ear to ear. Maybe the missing Schmidt was on the shores of Lake Starnberg waiting for his little green men to return. If so, Becker would soon have the professor back in custody and he would be the shining star of BKA.

***

Monday morning, the second full day of work for Jim and his new team, began with a surprise visit from the base commander, Captain Stukey. The Captain had elected to personally escort the final two full time members of the team to their new duty stations. Jim was surprised at how intimidated his team seemed to be by Captain Stukey. To Jim, Stukey was just the "guy in charge" and nothing more.

"It's a good thing I was never in the military," Jim smiled to himself.

Captain Stukey introduced Howard Donaldson, the team's new metallurgist, and Naomi Stevens, a chemical engineer. Both had been transferred in from other facilities on very short notice—and both seemed very surprised to be at the Naval Research Lab this morning. Until yesterday, Donaldson had been working at the Army's Adelpi Laboratory Center, only a few miles from NRL. Stephens had flown all night from the Army's Desert Test Center near Salt Lake City, Utah.

After the introductions, the two new teammates were turned over to Chip Davis for thumb printing and ID card processing.

"They'll be on Team 1," said Jim, indicating that Chip should grant them access to the lab at the back of the facility.

As Donaldson and Stevens followed Chip to his workstation, Captain Stukey motioned towards Jim's office with his head.

"Let's chat for a minute," he said as he led the way. When they reached the sliding door to Jim's office, Stukey stepped aside so Jim could place his thumb into the biometric reader. Once inside, the Captain slid into one of Jim's guest chairs and indicated that Jim should assume his regular chair behind the desk.

"So," began the Captain, "How are things going? Do you have everything you need?"

Now a little intimidated himself, Jim tried to smile.

"Yes, Sir, as far as I can tell we're in good shape. Today's really only our second day of work, but now that the last two are here, I'll get my triangle team up to speed quickly. I hope to have them breaking new ground before quitting time today. The folks working on the Schmidt file are still doing the necessary fact-checking but I hope to be able to start bringing some individuals in for interviews by mid-week."

"Good," nodded the naval officer. "And what about this intelligence guy—Blass is it? Has he been of any help?"

"Actually, he has, Sir," replied Jim cautiously. "He's already verified some important facts for me and today he's going to start vetting our interviewees at the national security level. I wouldn't want to accidently invite a card-carrying member of the Six onto the NRL campus."

"No, you certainly wouldn't!" exclaimed Stukey. "In fact, they shouldn't be in this office at all. I'll make arrangements for a video conferencing room to be set up somewhere away from the NRL facility. That way I can keep you inside, where I can protect you, and we'll keep your interviewees outside, where they can't do any of us any harm."

"But Sir, I'm hoping to talk some of them into handing over any artifacts they may possess and I need to be in physical contact with them in order to do that."

"No, that's what we have SPs for. Our local security team will manage the remote location and, if necessary, shuttle things back and forth. They can also take care of the non-disclosure agreements and other paperwork so all you have to do is conduct your interviews and collect the 'artifacts,' as you call them."

"But Sir..."

"Sorry, Smith, but that's the way it has to be. You stay in and they stay out. The President has made me personally responsible for your safety until this project is over and I'm not taking any chances."

"Yes, Sir!" replied Jim, mocking the military form of reply.

"Look, Jim, I know you don't like to be told what to do and I know you don't get the military lifestyle. I'm trying to give you as much slack as I can but there must be boundaries. You still don't understand how much danger you're in or how important this project is to the safety of the United States and its allies. And that brings me to the real reason for my visit this morning.

"What I'm about to tell you is so sensitive that I couldn't share it with you electronically—this has to be done face-to-face—and you are never to repeat this information to anyone, do you understand?"

"Of course, Captain," replied Jim.

"The President has a lot of confidence in you, Son, and he's decided that you should be one of a very small number people on this planet to know about *Operation Starlight*. He believes that if you are successful here you will begin to put the pieces together anyway and if you were to find out about *Operation Starlight* on your own, you would naturally wonder why you had been kept in the dark. He hopes that by sharing the details now, he will save you some precious time."

Truly stunned, Jim didn't know what to say.

"So here it is. *Operation Starlight* is probably the darkest secret in U.S. history and dates back to the Wilson administration. It has been passed on from President to President and shared with only a tiny handful of citizens in all those years. *Operation Starlight* is a secret alliance between the U.S. Government and a race of extraterrestrials we call the "Starfolk." They have been here a long, long time and they have provided our country with invaluable assistance at some critical times in the past eighty-eight years.

"You can imagine our shock when you waltzed into my office last week and started talking about *the Teachers* and telling us that their artifacts had apparently been turning up all over the world for thousands of years. Until seven days ago, we believed we were the only ones on the planet in contact with these beings."

"Now I get it!" exclaimed Jim. "The President and his predecessors have been working so hard, for so long, to protect this secret and now it appears that it may have been known to a lot of people for a very long time. I can see where that would be a bit of a shock!"

"It's not just that. If the *Starfolk*, or *the Teachers*, or whatever you want to call them made an alliance with the United States, maybe they also made alliances with other governments, past and present. The strategic advantage we thought we had may be non-existent."

"But you said you were in contact with them. Why don't you just sit down around the campfire and discuss it?"

Jim's tone was more mocking than he had intended, but his skepticism about governments in general and the military in particular, had been restored.

Stukey frowned but seemed more embarrassed than angry.

"Well, it's not so much that we're in contact with them as that they're in contact with us. They always initiate our brief dialogs and they always terminate them. And the alliance I mentioned is actually more like an agreement in which we agree to do whatever they ask us to and in return we don't have to find out what they would do if we made them mad."

"Wow!" smiled Jim, knowing how much that situation must frustrate a bunch of folks who are used to being in charge of every situation. "I'm beginning to like these creatures more all the time."

"Yes, well, like them or not," grumbled Stukey, "we need to know to what extent they've made commitments to other governments and what their real intent is here on Earth. That's why you're here and that's why the President is providing you with access to this ultra-sensitive information."

Jim thought about his response for several seconds before replying.

"Please tell him that he can count on me," said Jim finally.

Expecting an objection, or at least a challenge, Captain Stukey stammered, "Er, well, yes, I'll do that. And now I need to get out of your hair and let you and your team get to work. Keep me posted, Dr. Smith."

Feeling like he had the upper hand for the first time in days, Jim waited until the Captain was almost through the door before he said, "That's not my real name, you know."

***

Sophie and Manny had reviewed the last minute of the video tape a dozen times but nothing more revealed itself. Someone had clearly been in Schmidt's apartment with the BKA agent and that person appeared to have been wearing a traditional German alpine-style hat. Beyond that, everything was purely speculation.

"I sure wish I could get a look at that camera," sighed Manny. "If we knew what happened to it, maybe we'd have a better idea of what went on in there."

"Well, you probably won't be able to get near that place for days, thanks to my call to the Munich police," frowned Sophie. "Maybe that wasn't such a good idea, but I was concerned for that woman."

"No, you did the right thing. If she was in trouble, you may have saved a life—albeit a BKA life—but a life, none the less. And your call will probably keep Becker and his friends out of the apartment for a day or two. I'm guessing the police will be keeping a close eye on the place until they finish their investigation. And for all we know, it might be an actual crime scene by now."

"You know," said Sophie thoughtfully, "maybe we *should* contact Becker and tell him about our video. We don't know what happened after the camera went off and he may actually have an agent in trouble. Besides, I'd really like to know who else was in that room with her and maybe we can work out an information trade. Maybe we can even get the scoop on the camera."

"Are you kidding me?" asked Manny. "After all that's gone on between the BKA and our group—and you in particular—how can you even consider helping them out?"

"I know, but we aren't turning up any leads on our own and there's obviously something suspicious going on in Schmidt's apartment."

"Well, do me a favor, okay? Sleep on it and don't do anything until tomorrow. Maybe by then this will sound as crazy to you as it does to me."

***

Becker exited the autobahn at the south end of Lake Starnberg and headed a mile east to St. Heinrich. From there he followed the main road around the south end of the lake until he came to a fork where the highway continued east, away from the lake, and a smaller country road continued north, along the east side of the lake.

He found a wide turn-out and pulled off the road to retrieve his GPS unit from the back pack. After checking his current position against the coordinates where Agent Braun's phone had reactivated, he slammed his car into gear and continued on with a renewed sense of urgency. He was just a kilometer or two away!

A few hundred yards ahead the road curved sharply left, away from the lake but Becker spotted a gravel road that seemed to stick closer to the lake. It could just be a long lane leading to one of the many private homes in this area, but he decided to take a chance so he could stay as close to the water as possible. At another fork he again chose the branch that stayed closest to the lake. He drove through a heavily forested area and then suddenly popped out into a large clearing that sloped down one hundred yards to the water. He slid to a stop and then eased the car off the side of the road onto a grassy area. Grabbing his bag, he climbed through a barbed-wire fence and carefully made his way down the gentle slope until he felt the ground start to get soggy. Ahead lay a large patch of reeds and marshland that prevented him from getting any closer to the water.

"Hey!" called an angry voice from behind. "This is private property and you are trespassing!"

Becker spun to inform the poor, misguided sole that he was a BKA agent and that he could go pretty much anywhere he wanted to but decided against it when he realized he was looking into the business end of a double-barreled shotgun.

"I'm terribly sorry," he said instead. "I guess I missed the 'No Trespassing' sign. I'm following some GPS coordinates and I guess I got so excited when I saw this clearing that I didn't think. There's no reason to point a gun—I'll move along."

"You bet you will!" shouted the old man who had emerged from a small stand of trees. "I'm tired of all you city folks coming down here and stomping all over my pasture. I'll tell you just what I told that other fella—if you want to look at the lights so darn much, why don't you just rent a boat and go on out there?"

"Lights? Boat? What other fella?"

"You're not fooling me, mister. I'm sure that glow at night is just some pollution from the north end that's drifted down here. But that other fella wouldn't take 'No' for an answer. I caught him down here three or four times and the last time I told him that if he ever came back here I was going to fill him with buckshot."

"And how long ago was that?" asked Becker as he inched his way back up the slope.

"About fifteen minutes ago. He headed north towards Bernried and I suggest you do the same."

Chapter 16

Rather than waving his BKA badge around and tipping his hand, Becker made his way back to the road and climbed into his car. With one eye on the stranger in the field, he rechecked his position on the GPS unit with the coordinates he had written down back in his office. One glance confirmed that this had to be the same place where Braun—or whoever had her phone—had stopped to reactivate it.

He quickly decided he needed more information, even if it meant throwing his weight around a little, so Becker opened the car door to ask the stranger if his recent "guest" had been accompanied by a woman. He had only taken his eyes off the other man for a few seconds while he climbed out of the car but when he looked up the field was empty.

Realizing that he should have also gotten a description of the vehicle, Becker hit the roof of his own car with his fist and climbed back in.

Back on the gravel road, he continued slowly north, scanning both sides for any signs of another vehicle. He suspected that if the person in the other car really wanted to get near the shoreline he wouldn't let a crazy old farmer stop him—he'd just move up the road a bit and try again.

"That's what I would do," Becker said to himself.

The farmer had alluded to some lights, apparently coming from the water, and while that fascinated Becker his immediate objective was to find Braun's phone and, hopefully, the agent herself.

Twice he stopped to examine tire tracks that led off the road and into the damp grass, but on both occasions he came to the end of the tracks without finding the vehicle that had made them. Eventually the gravel road rejoined a paved highway and a few hundred yards later he caught his first glimpse of the small Bavarian village of Bernried.

At the first opportunity, Becker pulled into the parking lot of an inn and called his office. When the operator answered, he asked to be connected to his secretary.

"Mr. Becker, where are you?" exclaimed Annette Fischer, his assistant of more than ten years. "Colonel Kruger is looking for you and he's very angry!"

"Well, I'm sorry, but I'm on a very important mission and I don't have time for his nonsense. Listen, I need everything we have on a village called Bernried. It's at the south..."

"The south end of Lake Starnberg, yes, I know the place," Annette interrupted. "Let me pull up some information. Is that where you are right now?"

"Yes, but you must not tell Kruger that. As far as you're concerned, this call never happened and you haven't heard from me, okay?"

"Yes, but I've never seen him like this. Okay, here's what we have in the computer. The village covers slightly less than fourteen square kilometers and has a population of about two thousand people. There are five lodging establishments with restaurants and one without. There is one elementary school with..."

"No, no, I'm looking for something out of the ordinary. Are there any unusual businesses or government facilities down here?"

"Let me look. No, I don't see anything. The only complex of any size is the Höehenried Hospital. I've been by there and it's a huge place."

"And what do they treat at this hospital?" asked Becker.

"Well, here's what our file says. 'Our clinic is one of the most modern centers in Germany for the rehabilitation of critically ill patients. An interdisciplinary team of cardiologists, psychologists, physiotherapists, dieticians, nurses and educators are on hand to care for all the needs of the patient.' Like I said, the place is huge but it's a private facility owned by an insurance company and it keeps a pretty low profile."

"Okay, well, that's something. What about an airfield?" asked Becker.

"No, the closest airport is here in the city. There's rail service from here to there, but no air service of any kind."

"Are you sure?"

"I'm positive, why?"

"I'm tracking one of our new GPS-equipped cell phones that went offline in Munich and came back on briefly just a couple of miles south of here. However, it made the trip from the University district to here in less than fifteen minutes and it took me more than an hour to make the trip by car."

"And the train takes even longer," said Annette. "The time I went we were on the train more than two hours, including the stop at the north end of the lake. Could you be looking at a computer malfunction?"

"I don't think so, but if you hear anything from Agent Braun, I want you to call me immediately, do you understand? And do not say a word about this to anyone else!"

"Klaudia Braun? Is it her phone you're tracking?"

"Yes," Becker replied curtly. "But not a word to anyone about that, either. I'm going to find this hospital you mentioned and check it out. Call me if you hear anything or turn up anything unusual about this village."

***

As soon as Manny left, Sophie grabbed her scarf and jacket and headed for the campus. It was early May and the mornings could be chilly, but she wanted to be alone and think and the forty minute walk was the perfect opportunity to do both.

This whole Schmidt disappearance had Sophie really stumped. The professor wasn't a high-profile researcher, so kidnapping wasn't a likely motive. He had been outspoken about his "alien encounters" but nobody took his stories very seriously and they certainly weren't reason enough for anybody to harm the professor. But if he hadn't been kidnapped and he hadn't been otherwise taken out of action, where was he? For a while everyone assumed he was in BKA custody but that obviously wasn't the case now that they, too, were looking for him.

And what about Schmidt's interest in Jim Barnes, the American researcher? Their areas of scientific interest were completely different and Sophie wondered how Schmidt even knew of Barnes. And yet he did! In fact, he apparently trusted Barnes with a very important file. What did the two men have in common and what was it about both of them that interested the BKA? Did Schmidt steal classified secrets and hand them off to Barnes? Sophie rejected that idea almost before the mental question had formed. In the brief time she had spent with Dr. Jim Barnes, she had developed a respect for the man and it didn't seem possible that he was a U.S. spy posing as a scientist investigating ancient civilizations and whether or not they had received help from aliens.

And there it was—the connection she hadn't been able to make earlier! The connection between Schmidt and Barnes was a common interest in aliens. Barnes had mentioned some documents he'd received from Schmidt and Sophie now suspected that they might relate to Schmidt's wild stories about aliens. As she passed through the large stone gates that marked the entrance to the University, she began to wonder if Schmidt's alien encounter stories were so crazy after all.

***

Monday turned out to be a very interesting day at the new Project Chalk Flyer facilities. After his tense meeting with Captain Stukey, Jim spent the rest of the morning with his lab team—Team 2—doing actual analytical work for the first time in several weeks. He began by revealing the triangles to his four staffers and explaining his theories about the possible origin of the mysterious objects.

"As I mentioned," explained Jim, "some people have a violent reaction to these artifacts and, so far, I have no explanation for this phenomenon. Frankly, there haven't been enough situations to establish a pattern, much less a cause, but I assure you they can be very dangerous. They've already killed a man in the Bahamas and made several other people very ill. If at any time you feel strange in any way, let someone around you know and then get out of this lab. The room is sealed and does not share air with the office area, so you should begin to feel better as soon as you're out there. However, most people have no reaction at all to these little beauties, so let's hope you all fall into that category."

Next, Jim placed one of the triangles onto a glass dish and set the others aside. He had Andrew Jones, the team's linguist, photograph the solitary triangle using a digital camera. Jim then placed the dish into a rectangular glass chamber about the size of a bread box and sealed the front opening.

"Over the past five years I've experimented with many different gas mixtures, but only a few produce the result I'm about to show you."

After adjusting the valves of several small compressed gas cylinders at the end of the bench, Jim nodded to the lab tech, Justin Burgess.

"Okay, Justin, please evacuate the chamber and then return it to normal pressure with regular air."

A couple of minutes later, Justin nodded.

"It's ready, Dr. Smith, er, Jim," said the young man.

"Naomi, carefully remove the sample from the chamber and tell us what you see," instructed Jim.

Cautiously, the chemical engineer opened the chamber door and removed the dish with a pair of tongs. She studied the triangle on the dish for a minute and then shook her head.

"Without running a complete analysis I can't say for sure, but it looks the same to me. What were we expecting?"

Jim smiled. "Actually, it's what we weren't expecting! Anybody else want to weigh in here?"

The other three leaned in over the stainless steel workbench and visually examined the triangle. Finally Andrew picked up the camera and checked the image he had snapped.

"The symbols have changed," he exclaimed. "How can that be possible?"

After passing the camera around to allow the others to verify Andrew's claim, Jim tried to answer the question.

"Andrew asked how this is possible. My theory—and it's just a theory—is that these triangles each carry a series of messages encoded into the symbols around the perimeter. I believe that each message is intended for a different reader and the atmosphere surrounding the triangle determines which message is displayed."

"Why doesn't it change back once it's removed from the foreign atmosphere?" asked young Justin.

"An excellent question, and one I struggled with for a long time after I learned how to alter the symbols," replied Jim. "My current theory is that our particular air mixture here on Earth is neutral. Once the symbols have changed as a result of being subjected to a specific atmosphere, they remain in that configuration until they encounter a different specific atmosphere. Our atmosphere on Earth isn't one of those specific mixtures, so, therefore, no change. But that's based entirely on my observations and not on any scientific knowledge that would support the behavior."

"Are the messages always the same for the same atmosphere?" asked Naomi.

"For a given triangle, yes!" replied Jim. "Each of the five triangles displays a specific message when exposed to atmosphere A1, and a different specific message when exposed to atmosphere A2." Jim paused for effect. "However, triangle T1 displays a different message than triangle T2 when both are exposed to atmosphere A1 and likewise for the other triangles and the other atmospheres. In other words, the five triangles appear to be a set rather than five identical objects."

"I think I know the answer already, but have you determined the chemical composition of the object?" asked metallurgist Howard Donaldson.

"No," replied Jim, with a frown. "And that's precisely why you are here. I'm an anthropologist by training and that sort of work is way out of my league. My specialty is ancient languages so my main interest has been with the inscriptions themselves in the hopes that they would lead me back to the original owners of these things."

"And how has that worked out?" asked Justin.

His comment invoked an unintended chuckle from the group and he quickly added, "I meant no disrespect, Sir."

"No, that's certainly a fair question. As I mentioned, I've discovered a number of alien atmospheres that will cause the messages to change and Earth's atmosphere doesn't appear to be one of them. From that I deduce that Earth wasn't the intended destination for these objects so I've already eliminated one possibility out of the billions that probably exist."

He waited for the chuckles to die down again before continuing.

"So if the triangles weren't being sent *to* someone on Earth, is it possible they were being sent *from* someone here? Hold that question for a minute.

"So far, I've found eleven different artificial atmospheres that will cause the glyphs to change, but there could be hundreds or thousands more that I haven't discovered. For now we're not going to concern ourselves with what the total number could be and instead focus on why there's more than one. Why would an object be created that would display one message in one location and a different message somewhere else?"

"Well, one possibility is that each message is in a different language," suggested Andrew.

There was head bobbing by all.

"A possibility," acknowledged Jim, "but my observations have confirmed that certain graphic elements appear in more than one message on a single triangle and in messages on other triangles as well. I suppose we could be looking at a number of different dialects all built on a single language, but I doubt it. Andrew, I'm hoping you will be able to shed some light on this question as you begin to analyze the fifty-plus messages I've documented."

Jim handed a thick folder to the linguistics expert and smiled.

"Here are photographs of each triangle after being exposed to each of the currently known 'trigger' atmospheres. They are all keyed—T1 is triangle number one; A1 is atmosphere number one and so on."

The oldest member of Team 2 accepted the folder with a smile, eager to get to work.

"Before I turn you all loose on these things, I have one more puzzle to show you."

Jim retreated to the small, private lab immediately behind his office and removed something from the safe. When he returned to the main lab, he was carrying a small metallic box that appeared to be made out of the same material as the triangles.

"So far, no one has asked where the triangles were actually found, so I'll save that story for another day. For now, let me just say that all five triangles were inside this box and the lid was very difficult to remove due to some sort of internal vacuum. When we finally got the box open, it was clear from the smell that we were the first ones to peer into the box in eons. Although the box was found at a considerable depth in salt water, there was no apparent corrosion or other damage. In fact, this box is essentially just the way it came out of the water. The only thing I did was to rinse it off in fresh water and dry it."

Jim moved the box to the center of the work space and motioned for the others to gather around the table. He picked up the triangle with the tongs, gently lowered it into the box, and closed the lid. Stalling for a few seconds, he scanned each face to see if anyone had guessed what was coming. Only Andrew had a smile that indicated he might know.

After about thirty seconds had gone by, Jim opened the box's lid and removed the triangle.

"What do you see?" he asked. Out of the corner of his eye he saw Andrew's smile widen.

When no one spoke up, Jim frowned.

"Really? After the last demonstration you still don't see it?"

"Did the symbols change again?" ventured Naomi.

"Tell them, Andrew," said Jim.

"Yes, the symbols changed, and this pattern is different from either of the two we've seen so far," replied the linguist.

This pleased Jim.

"Excellent! I'm glad someone was paying attention. The subtle changes in the glyphs will become easier to recognize as you work with the triangles, but until then most of you shouldn't trust your memories—use the camera before and after you do anything that involves the triangles and refer to the digital images frequently.

"Now then, back to the box. This is actually the way I originally discovered the triangles' ability to alter their messages. Obviously there's no foreign atmosphere at work here, so what is it about the box that causes the change in the triangles? And what is the purpose of the box other than serving as a storage container?

"Now you see what's been driving me crazy for the past five years," continued Jim. "Until today, I've been the only person on the planet seeking answers to the questions I've posed to you. But as of now, the brain power increases dramatically, and I've promised the President that we'll come up with some answers, so don't let me down. Are there any questions before I turn you all loose?"

"Jim, on Friday I think you mentioned something about additional artifacts to analyze. Are there more of these triangles out there?"

The question was asked by Team 2's youngest member, lab technician Justin Burgess and Jim made a mental note that the young man had an excellent memory and a knack for details.

"Actually, no—at least not that I know of. But there are definitely other artifacts out there. I have personally been involved in the discovery of two other types and I know of at least one other, but we have reason to believe there may be many more. Your associates on Team 1 are currently sifting through a list of names that we hope will yield the additional artifacts I mentioned last week. Of course if that happens we may need additional space and additional staff."

"Wow," commented Howard. "Yesterday I was sipping coffee on my back porch and today I'm part of the biggest mystery in human history—not bad for a country boy!"

"I've been involved a little longer, of course, but I feel that same way every day," smiled Jim. "And don't forget that we're working directly for the President of the United States. This is quite a gig, all right! So how about if you all get to work and I'll go see how Team 1 is doing. Justin, I'd like you to act as support staff back here in the lab. Get to know where things are and how the equipment operates so you can assist anyone who's actively working back here. When some of the other items come in I'll assign you your own project but for now I think it would be good to have some continuity back here."

Except for the folder he had given Andrew, Jim intentionally hadn't assigned the tasks he had outlined to specific individuals because he wanted to see where his new staff gravitated and how well they cooperated. He was also waiting to see who bubbled to the top as the group leader.

He quietly slipped out of the main lab through the door that opened into his smaller, private lab next door. After returning the four extra triangles to the safe under his workbench, he moved into his office, which was directly in front of his personal lab. He noticed the blinking message light on his phone and picked up the handset.

"Norma, this is Jim. Do you have a message for me?"

"Yes, Sir," replied the new receptionist. "A Mr. Ben Kingston called to say that he had been able to catch an unexpected flight and that he had just landed at Andrews Air Force base. He said he wasn't sure exactly what time he'd be here, but that he was sure he'd be here before quitting time. I asked him for his telephone number but he said his cell battery was dead. However, he did ask me to tell you that he was bringing you a surprise."

"Thank you, Norma. Please let me know as soon as he arrives, even if I'm in a meeting or on the telephone."

Jim was looking forward to chatting with Ben again. The two hadn't spoken since the end of Jim's first "mission" with NWIDI and so much had happened since then! Jim had examined the *tsubutes* and ancient murals on Yonaguni, and later the triangles from the Caribbean. And of course there was Ben's work on the prize artifact of them all!

Jim's thoughts were interrupted by the ring of his telephone.

"Jim, this is Bill. I don't know what your office protocol is, so I didn't know if I should call or just come back and knock on your door. Do you have a minute to talk?"

"Of course, come on back," replied Jim.

When Blass approached the transparent sliding door, Jim pressed the button to open it. He never got tired of the Star Trek effect of that door.

He nodded for Blass to take a seat and waited for the door to close automatically.

"What's up?"

"I just wanted to give you a quick update," replied the intelligence analyst. "First of all, I can now confirm that the BKA has a formal interest in one Dr. James Barnes. He's wanted for questioning regarding the unauthorized possession of German classified documents. Also, on Friday afternoon you asked me to look into the whereabouts of your former NWIDI teammates. So far, I haven't been able to locate any recent information on any of the primary figures—Linda McBride, Tony Nicoletti or Frank Morton. However, I did turn up some news on the Fiztgeralds and the Learjet that was left in their custody."

"No kidding!" exclaimed Jim. "What do you have?"

"Well, apparently both the plane and Mr. Fitzgerald have been reported missing by Mrs. Fitzgerald," replied Blass.

Chapter 17

Jim was floored by Blass' news about "Fitz" Fitzgerald and the Learjet he and his wife had inherited when NWIDI had been dissolved.

"Missing?" exclaimed Jim. "When did this happen?"

"From what I've been able to determine," replied Blass after a glance at his notes, "Mr. Fitzgerald went to the hangar yesterday morning to do some routine maintenance and hasn't been seen or heard from since. He and his wife had a 2:00 p.m. meeting with a prospective client and when Mr. Fitzgerald didn't show, she started making calls. Apparently the tower at the small regional airport where the plane is kept reported that the plane took off at 10:07 a.m. and has not yet returned."

"Did Fitz file a flight plan?" asked Jim.

"No, but the airport officials didn't realize that until Mrs. Fitzgerald started making inquiries because they often take it out for quick check-out flights when they're doing maintenance. The plane has now been missing for more than twenty-four hours, far longer than it could fly without refueling, so the FAA is contacting all surrounding airports. There haven't been any crashes reported, so if it didn't refuel I'm afraid we have to assume it went down somewhere in the Atlantic or the Caribbean."

"Oh, my God! Bill, please stay on top of this for me and make it your number one priority, regardless of how else I ask you to help out. With all your resources, maybe you'll be able to turn up something the FAA might miss. Do you have a phone number for Susan—ah, Mrs. Fitzgerald?"

"Yes, but given the nature of your project here, I don't think you should contact her directly. Give me your message and let me make contact using an untraceable line outside the Washington D.C. area."

"Good idea," mumbled Jim, as he scratched a note to Susan and handed it to Blass. "And thanks again. Anything— and I mean absolutely anything—that we can do to help locate

Fitz is on the table. If we need to involve the U.S. military, I think I have the connections to do that right now."

"Oh, I'm sure you do," smiled Blass, "but let me see what I can turn up first. I'll let you know the second I hear anything."

With that, Blass collected his papers and left Jim to ponder this newest development—as if he didn't have enough to worry about already!

***

Once Sophie realized that her new friend Dr. Jim Barnes and the missing Professor Schmidt might be connected through a common interest in aliens, her resolve to locate Schmidt increased ten-fold. If anything had happened to Schmidt, she needed to warn Jim before he suffered the same fate! Sophie quickened her pace and reached her small office on the University campus in record time.

When Becker had visited Sophie at her apartment building he had posed as a friend of Schmidt's named Max Weber but Manny had long since determined that the man's real identity was Max Becker, BKA Special Agent assigned to none other than Colonel Wilhelm Kruger, the Munich branch's infamous director.

After rummaging around in her purse, she finally found the piece of paper Manny had given her with the information about Becker. She studied it for several minutes before finally coming to a decision she knew Manny wasn't going to like. Sophie dialed the number on the piece of paper and waited for an answer.

"Becker here," said the voice at the other end.

"Good morning, Agent Becker. My name is Sophie Hoffman and I believe we met a few days ago although you were using a different name at the time."

After a noticeable pause, Becker barked "How did you get this number?"

"That's not really important, Max. May I call you Max? What is important is locating Professor Karl Schmidt.

I understand the BKA would like to find him and so would I. I'm calling to suggest that we work together on this task."

"Listen," replied Becker angrily, "I don't know what your game is, but I could have you taken into custody just for dialing this telephone number."

"You could, but you won't because I have something I think you will want and I also think my friends and I can help you canvas the city. And we will be welcome and inconspicuous in places where BKA agents would stick out like sore thumbs."

"What could you possibly have that I would want?" scoffed Becker. "Do you have any idea what resources are available to me?"

"Yes, I think I do, but I have a video of a female agent searching Schmidt's apartment this morning. Would you like to have a copy of it?"

There was another long pause and then, in a more subdued tone, "Yes. When can we meet?"

***

Jim's thoughts were consumed by the plight of Fitz and he found it hard to concentrate on anything else but he forced himself to review a partial list of "Those Who Know" that Danny Miles had prepared based on the work of the data analysts. As he scanned the list, his eyes locked onto one specific entry—not because of the name, but because the individual's address was listed as Seattle, Washington. The man's name was Phillip Dorado, an eye surgeon with the Eye Institute at Harborview Medical Center—the teaching hospital connected to the University of Washington where Jim had been a professor before joining NWIDI.

Another thing about Dorado that peaked Jim's interest was the fact that the analyst who had researched him had turned up information indicating that the Seattle eye surgeon was interested in amateur underwater archaeology and had a particular interest in South Bimini Island, in the Bahamas—

the very same island where Frank Morton, the founder of NWIDI, has disappeared more than five years ago!

Jim forwarded the information about Dorado on to Bill Blass' computer with a note that read, "I need to see this person ASAP. Please vet and advise."

Leaning back in his chair, Jim closed his eyes for a moment to let his brain catch up with everything that was happening around him. He had read an article about using breathing to control the body and he had just inhaled deeply for the second time when the buzzer on his phone startled him and almost made him choke.

"Jim, Mr. Kingston is here to see you."

"I'll be right there!" replied Jim, suddenly renewed.

He buzzed Chip Davis and alerted him to the fact that Ben had arrived and then hurried out to greet his old friend.

The Indian-American exobiologist smiled from ear to ear when he saw Jim and the two men shook hands for a long minute before Jim stepped back and introduced Chip and Norma.

"I'm glad to have you on the team, even if it's only part time!" beamed Jim, as he accepted an official looking envelope from Ben. "Chip will get you set up with the necessary credentials and then we can talk privately back in my new office."

As Jim and Ben waited at Chip's desk for a badge to be printed, Ben indicated the office and said, "This is quite a setup you have here. Everything looks brand new."

"It is," nodded Jim. "A week ago today I was in...well, let's just say I was a long way from Washington, D.C. and none of this was here. It's been a crazy week, Ben."

Chip handed Ben a clip-on identity badge and indicated the colored stripe across the bottom.

"Jim asked me to assign you to Team 2 and that's what this yellow stripe means. You have access to the lab area whereas those wearing badges with a green stripe don't."

Confused, Ben wrinkled his brow at Jim.

"Don't worry. I'll explain it all in my office. Are we good to go, Chip?"

"Yes, Sir! I'll code his thumb print into the door access system while you two are talking but he has everything he needs from me. Nice to meet you, Ben."

On their way from Chip's desk to Jim's office, Ben remarked, "Everyone seems so friendly here! It's hard to believe this is a government operation."

When they reached Jim's office he touched his right thumb to the sensor and the door slid back into the wall.

"Whoa!" exclaimed Ben. "I've got to get me one of those!"

Inside and comfortably seated at Jim's small, round work table, Jim sighed.

"Wow, there's so much to tell you that I don't know where to begin. The last time we were together we were in the cafeteria at Mercury Base Camp on the Nevada Test Site property. We were still struggling with the mystery of the alien spheres at that point. Little did I know that my NWIDI teammates and I would later come in contact with two more types of artifacts each totally and completely different from the spheres."

"How are the other folks?" asked Ben. "Are they working here with you?"

"No," frowned Jim. "Didn't you hear about Frank's accident?"

Jim spent the next fifteen minutes catching Ben up with the events of the past five years, as best he knew them.

"So you have no idea where Tony and Linda are?" Ben finally asked.

"No idea at all, Ben! In some ways it's been the worst five years of my life, even though the research part of it has been incredible. And what about you? How's your research coming?"

"To tell you the truth, I haven't accomplished much in the past year or so. I seem to have run out of things to test and analyze and there haven't been any real breakthroughs in a long time. The DOD is only interested in the propulsion system and I can't seem to make any headway there. As an exobiologist, I'm more interested in where it came from and who—or what—was in it."

Ben was talking about the "flying saucer" he had been investigating for a number of years in a secret laboratory at the Air Force facility commonly known as "Area 51."

"Well, this entire project," Jim said, indicating the office complex, "is dedicated to learning just that, my friend. The folks on the right side of the room are analyzing the triangles I told you about and the others are following a paper trail that we think will lead us to the beings that brought the triangles to Earth. Maybe we should have your craft shipped out here and we can all work together."

"I don't think the DOD would stand for that," smiled Ben, "but I did bring you a little present that may help you along. At the time I didn't understand the note attached to my travel orders, but now that I understand what you're up to it makes a lot more sense."

Ben reached into a small carry-on bag he had brought with him and pulled out an object about the size and shape of a thick magazine.

"I was told to bring something with 'hieroglyphics' on it and this was the best I could come up with. I assume whoever made that request knows about your triangles and their changing messages."

Jim accepted the rectangular object and studied it carefully. Even at first glance he recognized some of the characters from the triangles.

"The Rosetta stone?" he asked.

"I have no idea. I gave up trying to decode those symbols years ago. I've always assumed it was a pre-flight checklist, given where I found it. It doesn't seem logical that a dictionary would be located on the flight deck, but who knows?"

"It looks like it's made out of the same material as the triangles," observed Jim. "If it is, that would be a revelation in itself. Let's go back to my lab and check this out."

In the small lab behind his office, Jim opened the safe and withdrew the tray containing four of the triangles.

"You're right, the material looks identical to me," agreed Ben. "But I thought you said there were five."

"One is next door in the hands of my new staff. The set of five originally came packaged in this handy carrying case," added Jim as he pulled the storage box from the safe and handed it to Ben.

Ben rolled the box over in his hands several times and examined it inside and out.

"Where did you say you found this?" he asked.

"Frank recovered it off the northwestern tip of Cuba, in about two thousand feet of water. He had access to a special ship at the time, one with an ROV capable of exploring at those depths. I wish you could see the pictures they took of the city, or what's left of it. They were really incredible."

"You say 'they'—weren't you with the team?"

"Not at the time of the actual discovery, but I arrived by helicopter a few hours later. I was in Florida waiting to be secretly inserted into Cuba, but that's another story.

"Are you planning to leave this with me or do you need to take it right back?"

"It's yours to keep," replied Ben. "You must have friends in pretty high places because for nearly ten years I've been the only person allowed to touch that craft and then suddenly the DOD tells me to break off a piece and bring it to you."

"I'll tell you about that situation at dinner, my friend. It's just one of many unbelievable things that have happened to me lately. Have you done any type of chemical or other analysis on any portion of the craft?"

"If you're asking me if I know what it's made of, the answer is no. Early in my investigation I tried to get a chemical analysis done but the DOD wouldn't allow any piece of it to leave my remote lab. That's why I was so surprised when..."

"I have a metallurgist and a chemical engineer on the team," interrupted Jim. "Maybe we can figure something out that will help you."

"All my bosses want to know is what makes it go. The incredible fact that what I have in my lab is a flying machine from another world is completely lost on them. All they care about is the motor."

"Listen, let me switch gears on you for a moment. How well did you know Buzz Edwards?"

"Not well at all," replied Ben. I think it was Gene Carlson that introduced us and that would have been over at the Yucca Mountain project while I was on loan to the Department of Energy. I think that would have been about the same time I met you. In fact, when I was ordered back to my own lab you were still in Nevada, weren't you?"

"Yes, I think so," nodded Jim. "And we ran into Edwards again during each of our two subsequent missions. Did you ever go back to Yucca Mountain to work with the spheres?"

"No, never," said Ben. "And after Carlson's accident they sealed off the underground facility and I'm pretty sure the whole Yucca Mountain project has been abandoned."

"Accident?" asked Jim. "What accident?"

"Well, I guess it's my turn to give you some bad news. About a year after you and I made our interesting little trip to the bottom of that facility, there was a catastrophic radiation leak in one of the storage tunnels. I didn't even know they had started storing nuclear waste down there, but obviously they had. Anyway, the contamination was so bad that they had to seal off the tunnel. A few weeks later a team from the Nuclear Safety Commission went down to check for leaks, there was an explosion and they never came back up. At that point, the Department of Energy made the decision to close all the safety doors in the shaft and seal the facility at ground level. As far as I know, that's still the situation out there."

"But what about Carlson?" asked Jim.

"He was leading the team that never came back to the surface. I assume he died down there."

"He was murdered!" exclaimed Jim. "He was one of the few others who knew that the spheres were being stored at the bottom of Yucca Mountain. They engineered the radiation accident to force the closure of the facility and they probably arranged for Carlson to be lost with the spheres. Two birds with one stone!"

"You keep saying 'they.' Who are they and why would anyone undertake such a huge operation just to get rid of one man?"

"No, you don't understand. They had to permanently dispose of the spheres without letting anyone else know they existed. By playing their cards right, they were able to get Carlson, too, in what to all outward appearances was a terrible accident. One that probably never made the news, am I right?"

"Well that's certainly true," agreed Ben. "The whole incident was covered up with a Top Secret blanket and the closure of the facility was explained away as the result of pressure from environmental groups. I only heard about it because some of our radiation people were called in to assess the damage both before and after the explosion that killed Carlson and the rest of the safety team. But you still haven't told me who 'they' are?"

"They are an international terrorist group, probably led by none other than Buzz Edwards himself. And now that I've told you that, you'll have to trade in your security badge for a new one with both yellow and green bands, because you just crossed over into Team 1 territory. Let's grab my security chief and go get some dinner. Then I'd like to come back here and run a couple of tests on this present you brought me."

***

Sophie had agreed to meet BKA agent Max Becker at a coffee shop just off campus at 5:30 p.m. but as she waited at a small table near the back of the student hang-out, she was having second thoughts. She should have at least brought along Manny in case Becker decided to make trouble. She glanced at her watch and noted that he was already ten minutes late and the longer she waited the more uncomfortable she grew with her decision.

"Good afternoon, Miss Hoffman," said a male voice from directly behind her.

Sophie jumped and spun in her chair to be greeted by the smiling face of the same man who had visited her at her apartment building.

"How did you do that?" she demanded angrily.

"I've been here for nearly an hour," smiled Becker calmly. "I didn't want to get ambushed by a bunch of unruly college students."

Taking a seat opposite Sophie without waiting for an invitation, he continued.

"Now what's this about a video recording?"

Sophie took a deep breath to calm down.

"Not so fast, Mr. Weber or Mr. Becker or whoever you really are. Before I turn over anything, we need to talk about our mutual friend Professor Karl Schmidt."

"You do realize that I could arrest you on the spot for possession of that video, right?"

"And you realize that I could have you beaten into a coma by simply yelling 'BKA agent,' right?" whispered Sophie.

"Touché," replied Becker. "So let's get our cards out on the table and see what kind of game we're playing, shall we? What's your interest in Schmidt?"

Sophie considered her response before replying.

"I have reason to believe that your agency has connected Karl Schmidt to a friend of mine and I want to know why."

"Then why not simply ask me?" challenged Becker.

"Because I want the truth, Mr. Becker, and I'm not sure you're capable of that."

"Okay, young lady, let's knock off the innuendos and talk frankly, because otherwise I'm out of here. Perhaps we got off on the wrong foot, but you and your friends don't exactly hold a place in the BKA Hall of Fame. When I visited you last week I was trying to locate Schmidt and I had hoped that I could intimidate you by implicating the visiting

American lecturer that you have apparently become friendly with."

"Become 'friends' with," corrected Sophie. "And I resent your implication. Isn't it true that the BKA has an arrest warrant out for Dr. Barnes based on some sort of espionage charges?"

"Yes," nodded Becker, "but Barnes was the last person to see Schmidt before he disappeared and that makes him a person of interest."

"You're lying again," replied Sophie. "Schmidt was in BKA custody more than twelve hours after he met with Dr. Barnes. He was being detained in a private interrogation room near Kruger's office and you personally questioned the two agents who were assigned to guard Schmidt."

Becker stared into the young woman's eyes in disbelief but saw only defiance starring back at him.

"There's no way you could possibly know that," he finally said.

"And yet I do, Mr. Becker. I also know that your agents searched Dr. Barnes room looking for a packet—the alleged classified documents you think he was given by Schmidt. However they didn't find anything because the packet was still down at the hotel's front desk waiting to be delivered. He did eventually receive the package but I'm reasonably sure they weren't classified at the time Dr. Barnes took possession of them."

Becker was temporarily at a loss for words. "Where are these documents now," he finally uttered.

"Dr. Barnes took them with him when he returned to the United States last Monday," smiled Sophie. "But I'm telling you, they are nothing more than the ramblings of a slightly maladjusted Karl Schmidt. The only piece of information in the whole packet that related to Germany was your boss's name scrawled on one of the sheets."

"Kruger?" exclaimed Becker. "Why would Schmidt have written Kruger's name?"

"I think you'd better ask your boss about that. I never actually saw the papers but I'm positive they were the personal creation of Schmidt and that they had nothing to do with German State secrets."

Becker's head was reeling. He already knew that Schmidt had somehow learned about a group called "the Six" but had the professor also connected Kruger to this group? And was Becker's name mentioned in Schmidt's ramblings?

Becker saw Sophie's lips moving and realized that she was speaking to him.

"I'm sorry, what did you say?" he asked.

"I said, are you ready to work together in an effort to locate Karl Schmidt? He's the only one who can answer some important questions we both have."

"Absolutely!" replied Becker without hesitation.

The directness of his answer surprised Sophie and caught her off guard.

"Er, well, good! I'm glad you see it that way." Sophie reached into her purse slowly, so as not to spook the BKA agent. "I will give you this video of your agent in Schmidt's apartment in exchange for you telling me what she was looking for."

"It was just a routine search of a suspect's residence," replied Becker as he reached for the compact disk Sophie was holding."

"Wrong answer again!" she hissed as she pulled back the CD. "She was looking for something very specific on the shelf behind the recliner and she was talking to someone on her cell phone. Was she talking to you?"

Becker slumped back into his chair. He was very frustrated but he also realized that the woman had the advantage.

"Yes, she was talking to me! She was looking for an appointment journal that I had torn a page from a few days earlier." Reaching into his jacket pocket, he produced a folded piece of paper, slammed it down on the table and slid it across to Sophie. "This page!"

Sophie cautiously reached into her purse a second time. Becker's eyes followed her hand carefully, ready to go for his weapon if necessary.

"Do you mean this journal?" asked Sophie, as she slid Schmidt's appointment book across the table to Becker along with the CD containing the video.

Chapter 18

The first thing Tuesday morning, Jim introduced Ben Kingston to the rest of the staff and then convened a meeting with his lab team. When everyone had found a place to sit or lean in the main lab, Jim pulled back a white towel and exposed the object Ben had brought from Nevada.

"Ben was kind enough to bring us our first artifact that's not part of the triangle collection. This object comes to us from, well, from a different geographic location but as you can see, it looks to be made from the same material as the triangles. Our task for this morning, or for however long it takes, is to determine if they are, in fact, made of the same material. As I'm sure you can see, Ben's gift contains rows of symbols that appear to be similar to those on the triangles. Before we go any further, I'd like Andrew to take as many photos as he thinks he needs because he's going to be working independently trying to correlate the glyphs here with those on each of the five triangles. Andrew, please proceed whenever you're ready."

"Mr. Kingston, where was your object found and do you know what its purpose might be?" asked metals expert Howard Donaldson.

"Please call me Ben. Unfortunately, I'm not at liberty to give you all the details about this object, but I can tell you that it was found inside a larger, somewhat portable object so the actual location where it was found probably isn't relevant. I'm afraid I can't help much with the second half of your question, either. Jim hopes this will turn out to be a dictionary of the alien languages you're working with, but I think it's nothing more than a set of notes or a checklist of some sort."

By the time Ben had finished his explanation Andrew had also finished his photos and was headed out the door toward his desk to begin work.

"Okay, then, let's see what we can make of this bad boy," smiled Jim. "Howard, you have the lead for now, with

Naomi and Justin assisting. Ben and I will observe and throw in our two cents worth here and there."

Howard seemed to be a natural leader as he directed the other two through various physical tests of the object Ben had provided. He carefully documented every move they made and every result they accumulated in a bound journal he always seemed to have with him.

As they worked, Jim silently nodded his approval several times. About thirty minutes into the analysis, Ben handed Jim a folded note.

"They must never know about the craft or its current location," read the note.

Jim nodded and stuffed the note into his shirt pocket.

After about forty-five minutes of poking, prodding and examination, Howard addressed Jim and Ben.

"Short of breaking off a corner and melting it down, I think we know everything about the physical characteristics of this thing that we're going to learn today. Now we need to run the same set of tests on the triangles and then compare notes. However, I have a suggestion."

"What's that?" asked Jim.

"I suggest we do out testing on the lid of the box that originally contained the triangles. The triangles themselves are some sort of mechanism and until we understand how they work, I don't think we should subject them to any unnecessary physical abuse."

"Interesting idea," nodded Jim, "although I may have already abused them years ago. And there's something odd about the box that makes the triangles do their thing so how do we know it's not also a mechanism of some sort?"

"And for that matter," interjected Naomi, "how do we know the tablet we've just been testing doesn't exhibit the same properties observed with the triangles? If we put it into one of your alien atmospheres would all the characters on it change?"

"Now *that's* an interesting possibility," grinned Ben. "If it did, that would certainly establish an undeniable link between the tablet and the triangles, wouldn't it?"

"Well, let's give it a try!" urged Jim. "Andrew, you and Justin run the second set of physical tests on the lid—a good suggestion, by the way—and I'll help Naomi test the tablet. I'll get the lid from the safe while you two get set up in here. Ben, can I have a word with you?"

Once they were securely in Jim's private lab and the door had hissed shut, he took Ben's note out of his pocket.

"You know, this is going to be very difficult to keep quiet if it turns out that these two samples are made from the same stuff."

"I know, but you understand how incredibly classified my project is, right? If the word got out that the Department of Defense has been keeping a flying saucer hidden for more than eight years, the *you-know-what* would hit the proverbial fan."

"But these folks already know they're dealing with alien artifacts, Ben. They're all bright people and it won't take them long to begin wondering how all this stuff ended up on Earth. And I dare say that we have secrets here that even the DOD doesn't know about."

"Sorry, Jim, but my orders are to keep the source of the tablet secret and that's what I have to do. If you decide to let your staff in on this, please wait until after I'm gone."

"Understood," agreed Jim. "And if we don't come up with some matches, it won't matter anyway."

A little more than an hour later, Jim, Ben and the members of Team 2 reconvened to compare notes.

"So what have you learned, Andrew? Do the symbols on Ben's tablet have anything in common with the messages on the triangles?"

"Oh, most certainly," beamed the linguist. "I accepted Ben's premise that the tablet contained notes or other coherent writing and did some frequency of occurrence and pattern recognition analysis. Because there is so much more text on the tablet, I was able to make some real progress there. Then I took what I had learned from the tablet and applied it to the triangles. For each of the five, I was able to predict characters based on patterns from the tablet. But this is only true for one atmosphere, the one you refer to as A3."

"Excellent!" exclaimed Jim. "Excellent work! Were you able to decipher the messages on any of the triangles?"

"Not in the short amount of time I had with such a limited amount of text. But maybe, with more time…"

"You have as much time as you need, my friend. I'm sorry to say that our results with the atmospheric testing were negative. The text on the tablet did not change with any of the seven different atmospheres we tested. Howard, how did your comparison testing go?"

"Inconclusive, I'm afraid, but with a definite bias towards a common base material. In other words, I would have to say that they are almost the same, but not exactly identical. Perhaps the two samples have been subjected to different environmental factors since arriving here and this has slightly altered one or both objects so they no longer test as exact matches. Another possibility is that the slight differences we see between the lid and the tablet are what account for one being able to change characters and the other not being able to."

"And were you able to identify the tablet material?" asked Ben.

"No, I'm afraid not. The material is an alloy of some sort with trace amounts of aluminum, zinc and rhodium but the main component is completely foreign. Perhaps with an electron microscope we could identify the atomic structure, but I'm pretty sure we aren't going to have a name for it on our periodic table of the elements."

"That's disappointing, but we need to continue this investigation," frowned Jim. "I don't exactly know what an electron microscope is, but I assume it's a pretty sophisticated device. Should we look into requisitioning one for the lab?"

Both Naomi and Howard laughed out loud at Jim's comment.

"Jim, an electron microscope is a huge device that would fill most of this room," offered Naomi, "and it would take weeks to set up and calibrate, even if we did have the space."

"Okay, then, we'll have to get you access to one somewhere else. Whatever you need you shall have. It's about lunchtime, so let's knock off for a while and pick this up a little later. Good work, team!"

Jim, Ben and Danny Miles went to the cafeteria in the building for a quick lunch but ended up getting box lunches to go because Jim wanted to bring Danny up to speed on the morning's lab analysis and the subject was taboo outside the secure walls of the office.

Seated around Jim's small table, they ate and discussed the implications of what they had learned.

"I was sure disappointed when the tablet didn't react to the atmospheres the way the triangles do," commented Jim between bites of roast beef sandwich.

"Frankly, I would have been very surprised if it had," replied Ben.

"Why is that?" asked Danny.

"Well, Jim suspects the triangles contain messages created here on Earth to be sent to a variety of other locations. Hence the message changes to the correct 'language' upon arrival in the alien atmosphere. The tablet, on the other hand, arrived from another world aboard a …"

Realizing that he was about to give away the secret of the alien craft back in his Nevada lab, Ben stopped in mid-sentence.

"It's okay, Ben, he already knows. And he's seen the triangles do their trick and he's read the entire Schmidt file."

"Oh," said a surprised Ben. "Well, in that case, I was going to say that the tablet arrived from another world and its intended readers—the crew of the craft—were a known constant. The tablet wouldn't have to change languages because the language of the crew would have been known in advance."

"That's correct," agreed Jim. "And we learned something huge this morning, guys. Something really, really huge!"

Ben and Danny stared at Jim questioningly.

"As soon as we find the planet with atmosphere A3, we'll know where your flying saucer originated!"

***

Sophie left the coffee shop with an uneasy feeling about her meeting with agent Max Becker. Although they had agreed, in principle, to work together in the search for Schmidt, Sophie was never really sure the BKA agent was being honest with her.

"Well, what's done is done," she said to herself as she stepped into the warm mid-day sun. She needed to know what had happened to Schmidt and she was getting nowhere on her own. Maybe her alliance with Becker would result in some information.

As she slowly walked back toward her apartment building, her cell phone rang.

"Sophie, it's Manny. Where are you?"

"I just left Vee's Coffee Shop and I'm headed home, why?"

"I'll be right there! Watch for my van!"

With that, the line went dead, leaving Sophie speechless.

Ten minutes later screeching tires at the far end of the block signaled the approach of Manny's VW van.

He stopped abruptly in the middle of the street and yelled, "Get in! Hurry!"

As Manny careened through traffic on his way back to the apartment, Sophie tried to get him to tell her what all the excitement was about but the only thing he would say was, "You have to see this to believe it!"

As they stepped through the front door of the apartment building, Sophie grabbed Manny by the arm and demanded to know what was going on.

"In here," Manny said, pointing to the multi-purpose room known as room A-1. "In here!"

Sophie entered the room not knowing what to expect, but she certainly didn't expect to see Professor Karl Schmidt seated quietly at the far end of the large conference table. When he saw her enter the room, he politely stood to greet her.

"Professor Schmidt!" exclaimed Sophie. "A lot of people are looking for you, including me."

"I know," replied the professor softly. "The BKA would really like to have me back in custody, and I'm running out of options. I was hoping you would allow me to stay here for a couple of days until I can make other arrangements."

"Here?" cried Sophie. "Do you realize what kind of risk we would be taking if we allowed you to stay here? We would be breaking a dozen laws, at least!"

"Yes, I know what I'm asking is a lot, but I truly have nowhere else to turn. I will only be here two or three days and then I'll be leaving Munich for good. In the mean time, I will provide you with some information that I think you'll find very interesting. Perhaps you'll even be kind enough to pass it along to your American friend, Jim Barnes. And I assure you the BKA won't be looking for me here. In fact, I've taken measures to convince Agent Becker that I'm miles south of here on the shores of Lake Starnberg."

"And just how did you do that?" asked a dubious Manny.

"By arranging for the GPS-enabled cell phone of one of his agents to be briefly activated there," smiled Schmidt. "He raced down there this morning after the agent went missing from my apartment and, as far as I know, he's still down there."

"That was you?" shouted both Sophie and Manny at the same time.

"And he's not at the lake any more, Professor, because I just came from a meeting with him!" added Sophie.

"I see. Well, he must have been very interested in what you had to say to drive all the way back up here for the meeting. However, I'm sure he'll be resuming his search for me very soon. I've left enough clues scattered around down there to keep him busy for days."

"Wait a minute!" demanded Sophie, just realizing the significance of all Schmidt was saying. "Were you the person in our video? Did you disable our camera? And what happened to that agent that was searching your apartment?"

"Yes, yes and she's fine," replied Schmidt. "And I should be asking you why you placed a camera in my private residence, young lady!"

"We—my friends and I—have been looking for you ever since we heard that you had escaped from BKA custody," replied Sophie, moderating her tone a bit. "We went to your apartment to look for clues but discovered that Becker was already inside so we waited for him to leave and then installed the camera to keep tabs on the BKA. We had no intention of spying on you, Professor. We assumed you had already left the area for good."

"If you and your friends are at odds with Agent Becker and the BKA, why were you meeting with him today?" challenged Schmidt.

"I met with him to negotiate an informal partnership and to give him the video we captured seconds before his agent disappeared," admitted Sophie.

"You what?" shouted Manny. "My God, Sophie, are you completely out of your mind?"

"Yes, young lady, what could possibly possess you to join forces with the BKA?" demanded Schmidt.

"Listen, I know this sounds bad on the surface, but please hear me out," pleaded Sophie. "When I heard that the BKA had picked you up, Professor, I was of course concerned. But when I learned that you had escaped, I figured you were temporarily safe and my concern subsided. Then Max Becker, using an alias, showed up here and implicated both you and the American, Dr. Barnes, in an espionage plot. I didn't believe it, but Dr. Barnes had already mentioned his meeting with you and Becker made a good case. I decided that the only way to get the truth would be to find you, and since Becker had already initiated a city-wide manhunt for you, it seemed to make sense to team up with him. Obviously he would never share information with me under normal circumstances, but when I offered the video of his agent, just seconds before she disappeared, he changed his tune completely."

"And you actually trust that man?" asked a still angry Manny. "I don't believe it!"

"Well, no, of course I don't trust him, but when I gave him the video we captured, I told him there was another ninety seconds that showed the abductor's face and that he could have it as soon as Professor Schmidt was located and I was able to question him."

"But there isn't any..." began Manny.

"Yes, I know, and we'll have to cross that bridge when we come to it," interrupted Sophie.

She turned to a confused Schmidt. "You see, Professor, there isn't any additional footage. Until a few minutes ago we had no idea who the abductor was."

Schmidt smiled his approval and then frowned again.

"But why are you so interested in talking to me?" he asked.

"Because I promised Dr. Barnes that I would try to find out why the BKA had an arrest warrant out for him and whether or not you had, in fact, transferred classified information to him without his knowledge. I know about the file you had delivered to his hotel, Professor. Dr. Barnes didn't share with me what the file contained, except to warn me that Wilhelm Kruger's name was mentioned and I've always considered Kruger to be a very dangerous man. I suspect that the connection between you and Dr. Barnes is related to aliens and not the theft of classified documents, but I need to be sure. It's as simple as that."

"Well, let me put your mind at ease right now," replied Schmidt. "Since everything in the file I gave Barnes was written or typed by me, personally, and since I have no authority to classify material of any kind, I can assure you that the information was not classified at the time I turned it over. The file contains my personal research on a number of people and organizations, but, in most cases, the information is just my opinion. As I mentioned, I'm going to be leaving soon, and I wanted to put what little I've been able to learn into the hands of someone more capable of pursuing the truth. Having said that, I'm quite sure that if Kruger knew everything the file contained, he would do anything—and I mean *anything*—in his power to retrieve the file and silence those with knowledge of it. That's actually the main reason I've decided to leave."

"So Dr. Barnes *is* in danger!" exclaimed Sophie.

"Only if Kruger had access to my notes," replied Schmidt, "and I doubt if that happened. Dr. Barnes has my original file and I never made copies of anything."

Sophie opened her purse and withdrew a folded piece of paper. She laid it on the table in front of Schmidt and tapped her finger on the words "Turn over files to Dr. Barnes."

"Is this your writing, Professor?" she asked.

"Yes, that looks like a page out of my appointment book," stammered the obviously surprised Schmidt.

"That's exactly what it is," nodded Sophie. "Max Becker gave this to me earlier today in exchange for the rest of your book."

She slowly turned the page over to reveal the words "THE SIX" printed in large block letters.

"And what about this, Professor? Do you think this might cause Kruger any concern?"

***

After lunch, Ben went back out into the lab to observe some additional testing Howard was doing and Danny went to tend to another shipment of supplies that had arrived earlier.

Alone in his office for the first time in the day, Jim stared at the pile of paperwork in his In Basket and slumped into his chair. Every time something arrived at the office, Norma signed the delivery receipt and Danny initialed the packing slip when a security check had been completed but Jim had to personally sign a formal Navy document acknowledging receipt for everything that arrived. He was sure that somewhere, in a drab government accounting office, a clerk was diligently charging every single item to Jim's personal account. Electing to ignore the paperwork for the time being, Jim instead picked up his phone and dialed Captain Stukey's office.

"Hi, Sharon, it's Jim Smith again. Listen, I don't know who to call about this, but one of my folks needs access to something called an electron microscope. Do you know if there's such a thing here at NRL?"

Jim had called the Captain's office so many times in the past few days that he was on a first name basis with the Captain's secretary. She knew more about the research facility than almost anyone and if something like an electron microscope had to be run past the Captain for approval, she was the one to get it done.

"You've finally stumped me, Dr. Smith. I've never heard of any such thing, but I'll check it out and get back to you. Anything else you need while we're on the phone?"

"Just a fifty-five gallon drum full of aspirin," replied Jim wearily.

"Be careful what you ask for," laughed the secretary before she hung up.

Jim replaced the phone in the cradle and looked up to see Bill Blass, his new Intelligence analyst, approaching his door. Jim pressed the button to open the door, happy for anything that would keep him away from the pile of paperwork.

"Good afternoon, Bill. What disturbing news do you have for me today?"

"If you're referring to the Fitzgerald situation, there's been no change. He and the plane are still missing and the FAA is still polling airports. They've broadened the search area, but still no news. "

"I'm really sorry to hear that," frowned Jim. "It's beginning to look bad, isn't it?"

"I'm afraid so," replied Blass. "But I do have some good news for you, I think. Yesterday you asked me to vet a person named Phillip Dorado and I've done so. The analyst's preliminary research proved to be very accurate. Dorado is a well-respected eye surgeon at Harborview in Seattle and he has a long-time interest in underwater archaeology with a particular interest in South Bimini. The analyst listed him as an amateur scientist but I would have to say that the only thing separating Dorado from the pros is that his degree is in medicine instead of anthropology or archaeology. He's published some of his work and it seems to be generally well accepted. Now here's the good news.

"Dorado left Seattle a week ago on one of his exploration trips and he's scheduled to begin his return trip from the Bahamas this afternoon. Would you like me to have him diverted to Washington D.C. for an interview?"

"Can we really do that? Can we just kidnap someone and make them come and talk to us?"

"Actually, yes, *you* can. Although in this case I might suggest that we use the term 'invite' and that we make arrangements to get him back to Seattle more or less on time so we don't disrupt his surgery schedule."

"Well, I don't know how we do all that, but if we can make it happen, let's do it! I'm very curious to learn why this man's name is on Schmidt's 'Those Who Know' list."

***

The reaction on Schmidt's face after seeing the page from his appointment book helped Sophie convince Manny that they should allow Schmidt to stay, but only until he could make whatever travel arrangements he had eluded to. As they got him settled into the unoccupied apartment, Sophie couldn't help but point out the irony—this was the same room where they had hidden Jim Barnes just a few days earlier.

"In fact, I think he sat right there at that table the first time he examined your file, Professor," she smiled as she closed the door and left a noticeably nervous Schmidt alone in the room.

After they turned the corner in the hallway, Manny asked, "So what about your deal with Becker? Are you going to tell him Schmidt is here?"

"No, I don't think so. If Schmidt is telling us the truth—and I think he is—then the charges against him are unfounded. Perhaps the BKA received some bad intel or, more likely, Kruger is after Schmidt for entirely personal reasons. In either case, Schmidt should not be in BKA custody."

"But you made a deal with Becker. In all the time I've known you, Sophie, I've never known you to go back on your word."

"I know," she replied softly.

Chapter 19

Jim was totally absorbed in the updated list Danny had just brought him from the analysts when Blass appeared at his door again. He pressed the button to let the older man enter.

"What's up, Bill?"

"I just wanted to let you know that Dorado is on his way in. We were able to catch up with him while he was between flights in Fort Lauderdale and he's agreed to divert to D.C. in exchange for a first class ticket back to Seattle later this evening. He's on a Navy T-39 at this moment and should be on the ground in about ninety minutes. I've arranged to have him transported directly to the remote interviewing facility and after you've finished questioning him he'll be taken to Dulles to board a flight back to Seattle. Unfortunately, the only flight we could get him on leaves Dulles at 7:25 p.m., so you won't have a lot of time to talk to him—probably no more than an hour, given the travel time back to the airport."

"An hour should be plenty of time as long as I get my act together beforehand and make a list of specific questions. But what's a T-39? Did you put him on a fighter jet?"

"No," laughed Bill, "a T-39 is the military version of a Saberliner corporate jet. It carries a crew of two and has seating for four passengers. They're primarily used to move general officers around, but there was one already in place at Fort Lauderdale, so you commandeered it to transport Dorado."

"I did what?" exclaimed Jim. Then, seeing Bill's smile, he decided he didn't want to know the details. "Very well, where's the other end of this remote interviewing setup?"

"Actually, it's right here," replied Blass, pointing to Jim's computer monitor. "Chip will patch everything into your workstation so you won't have to leave your desk. He will also make a digital recording of both sides of your video conference in case you need to review it at a later time."

"Way to go, Chip! Well since we have some time, how about going over this new list the analysts have prepared? With your security okay, I'd like to bring in another five or six people as soon as possible."

***

After the Professor had had some time to rest, Sophie knocked on his door to make sure he was okay and to arrange for an evening meal.

"Come in," called Schmidt from behind the door.

"Good afternoon, Professor. I hope the room meets with your approval. I assume you won't be going out for dinner, so may we order you something and have it delivered?"

"Yes, that would be very nice," nodded Schmidt. "And I want to thank you, young lady, for allowing me to shelter here while I make some final arrangements. I also need to have a few minutes of your time to pass along some information for Dr. Barnes. I assume you know how to reach him, correct?"

"Yes, I have his cell phone number and Manny—the gentleman you met earlier—has a way to make my call appear to originate in the United States so it can't be traced to this location."

"Excellent!" beamed Schmidt. "Give me this evening to put together some notes and maybe we can talk in the morning. The sooner the information gets to Dr. Barnes, the sooner he can review it and take the appropriate action. Now what do you suggest for dinner?"

***

Jim had been alerted when Phillip Dorado's plane touched down and he sat at his desk impatiently waiting for the video conference to start. He had asked both Danny and Bill to sit in on the conference, but on the other side of his desk so their faces wouldn't appear on the small camera built into Jim's monitor. Suddenly, Jim's monitor switched from his desktop to a live video of a middle-aged man with wavy hair that was just starting to gray at the temples.

"Hello!" said the man at the other end who was obviously surprised by the sudden appearance of Jim's face on his own screen.

"Hello, Dr. Dorado. My name is Jim and I'd like to thank you very much for agreeing to chat with me for a few minutes. I understand we've made arrangements for you to get back to Seattle tonight, so I'm going to jump right into this. I hope you don't think me rude, but I'm very interested in your work around South Bimini and I have a list of questions that I'd like to get through before they have to rush you off to the airport."

"Not at all! It's not every day that you're asked to make an unexpected trip to Washington D.C. to help out the Government. I'll be glad to tell you whatever I can."

"Great! First of all, could you start by briefly describing the nature of your research near South Bimini?"

"Of course. I first became interested in the area more than twenty years ago when I read an article about an underwater feature off the coast of North Bimini that had been discovered in the late nineteen sixties. From the air Bimini Road appears to be two tracks on the ocean floor and when it was first explored the consensus was that it was nothing more than oddly shaped but naturally occurring beach rock. Later, amateur explorers took an interest in the feature and claimed that it was *not* naturally occurring but was, in fact, a man-made structure built to protect an ancient harbor."

"What exactly do you mean by 'ancient'" interrupted Jim.

"It appears that the structure—and there's no doubt in my mind that it is a man-made structure—is at least three thousand years old. I spent several years diving the site and taking video and still pictures of the structure. It was on one of these trips, about ten years ago, that I made the discovery that currently keeps me awake at night."

"You mean the discovery of a three thousand year old man-made structure fifty-five miles off the coast of Florida wasn't enough for you?" laughed Jim.

"Well, it was, until I discovered the foundations of a large number of buildings, arranged in a grid-like pattern on the ocean floor. Their rectangular shape and right angle corners left no doubt that these megalithic structures had been man-made!"

"I see, but how are these foundations so much more exciting than the Bimini Road structure?"

"Because of their depth," replied Dorado. "Unless they were inhabited by fish, one must assume that the land under the foundations was once above the surface. Almost all scientists agree that the oceans rose substantially after the last ice age and they even agree on the rate and amount of this rise. Given the depth of the structures I have been exploring, they have to be at least twelve thousand years old."

"But that implies that an intelligent culture lived in the Americas thousands of years before our modern civilization walked out of the desert!" interrupted Jim again. "How is that possible?"

"All I can tell you is that the evidence is down there in the sand for anyone to see. I've mapped, photographed and examined these structures for a while now and there is simply no other explanation except to assume that an as-yet unknown advanced civilization lived in that area long before the Sumerians appeared in Mesopotamia."

"That's an incredible find, Dr. Dorado! Why are you doing this alone, with your own money, when you should have the backing of a major university?" Jim knew the answer but he was curious what Dorado's response would be.

"For exactly the reason I just mentioned—because there is simply no other explanation except to assume that an as-yet unknown advanced civilization lived in that area long before the Sumerians appeared in Mesopotamia. Since this explanation doesn't fit the history archaeologists and anthropologists have prepared for us, they will not accept the obvious and no major university will touch the subject."

"This would probably be a good time to mention that I'm a professor of anthropology associated with a major university," said Jim, trying to keep a straight face.

"I'm sorry, Professor, but the facts don't lie. On this subject, the scientific community seems to have a very well coordinated attitude of 'don't confuse me with the facts' and it's just plain ignorance on their part."

Jim broke out into a wide grin and let the eye surgeon off the hook.

"Please don't apologize, Doctor. I was actually just testing your resolve a bit. I, too, have been involved in some discoveries that would be summarily rejected by traditional anthropologists and I share your frustration with mainstream academia. In fact, the reason I asked to speak with you is that we were indirectly associated with the same institution. I was a professor of anthropology at the University of Washington, which oversees your Harborview Medical Center. However, I took an extended leave of absence from UW several years ago and I no longer consider myself a member of the traditional scientific community. These days, I'm much more of a maverick, like you.

"If we can shift gears for a moment, I'd like to ask you some questions about a specific area. Have you ever done any exploring off the south end of South Bimini Island? Specifically, in the area known as Nicholas Harbor?"

"That's between Port Royal and the air strip, right?" asked Dorado.

"Yes, that's the spot. Have you done any diving there?"

"No, I'm afraid I haven't. My work has all been on the western side of the island, on what would have been the river bank back when the Gulf Stream was actually a river."

"I see," frowned Jim. "Have you ever talked to anyone who's been diving over there? Maybe even a recreational diver?"

"No, I'm afraid not. What's so interesting about that area, if you don't mind my asking?"

"I have a good friend who went missing there about five years ago and I'm trying to understand the topology of the area, that's all," explained Jim, trying to back away from the subject so as not to arouse Dorado's interest too much.

"I'm sorry to hear that," replied Dorado before his head disappeared from the screen. When it returned he was holding a large rolled up paper.

"I have what is supposed to be a pretty good map of South Bimini that I always carry with me. Let me check it out."

Dorado unrolled the map and examined it for a minute before laying it in his lap.

"Huh!" he grunted. "The map says that area has a long, sloping bottom that gradually drifts off into deep water between Bimini and Andros. In the area you mentioned the water isn't any more than seventy-five feet deep."

"Is that the map prepared by the Navy about seven or eight years ago?" asked Jim.

"Yes, it sure is and it's one of the few detailed maps of the South Bimini area. Everybody over there uses it."

"Well, I wouldn't put too much stock in it. Does that map suggest why my friend and another person would have been using rebreather equipment the day they went missing?"

Dorado looked at the map again.

"No, not really. Rebreather gear is normally only used for one of two reasons: really long dives or really deep dives. In the Nicholas Harbor area, the depth is easily accessible with normal SCUBA gear, but maybe they were planning a long dive. Perhaps they were searching for something on the bottom and used the rebreathers to expand their search area. Another possibility is that they were just training with the equipment."

"Doubtful," replied Jim. "My friend and his companion hitched a ride on a Coast Guard helicopter all the way from Andros Island to make that dive. If they were just practicing, they could have done it anywhere along the coast of Andros."

"That's true," agreed Dorado. "If you'd like I can check it out the next time I'm on Bimini but I don't have anything planned for a couple of months."

"No, that's okay, I was just curious about the area. Let me shift gears one more time before you have to leave for the airport. What's the strangest thing you've ever seen in the waters over there? And now I'm referring to anywhere in the Bahamas."

"Hum, let me think about that. The megalithic structures are pretty strange, of course, but I've already mentioned them. Other than some odd-looking marine life, nothing really comes to mind."

"What about lights, metallic spheres, or fast moving disks?" asked Jim, coming bluntly to the point.

There was a long pause from his guest—*so* long that Jim thought maybe his question hadn't been heard.

"Dr. Dorado, what about..."

"I heard the question, Jim. Listen, if you're intent is to discredit my research by making me out to be a crazy I'm not going to fall for it!"

Dorado's response caught Jim off guard and apparently his surprise showed.

"Please let me assure you that I have nothing but respect for your work. No, my question was a very sincere one. You see, my friend—the same one who disappeared off South Bimini—witnessed a spherical shape traveling underwater at a high rate of speed directly toward the spot where he would disappear ten days later. I was just wondering if you had seen anything out of the ordinary during your own dives."

For the next fifteen minutes Dorado described numerous encounters with small, shiny spheres. Most encounters occurred at some depth and there was never any interaction with Dorado but his description of the objects sounded exactly the way Frank Morton had described the sphere he had spotted off the coast of Cuba when he was exploring the sunken city where the triangles were found.

Dorado explained each incident in detail, almost reverently, and Jim sensed that there was more to the encounters than the other man could express. However, before he could ask, he spotted Blass tapping his watch. It was time for Dorado to go!

"Listen, I hate to interrupt you, but one of my associates is signaling me that if you don't leave for the airport immediately, you'll miss your flight. Perhaps we can continue our discussion another time?"

"Yes, of course!" replied Dorado. "If I didn't have a surgery scheduled for tomorrow morning, I'd say 'screw the flight' but I really do have to get back into Seattle tonight. But please call me. You found me in Fort Lauderdale, so I assume you can find me again."

"Yes, I'm sure we can, but someone will get your preferred contact information anyway and we'll be in touch. Thank you for your help and I'd really appreciate it if you kept this meeting to yourself."

"Understood," nodded Dorado. "Good luck finding your friend."

Jim's monitor switched back to his normal desktop and he leaned back in his chair with a smile.

"Well, that was certainly interesting. What did you guys make of it?"

"I think there's something about the spheres he wasn't telling us," said Danny. "I think his experiences went beyond mutual observation. Maybe he's had actual contact with them."

"Them?" questioned Bill. "Are you suggesting that these spheres actually exist? Or that they are capable of having contact with a human?"

Jim sighed and looked at Danny.

"I guess it's time we filled him in on the other half of our little project. Danny, will you let Chip know that Bill needs a dual-team access badge like yours and mine? I'll bring him up to speed and then let's get busy rounding up these other folks I want to see."

***

As she approached his door, the smell of freshly brewed coffee told Sophie that the professor was still with them. The night before, several of the tenants had put together a breakfast basket to tide Schmidt over until Sophie could return from her regular Tuesday morning meeting with the editorial staff of the University newspaper but the meeting had been pushed back to early afternoon and Sophie had stayed at the University rather than walking back and forth. Now she worried that the old man hadn't eaten all day. As she knocked on Schmidt's door, she glanced at her watch and was surprised to see that it was already 5:00 p.m.

"*Fräulein*, please come in!" greeted the friendly old man. "May I offer you a cup of coffee?"

"No thanks, Professor, I've already had too much coffee today. Have you had any lunch?"

"Yes, one of your young friends brought me a delicious salad and some dark bread. I sincerely appreciate the hospitality of everyone here."

"It's our pleasure, Professor. You're becoming something of a legend around here. In fact, I just came from a long meeting that was mostly about the search for you and it was very difficult not to be able to tell them that you have been found!"

"I'm so sorry, my dear, but I hope you remembered your promise of last night. It's very important that I not be taken back into BKA custody now that Kruger knows that I am aware of the Six. I think I will be leaving sometime tomorrow so you just need to keep my secret a little while longer."

"Don't worry, Professor, I didn't say a word. Did you have time to put together the information you want me to pass along to Dr. Barnes?"

"I did, indeed," said Schmidt as he reached for a sheet of paper on the table. "I don't know how much he's told you, but he's been involved in some very interesting research and I provided him with a list of others who I believe have had similar—and yet different—experiences. I hope he'll make the connection on his own, but I can no longer take that chance, so I want you to impress upon him that each person on my list titled 'Those Who Know' have had in their possession, at one time or another, items similar to his triangles. That's my 'Item One' here on this paper.

"It's also important that he realize the grave danger he's in because of my carelessness with my appointment book. Kruger will assume that I passed information to Dr. Barnes connecting him—Kruger—to the Six and that could prove fatal to Dr. Barnes. Please apologize for me and explain that it was a momentary lapse on the part of an old man. 'Item Two' also provides the names of some additional people Dr. Barnes should be on the lookout for.

"And that brings us to 'Item Three.' Dr Barnes will soon realize the full implication of my notes regarding *the Teachers* and he must work to protect their secret and expose the Six. Any other outcome will be disastrous for all of human-kind."

"Sophie scanned the list and nodded. "I understand, Professor, and I'll make sure he understands, too. Are *the Teachers* the aliens you've been trying to warn everybody about for the past few years?"

"Warn? No, no, no, young lady! *The Teachers* are here to help us—to save us, actually—but there are forces at work throughout the world that want to destroy them."

"But why would anybody want to do that?" asked Sophie.

"Because they profit from human misery. They sell the drugs that poison our youth, they manufacture the weapons of war and they infiltrate the governments that control our lives. And they kill anyone who gets in their way without a second thought."

"The Six?"

"Yes, the Six! And they are too strong to fight, I'm afraid. That's why I must leave."

"But Professor, if this group is such a threat to humanity, isn't it your duty to stay and fight, regardless of the personal risk? Please excuse me for being so frank, but it seems like you are taking the cowardly way out."

"I'm not giving up the fight, *Fräulein*, I'm just taking up the fight from a different location. Here I am only one, but over there..."

A loud knock on the apartment door startled them both.

"Sophie, are you in there? Becker just pulled up across the street and he's heading this way."

"On my way!" yelled Sophie. And then to Schmidt, she whispered, "You stay right here and don't unlock your door until he's gone. I'll get rid of him and be right back."

***

Jim still wasn't sure how it was possible, but individuals who had been just names on a list the day before started showing up at the remote video conferencing facility the very next morning. By noon he had conducted five interviews and a pattern was already starting to emerge.

His first interview had been with a woman named Karen Koenig who had served as a Christian missionary in Southeast Asia for more than forty years. Now in her late eighties, she had spent most of her adult life in Cambodia before, during and after the Viet Nam war. It was during this tumultuous time that she first became interested in the ancient temple at Angkor Wat, in the northwestern region of the country. Dating back to the early twelfth century, the complex started as a Hindu temple but eventually became a Buddhist religious center and today still remains the world's largest religious building.

On one of her first trips to Angkor, Karen had discovered a small, intricately carved ivory statue in the dirt near a path in a remote corner of the complex. When she tried to return it to one of the monks at the temple, he waved her away and scolded her vigorously; but she didn't speak whatever dialect he was using so she left for home that night with the statue still in her shoulder bag.

For the next few years, the statue occupied an inconspicuous space on a bookshelf in her living room until one day when a visiting Cambodian friend spotted it and demanded to know where she had found it and why she had it in her house. It turned out the statue was the image of an ancient god and it was considered bad luck by both the Hindu and Buddhist religions. Karen had always considered it a soothing addition to her house but in deference to her friend she stored it away in a box and didn't see it again until years later when she was packing up her house for the move back to the United States.

Undecided about what to do with the statue, she set it on her nightstand and went to bed. Early the next morning a violent head-on crash on the street in front of Karen's house sent one of the vehicles careening into her living room, destroying almost the entire structure—except for the bedroom, Karen and the statue on her night stand! From that point on Karen had kept the statue close by and she swore it had provided protection numerous times. She even had it in the remote interviewing room with her, so Jim was able to capture its image as a part of the video conference recording.

Each of the other individuals had a similar story about an artifact that had been found near a historically ancient site. In each case, the artifact seemed to provide knowledge, protection or emotional comfort to the bearer. In each case, the person in possession of the object had kept it out of the public eye for personal reasons. Since 8:00 a.m. Jim had been shown artifacts from northern Europe, Easter Island, central Africa and the shores of Lake Titicaca, high in the Andes Mountains near the Peru/Bolivia border.

When the last of the morning's interviews were over, Jim challenged Bill and Danny for an explanation.

"What's the verdict, guys? Are these people all whackos or is there something real going on here? "

"The stories are too similar to be made up," suggested Danny. "Like the hundreds of UFO stories we've all read, right?"

"Yes, except for one big difference," replied Jim. "These people all have hard, physical evidence and they're willing to produce it. We now have video images of five more artifacts and I suspect that every name on Schmidt's list will be a similar situation. If the artifacts we saw today were originally associated with the culture where they were found, then it appears that someone—or something—has been helping out humans for a long, long, time. And it would also appear that this help was offered in a wide variety of locations to specific cultures. Every site we heard mentioned today was once the center of a great civilization that is now either gone or very much diminished."

"I wonder if they're helping *us*?" asked the always skeptical Bill Blass.

"They sent us Schmidt's notes, didn't they?" replied Jim.

Chapter 20

Sophie flew out the door of Schmidt's temporary sanctuary to meet Manny and two other male occupants of the building he had managed to alert on his way to notify her. By the time the four reached the main floor, Becker was pounding on the door and demanding to be let in.

"Let me try talking to him," insisted Sophie, "but be prepared for anything. In my meeting this morning, it was obvious that he's right on the edge."

Sophie positioned herself so she could talk to Becker through the tall, glass panel just to the left of the door.

"What is it, Mr. Becker?" she shouted.

Becker quickly moved to the side and confronted Sophie through the glass.

"Open up! I know he's in there with you and I'm going to take him into custody, one way or another."

"Who, Mr. Becker? Exactly who do you think is in here with us?"

"Don't play games with me!" shouted Becker. "I know Schmidt is in there. Open this door!"

Taking a chance, Sophie shouted right back, "Place your search warrant against the glass so I can read it and I'll gladly open the door. Otherwise, you have about one minute to get off my property before I call the local police and file a complaint."

"Open this door!" shouted an angry Becker. "You know I can have a warrant here in a matter of minutes so why prolong the inevitable?"

Sophie breathed a silent sigh of relief that Becker didn't already have a warrant in his possession.

"And if Schmidt really is here, you know we can have him safely away in less time than it will take you to get your warrant, so let's stop making idle threats and discuss this. What is BKA's interest in Schmidt, Mr. Becker? What is it that he's supposed to have done?"

"I don't have to answer to you or anyone else! The man is wanted for questioning and that's all you need to know."

"In that case, Mr. Becker, I suggest you toddle off and get your warrant. Good evening!"

Sophie abruptly turned and started to walk away from the glass.

"Wait a minute!" yelled Becker.

Sophie stopped, turned and slowly returned to the glass with a stern look on her face.

"Yes?"

"I don't have to tell you this, but if it will speed the process along I will tell you that Schmidt is wanted on espionage charges for passing classified information to a foreign national."

"And would that foreign national be Dr. James Barnes, of the United States?" asked Sophie.

"Again, that's really none of your business, but yes, it's Barnes."

"Well, for your information, Mr. Becker, I happen to know that those charges are totally false. I also happen to know that this arrest order you seem to think you have has never been put on the BKA Federal Docket. The only office interested in either Schmidt or Barnes is the Munich office and I'm guessing your orders are coming directly from Kruger himself. How am I doing so far, Mr. Becker?"

With a little of the wind taken out of his sails, Becker calmed down a bit.

"Regardless of what you think you know, you have no right to stand in the way of law enforcement activity. Now please open the door."

"Actually, I have a moral obligation to stand in the way of this particular investigation, Mr. Becker. Your boss is up to something very sinister and if you're involved you are just as guilty as he is. The page you gave me from Schmidt's appointment book has the words 'The Six' printed on one side. Do you know who this group is or what they stand for?"

"That's none of your business!" shouted Becker with anger returning to his voice.

"But it is, Mr. Becker. And it's the business of every citizen on this planet, if my information is correct. And unfortunately for you, a lot more people than just Schmidt are now aware of this group and its intentions. Rather than standing here hassling me, you should be packing a bag for someplace far, far away. Everything Schmidt knows about the Six and its members went back to the United States with Dr. Barnes and I'm sure it's now in the hands of people who will not take the information lightly. In fact, they will probably see it as a major international terrorist threat. If I were you, Mr. Becker, I'd be thinking about finding a place to hide!"

Frustrated, but noticeably concerned, Becker yelled, "This isn't over! I'm coming back here and I'm going to tear this place apart until I have Schmidt. And when I return, I'll also have a warrant for your arrest on charges of obstruction of justice!"

Becker stormed down the steps to the sidewalk and stomped across the street to his car. As his tires squealed down the street, Sophie turned to find Manny's two companions staring at her in shock.

"What?" she smiled. "Haven't you ever seen an angry BKA agent before?"

"It's not that, Sophie," one of them finally stammered. "What's all this stuff about Professor Schmidt and international terrorists?"

"It's best that you forget what you just heard, guys. The more you know, the more danger you will be in. Where's Manny?"

"He's probably half way across town with Professor Schmidt by now," mumbled the other man.

***

Becker fumed all the way back to his office. He was angry at Karl Schmidt; he was angry at Sophie Hoffman; and he was angry at himself. It didn't seem possible that the woman could know anything about this group called "the Six," especially since he, himself, didn't really know who they were. But if she was even a little bit right his whole career could be in jeopardy just because of his association with Wilhelm Kruger.

He closed his office door and slumped into his chair. After calming himself for a minute, he called an old friend who was now assigned to the BKA office in Berlin.

"Hey, Max, it's been a long time! What's up?" asked the other man.

"I just need a little information, Kurt. What have you guys up there learned about the Schmidt case?"

"Sorry, the what?" asked the Berlin agent.

"Schmidt. Professor Karl Schmidt, a university professor from here in Munich that's wanted for questioning on espionage charges. He might have passed classified information off to an American named Barnes. I have the memo right here in front of me—haven't you seen it?"

"No, sorry, but I haven't. Hold on a minute."

Becker drummed his fingers while he listened to on-hold music.

"No, nothing like that made it up our way, Max. I just pulled the file of open cases and there's nothing in it about a Schmidt or a Barnes. Are you sure you have the right names?"

"Yes, I'm pretty sure," replied Becker, reigning in his growing anger. "Do me a favor, will you? If anything shows up in the next few days, give me a call. In the mean time, I'll double-check those names."

Becker hung up, put his elbows on his desk and rested his head in his hands. It could just be a case of sloppy filing in Berlin, but if the Hoffman woman was right—if this were a Kruger personal vendetta—then he had to get as far away from it as possible as fast as possible. But he had to be absolutely sure because if he defied Kruger and there wasn't any wrong doing, more than just his career would be destroyed.

Becker studied the memo again and noticed something he'd seen a hundred times before but never paid any attention to. Every official BKA memo had a control number printed in the lower left corner of each page. This number was automatically assigned by the BKA central computer system and it tied the memo to one or more case numbers. Becker quickly logged into his workstation, found the correct inquiry screen and entered the control number from the Schmidt memo on his desk.

"Record not found," displayed the computer. Becker cleared the screen and tried again. "Record not found" appeared again. Becoming increasingly suspicious, Becker yanked open his file drawer and pulled out another memo. When he entered its control number, the correct information displayed as expected, so it wasn't a problem with the computer system. The problem was that the Schmidt control number really wasn't in the BKA database!

But how could that be? Either he was missing something or Kruger was taking a huge risk by falsifying a BKA document. Even Kruger's status as a retired Army colonel wouldn't protect him if he got caught. There had to be another answer.

***

After Becker left, Sophie went immediately back to her room and called Manny on her cell phone.

"Becker is gone. He's supposedly going after a search warrant but I doubt if he can get one this late in the day. Is everything okay on your end?"

"Yes, as good as can be expected. There are some personal belongings I'll need to pick up if we're not coming back to stay and I'll also need to know where to drop the package."

Sophie knew that Manny was deliberately trying to be vague, but if the BKA had their cell phones tapped none of this double-talk was going to fool anybody.

"I think we have plenty of time and I need you to set up the internet phone for me, anyway, so why don't you come back here? Come in through the service entrance and we'll be waiting for you."

"Are you sure?" questioned Manny. "At least out here I'm off the radar."

"Maybe, and maybe not. But you can't drive around forever and I have a better plan. Remember, use the service entrance."

Sophie ended the call and raced down the hall to the apartment of one of the guys who had witnessed her conversation with Becker.

"Lukas, Manny is on his way back and he's headed for the back door. Can you meet him and help him secure the professor in case the BKA shows up here? If Henri is still here, get him to help you. I'll see who else I can find and send them along shortly."

Sophie returned to her room and began calling every apartment in the building from a list she kept in her desk. It was early evening on Wednesday, so she was only able to contact three other students. Following the same instructions she had just given to the other three, she went down to the main floor and made her way to the basement door.

The apartment building had been built right after World War II during a time when many Germans privately feared that the British might bomb their cities as retribution for the Luftwaffe bombings of London in 1940. Consequently, it had a large, very secure bomb shelter built two stories underground. The shelter had never actually been used, but the building's current tenants kept it clean and stocked as a refuge in case of severe weather. Access was through a solid steel hatch in the basement floor that could be secured against the harshest wind, weather or war.

The plan was for Manny to race down an alley behind the apartment building and stop at a little-used back door just long enough to push the professor out of the van and into the arms of waiting students. While Manny sped away and circled the block a few times to distract anyone who might be following him, the Professor would be spirited down the back stairs into the basement and from there into the shelter. One student would enter with him and the others would replace the carpet and furniture that usually disguised the portal in the floor. When Manny received the all clear, he would park the van out on the street, where it normally sat, and come in through the front door calmly carrying a grocery bag full of empty food boxes that was kept in the van for just such occasions.

Unfortunately, even the best laid plans sometimes fail.

***

As Becker sat glumly pondering his next move, the telephone solved his problem for him—it was Kruger, summoning him to his office.

"What's happening with the search for Schmidt?" demanded Kruger.

"I'm following up some leads, but we still haven't found him, Colonel. I have a lot of agents on the street, but my personal involvement has been limited due to the disappearance of one of our agents. Klaudia Braun was conducting a routine search of Schmidt's apartment when she was apparently overpowered and kidnapped. Rather than divert the efforts of the field agents, I've been attempting to track down Braun while the others continue their search for Schmidt."

"Braun can wait!" bellowed Kruger. "I want all your energy focused on this search for Schmidt, do you understand?"

"Yes, Colonel, but..."

"Do you understand, Agent Becker?" yelled Kruger.

"Yes, Sir," replied Becker.

"As for Schmidt's accomplice, I'm closing in on the American in my own way. In fact, I already have one of his associates in my grip in case I need some bargaining power but I hope to have the American, himself, very soon. It's absolutely critical that the documents Schmidt gave to the American be recovered immediately, along with anyone who has had access to them."

"Colonel, I hope I don't have to remind you that the BKA has no jurisdiction in the United States. You can't just start rounding up Americans, especially on American soil."

"You don't need to remind me of anything, Becker! You just do your job and leave the American to me. And if you can't do your job, I'll find someone who can! Now get out of here and find Schmidt!"

On his way to Kruger's office, Becker had made up his mind to question the Colonel about the Schmidt memo and why it hadn't been properly logged. On his way back to his own office, Becker was confident that he had the answer. This manhunt wasn't so much about finding Schmidt as it was about eradicating all knowledge of the contents of his file. Becker now believed that if he brought Schmidt in, it would amount to a death sentence for the old man. And while that might be justified, Becker wanted to know more about Schmidt's file before he facilitated the professor's illegal execution.

***

By mid-afternoon on Wednesday, Jim had interviewed a total of eight people, each with a physical knowledge of a different type of artifact. Each artifact was attributed to a different culture that ranged in age from the ancient Egyptians to the more contemporary Incas of South America. But in every case, the artifacts' original purposes seem to have been to provide information or knowledge of some kind to the culture where they originated.

Even Jim's three experiences matched this pattern. The spheres he and his comrades had investigated in Nevada and the Yucatan provided solar eclipse information to the ancient Maya and also seemed to be collecting current data to be returned to their makers.

Under Japan's Yonaguni Island the *tsubutes* they had discovered provided Jim with enough information to allow him to partially decode the remarkable ancient murals. The murals, in turn, proved beyond any shadow of a doubt that beings from another planet had visited Earth at least once.

And, of course, the triangles found near Cuba had turned out to be messages intended for the "home world" or "worlds" of the visitors.

As Jim studied the results of his interviews, he jotted a question to himself in the margin.

"How many civilizations?" he wrote. He wasn't sure he'd ever know the answer to that question because there was no guarantee that Schmidt's research was complete. The German professor had listed twenty-three names but there was no way to know if that was the entire list or not. Some of the names on Schmidt's list shared knowledge of the same artifact, and at least one name, Jim's, had knowledge of more than one artifact. If there were no more duplicates, Schmidt's list would represent twenty different cultures that had been helped along by *the Teachers* but how many more had there been?

While Jim was pondering that question, his cell phone rang. When he answered it, he was surprised and pleased to hear Sophie's voice."

"Hello, Sophie! It's kind of late where you are—how are things going?"

"Well, not so well at the moment," she replied, "but before we get to that I need to pass along some information from Professor Schmidt. He showed up here at the apartment building yesterday seeking sanctuary and, of course, we obliged. I'm reading from his notes and he insists that this is quite urgent, so let me finish before we catch up on the news.

"First of all, he wants me to make sure you realize that each person on his list titled 'Those Who Know' had in their possession, at one time or another, items similar to your triangles. He said he thought you'd figure that out by yourself, but he wanted to be sure.

"Secondly, he wants you to know that you are in grave danger because of your knowledge of his file. This somehow relates back to the Munich BKA bureau chief, a man named Wilhelm Kruger.

"And lastly, Professor Schmidt assumes that you will soon realize the full implication of his notes regarding *the Teachers* and he insists that you must work to protect their secret and to expose the Six. In his words, and I quote, 'Any other outcome will be disastrous for all of human-kind.'"

"I see," replied Jim, not really knowing what else to say. "You can tell the good professor that I've started interviewing people from his list and a clear pattern is already emerging.

"You can also tell him I'm not happy about the danger I'm apparently in, but I'm beginning to understand why he felt he had to pass the file on. I'm now in a very secure location and I have the resources of the U.S. Government at my disposal but I still don't know if I can protect *the Teachers* or defeat the Six. However, please tell him that I will try."

"I'll tell him if I can, Dr. Barnes, but that's the not so good part I mentioned when you asked me how things were going. Things have been a little crazy here in Munich and this evening we had to get the Professor out of the apartment building in a hurry to avoid his recapture. In all the excitement I'm afraid he may have suffered a heart attack. He's safe here in the apartment building, but we can't risk taking him to the hospital and he's clearly not well."

"I'm sorry to hear that," frowned Jim, "but if he needs medical help, you may have no choice but to risk hospitalization. Is there any chance you can get a doctor to see him there?"

"We're looking into that right now. The Professor keeps insisting that he's leaving soon and that it's imperative he not be recaptured by the BKA, but I really think he needs some medical help."

"Sophie, let me see if there's anything I can do from this end. Can you call me back in an hour?"

"Yes, of course. I'm using some kind of Internet phone that Manny rigs up to make it appear like I'm calling from the United States. We'll just leave it connected up until we get the Professor's issues resolved."

"Give me your exact street address and then let me see what—if anything—I can do to help."

As soon as Sophie was off the line, Jim buzzed Bill Blass and asked him to come into his office. After explaining the developing situation in Munich, Jim asked the question of the hour.

"So, is there anything we can do to help?"

"Officially, probably not," replied Blass. "But unofficially, I know some folks in Munich who might be able to lend a hand. However, this has to be completely off the record, okay? If word about this got out, heads would roll on both sides of the Atlantic."

Jim handed Blass the address Sophie had just given him and nodded.

"Okay, agreed. It's off the record. Anything you can do would be greatly appreciated. The professor is the only one who really knows what all this business about the Six means, and we need to do whatever we can to protect him—or in this case, maybe save his life."

**

Just as Jim was getting out of his chair to head for Danny's desk and the short drive back to the house, his cell phone rang again.

"Hi, Sophie, how are things going? Is there any change in the professor's condition?"

"Ah, yes, and thank you very much! I don't know how you managed to pull this one off, but thanks."

"Managed to pull what off? I just asked one of my guys here to see if anything could be done. I didn't know any wheels were in motion yet."

"Well, your guy did a great job! About forty-five minutes ago two ambulances pulled up in front of the building and four medical technicians rolled in two gurneys. Or at least they looked like gurneys. Together they were carrying enough equipment and supplies to stock a small clinic, and that's exactly what they did. We had the professor resting in an old bomb shelter under the basement and they turned it into a trauma room in a matter of minutes. When they were all set up, two of the building's residents climbed on the gurneys and pretended to be patients while two more took the places of two of the techs and away they went, red lights flashing and sirens wailing. The professor now has full-time medical assistance, but whatever they gave him has already made a huge difference and he's feeling much better."

"Huh! I guess we were able to help, after all," mumbled Jim. "That's great news, Sophie. I was just getting ready to head out but if there's anything else you need, please feel free to call my cell at any time."

"Okay, and thank you again. I don't know where these two medical techs came from, but they seem to be very well connected, so I think we'll be fine."

As he passed Blass' desk on the way out, Jim nodded and said, "Thank you."

"Glad it worked out," replied Blass, turning back to his workstation monitor.

As usual, Danny drove the Navy staff car and Jim rode in the front passenger seat. On the way back to the house they shared in the military housing section of adjacent Bolling Air Force Base, Jim solicited Danny's opinion of Bill Blass.

"He's a hard one to read," suggested Danny. "He keeps to himself; he's quiet; and he seems very confident. Almost too confident—like he knows what you're going to do before you do."

Jim told Danny about the most recent Blass achievement involving medical care for Schmidt.

"How could he do that?" asked Jim rhetorically. "Less than fifteen minutes after I asked him to see what he could do, there were ambulances in front of an apartment building in Munich, Germany. And yesterday, when I asked him to see if he could arrange a meeting with the eye doctor from Seattle, he found the guy and had him on a military flight to D.C. in less than two hours!"

"Well, all I can say," said Danny as he turned into the driveway, "is he sure makes your side look a lot bigger!"

Taking the lead, Jim opened the door and stepped inside. He only felt the pain from the blow to his head for a second before he lost consciousness.

Chapter 21

Jim slowly opened his eyes and tried to focus but everything within his field of view was a stark white. He slowly rolled his head to the right and darker objects became visible. As his vision began to clear he realized he was in a hospital room. Struggling to figure out why, he tried to recall his most recent memories. He remembered talking to Sophie and to his intelligence expert, Bill Blass. He remembered leaving the office and riding back to the house with Danny and then...nothing.

"Dr. Smith? How are you feeling?" It was a female voice but she was out of Jim's line of sight and he didn't have the energy to turn his head again.

"Where am I? What happened?"

You're in the Bolling Air Force Base hospital, Dr. Smith. You had a nasty blow on the head, but there doesn't seem to be a concussion, so you should be fine after a little rest. Would you like a drink?"

Jim nodded and the nurse lifted his head.

"Slowly, please," she cautioned as she lifted the paper cup to his lips.

"What happened to me?" asked Jim again.

"I think I'd better let the Captain bring you up to speed, Sir. Let me get him for you."

Moments later, Jim was staring into the face of Captain Stukey, his most recently appointed military boss.

"Welcome back, Son! We were pretty worried about you. Are you feeling well enough to talk?"

"Er, yes, I guess so, but I'd still like somebody to tell me what happened. Can I have some more water?"

The nurse's face replaced the Captain's and she held another cup of water for him.

"Thank you," he said as he tried to smile. "Captain?"

"Here, Jim," replied the naval officer, returning to Jim's view.

"Okay, here it is in a nutshell. A few hours ago you and Sergeant Miles left your office and returned to your base housing unit. You were clobbered with something hard and rendered unconscious. Apparently, Sergeant Miles saw what was going down and was able to take defensive action. After what was probably an extended hand-to-hand combat engagement, Miles finally subdued the two attackers and called base security. I was hoping you might remember some details of the attack that would help us figure out how these intruders managed to get into a base housing unit."

As the Captain described the events, Jim's memories flooded back to him.

"I didn't see anything, Captain. I was hit before I was even through the doorway and I don't remember anything after that," replied Jim, barely able to follow the conversation. "How's Danny?"

After a telling pause, the Captain replied, "He's not doing too well, I'm afraid. Both attackers were armed with nasty knives and Sergeant Miles took a pretty deep puncture wound to the abdomen. He had lost a lot of blood by the time the paramedics arrived and it appears that some vital organs were also damaged. He came out of surgery about an hour ago and he's in intensive care right now, but I'm afraid it doesn't look too good."

"Can I talk to him?"

"No, not right now. Miles is still heavily sedated and you shouldn't be moving around, either. Just let the good folks here take care of you until you get your strength back and then we'll see about a visit."

"But what about my work at the lab?" Jim protested weakly.

"Don't worry about that right now. Obviously we'd like to get you back to work as soon as possible but not until the doctors say you're fit for duty. In the mean time, your staff can press on without you. They're all very concerned about you and Sergeant Miles, by the way, and they send their best wishes.

"I've been here since they brought you and Miles in because I wanted to be here when you regained consciousness but now I really must get back over to NRL and take care of some things, including finding you a new—and safer—place to live. I'll check in every few hours and I hope to see you back on your feet in no time."

"Did you say that Danny subdued the attackers? Do you know who they are?"

"Not yet," frowned the Captain, "but our best interrogators are with them right now and I promise you they will be talking very soon. Now get some rest. I'll talk to you in a few hours."

After the Captain left the room, the nurse returned to ask if Jim wanted to try to eat something.

"Maybe something light—do you have any applesauce?" replied Jim. "What time is it?"

"It's just past two in the morning, Sir. I'll see about the applesauce and be right back. Please try to rest."

When Jim was alone in the room, he slowly rolled to his right and slid the drawer of the metal night stand open. With his left hand, he rummaged around until he felt his cell phone and glasses. Once he had his glasses on, his vision improved significantly and he studied the room briefly before closing the drawer and stashing the cell phone at his side under the sheet.

"You're in luck," announced the nurse as she burst back into the room carrying a cafeteria tray. "Apple sauce seems to be something we have plenty of and the doctor on duty thinks it's a good sign that you're hungry."

"Why?" questioned Jim. "I haven't eaten since lunch yesterday—shouldn't I be hungry by now?"

"Yes, of course, but head injuries can do strange things to a person. I think what he meant was that it's a sign your injury hasn't caused any secondary complications. Let me raise the head of your bed a little and then I'll leave you alone and let you sleep."

She adjusted the bed, positioned a bed table and placed the tray in front of Jim. On her way out, she turned off the overhead lighting, leaving only some indirect light so Jim could see to eat.

The kitchen staff had been thoughtful enough to include a glass of cold juice and Jim ate and drank everything he had been provided. After pushing the small, wheeled table away from the bed, he retrieved his cell phone and scanned his log of recently received calls. Sophie had said Manny was going to leave the Internet phone hooked up for a while and Jim hoped it was still working.

He was about to give up when, on the fifth ring, someone answered the line in Munich.

"Hello, who is this?" asked a gruff male voice.

"This is Jim Barnes calling for Sophie Hoffman."

"Oh, hey, Dr. Barnes, it's Manny here. Obviously I forgot to disconnect this line, but I think Sophie will be glad I did. She's just down the hall, let me get her."

While Jim waited, he tried to make some sense of the last nine hours. Who had attacked him, and why?

"Dr. Barnes, this is certainly a surprise! And since it's the wee hours of the morning in America, I'm guessing this isn't a social call. Is everything okay?"

"No, actually it's not, Sophie. An associate and I were attacked last night and I think this incident may be related to what Professor Schmidt was warning me about. I'm calling because you should know that the people behind last night's attack are not fooling around. My associate is in intensive care, Sophie, and I'm told he may not survive so you guys need to increase your security."

"I'm so sorry, Dr. Barnes, but I can't say I'm surprised. Becker was around here yesterday threatening searches and arrests if we didn't hand over the professor and when I suggested that this whole BKA witch hunt might be a plan fabricated by his boss I think I hit a nerve. He's had nearly twelve hours to get his search warrant and, so far, we haven't seen or heard from him or anyone else at BKA. I'm guessing he won't be back. Personally, I think everything that's going on here as well as the attack on you last night revolves around Professor Schmidt's file. Whatever's in that file is very important to somebody!"

"Kruger?" asked Jim.

"That would be my guess. Yesterday I found out that the BKA arrest warrant for Schmidt was never formally filed. The only office looking for the Professor is Munich—in other words, just Kruger's office!"

"That's very interesting information, Sophie. My team has been trying to untangle part of Schmidt's file and so far we haven't made much progress. However, Kruger might just be the key we need to open this case up and I have an intelligence guy here that can find out anything about anybody. By tomorrow he'll know everything there is to know about Kruger including any dirty little secrets he may be keeping. By the way, this intel guy is the same person who got you the medical help last night. How is Schmidt doing?"

"He seems to be much better, thank you. The medical techs are still here, but I suspect they will leave sometime today. They've already removed the IVs and Schmidt was sitting up in bed the last time I was down there, so he's definitely on the mend. He still claims he's leaving soon, although he won't tell anyone where he's going. Maybe he has a safe house lined up and he doesn't want anybody to blow his cover."

"Maybe. Listen, it's very important that you—and all the tenants there at the apartment building—be on guard. If our incident here really is related to Schmidt's file, they will be coming for him soon and they are obviously interested in anyone else that may have had access to the file. That will include you and all your friends, I'm afraid."

"But none of us has ever seen the file," protested Sophie.

"But they don't know that and if they find out that Schmidt's been there, they will assume you know everything. And you actually do know something about the contents just from reading Schmidt's notes to me yesterday so please be careful!"

"You too!" replied Sophie. "Even if Becker does suspect that Schmidt is here, I don't think he's passed that information along yet. I've been expecting a BKA SWAT team to pull up ever since he left yesterday but every hour that goes by strengthens my belief that he's sitting on this information for some reason. Maybe he's beginning to doubt Kruger's motives, too."

"Maybe, but you can't be too careful. You mentioned yesterday that you have a secure place to hide Schmidt. Is that place big enough to hold all of you?"

"Yes, and then some! It's actually a bomb shelter under the basement of the building but right now the only people down there are Schmidt, his medical team and one volunteer tenant. The rest of the group is going about their regular routine to make things look as normal as possible."

"Okay, it sounds like you have things under control. Just remember that whoever hit us last night is playing for keeps. If you decide to disconnect this line, please check in with me a couple times a day or at any time if something comes up."

Without his personnel files, Jim had no idea how to contact Bill Blass outside the office so he called Bill's desk phone and left a message asking him to look into Kruger's activities as soon as possible.

Feeling suddenly very tired, Jim put his glasses and cell phone back in the drawer beside his bed and laid his head back on the pillow. He was sound asleep less than a minute later.

***

Michael "Buzz" Edwards was always the first one to arrive each morning and the last one to leave each night. His staff had several theories to explain this behavior but none were even close to the truth. Always an over-achiever, Edwards had risen through the ranks of career federal employees by completing tasks better and faster than his peers and he had attained his current pay grade of GS-13, the civilian equivalent of a lieutenant colonel, seven years ago at the age of thirty-five. Along with his promotion from GS-12 to GS-13 had come a new position as a Section Head at the Department of Defense's Defense Contract Administration Agency in Washington, D.C.

Less than a month after relocating to the nation's capitol, Edwards was approached by a man named Wagoner who suggested that a "group of concerned patriots" had been following his career and wished to speak with him about a unique opportunity. Reluctant at first, Edwards had finally agreed to meet with his secret admirers and he soon began joining them on a regular basis. Informal meetings were usually held in a quiet corner of one of the many private clubs in the Beltway district and the ultra-conservative group seemed to be genuinely concerned about the state of the country and their world views seemed to be very consistent with his own.

While the other members of the group were obviously familiar with Edwards, he was never given any details about any of them. Everyone was addressed by their first names only, except for Edwards, who was known by his childhood nickname of Buzz. Judging by their level of education and their dress, any one of them could have been a banker, an attorney or a congressman but no one offered any explanations and he never asked. This added to his surprise when one dark, dreary Friday afternoon he was asked to represent the group at a meeting in London. The meeting, he was told, was the annual get together of like-minded representatives from several other countries and his new Washington friends wanted his opinion of the group.

That was his first exposure to the Six, and now, seven years later, Edwards was the chairman of the U.S. division and in line to be the Chairman General soon.

But that was then. This morning, Edwards was at work as usual at 6:00 a.m. to put in a couple of hours for the Six before his staff arrived and his boring day of government contract administration began.

Logging into a private webmail account, Edwards scanned his new messages. The third one was from his counterpart in London and it was marked Urgent. Edwards opened it and began to read.

"Buzz—I received a call this morning (last night, your time) from Kruger, our German contact. He's really pushing for us to admit Germany at the next annual meeting, and he wanted me to know that he's on the verge of recovering a German professor and his file that apparently speaks unfavorably of our organization. He also told me that he's holding a pilot named Fitzgerald and his private jet to use as leverage in recovering the file, which has apparently found its way to the U.S. I thought you might want to know what's going on in your own backyard."

Edwards reread the message twice before pounding his fist on the desk. Just what he didn't need was a rogue wanna-be stirring up trouble!

He retrieved a number for Kruger from his personal Blackberry cell phone and dialed the number.

"Colonel Wilhelm Kruger," greeted the voice at the other end.

"Kruger, my name is Buzz Edwards. Do you recognize my name?"

"Ah, yes Sir!" replied Kruger. "How may I be of service?"

"I just received some interesting news from a mutual friend in London. Is it true that you know the whereabouts of a certain aircraft and its pilot?"

"Yes, Sir!" replied Kruger. "And very soon I expect to receive confirmation that the file prepared by an unguided countryman named Schmidt has been recovered, along with its new guardian."

"Now you listen to me, you moron," began Edwards. "You have no authority to conduct operations of any kind outside Germany. Your job is to provide us with BKA resources when requested and to otherwise keep a low profile. If you draw unwanted attention to our group, Kruger, so help me I'll personally put a bullet in your head!"

"But Mr. Edwards," stuttered Kruger, "you don't understand! I didn't sanction the kidnappings, but once the play was in motion I intervened to make sure we wouldn't be implicated in any way."

"Then who *is* responsible for this?" demanded Edwards.

"One of my over-zealous field agents named Max Becker," lied Kruger. "He's been working on the Schmidt case and when he let the Schmidt file slip out of the country, he felt compelled to retrieve it any way possible."

"Wait a minute, did you say kidnappings? As in plural? My God, Kruger, what have you and your band of idiots done? Who's the other target?"

"Becker believes that an American named Jim Barnes has the folder and apparently the plan was to grab both the file and Barnes. I'm waiting to hear from the operatives in Washington right now."

By now, Edwards was pacing his office in a rage.

"And you didn't stop this misguided plan even though it was clearly taking place far outside your area of responsibility?"

"Well, as I said, Mr. Edwards, I wasn't aware of the plan until it was too late to stop it. However, I have since taken control to avoid any unpleasant fallout for our group."

"Our group?" yelled Edwards. "It's not our group, you imbecile, it's *my* group and I won't have you endangering years of very hard work. As of this second you are to put a stop to any plans currently in place and then cease all communication with anyone outside Germany except me. I want a detailed briefing in my Inbox in thirty minutes, do you understand?"

"Yes, Sir, but…"

"End of discussion! And your report had better include the location of the pilot, the names of those holding him and how to contact them. I also want a list of any other people your agent may have contacted over here. If you can't control your own agents, Colonel, I don't know how you expect to run a new division. Goodbye!"

Edwards punched the End button on his cell phone and slid it back into his inside suit coat pocket. He only had about ninety minutes before his staff arrived and he couldn't even begin to clean this mess up until he received the information from Kruger. However, he could use the time to make sure that Kruger never pulled a stunt like this again!

***

Jim awoke with a start and it took him a minute to remember why he was in a hospital room. As he lifted his head to look around he had the feeling this wasn't the same room he had been in earlier.

"Can I get you something, Sir?" inquired a deep male voice from a shadowy corner of the room.

"Who are you?"

"I'm Agent Rogers, Sir, and I'm your security detail for the next few hours."

"Agent? Great, now there's even more government in my life. So which agency are you with?"

"The Secret Service, Sir," replied the agent as he made his way to the foot of the bed so Jim could see him.

"The Secret Service? Aren't you the guys who look after the President?"

"Yes, Sir, and the Vice President and a number of other high profile individuals, as well. But our protection can extend to anyone if the President issues an Executive Order as he did in your case, Dr. Smith."

Jim laughed out loud. "Ha! I'm being protected by an Executive Order that probably doesn't even have my real name on it. Don't you find that funny, Agent Rogers?"

"No, Sir, I don't. The Secret Service is frequently called on to protect high-profile individuals in the federal witness protection program and they all have fictitious names."

Jim raised his eyebrows. "Good point! Hey, do you think I could get some breakfast? I had a snack about two but

I'm feeling much better now and I think I'd like to try some real food."

The agent moved to the head of the bed and pushed the call button clipped to Jim's pillow. A couple of seconds later, a female voice from a ceiling-mounted speaker asked, "May I help you, Sir?"

"Dr. Smith would like to order breakfast," replied the agent, nodding to Jim.

"Uh, Hi! How about just a regular American breakfast? You know, bacon and eggs, toast and coffee," said Jim to the ceiling.

"Yes, Sir! Your breakfast will be there in about 15 minutes," replied the ceiling. A faint click told Jim the connection had been terminated.

"So, Agent Rogers, pull up a chair and let's chat while we wait. Am I still in the base hospital where I found myself the last time I woke up?"

Rogers moved a gray metal straight-back chair closer to Jim's bed and smiled. The tall black man had an athletic build and a face that was very hard to read. Even when he smiled his eyes remained cold and alert, constantly scanning his surroundings.

"Yes, you are still at the base hospital but I guess you've figured out that you've been moved. This room is in the interior of the building on one of the lower floors and it's normally reserved for high-risk patients. We chose it for you because it's more defensible than the room you were in."

"We?" asked Jim.

"The Secret Service, Sir. We have assumed responsibility for your security until further notice. One of the first things we did when we took over was to move you here."

"But what happens when I go back to work? I'm actually feeling much better and I think with some breakfast and a shower, I'd be ready to get back on the job."

"You will have a security detail with you at all times, Sir, and your movements will have to be approved by them in advance. You will be treated just like any other dignitary we protect."

"And this is all because someone broke into my base housing unit and hit me on the head?"

"No, Sir," replied Rogers. "It's because the President of the United States values you as an extremely important asset and he feels that only the Secret Service can provide the level of protection you require."

Jim studied the man's face, waiting for a smile to indicate the agent was being sarcastic but no smile appeared.

"Have they identified those guys from last night?"

"I don't know, Sir. That part of the investigation is being handled by Naval Intelligence, but I understand through the rumor mill that the plan was to grab you, force you to turn over some file, and then kill you. The young Marine who was with you definitely saved your life."

"Sergeant Danny Miles," replied Jim. "Any word on how he's doing?'

"No, Sir. He was still in intensive care the last I heard, but his security falls under the jurisdiction of the Department of the Navy so we would probably only be notified if he…"

Rogers' morbid explanation was interrupted by the ringing of Jim's cell phone, which was on a night stand similar to the one in his previous room.

"Hello?" he answered.

"Jim, it's Captain Stukey here. I understand you just ordered breakfast, so I assume you're feeling better. Are you getting acquainted with your new security team?"

"Yes, one member of it, at least. Is there any news on Danny?"

"There's been no change, I'm afraid. But that may be good news, because he seems to be hanging in there and fighting."

"What about the men from last night? Any information from them yet?"

"They've turned out to be pretty tough cookies. They're definitely pros and they appear to be Americans, although we still don't have their names. However, a name that seems to come up a lot is Kruger. Does that mean anything to you?"

"Yes! Colonel Wilhelm Kruger is the head of the BKA office in Munich," replied Jim.

"Well, he's likely the one who ordered the hit on you, although we're still confirming that."

"Ah, thanks, Captain. Listen, I need to make a quick call, but I'm feeling much better. Can you see about getting me out of here soon? There are some things I need to look into at the office and I'd like to meet with Bill Blass as soon as I get there."

"Sure, Son, glad to see you back on your feet. I'll put the wheels in motion and get back to you in about an hour. Enjoy your breakfast!"

Jim dialed Sophie's Internet phone, but this time there was no answer so he composed a simple text message and sent it to the cell number she had given him the day he left Munich.

"Beware of Kruger" read the three-word message.

Chapter 22

True to his word, Captain Stukey had Jim out of the hospital and on his way back to the office by 10:00 a.m. Agent Rogers had never been more than a few feet away and now he was seated opposite Jim in the back seat of a dark colored sedan.

"Bullet proof?" asked Jim as he wrapped the side window with his knuckle.

"Of course," smiled Rogers, who was beginning to realize that Jim didn't really grasp the seriousness of the situation. "Nothing but the best for you, Dr. Smith."

Jim leaned toward the center of the car so he could see out the windshield and noticed that there was an Air Force police truck leading them as they made their way from the Bolling base hospital to the adjacent Naval Research Laboratory facilities.

"Is there one of those behind us, too?"

"Of course," replied Rogers again.

When Jim's vehicle eased to a stop in front of the building housing his office complex, two men dressed in dark suits and wearing earpieces approached the vehicle and one of them opened the door on Jim's side.

"This way, Dr. Smith. Please walk briskly inside but do not get ahead of us."

Once inside, Jim looked back over his shoulder and saw Agent Rogers standing outside the car on the opposite side.

Before he could ask, the second new agent replied, "His shift is over. We have you for the rest of the day, Sir. I'm Agent Graves and to your left is Agent Easton."

Outside the actual office door another "dark-suit," as Jim now mentally called them, was standing with his back against the wall. He nodded to the agents escorting Jim, keyed a code into the lock and swung the door open. Inside, Norma Massey, Jim's receptionist of just a week, stood as the entourage entered.

"Good morning, Dr. Smith!" she greeted. "Welcome back!"

"Thank you Norma, but wasn't I here just last evening?" Jim replied with a smile.

"It seems like it's been forever," the woman frowned as she nodded towards yet another dark-suit standing at the far end of the reception area.

Once inside the office proper, the Secret Service agents eased up a bit, taking up positions in the two front corners of the large room and allowing Jim to move more or less freely among the staff. He spoke with each one personally as he made his way towards his office. When he reached Bill Blass' desk, he stopped.

"We need to talk," he said, quietly. "Give me five minutes and then please join me."

Blass nodded and Jim pressed his thumb into the pad beside his door. As it hissed open he turned to see everyone in the office staring at him.

"Well, let's get to work," he said in the most cheerful voice he could muster. "Let's make some real progress today, and let's do it for Danny Miles!"

Jim checked his voice mail for any information from Sophie, but there were no messages so he took the next few minutes to collect his thoughts and map out a rough strategy.

When he heard the knock on his door, he pushed the button and admitted Bill Blass.

"Tough night," commented the older man. "Is there any word on Sergeant Miles' condition?"

"No, not yet. Captain Stukey told me the two who did it were being 'interrogated' but it doesn't sound like much progress is being made. However, we do have the name Kruger. What have you been able to dig up on him?"

Blass laid a thick folder on Jim's desk.

"I took the liberty of enlisting the help of the other analysts and we pulled together this as a starter," replied Blass. "Based on our preliminary research, there's probably a lot more, but we started with the most current stuff first and it wasn't long before we picked up a vague trail to someone I think you already know. A man named Michael Edwards."

"Edwards?" replied a surprised Jim. "Do you mean Buzz Edwards?"

"That's the guy. Apparently Kruger got wind of Edwards' group a couple of years ago and he decided that Germany should be the seventh member. At least that's what it looks like so far."

"Wait, are you telling me that Edwards was behind last night's attack on Danny?"

"No, we don't think so. It's more likely that Kruger initiated some sort of covert operation on his own designed to impress Edwards and his associates, but we don't have anything concrete that would implicate Edwards—at least not yet."

Jim glanced at the folder and frowned.

"Is that for me?"

"No, it's actually for me, unless you want to review it. As the team comes up with new leads, I run them down through my own channels and the good stuff goes in here. They've been going strong ever since I received your message this morning."

"But that was at 2:00 a.m.!" exclaimed Jim.

"It was actually about 4:30 a.m. by the time I got here and listened to it. Captain Stukey called each of us just after midnight and the entire staff was back here at work by 4:00 a.m. He came down to brief us soon after everyone had checked in."

"Didn't he mention the name Kruger?"

"Yes, but he didn't give us the information from the interrogation team until about 5:00 a.m. Thanks to your message, we were already on it by then."

A knock on the door startled both Jim and Blass. Jim pressed the button to open for Albert Lund, the team's senior analyst.

"Sorry to interrupt, gentlemen, but Bill asked us to let him know if we came up with anything and we just got word that the missing Learjet has landed at the Naval Air Station in Key West, Florida."

"Great news!" shouted Jim. "What about the pilot?"

"Our information is that Mr. Fitzgerald was the only occupant of the plane, Sir. He's being debriefed by the Navy right now and the plane has been quarantined until it can be searched, but it appears that both the plane and the pilot are in good condition."

"Thank you very much, Albert! Great work and please keep us updated."

When the door had closed behind the analyst, Blass spoke.

"We need to keep a tight lid on this until we've had a chance to talk to Fitzgerald personally. Maybe you should contact the Captain and let him know what's happened."

"Absolutely! Are we done with Kruger for now?"

"Yes, unless you want to plow through all these details."

"No," replied Jim, shaking his head, "that's your area of expertise, not mine. Listen, I want you to know that I realize how much you're doing here and also I want you to know how much I appreciate it. You're doing a great job of making it look like I'm in charge around here, but without your efforts we'd still be trying to open the front door to this place."

Blass flashed one of his very rare smiles.

"Thank you, but I'm just doing my job. I've been digging around in other people's business for almost forty years, and I'm glad some of that experience is proving useful. But your strength is the world of wacky science in the lab next door. That stuff scares the crap out of me."

Jim smiled and accepted the reciprocal compliment with a nod. As Blass headed for the door, Jim reached for his phone to call Captain Stukey.

"You understand that if we clear him and admit him to your facility, he's not going to be leaving NRL anytime soon, right? Don't you think his wife will be a little upset about that?"

"Yes, I understand, Captain, but under the circumstances, maybe we should consider bringing her in, too. Until we know more about his disappearance, I think we have to assume that whoever grabbed Fitz could also grab Susan."

"Yes, well, I suppose there is that to consider, but housing is also an issue. I've managed to create a living space for you in the basement of this building that's acceptable to the Secret Service, but I don't know how many more folks I can accommodate."

"Sorry, Captain, but I think you'd better plan on at least three more after the Fitzgeralds. If we can find the rest of my former teammates, I'd like them here, too, at least until we get the Six shut down."

***

As soon as Sophie read the text message from Jim Barnes, she immediately dialed the cell phone number she had used to set up the meeting with Max Becker at the coffee shop five days earlier.

"Becker, here," answered the BKA agent.

"This is Sophie Hoffman, again, and…"

"Miss Hoffman, I thought I told you not to call this number again!"

"Becker, just shut up for a minute and listen to me. I have some information I think you will find very interesting and it might even affect your personal safety."

Sophie paused and Becker was silent.

"I just received a message from Dr. Jim Barnes, the American you BKA folks think is a spy. He and an associate were attacked last night at his residence on a military installation in the United States and the other man may not live. Fortunately, the attackers were apprehended and are currently being questioned. Would you like to take a guess who ordered the attack?"

"I'm in no mood for games, Miss Hoffman. If you have…"

"Your boss, Colonel Wilhelm Kruger, has been named by the attackers, Agent Becker, and my guess is that the CIA and the German Federal Police will be arriving at your office very soon. I warned you the other day that Kruger was up to no good, but this time he's gone too far. I'm only telling you this because I think you've become a pawn in whatever evil business Kruger is mixed up in and you may be the only person who can stop him."

There was a long pause before Becker finally replied, "Thank you Miss Hoffman. I have to go now."

And with that, the line went dead.

**

Becker abruptly ended the call with the Hoffman woman and started for Kruger's office. He had no plan and no ideas other than to confront Kruger and demand an immediate transfer.

"Is he in?" he asked Kruger's secretary.

"No, but he does want to see you and he'll be back in a few minutes. I was just about to call you. You must have ESP."

"Yeah, something like that. I'll wait inside."

Becker let himself into Kruger's private office and closed the door. He immediately went to the Colonel's desk and started rifling through the other man's Inbox. He would need something concrete when he confronted his boss.

After scanning through everything in sight, he instinctively opened the shallow center drawer of the ornate wooden desk and there, on top of everything else in the drawer, was a stapled set of pages titled "Becker's Plan." Becker snatched the typed document out of the drawer and began to read. Before he finished the first paragraph he was furious.

Sliding the drawer shut, he stuffed the document into his shirt and quickly exited the office.

"I just received an emergency call. Tell him I'll be right back," Becker said as he dashed into the hallway.

Instead of returning to his office, Becker headed directly to the parking lot. Once inside his car, he locked the doors and tried to control his breathing. Fear and anger had combined to bring him almost to the point of hyperventilation. He removed the document from his shirt and began reading again. Kruger had apparently prepared the report for someone outside the agency because the report wasn't in the usual BKA format. In fact, it read more like a letter except that it described a totally unrealistic set of events in which Becker had devised and implemented a plan to kidnap an American pilot named Fitzgerald. The report went on to explain how Becker had allowed a file containing sensitive information about the Six to slip out of the country and in a frantic effort to recover it had also ordered the kidnapping of a Dr. James Barnes, who allegedly had control of the document. It listed contacts within the United States, complete with telephone numbers. Throughout the report Kruger explained how he had used his own initiative to manage the plot, once he had discovered it, to prevent exposing the Six.

Becker threw the papers into the passenger's seat and started his car. Just as he was about to back out of the parking spot he noticed Kruger's dark Mercedes pass by. The old man was returning to his office and as soon as he discovered that the report was missing, Becker would be a marked man!

As soon as the Mercedes rounded the bend to descend to the next level of the underground parking facility, Becker slammed his car into gear and raced up to the ground-level exit. Recognizing the car, the guard at the exit opened the gate and Becker burst onto the street with no idea where he was going. He continued for several blocks with his eye on the rear view mirror and even lurched into a parking spot along the street to see if he was being followed. So far, so good but he had nowhere in the city to run and no way out without revealing himself. He was becoming frantic when he remembered the recent call from the Hoffman woman.

"Miss Hoffman, this is Max Becker. You're absolutely correct about Kruger. I just came from his office where I found a detailed report of the activities you described in

America except that this report describes these plans as being mine, not his—he's trying to blame this all on me!"

"Does he know that you know?"

"Not yet, but he will soon, because I took the report. It specifically mentions the Six and it's addressed to someone named Edwards."

"Where are you?" asked Sophie.

Becker glanced at the street signs as he flashed through an intersection and reported his location.

"You need to get off the street and away from that car as quickly as possible. Pull into the next parking structure you come to—the bigger the better—and try to hide your car among the others. Then get down to the street, hail a taxi and take it to the southwest entrance of the *Englischer Garten*. Once the taxi is out of sight, cross the avenue and wait at the bus stop. Someone will pick you up there."

"But I need a place to hide! Kruger's going to turn this city upside down when he realizes that I have this letter."

"I have just the place," replied Sophie. "Now, go!"

Using the same rear entrance plan that had worked so well with Professor Schmidt, Sophie and her comrades covertly brought Becker into the apartment. Before allowing him to enter the sub-basement shelter, Sophie went down and had a talk with the Professor because she didn't want the shock of seeing his nemesis to cause a relapse.

When the two finally came face-to-face, it was Becker who spoke first.

"Professor, I'm truly sorry if I caused any of this. I was led to believe that you had committed a crime against your country but I now realize that the information I was given was all fabricated by my boss, who apparently has other reasons for wanting you locked up."

Still a little surprised by the sudden appearance of a BKA agent, Schmidt nodded and tried to smile.

"I'm afraid I caused some of my own problems by carelessly making that note in my appointment book, but your Kruger was after me long before that and I don't know why."

Becker pulled Kruger's report out of his jacket pocket and offered it to Schmidt.

"This may help explain his obsession with you. He says here that he was afraid your comments to the media about UFOs would hurt Germany's chances of becoming the newest member of the Six. He clearly doesn't believe in flying saucers and he couldn't have this kind of publicity coming out of his own home city."

"Well, the loss is his," replied the Professor, "because the stories are true. However, I now realize that it's not in *the Teachers*' best interest for me to be shooting my mouth off."

"I'm, sorry—did you say '*the Teachers*'?" asked Sophie. "The same '*Teachers*' you mentioned in the file you gave to Dr. Barnes?"

"Yes, that's correct. I don't imagine either of you have had an opportunity to read my notes, but it doesn't matter because I was only speculating back when I prepared that file. Since then, I've gained a great deal of first-hand knowledge."

Sophie and Becker looked at each other and then back to Schmidt.

"Yes, well, that's interesting, Professor," smiled Sophie, "but I think we should expose Kruger's bogus report for what it is as soon as possible. Agent Becker, would you mind if one of my associates scanned that document and sent if off to Dr. Barnes? Maybe you should also write a short explanation of what really happened that we could send with it."

"Of course," replied Becker. "I'd also like to send the same information to a friend in the Berlin BKA office so they can start taking the steps necessary to shut Kruger down."

As Sophie and Becker wandered off to a far corner of the shelter, Schmidt offered a feeble protest.

"Doesn't anyone want to hear about *the Teachers*?"

***

Jim was very relieved to learn that Fitz Fitzgerald had been released and that he was at least healthy enough to have landed the Learjet at a Navy base in Florida. It would be several hours before he would be able to talk with the pilot face-to-face, but Blass had just delivered a copy of the debriefing transcript.

Jim scanned the file, hoping to find some information he could use.

As everyone already assumed, Fitz had been kidnapped from the hangar while he was performing routine maintenance on the aircraft. At gunpoint, his captors had ordered him to fly south at a very low altitude—so low that the plane had been missed by the commercial radar network.

When the Learjet was over water, Fitz had been provided specific GPS coordinates which turned out to be a small, regional airport about one hundred miles south of Miami. Fitz had been very surprised to discover that the remote facility had a runway more than ten thousand feet long.

Once on the ground, Fitz had been whisked away in a dark SUV to a nearby town where he had been held in a small, private house until this morning. Then, with no warning, he had been loaded up, hauled back to the airport and told to fly north until he got to the United States.

Thankfully, Fitz had had the presence of mind to log the GPS coordinates of the airport before takeoff and the Navy had confirmed that it was the Varadero Airport, about sixty miles east of Havana, Cuba.

The report concluded with a brief summary of the aircraft inspection which had turned out to be negative. The captors hadn't planted any explosives or locator beacons on the Learjet and had apparently been interested only in Fitz.

Jim closed the thin file and leaned his head back against his chair. The fact that Fitz had been held in Cuba reminded Jim of the time, more than five years earlier, when he had been poised to undertake a solo mission into the island country to search out the origin of some unusual radio signals. Thankfully, that mission had been scrubbed at the last minute and Jim had instead joined the rest of his teammates on a ship off the northwestern tip of Cuba where the triangles had just been discovered.

A pop-up window on his laptop indicated that he had new email and when he saw that it was from Sophie, he quickly jolted back to reality.

"Dr. Barnes," the email began, "please see the attached documents. The first is a report Kruger prepared for someone named Edwards and offers his version of the kidnapping of an American pilot and the attempted kidnapping of you. You'll notice that all the blame is placed on a BKA agent named Max Becker.

"The second document is Becker's statement about these events. We just sent a copy of these documents on to the Berlin BKA headquarters.

"In one way or another, these documents seem to tie both Kruger and this Edwards guy to your assault last night. They also provide some contact information that should prove useful."

The email was signed, "Stay Safe! Sophie."

Jim printed the email message and its attachments and then raced out to Bill Blass' desk.

"I think this will make your job a little easier," he said as he laid the pages down on the intelligence officer's desk. "There are names, phone numbers and even a positive connection to Edwards. I'm going to spend the rest of the day in the lab, but let me know if you hit the jackpot with this."

Returning to his office, Jim opened the small safe to retrieve the triangles and discovered the Schmidt file lying right where he had thrown it Wednesday afternoon after the interviews. As he flipped through it, he ran across the page where he had written "How many civilizations?" in pencil in the margin. However, after his note someone had printed the number "37" in neat red numerals!

Chapter 23

Jim dialed Bill Blass' desk and waited for the other man to pick up.

"Didn't you tell me you and the others returned to the office this morning at 4:00 a.m.?"

"That's correct," replied Blass.

"Who was the first one into the office?"

"Well, technically I was the first one through the door, but Norma, Miguel and Justin came in with me and the others trickled in over the next thirty minutes or so. Why, is something wrong?"

"Yes. Were the Secret Service agents here when you arrived?"

"No, they surprised us about 6:00 a.m.," replied Blass. "Shall I come back there?"

"Yes, I think you should."

When Blass was inside and the office door had closed, Jim handed him the Schmidt file.

"Do you see my hand-written note in the margin?"

"Yes, and it looks like you've written the number thirty-seven after it," nodded Blass. "What's the problem?"

"The problem is that I didn't write that number. I wrote the question yesterday afternoon and I'm no closer to knowing the answer now than I was then and I certainly don't know whether or not the answer is thirty-seven. Someone has been into my secure safe, inside my secure office and we need to find out who it was."

"I can't imagine how anyone could get in here without your knowledge, but let me do some checking. Are you positive the safe was locked?"

"Absolutely! I opened it just now to get the triangles out and I actually tried the door before I dialed the combination. As far as I know, Danny and I are the only two who have the combination and I don't think he was in any condition to sneak into the office last night and write on the file."

"No, of course not," frowned Blass. "And you set that combination into the lock yourself?"

"Yes, yes, Danny and I did that the first day we were in the office. In fact we discussed what to use for a combination so it would be easy for both of us to remember."

"You discussed it out loud?" asked Blass, carefully surveying the ceiling of Jim's office.

"Well, yes, I suppose we did, but we were the only two in the office at that time."

"Maybe you were and maybe you weren't. I'll get back to you as soon as possible. In the mean time, don't mention this because if we freak out the Secret Service guys it will be even harder to do any work around here."

Blass left and Jim returned the Schmidt file to the safe after removing the tray containing the box, its five triangles and Ben's artifact. He convened a meeting of his lab team and linguistics expert Andrew Jones in the main lab.

"Let's try a new approach. I want each of you to take one of the triangles, find your own spot here in the lab and go to work. Today's objective is to learn as much as we can about these objects and I'm hoping a little parallel processing will get us some results. No idea is off the table and no theory is too whacky. The only rule is that you can't destroy any of the triangles or the box they came in. You can all share the box in case you want to experiment with it and, Andrew, I'm giving you Ben Kingston's tablet because you had some decent success with it a couple of days ago. Okay, team, let's get to work!"

Picking one of the triangles at random, Jim retired to his private lab and plopped down on a stool in front of the workbench. He turned on the flat-panel monitor mounted on the wall behind his small workbench, slid a keyboard tray out from under the work surface and brought up a spreadsheet he'd created based on Schmidt's "Those Who Know" list. Next to some of the names Jim had noted the artifact or artifacts that each individual was aware of. Some names, like his own, included several items—the spheres from the Mayan cave, the jewel-enhanced clay *tsubutes* from Yonaguni, Japan, and the triangles from the waters off northwestern Cuba.

Thinking back to his interviews of the previous day, each new artifact he learned about had been associated with a different ancient culture that had, for whatever reason, disappeared. Each of them had risen to relative greatness based on a special skill or talent its people had developed for no apparent reason. The Maya, for example, had developed highly sophisticated astronomical and mathematical skills for a people that never used the wheel as a mode of transportation. So what was it that caused the Maya to leap ahead of other cultures of their time? Where did they get that first spark that propelled them down a completely unlikely path that would eventually allow them to predict the time and location of solar eclipses? Obviously, there had to have been some outside influence!

Jim scanned his small list of identified cultures and realized that none of them had flourished at the same time. Was it possible that each of them was an experiment of some sort and when one experiment failed another was initiated somewhere else on the planet?

Glancing back and forth between the triangle on his bench and his list of twenty-three names, Jim wondered again about the mysterious appearance of the number thirty-seven in the margin of the original Schmidt list. Disregarding for the moment the problem of how the number got there—was the number even relevant? Are there thirty-seven artifacts or thirty-seven people who know about artifacts or was the number completely meaningless?

On a hunch, Jim opened a Web browser. He navigated to Wikipedia and typed in the number thirty-seven. He was more than a little surprised by what he read.

It turns out that *thirty-seven* is the first irregular prime number. It's also a factor of all three-digit repdigits (one hundred eleven, two hundred twenty-two, and so on), it's a star number (the basis of the game of Chinese checkers), it's a Størmer number and it exhibits the unique quality that when it is multiplied by two, subtracted by one, and then read backwards the result equals the original two digit number. It's also the temperature, in Celsius, of the normal human body.

***

Once Kruger's bogus report was sent off to Dr. Barnes and the Berlin BKA office, Becker surprised Sophie by asking if he could talk with Professor Schmidt.

"Of course," she replied. "I'll be in my apartment if you need anything. Whoever's on duty down here will be able to reach me."

"Actually, I was hoping you could stay for a while. I think it would make Schmidt feel more comfortable if you were here."

"Sure, I can do that, too," replied Sophie. "And later maybe you and I can discuss your plans—specifically how long you plan to stay here in what is quickly becoming Munich's most popular safe house."

When they returned to Schmidt's bedside, he was talking one of the doctor's ears off. Relieved to see someone actually willing to listen to the old man, the doctor quickly busied himself with some medical equipment away from Schmidt's bed.

"Professor Schmidt, I was wondering if I could ask you a few questions. I wouldn't blame you if you said 'No' but now that I have a slightly different perspective on things, there are a few things bothering me."

Schmidt, who was obviously hungry for human interaction, motioned for Becker and Sophie to be seated in the two straight back chairs someone had placed near his bed.

"What can I do for you?" asked the Professor.

"Well, my biggest concern is for my missing agent. You indicated that she's safe, but if you're holding her someplace, don't you think you should let her go? I mean, given your condition and all."

Becker indicated the make-shift medical clinic with a sweep of his arm.

"Oh, I'm not holding her, young man! She's perfectly free to do as she pleases, but I wouldn't expect to see her in Munich any time soon."

"So she's out of the city?" asked Becker.

"Yes, I think that would be a fair statement," smiled Schmidt with a twinkle in his eye. "I'm not at liberty to disclose her current location, but please believe me when I tell you that she's very happy where she is and she's not being held against her will."

"Well, that's comforting, but I'd still like to know where she is and have the opportunity to speak with her," Becker frowned. "Maybe we can come back to that in a minute.

"Another thing I'm curious about is how Agent Braun's cell phone found its way to the southern end of Lake Starnberg, some thirty kilometers southeast of here. In particular, I'd like to know how it got there so fast and where it is now."

"Young lady, would you be kind enough to hand me my leather bag? I think it's against the wall over there."

Sophie retrieved Schmidt's bag but when she tried to hand it to him he shook his head.

"No, you can get it. Open the flap and reach down the front. I believe the phone is all the way at the bottom."

Following his instruction, Sophie soon produced an industrial-looking cell phone and handed it to Becker.

"I tried to give it back to Miss Braun, but she didn't want it and I certainly don't need it. I only borrowed it to throw you off my trail. I had hoped you would stay down at the lake for several days until I was able to get out of Munich myself."

"And he would have," smiled Sophie, "if I hadn't talked him into coming back to the city to meet with me. And I convinced him to come back because I was desperate to find you, Professor. It seems that we've been leading each other in circles!"

Becker stared at the phone for a minute before looking up at Schmidt.

"Why did you activate the phone at the south end of the lake, Professor? And how did you get there so fast?"

"Well, I had some other business in the area and that was a convenient time and place to alert you that the phone was still working," replied Schmidt. "While you were racing down the east side of the lake to find the phone, I was returning to the city via the western route."

"And how did you get there so fast?" repeated Becker.

"Let's just say I know a short cut."

"You're not giving me much to go on, Professor!" admonished Becker.

"Perhaps not, but as you said earlier, I don't have to give you anything. I suggest you take what you can get while I'm still here."

"Professor," interrupted Sophie. "You've been alluding to the fact that you're going to be leaving since the minute you set foot in this building. If you don't mind me asking, where and when are you going?"

Schmidt looked at his watch before replying.

"I'll be leaving in precisely two hours and eleven minutes, young lady," replied the Professor.

"And where are you going?" pressed Becker, tiring of Schmidt's mind games.

"Again, Mr. Becker, I'm not at liberty to disclose that information, but I would be happy to pass along your concern to Miss Braun."

Before Becker could fire back, Sophie interrupted the exchange with a question of her own.

"Professor Schmidt, several days ago you asked me to pass some information along to Dr. Barnes, which I did. One of the items spoke of a group called '*the Teachers*.' Who or what are *the Teachers* and why is it so important that Dr. Barnes protect their secret. And for that matter, what is their secret?"

Schmidt chuckled.

"Young lady, your question involves hundreds of thousands of years of time and you expect me to answer it in a sentence or a paragraph? Even if I were at liberty to answer you..."

"That's enough!" interrupted an angry Becker. "I've heard enough 'I'm not at liberty' from you, Professor. We're all friends, here. We're all on the same side, and you're sitting on information about people we each care about. Sophie is clearly concerned about her friend in America and I am concerned about my agent. So stop playing games or we're out of here and you can go back to talking to the doctors."

There was a long pause before Schmidt answered.

"You're, right, Mr. Becker; you're absolutely right. When I was afraid for my life and had nowhere to turn, I came here and Miss Hoffman took me in with no questions asked. And when you started to get too close, I took from you someone you obviously care a great deal for. I owe you both better answers than I'm providing so I'm going to do something that violates all established protocols—I'm going to show you what I can't possibly explain in words. But I have to warn you that once you've seen it you may not want to come back, just as Miss Braun doesn't."

"Professor, it's too dangerous for any of us to leave this facility right now," protested Sophie. "I'd love to know what you are talking about, but it's just not possible at this time."

"Leave me," responded Schmidt, shooing his two companions away with the flick of a hand. "I need to rest, but be back here in exactly two hours."

With that, Schmidt laid his head back on his pillow and closed his eyes.

Frustrated, Sophie and Becker moved away from the hospital bed.

"So, I guess we have a couple of hours to kill," said Sophie. "Maybe you should get some rest, too. There's a cot behind that curtain. I have some things to do but I'll be back in a couple of hours and we'll see what happens. Personally, I think he's finally lost his mind. Maybe the heart attack did some damage to the part of his brain that deals with reality."

"I agree," replied Becker, yawning. "But I don't really have anything else to do tonight and I wouldn't miss this for anything. I'll see you in a couple of hours."

***

Jim sat at his small workbench and studied the solitary triangle as if staring at it would somehow force it to give up its secrets. The message—or whatever it was—around the perimeter of the object was one he'd studied so much that he actually recognized it. But what did it say, and why did it change?

Thinking back to the discovery of the triangles, Jim worked through the events mentally. He hadn't been aboard the merchant ship with NWIDI teammates Frank, Tony and Linda when the triangles were actually located off the coast of Cuba, but he knew the story well and he had arrived by helicopter shortly after the discovery.

Frank had accidently bumped a control in the ROV command post and caused the ROV's robotic shovel to move and strike something in the sand. A little intentional digging uncovered the silver covered box containing the triangles and it was brought aboard when the ROV surfaced. When the lid was finally pried off the box, it emitted a horrific smell and something caused immediate and severe medical problems for Javier Reyes, the team's temporary fifth member for that expedition. Javier had recovered and he eventually married Linda. The wedding was the last time Jim had seen either of them.

Since the discovery of the box had been a freak accident, the box certainly wasn't in plain sight, waiting to be found. In fact, it was buried in the sand more than two thousand feet below the surface of the Gulf of Mexico! It wasn't even hidden in the huge underwater ruins they had explored using the ROV—it was buried some distance from the nearest structure and the discovery occurred while the ROV was on its initial "approach" to the ruins.

So either Frank's bump against the control was the coincidence of the century or someone…

Jim struggled to return to his analytical line of thinking. He had suggested to his team that the triangles were encoded messages destined for a home planet, or planets, but suddenly that didn't make any sense to him. How would important messages waiting to be shipped off-world end up buried in the sand off the tip of Cuba? Could it be that the triangles were actually inbound messages that never got delivered for some reason? The underwater city had obviously been an important site at one time, and some catastrophic event had caused it to sink. Some geologists believe that Cuba and Mexico's Yucatan Peninsula were once connected by a land bridge, but even conservative estimates put the volcanic destruction of that feature more than fifteen thousand years in the past and some scientists suggest that the bridge sank more than fifty thousand years ago!

If the messages encoded into the triangles were incoming, rather than outgoing, then they probably never got delivered and instead ended up lost in the ancient sands off Cuba. And, in that case, Jim was quite possibly the first person on Earth to ever view them. Too bad he didn't have a clue what they said.

On a whim, he retrieved the digital camera from the main lab and snapped pictures of both sides of the triangle. Moving to his desk, he downloaded the images and emailed them off to Sophie. He then called her to make sure she checked her email.

"Is Professor Schmidt still with you?" he asked.

"Yes, but he claims he's leaving pretty soon and he thinks he's taking Becker and me with him. We think he's off his rocker, of course, but we can't wait to see what he thinks he's going to do."

"Wait, did you say Becker is there? Isn't he the BKA agent you've been feuding with?"

"Yes, it's a long story, but he's come over to the good side after learning the truth about Kruger. Kruger has even written a memo blaming Becker for the assault on you and your friend. How is he, by the way?"

"There's still no change in Danny's condition. Listen, I hate to change the subject, but I would really appreciate it if you could print out the two images I just emailed to you and show them to the Professor. They may not mean a thing to him, but I need to know."

"Sure, I'll take them down to him right now. His mysterious departure is just a few minutes away and I don't want to miss that. Talk to you later."

"Be careful over there, Sophie. Things are getting pretty crazy."

***

When Sophie reached the sub-basement bomb shelter, Becker was already there, talking to the Professor who was out of bed for the first time since the paramedics had arrived. She nodded to Becker and then handed the two pages to Schmidt.

"Dr. Barnes just sent these over and he'd really like you to take a look at them. I have no idea what these things are, but Dr. Barnes seems to think they are important."

Schmidt scanned the pages and shook his head.

"Looks like some kind of hieroglyphics but it's not something I'm familiar with. These are interesting looking objects, though. I wonder where Dr. Barnes found them."

"Sorry, but he didn't say. Are you sure you don't know anything about these symbols?"

"Positive, but let me hang onto these. I may know someone who can help out." Schmidt folded the two pieces of paper and slipped them into his tweed sports jacket pocket.

"Are you two ready for an adventure?"

Sophie looked at Becker and smiled.

"Sure, Professor! Is a magic carpet coming by to pick us up?"

"Something like that, my dear. I've made the necessary arrangements for the two of you, but I'm going to have to insist that you stay very close to me and do not wander away.

Now, make a circle by locking arms and hold on for a minute."

The other two did as instructed, still smiling at the silliness of it all. And seconds later, all three vanished from the steel-walled bunker two floors below ground.

***

Jim waited an hour for Sophie's reply and finally decided to check in with his crew and see if anybody had come up with any new ideas.

"So, how's everybody doing?" he asked as he entered the lab. The shrugs and frowns told him things weren't going so well.

"Okay, does anybody have anything new?" he asked.

"Well, I might be on the trail of something," offered Andrew. "I've been analyzing the messages not as individuals but as streams of data and then comparing them to the tablet Mr. Kingston left with us. Some of my pattern recognition algorithms seem to suggest that a message from one triangle might be continued on another triangle. That would seem to suggest that the five triangles aren't individual messages at all, but rather a set containing a single, more complex message."

"Interesting," nodded Jim. "Do you have any hints as to what these more complex data streams might mean?"

"No. There just isn't enough content to do that. Unlike our modern writing, where sentences are made of words and words are made from individual characters, these are glyphs. Each symbol may convey a whole thought or, at the very least, a whole word."

"And without a dictionary of what each glyph means, we'll never decode the messages," nodded Jim. "Well, I've been reconsidering the facts surrounding the initial discovery of these little three-sided mysteries and I think I've convinced myself that the messages must have been inbound rather than outbound. I don't know if that helps anybody or not, but I'm pretty sure we've been thinking about these things in the wrong context."

Jim was interrupted by the intercom on one of the lab phones.

"Jim, this is Norma. Sorry to interrupt but there's a woman named Sophie on the line and she insists on speaking to you."

"I have to take this, but keep looking. There has to be a clue somewhere that will unravel this puzzle."

In his office, Jim sat down and picked up the handset.

"Hi, Sophie. Was the Professor able to shed any light on the images I sent you?"

There was only silence on the other end and Jim thought he had lost the connection.

"Sophie, are you there?"

"Uh, yes, Dr. Barnes, I'm here. I just don't know where to start. We just visited the most awesome place! Schmidt said we wouldn't want to come back and he was right. It was amazing! No, it was more than amazing—it was absolutely incredible."

"Sophie, you're not making any sense. What was incredible?"

"Dr. Barnes, Schmidt took us to meet *the Teachers*! I don't know how he did it or where we actually were, but Becker and I were somehow transported to what Schmidt calls the 'Other Side' and it was unbelievable. Words can't begin to describe it. Neither one of us wanted to come back, but Schmidt insisted. However, he went right back and I don't think we'll be seeing him again."

Jim didn't understand what was going on, but he was sure Sophie was under the influence of something.

"What about the images?" he asked, trying to pull Sophie back to reality.

"Oh, yes! Your images caused a great deal of excitement, Dr. Barnes. Apparently they contain some missing information that has been sought for a very long time. I was asked if there were more of those triangles but, of course, I didn't know. I think you may be contacted soon."

Chapter 24

Jim was very confused by Sophie's call and her talk about the Other Side but it was late in Munich and she was probably very tired. Or maybe the stress of her self-imposed house arrest and the fact that she was harboring two high-profile characters had finally gotten to her. Jim made a note to follow up with Sophie in the morning and opened the door for Bill Blass, who was standing outside waiting for him to finish his call.

"Jim, the pilot of the Learjet has arrived. I've reviewed his Navy debriefing file but there are some additional questions I'd like to ask him, if you don't mind."

"Of course. Bring him back, Bill."

When "Fitz" Fitzgerald entered the office, Jim hardly recognized him. His face was thinner than Jim remembered and there was a distinct gray tinge to his hair. But then it had been five years since the two men had last met.

"Fitz!" exclaimed Jim. "Welcome to our little corner of craziness. I understand you had some excitement in Cuba."

Fitz nodded and looked around the office in awe before slowly dropping into one of the two chairs in front of Jim's desk.

"This is quite a setup you have here, Jim! What the heck is going on?"

"I'll tell you all about it," smiled Jim. "But first, my associate, Bill Blass, would like to ask you some questions about your recent adventure. I know you've already been grilled by Navy Intelligence, but Bill is helping me track down the people who nabbed you and he has some questions. He has your Key West file, so he won't ask you to go over all that again."

Fitz was still looking around, a little stunned.

"Have you assumed control of the Government or something?" he asked with a half-smile.

"Not quite, but our little project is pretty well connected. Bill, go ahead and then I'll catch Fitz up on our operation here."

"Mr. Fitzgerald, I've read the statement you gave the Navy but of course they were focused on the fact that you had recently flown a private aircraft into, and fortunately out of, Cuba. We are much more concerned about your kidnapping and those responsible. We already know who ordered your capture—and why—but I'm really curious about why they let you go. In your report, you state that they hardly talked to you during the four days you were held captive. Did they ever say why they grabbed you in the first place?"

"No," replied Fitz, shaking his head. "The whole thing didn't make sense right from the beginning. I was working on the plane inside the hanger when these two guys approached me and the next thing I knew there was a gun pressed against my side. They put a hood over my head after we landed in Cuba, but, of course I already had a pretty good idea where we were because I had communicated with the tower prior to landing. The two who came to the hangar spoke passable English but they had a heavy accent that I couldn't place. Once I was taken off the plane in Cuba I was handed over to some locals and I never saw the original two again. I don't think any of the locals spoke English and I had the feeling they had no idea why I was there or what to do with me."

"As Bill mentioned, we think we know why you were there" interjected Jim. "I recently came into the possession of a file that a particular retired German colonel wants back and you were going to be used as leverage to convince me to turn it over if they couldn't get it any other way. Last night an associate and I were attacked but the attackers were neutralized and are now in custody."

"My God, Jim, what are you involved in?" questioned Fitz.

"All in good time, my friend."

"But they never said anything to you about why they were holding you? Did they say anything when they released you?" continued Blass.

"No, the original two never said why and, as I mentioned, I don't think the locals in Cuba spoke any English. When I was released, they hooded me again, drove me back to the airport, escorted me up the stairs, removed the hood and indicated that I should leave. One of them pointed to the cockpit and grunted 'USA' in very broken English. Then they went back down the stairs, climbed in their old station wagon and drove away. In minutes I was airborne and streaking for Florida as fast as the plane would go."

"So you never heard the name Kruger?" pressed Blass.

"No, not that I remember, anyway."

"What about the name Edwards?"

"No, I don't…wait! I did hear one of the men at the house say Edwards several times while they were putting the hood over my head! I can't tell you what else he said because I don't speak Spanish, but I do remember hearing the name Edwards. At the time I thought it was a place, like Edwards Air Force base or something."

Blass and Jim looked at each other and nodded.

"Thanks, Mr. Fitzgerald. That's all I need. One of the staff members is preparing a set of credentials for you and everything you see and hear from now on is classified Top Secret. By the way, you wife will be here in about an hour."

Blass exited the office and Fitz looked at Jim and shrugged.

"What's going on Jim?"

Over the course of the next forty minutes Jim tried to bring Fitz up to speed on the operation and the events that had led up to it. He explained that due to Kruger's recent activities he had felt it necessary to bring Fitz and Susan into the relative security of the NRL facilities.

"And I'm really worried about Linda, Javier and Tony," added Jim. "Unfortunately, I have no idea how to warn them because I haven't heard from any of them in more than five years."

"Susan heard from Linda a while back, but she wouldn't say where she was or how to contact her. Susan thinks she and Javier went underground because we've tried to locate them several times since their wedding and we've never come up with anything."

"That's probably my fault," frowned Jim. "I called Linda the day they got back from their honeymoon and warned them that I thought their lives were in danger. A few days later I learned that they had heeded my call and fled their Cancun apartment but nobody knew where they had gone."

"So how long are we going to be held here?" asked Fitz. "We have a business to run and contracts to honor, you know."

"Ah, sorry, but you're here for the duration, I'm afraid. At least until we can get a handle on this terrorist group. They've already gone after you once and we can't take any more chances. I don't know if you noticed the suits out in the lobby, but they are Secret Service agents assigned to protect me from another incident like last night's. I don't like it, but it's a way of life for now. We'll get someone to deal with any contracts you have coming up, but you and Susan are off the street until the end."

"Well that sucks!" replied Fitz. "But as long as we're here, is there any way we can help? It looks like you have plenty of talent already, but there must be something we can contribute."

"I appreciate that, Fitz, and we'll certainly find something for you and Susan to do."

Pointing to the main office on the other side of his glass office wall, he said, "The folks on the left side of the room are data analysts who have been contacting and vetting people on a list that was in the German file I mentioned. The desks on the right belong to the crew you see next door in the lab. They are from a variety of disciplines, but they're all working on the mystery of the triangles. Those are our two big assignments and all our energy is focused on one of those two areas. In addition, there's Bill Blass, whom you just met. He's from the intelligence community and besides keeping tabs on the analysts, he's also working on a couple of special projects for me. On the far side, back against the lab, is Chip, our IT guy. He's the one working on your credentials. When you came in, you were met by Norma, our office manager and that just leaves Danny Miles, the Marine that was critically injured last night while saving my life."

"And you've been here how long?" asked Fitz. "Did you say a week?"

Jim glanced at his calendar and smiled.

"It will be two weeks next Wednesday but it feels like forever. Two weeks ago today I was calmly working away in a lab in the Bahamas and then my world turned upside down. I was flown to Washington in a military jet, had a telephone conference with several high-ranking government officials, including the President, and was assigned this office complex. Twenty-four hours later this whole team was assembled and we were hard at work! It gives me a headache just to think about it."

"That's incredible, Jim! I don't know how Susan and I will fit in, but at least we can help with some of the telephone work."

Jim's phone rang and he indicated to Fitz that he needed to take the call.

"What? Are you sure about that, Bill? Okay, well you're the expert in this area. How do you think we should proceed? Right. I agree, but now I'm more worried than ever about my former teammates. Have you had any luck tracking them down? Okay, well please keep me posted."

Jim hung up the telephone and sagged in his chair.

"The guy who ordered your kidnapping was assassinated about an hour ago," he replied to Fitz' questioning look.

"That's a good thing, right?"

"No, it's a very bad thing, Fitz. You see, he was the Munich bureau chief for Germany's version of the FBI and he was killed in his own office—in his BKA office! That means the folks who did this are getting much bolder and that also means that all of us are in a great deal of danger."

"What about Susan? You said she was on her way here—is she okay?"

Weakly, Jim lifted his arm and pointed to the front of the office.

"Yes, she and Sandstrom just arrived. Let's go say hello and then I'm going to find a place to crash. I only had a few hours' sleep last night and I'm suddenly very tired. My understanding is that the NRL has prepared quarters for us somewhere in this building, so let me find out where we're sleeping tonight and then I'll let you and Susan get caught up. Tomorrow's another day."

***

When Schmidt returned to the Munich apartment building with Sophie and Becker, he informed the medical team that he would no longer need their services. Skeptical, they insisted on checking him out and were amazed when he exhibited no signs of his recent heart attack. Bewildered, they began tearing down the makeshift clinic and packing it back onto two gurneys that had been recently returned. Before they were finished, Schmidt was gone again and Sophie had made her call to Dr. Barnes.

Becker, who was confined to the bunker due to his presumed "wanted dead or alive" status didn't receive the BKA alert that went out to agents all across the country, but one of the apartment house tenants caught a news bulletin on television and notified Sophie.

"Becker, are you awake?" she asked as she approached the screened off area that was his temporary bedroom.

"Yes, I'm awake, he replied, pulling the front curtain back and sticking his head out. "How can I possibly sleep after what we saw last night?"

"Someone upstairs just saw a news bulletin stating that Kruger was murdered in his office last night!"

"What?" exclaimed Becker. "Is this for real?"

"Well, I haven't personally seen the report, but you might want to risk coming upstairs and watching for yourself. If the report is true, you may not have to hide down here anymore."

A number of Sophie's confidants had gathered in the common study room and Manny had moved somebody's large flat-panel television to the far end of the room. As Sophie and Becker entered the room, the newscaster was just completing a live broadcast from outside the BKA offices.

"And so," concluded the newscaster, "as hard as it might be to believe, it appears that the Director of the Munich BKA division and three other individuals were killed by a bomb blast just before midnight last night. Live from the BKA office complex, this is Warner Klein reporting."

Someone turned the volume down as a commercial came on and all eyes shifted to Becker.

Surprised, he said, "Hey, it wasn't me! I was down in your bomb shelter the whole time."

Several people chuckled and that broke the awkward silence.

"What are you going to do now?" asked Manny from the end of the table.

"I don't know," replied Becker, realizing that he really didn't know. "While my initial reaction is shock, I have to wonder if whoever did this might be coming after me next. After all, I worked on a number of special projects for Kruger and it would be easy to assume I knew what he was up to. I didn't, of course, but it would be a logical conclusion to draw. I'm not sure whether I should return to BKA headquarters or remain in hiding."

The news came back on and someone yelled, "Turn it up! Turn it up!"

"We have just been informed that the Munich police are seeking another agent in Colonel Kruger's death. Apparently a senior member of the BKA office, a Max Ludwig Becker, is being sought as a person of interest because he was reportedly the last person in the Colonel's office before the terrible explosion that killed Kruger, his secretary and two other staff members. More news as..."

The volume went down again.

"Well, I guess that settles that!" sighed Becker. "Listen, I know you folks don't have a very high regard for the

BKA, but most of us are honest, hard working law enforcement professionals. The Munich office, thanks to its now infamous Director, hasn't always lived up to BKA standards, but I think you'll see a big change with a new person in charge and I encourage you to give them a chance. As for me, I think I'll see if I can join Schmidt and another friend."

***

After a fitful night, Jim left the makeshift dormitory in the basement at 6:15 a.m. and rode the elevator up to the third floor accompanied by his ever-present Secret Service escort. When he entered the inner office, he was surprised to see Blass already hard at work.

"Morning, Bill. I live here in the building now but what brings you in so early on a Saturday morning?"

"I was working on something last night but the pieces just wouldn't fall into place," replied Blass without looking up. "A couple of hours ago I received a call from an old friend over at NSA that connected the dots for me. I may have something for you soon."

"Regarding Fitz' kidnapping?"

"Regarding the inner workings of the Six. Just give me a few minutes."

Jim nodded and entered his office. Taped to his phone was the reminder he had left himself about calling Sophie.

"Sophie, good morning. Are you feeling okay? You were sort of out of it when you called me yesterday. I guess that would have been last night, your time."

"I'm fine, Dr. Barnes, and I don't know what you mean. I called to tell you about my visit to the Other Side courtesy of Professor Schmidt but I wasn't 'out of it' as you say. It's truly an incredible place and Becker is trying to figure out how to get back there as we speak. Did you hear about the bombing last night?"

"Bombing? What bombing? Are you all right?"

"Yes, of course," replied Sophie, "but Kruger was killed by a bomb that completely incinerated his office. Unfortunately, three other people were also killed in the blast."

"I heard about Kruger's death but I wasn't given any details. I didn't know it was a bomb or that there were other casualties. How is Becker taking all of this?"

"Apparently he's become a suspect because somehow the BKA learned that he was in Kruger's office yesterday afternoon just before he showed up here. The only other people to enter the office after he left were Kruger and his secretary and they're both dead so that leaves Becker holding the bag."

"Do you think he did it? Could he have planted a bomb?"

"No, I don't think so," replied Sophie. "Based on the little time I've spent with him since he arrived here, I don't think he's capable of it and he didn't know about Kruger's memo until he went to see him yesterday afternoon. He claims that as soon as he found the memo he fled and actually passed Kruger in the parking lot. His next stop was here."

"What's he going to do?"

"As I mentioned, he's trying to figure out how to join Schmidt and a friend on the Other Side. It's a long story, but Schmidt took one of his agents—a female agent he's apparently involved with—to the Other Side to distract him and now she doesn't want to come back. Besides, Becker is a wanted man and he can't hide here forever. His very presence in this building puts everybody in the building at risk."

"Sophie, what is this 'Other Side' you keep talking about? Are you on medication or something?"

"Dr. Barnes, I resent that!" shouted Sophie. "I am not on medication, or anything else for that matter. As I told you last night, Schmidt somehow took us to meet *the Teachers*. I can't begin to explain it, but Becker was there, too, and he can verify my experience. They are here, Dr. Barnes, and they are trying to help us but they are very concerned about this group Schmidt mentioned called 'the Six.' I don't know all the details, but Schmidt told us that little bit after he brought us back."

Jim didn't immediately respond because he didn't know what to say. When he did reply, it was with an apologetic tone.

"Sophie, I'm sorry. So last night when you told me that someone might be contacting me, you were serious?"

"Yes, Dr. Barnes. As I said, that triangle you sent photos of is apparently very important to *the Teachers* and they were very curious about whether or not there are more."

"Well, if it comes up in conversation again, I have five of them, plus a box they were stored in. I'd really like to talk to you more about this Other Side you mentioned but I'm under very tight security right now. Is there any chance you could make a trip to the United States?"

"I'd love to, Dr. Barnes, but I can't. There's too much going on here in Munich and with Becker in the building we're on very high alert."

"I was afraid of that," replied Jim. "Anything we can do to help?"

"Not that I can think of, but if something comes up I'll call you. Please tell your associate that the medical team he dispatched to help Professor Schmidt is just leaving. With the Professor gone, there's no reason for them to stay."

"You're not planning to join Schmidt are you?"

"No. I'd love to, but I'm more useful here right now. However, when things settle down a bit..."

"Sophie, promise me you won't do anything crazy! I don't know what Schmidt is into but please don't do anything until we have a chance to look into it."

"Relax, Dr. Barnes. Like I said, I'm needed here right now. Listen, I have to go see what's happening with Becker. We'll talk soon, okay?"

Reluctantly, Jim said good bye and hung up the telephone. It seemed like the whole world had suddenly gone mad and it was taking him with it.

His telephone buzzed and he grabbed the handset off the base.

"Sophie?"

"Ah, no, this is Bill Blass. Can I have a few minutes?"

Blass sat down in front of Jim's desk and opened another one of his now common dossiers so Jim could read it.

"I'm still firming up some details, but I thought you should see this."

Jim stared at the top page and recognized it as a copy of the list titled "The Six" from Schmidt's file.

"Obviously you've seen this before," began Blass, "but I'm now able to put names to it."

Blass flipped the page to another copy on which he'd hand-written names next to the countries.

"Here in the U.S. we've already identified Edwards as the cell leader, but I think you'll find some of these other names very interesting. Look at the United Kingdom, for example, or Mexico."

"My God, Bill, are you sure about this?"

"Positive. The Chinese name took a little extra work because we don't have a lot of good intel on their second-tier officials, but believe me, this information is correct. The bad news is that every one of these people dropped out of sight sometime during the past twelve hours."

"Dropped out of sight? What does that mean? A couple of these people are prominent government officials. They can't just disappear."

"And yet they have," shrugged Blass. "The lower profile players, such as Edwards, hastily created a cover story. For example, he called his office yesterday afternoon and said he had a family emergency. Nobody thought much of it until one of his staff members remembered that Edwards had never talked about any family. A check of his personnel file revealed no known family, so the issue got pushed up the chain of command. By then, of course, he was long gone. The FBI is at his apartment right now and it doesn't look like he's coming back."

"And the others?" asked Jim.

"We don't have immediate access to the foreigners' residences, but I expect we'll find the same thing. Jim, I think we have to assume that the Six, or at least its top leadership, has gone underground. Intel chatter picked up an obscure reference to a place called CV-13 but no one seems to know what or where it is."

"How credible is that intelligence?" pressed Jim.

"Oh, the name is credible enough because it showed up in multiple communications, but nobody has ever heard of it. Why?"

"On our last assignment as a group, my NWIDI teammates and I were summoned to a meeting with Edwards in Cancun, Mexico. Unfortunately, I was diverted to Florida before our Learjet ever crossed the border, but later the others told me about this incredible place several stories beneath the Cancun Airport that had been built to protect traveling heads of state. I think they called it MX-2. Are you familiar with the place?"

Blass' jaw dropped and he was momentarily stunned.

"Of course I've heard of it, but I can't believe you know about it or that your friends were actually there! MX-2 is part of a international network of PEOCs—Presidential Emergency Operations Centers—that were constructed around the world to provide a safe haven for local and traveling heads of state in case of a global emergency. There are twelve of them: CH-1 in China, MX-2 and MX-3 in Mexico, SA-4 in South Africa, RS-5 and RS-6 in Russia, UK-7 in the United Kingdom, and five in the United States—US-8 through US-12."

Suddenly Blass' eyes widened and he snatched up the file he had laid in front of Jim.

"There's at least one in every country on this list! Somehow, the Six has infiltrated every PEOC on the planet, which means that those twelve safe havens are probably traps just waiting to be sprung."

"And it looks like they built one more they forgot to tell the rest of the world about," frowned Jim. "It would appear that CV-13 is now *their* safe haven."

Chapter 25

Blass excused himself, returned to his own desk and began frantically dialing his telephone. As Jim watched through the glass wall of his office, he guessed that Blass was trying to alert as many intelligence contacts as he could about the compromised PEOCs.

Although the entire staff had offered to work through the weekend, Jim had insisted that they all get some badly needed rest and stay away until Monday morning. Now that Blass had determined the identities of the key figures in the Six, there wasn't a pressing need for the analysts to come in and the triangle researchers seemed to be suffering from a collective mental block so Jim was glad he had ordered the two-day break. With the main lab completely empty, Jim decided to spend a little one-on-one time with the triangles to see if he could come up with anything new.

As usual, he checked the safe door to make sure it was secure before dialing the combination. When the last number had been set, he twisted the latch handle and opened the door—and gasped. The tray that usually held the metallic box and its cache of five triangles was empty except for a small piece of paper.

Still bent down with his head near the safe, he took a long, deep breath and tried to calm himself. Slowly, he returned to a standing position and exhaled. Looking around, as if he might catch someone sneaking out the door with the box of triangles, Jim scanned his own office and small lab, the main lab and the rest of the office. The facility was empty except for himself, Blass and two Secret Service agents.

Jim removed the tray from the safe and set it on his desk. Then he dropped to one knee and reached his arm all the way into the safe in case the box had slipped off the tray and found itself a hiding spot in the back. However, the only things left in the safe were the Schmidt file and Ben's artifact.

Jim closed the door and locked it before returning to his desk. He carefully picked up the piece of paper and unfolded it. The words appeared to have been printed on a laser printer of some sort.

"We are grateful to you for locating and caring for our ancient relics. Please accept the information below as a small token of our appreciation."

Below the message there was a single line that read:

"24.126491N, 110.341370W -/- 18.427669N, 64.611647W"

Jim immediately recognized the numbers as two sets of GPS coordinates. He dashed to his computer and opened Google Earth. After entering the first set of numbers, he watched the image of the globe on his screen spin and zoom until it came to rest showing the roof of a house on Mexico's Baja Peninsula. After marking the location, he entered the second set. Again the globe spun and zoomed, this time indicating a commercial harbor in the eastern Caribbean. He marked the second location and glanced toward Blass' desk. The other man still had the telephone pressed to his ear, so Jim picked up the note and went to him.

When Blass saw Jim approaching, he held up his index finger to indicate he would be just a minute. Jim nodded and laid the note down on the desk so Blass could read it. After a quick glance, Blass interrupted the person on the other end of the line, apologized and hung up.

"Where did you get this?" he asked.

"It was in my safe where the triangles used to be," frowned Jim. "Someone paid us a visit again last night."

"These look like GPS coordinates."

"They are," replied Jim."The first one is a house in Mexico and the second one is a harbor in the Caribbean islands. Neither place means anything to me, but I think we'd better check them out as soon as possible. Whoever wrote this note thinks this information is a fair trade for ancient alien relics, so there'd better be big pots of gold in both locations."

Blass picked up his telephone handset again and dialed a number from memory. When he hung up, he handed the note back to Jim.

"We'll know in an hour or two."

"How do you do that?" questioned Jim. "Who has the connections to snatch people from airports and dispatch investigators to the four corners of the Earth with a single call? Who are you, Bill?"

Blass leaned back in his chair and smiled.

"Sit down, my friend, and let's chat."

An hour later, Jim still sat at Blass' desk, stunned.

Blass had opened with, "It was no accident that I was assigned to this project," and his story had gotten more and more bizarre the longer he talked.

Blass had been on the trail of the Six for several years but he had never been able to positively connect Edwards with the conspiracy. That information had first come from Jim when he blurted it out in Captain Stukey's office. In fact, it was Jim's revelation that had eventually allowed Blass to identify Edwards and the rest of the cell leaders. Blass had filing cabinets full of information he'd compiled on the terrorist organization's activities, plots, and intended targets but nothing that pointed directly to Edwards.

Jim was shocked to learn that he and his NWIDI teammates had been suspected co-conspirators of the Six for most of the past five years, including the time Jim spent at AUTEC. When Linda and Tony went missing just days apart, Jim had become a high-value asset and the government had decided it would be easier to keep an eye on him if he were inside the confines of a secret military research facility. They had provided him a place to conduct his investigations on the triangles in exchange for having him securely locked away at AUTEC. Whenever he traveled, he was always shadowed by CIA agents.

After hearing Blass' story, Jim realized how the other man had been able to connect his Dr. Smith alias to the real Jim Barnes so fast—he already knew! And it also occurred to Jim that the President and everyone else on the teleconference that day probably knew his real name, too. The whole Dr. Smith charade was merely for Jim's benefit—to make him feel secure and more willing to cooperate.

"You can understand why the government was suspicious," Blass had explained. "You and your friends were in regular contact with a man we already had under surveillance and you even conducted several unusual investigations for him. Unfortunately we lost track of you for a time at the beginning of your last mission. Otherwise, we would have made the connection between Edwards and MX-2 long before now."

"You mean before I told you today," Jim had fired back. "It seems as though I've provided all the missing pieces."

"Granted, and the President recognizes that now, but five years ago you and your friends looked pretty dirty. You were regular folks doing very irregular things and that raised a lot of red flags."

Jim had listened to the rest of Blass' narrative with just one ear. He was mildly interested in how the President's advisory panel had tracked the NWIDI team and followed their activities but he was infuriated by the fact that he and his friends had been used by both the Six and their own government.

Finally, Blass had ended with an apology.

"Jim, I'm sorry, but this is the way the real world works. We owe it to the citizens of the United States to investigate all credible threats and you and your friends appeared to be just that."

"And who do you work for, Bill?" asked an angry Jim. "Who decides what a credible threat is?"

"Jim, I work for the same man you do."

"Yes, yes, we all work for the President of the United States—I get the political double-talk. But who do you *really* work for?"

"I work directly for the President, Jim, just like you do. Officially, my title is Special Assistant to the President and normally I answer only to him. Regarding your original question, *that's* how I do that. And that's why I was assigned to your staff. The President wanted to be sure that you had every possible resource available because he recognizes that dealing with the Six is only half the battle. This other group—*the Teachers*—pose an equally large threat to national security and you may be the only person who can lead us to them."

"Wait, you expect me to lead you to *the Teachers* after what I've just heard? You're crazy, Bill, and so is the President if he thinks I would be a part of a plan to destroy *the Teachers*."

"We just want to talk to them, Jim. So far, all communications have been initiated by them and with the Six running for cover, we need some answers."

The telephone rang before Jim could respond and when Blass glanced at the caller ID display he said, "I have to take this—it's about your GPS coordinates."

Blass talked for several minutes and made a half page of notes before finally turning back to Jim.

"I have some good news, Jim. The house in Mexico belongs to a Mr. and Mrs. Moreno, formerly known as Linda McBride and Javier Reyes. And the dock in the Caribbean is currently being leased to a vessel named the 'Dolphin Diver' which was recently purchased by a non-profit research organization in Belize with funds we've traced back to Tony Nicoletti. I think it's safe to say that giving up the triangles for those two locations was a very fair trade!"

Jim's jaw dropped and his eyes widened.

"What? Are you sure about this? We need to contact them immediately and get them to safety until we find out where the Six is hiding out. If they can pull off the execution of Kruger from their new location, they could certainly do the same to my friends."

"The roundup is already under way," replied Blass. "This is still your operation, Jim, but I took the liberty of ordering them brought in rather than wasting another second. I know you're upset about being considered a suspect for so long, but I assure you all of that ended shortly after you arrived here at NRL. And your friends may have five years worth of information that could help us track down Edwards and his comrades. I think it might be a good time to set up a meeting with the President and bring him up to speed about this CV-13 situation. He should also know about the missing triangles because he was hoping they could be used to entice *the Teachers* to sit down and talk."

"It seems as though the best way to meet *the Teachers* is to crawl into my safe for a night!" exclaimed Jim. "And as for the President, you can bring him up to speed the next time you two play golf, or whatever it is you do together. I'm tired of being used."

"It doesn't work that way, Jim. As far as this project goes, I report to you and you report to the President. Like I said before, this is your operation and it's your duty to make the report. I'll help you prepare—or not—but you have to make the phone call. I suspect that things will get pretty busy for you once your friends arrive, so you should probably do it sooner rather than later."

Jim got up and walked the length of the office twice before replying. When he did, he locked eyes with Blass and spoke slowly and calmly.

"Bill, if I thought I could get away with it, I'd fire you right now. However, you've been a big help several times already and I suspect we're going to need you as long as this operation exists. Therefore, I'm officially asking you for your help in preparing me to brief the President. However, no more unilateral moves without my knowledge, understand? No more airport hijackings, no more personal profiling and no more roundups without my expressed authorization. Period. If this is my operation, then I'm in charge. Otherwise, I'm out of here and the President can go…"

"I understand," interrupted Blass. "And I apologize. If I've been overzealous it's only because I've been chasing these guys for so long that I've forgotten what it's like to do anything else. I'm also accustomed to working alone and not as part of a team but I will make an effort, I promise. Shutting down this group is more important to me than you can imagine, and you seem to be the key to making that happen. If I didn't believe that I wouldn't have spent the last hour telling you things I knew you weren't going to like. But I felt you deserved the truth and it didn't appear that anyone else was going to give it to you."

"Apology accepted," replied Jim curtly. "Now how do I go about telling the President I've lost his bad guys *and* his alien artifacts?"

***

Becker smiled and handed Sophie the letter he had prepared earlier that morning.

"I don't know how much this will help, but if the new Director has any brains he will see your small band of rebels as an asset and not a threat," he smiled. "At least give him a chance, okay?"

"I will, I promise," replied Sophie. "I sure wish I were going with you, but I'm needed here. Will you promise to check in now and then in case I change my mind?"

"Absolutely! It seems strange that they don't allow two-way communications, but I guess they have to do that for their own protection. I feel very honored to have been invited and it wouldn't have happened if Klaudia, er, Agent Braun, hadn't spoken for me. But soon you'll have me on the Other Side as *your* advocate, so don't worry."

Becker glanced at his watch and back at Sophie.

"It's about time, so please give my apologies to everyone, especially your friend Dr. Barnes. Good-bye, Sophie."

Becker disappeared, leaving Sophie alone in the now empty fallout shelter two stories below the Munich apartment building.

"Good-bye, Becker," she said to no one.

***

The hastily scheduled teleconference with the President's advisory panel was about to start and Jim was so nervous his sweating hands were leaving wet spots all over his desk. Blass had spent the last two hours preparing him, but Jim was suddenly feeling very insecure.

"Relax and stick to your notes," advised Blass from across the desk. "There will no doubt be questions, so listen carefully and answer the best you can. If you don't know the answer, say so. This isn't the time to make up stuff just to sound smart."

Jim's phone rang and he pressed the speaker-phone button.

"This is Dr. Smith speaking," he said, reminded to use his alias by the huge words Blass had written at the top of his notes.

"Good morning, Jim," said a friendly voice Jim recognized as his former boss, the director of the Office of Science. "We understand you have an update for us but before you begin, I have some news for you. I just got off the telephone with the Chief of Surgery at Bethesda Naval Hospital and I'm happy to report that Sergeant Miles is finally making some progress and his status has been changed from Grave to Critical. Now, please begin."

The news about Danny made Jim smile broadly but he tensed again as he glanced at his notes.

"Good morning," he read. "In the course of the past twenty-four hours several significant events have occurred that I feel you should be made aware of.

"As you may already know through other sources, it appears that the top leadership of the group known as 'the Six' has fled to a location identified in some intelligence chatter as CV-13. Mr. Blass and I believe this site is a complex similar to the twelve Presidential Emergency Operations Centers but one that was built in secret. At the present time we don't know any more about the facility or its location. However, we now suspect that the Six may be in partial control of the twelve legitimate PEOCs and we strongly advise against using them for their intended purpose until further notice."

Jim was interrupted by sounds of shock and several background conversations among his invisible audience. When the noise had subsided, he continued.

"Secondly, I'm afraid I have to report that I am no longer in possession of the alien artifacts known as the triangles. They were apparently removed from the safe in my office last night by a person or persons unknown."

This time the grumbling on the other end of the line was interrupted by a voice that Jim recognized as Captain Stukey.

"How is that possible?" he shouted. "Your facility is a Level 1 secure area and it's currently under the watchful eyes of the Secret Service. There must be some mistake!"

"I assure you there's no mistake, Captain," replied Jim as calmly as possible. "But please allow me to continue, because there's more to this story."

The background noise ceased immediately and Jim could picture the entire panel sitting on the edge of their collective seats.

"Somehow, in a manner unknown to us, the artifacts have been returned to *the Teachers*."

"How do you know that?" shouted an unidentified voice.

"Because they left me a thank you note," replied Jim with a smile. He was actually beginning to enjoy this!

"A what?" asked another voice. "What did this note say?"

Jim read the note out loud, omitting the line of GPS coordinates.

There was a pause while the panel members digested the message and then Captain Stukey asked, "Well, don't keep us in suspense, Dr. Smith! What was the token of their appreciation?"

"They provided me with two sets of GPS coordinates, Sir. The first turned out to be the house where Linda McBride, one of my former NWIDI teammates, lives and the other one is the location of an eighty-foot ship serving as the temporary home of another teammate, Tony Nicoletti."

This time, the background noise from the speaker phone was so loud that Jim reached over and turned the volume down a notch.

The teleconference was finally brought to order by a female voice.

"Ladies and gentleman, please come to order! The President has something to say."

The line instantly went silent.

"Mr. Blass, this is the President. Are these the same two individuals we've been trying to locate for the past five years?"

Surprised by a direct question from the President, Blass straightened in his chair.

"Yes, Sir, they are. It seems that *the Teachers* knew their whereabouts all along. Unfortunately, we never had the opportunity to ask them for this information."

"I see. Dr. Smith, what do you make of all this?"

"Well, Mr. President, *the Teachers* are the rightful owners of the triangles and I'm very grateful to know that my friends are alive and that they will soon be here in the relative safety of NRL, but I would have certainly liked to have been able to learn more about the messages on the artifacts. We have so many questions that will never be answered now."

"Many questions, indeed!" replied the President. "Do you have any more surprises for us, Dr. Smith?"

"No, except for the fact that Professor Karl Schmidt, the author of the now infamous Schmidt File, has apparently discovered a way to travel back and forth between our world and that of *the Teachers'* pretty much at will."

Again there was a commotion on the line, but the President's voice quickly brought things under control.

"Saving the best for last, Dr. Smith? How did you find out about this?"

"A couple of nights ago a friend in Munich accompanied him on just such a trip. She's back in Germany now, but Schmidt has apparently decided to stay in what he calls the 'Other Side'."

There was a long silence. The floor belonged to the President of the United States and no one dared to speak out of turn. Finally the President broke the silence.

"Is there anything else, Dr. Smith?"

"No, Sir, I think that's pretty much it."

"Dr. Smith, your country, this panel and I, personally thank you for all you've done. The panel and I need to discuss our next move but until we do I'm afraid I'm going to have to ask you and your friends to remain in the protective custody of Captain Stukey's facility. Captain, are you able to handle this growing group of civilians?"

"Yes, Sir, we're coping."

"Mr. President, if I may, I'd like to say something," said Jim.

"Of course, Dr. Smith, what is it?"

"After all my friends and I have done, I don't think it's fair to lock us in the basement of a building, even if it is for our own safety. This morning I learned that until recently we had been considered suspects in the biggest terrorist conspiracy in history and all the while we were just doing what we believed to be the right thing. Certainly we deserve better than this!"

"Your concern is duly noted, Dr. Smith, and I'll do my best to come up with a better plan as soon as possible. However, my top priority right now is keeping you all safe and the best short-term solution is to leave you right where you are. You and your friends can use the research facility, of course, but I think the rest of the staff should be relieved of duty immediately to minimize any potential security leaks. Mr. Blass, you may either remain at NRL with Dr. Barnes or return to your regular duties, but the others are to be debriefed and reassigned, effective immediately, is that clear?"

Jim started to object, but Blass waved his arms to keep him silent.

"Yes, Sir," replied Blass. "It's perfectly clear."

"I'm sorry, Dr. Smith, but this is much bigger than you or your friends. I will get back to you as soon as possible but until then please try to make the best of the situation.

"I'm dropping off the line," continued the President, "but I would like to schedule a panel meeting for 0800 tomorrow morning. I would like those of you who are in Washington to join me at the White House. The rest of you please join us the normal way. Good day, and thank you again, Dr. Smith. I'll be in touch."

One by one, the attendees dropped off the line with a click and Jim terminated his connection, too.

It was over, and Jim suddenly felt a huge sense of relief. Even though the Six remained a global threat, they had been forced underground. The triangles that had occupied so much of his time for the past five years were gone, but Jim took comfort in the fact that they were back where they belonged, with *the Teachers*. Danny, who had nearly given his life to protect Jim, was going to survive his injuries. And best of all, in a few short hours the old NWIDI team, minus Frank, of course, would be reunited. It didn't get much better than this!

THE END

Epilogue
(Sunday, May 11, 2008)

Linda and Javier had arrived an hour earlier and their daughter, Mariana, was currently occupied in one corner of the room with the Fitzgerald's small dog, Sandstrom. Tony had been escorted in about thirty minutes later, still upset about being hustled off the boat in the British Virgin Islands by U.S. Marshals. Together, Linda, Javier, Tony, Fitz and Susan were sitting at a six foot folding table catching up on the past five years when Jim entered the large, mostly empty room.

"Hey, there he is!" shouted Tony. "What's the big idea of interrupting my nap to drag me all the way back to the U.S.?"

Jim tried to smile, but he wasn't looking forward to the news he was going to have to break to his friends about being captives of their own government. After handshakes and back pats all around, he sat down at one end of the table and sighed.

"Listen, guys, I don't know how much you've been able to share with each other, but I have some news that you should probably hear sooner rather than later. Do you all remember Buzz Edwards?"

"You bet I do," replied Tony without waiting for anyone else to speak. "He had me locked up in that underground facility in Cancun from the day after Linda's wedding until about six weeks ago and I've been after him ever since. I almost had him, too, but a couple of days ago he slipped through my fingers and disappeared."

"What was that?" exclaimed a shocked Linda. "Are you saying you were held prisoner for more than five years?"

"Well, maybe 'prisoner' is a bit too strong, because I wasn't actually in a cell, but I wasn't allowed to leave the facility beneath the airport, either. I know every square inch of that place and I planned my escape for years, but the opportunity didn't present itself until a rainy Sunday night last March when the security system went on the blink and gave me a chance to get away."

"Incredible," replied Jim. "Well, your friend Edwards is in charge of an international terrorist group known as 'the Six' and he's used us—all of us—as pawns to further his plans."

"Yes, we were just talking about that," nodded Linda. "Javier and I have been intercepting coded messages from an Asian group for weeks now. We've leaked many of them to the press, in an effort to disrupt some of their plans."

"No kidding?" smiled Jim. "So, independently, we've all been causing him grief. Good! That makes me feel a little better. The reason he disappeared from your radar, Tony, is because an associate of mine here at NRL finally connected him to a crime that would have resulted in his arrest. We also identified the other key members of his organization and now they've all gone into hiding. We don't know where yet, but we think it's a facility similar to the one where you were held."

"No kidding!" remarked Tony. "Judging by the power you seem to wield here, I'm guessing you've faired a little better than me. What have you been up to since the wedding?

Jim gave them a quick recap of his time at AUTEC, his brief trip to Germany and his most recent experiences at NRL.

Everybody wanted to know more about *the Teachers*, so Jim told them what he knew and what he suspected.

"Wow, the 'Other Side,' huh?" said Tony. "I need to check that place out! Can you get me an invitation or a ticket or whatever it takes to get in?"

Before Jim could answer, a Marine assigned to guard the makeshift shelter in the basement of the NRL administration building stuck his head in the door and signaled for Jim. When he returned to the table, Jim pointed to a telephone on a small stand on the far side of the room.

"We have a call. I'll put it on the speaker phone, but please keep the chatter down."

Jim pressed the button and said, "Good morning, Mr. President."

"Good morning, Jim, and good morning to all of you. I understand that your old group is reunited except for your fallen comrade Frank Morton. I won't take much of your time, but I promised Jim I would get back to him as soon as my advisors and I had agreed on a new plan and we've just accomplished that.

"The six of you seem to have a knack for uncovering bizarre facts in an incredibly efficient manner. You've learned more about the Six—and done more to thwart their activities—than the entire U.S. Intelligence community. Jim knows more about *the Teachers* than we would have learned in a hundred years and he's even been directly approached by them.

"So here's the deal, folks. Your government would like to ask you to step up one more time and accept a very special assignment. We would like you, as a group, to make contact with these *Teachers* and establish a working dialog with them. We would like you, in effect, to become our ambassadors. Learn about them, understand them and gain their trust. And more importantly, get them to trust us. We have good reason to believe that the Six will stop at nothing to disrupt *the Teachers'* plans but we don't even know what those plans are or how they affect us."

"So you want us to be spies for you?" challenged Jim.

"Not at all, Jim," replied the President. "Tell them up front what your motives are. Tell them that your mission is to get them to agree, on their own terms, to a meeting with us. I don't expect or want you to be dishonest with them in any way. I don't know if you're a Star Trek fan or not, but we'd like you to be our 'away team' with *the Teachers*. You will, of course, have access to any resources you might need and we've even come up with a pretty decent place for you to hang out that will be a lot more comfortable than your current location. You'll even have access to the outdoors!"

"And what if we decline your offer, Mr. President?" asked Tony. "Not that we would, but I'm just curious."

"Jim can provide more details, but I suggest you all take a long look around and ask yourselves if you want to be confined to a windowless, underground environment such as your current location. I suspect you'll need to discuss this as a group before giving me a final answer, so take an hour or so and talk about it. The only thing I should warn you about is that this is an 'all or nothing' decision. Either you all agree to the new project or you all stay where you are for an indefinite period of time—at least until we bring down the Six."

"How do we get our decision to you, Mr. President?" asked Jim.

"Call Captain Stukey and let him know because if you decline he will need to arrange additional sleeping quarters there at NRL. Good-bye, ladies and gentleman. I wish you the best whatever you decide."

A click in the speaker signaled that the President had dropped off the line. Jim punched the speakerphone button on his end and then turned to face the group at the table.

"I can't believe it!" he shouted. "They're blackmailing us again!"

"What are you talking about?" asked a puzzled Tony. "We have an opportunity to be the first official emissary to an alien culture and you're complaining? As an anthropologist, I would think you would be ecstatic about this opportunity."

"Yes," echoed Linda. "This is ten times better than the finds in the Yucatan or on Yonaguni. It's even better than the discovery of the triangles because you get to interact with living beings instead of smelly metallic relics."

"But they are playing us again, don't you see? Once we've made contact and gained the aliens' trust, they will steam roller right over us and proceed with whatever agenda they already have cooked up. I'm not going to be their patsy again!"

"Well then we will take measures to guarantee that doesn't happen," said Tony.

"Like what?"

"Well, I don't know, off the top of my head, but we can figure it out as we go. If we know what's coming, we should be able to prevent it."

"Or we develop our own agenda," added Linda. "We decide how much information to share and we control the situation through our knowledge. Come on Jim, you can't possibly want to walk away from an opportunity like this. This isn't just the chance of a lifetime this is one chance in the history of human civilization. I vote to accept the President's offer."

The other four members of the NWIDI team all spoke at once, supporting Linda's vote.

Jim frowned but nodded.

"Okay, I'll go along with the group, but with some serious reservations. I can't help wondering how Frank would vote if he were here right now. I'm not sure he'd be so quick to jump into bed with the same government that's used us over and over."

Jim passed out some sheets of paper he'd been clutching since entering the room.

"These are menus from the cafeteria upstairs. I know it's been a while since some of you have eaten, so circle anything you want. Without credentials you can't roam around the building, but I can have it sent down here. While you're deciding, I'll go call the Captain and give him our answer."

Jim made the call and then returned to collect the sheets. As he was handing them to the guard outside the door, he noticed that there were seven sheets instead of six so he flashed through them. The very last piece of paper wasn't a menu at all, but instead contained a simple, handwritten note. As his eyes scanned the four short lines, he gasped out loud.

Read the entire Parallel Ops series:

The Scientists (ISBN 978-0977910922)   From their secret laboratory, scientists work to protect alien artifacts from powerful international terrorists.   [November, 2011]

The Informants (coming Spring 2012)   While on the run from international terrorists, a young couple stumbles onto a dark secret in the mountains of Mexico's Baja.

The Guardians (coming Fall 2012)   From their floating base in the Caribbean, a multi-national team struggles to protect a secret hidden deep beneath the sea.

The first three novels in this series take place at exactly the same time and may be read in parallel—a chapter from each book before moving on to the next chapter. They may also be read in series, the normal way.

The Teachers (coming December 21, 2012)   Sorry, but details about the exciting conclusion to the *Parallel Ops* series cannot be revealed at this time.

For more information about this series, please join us at
www.ParallelOps.com